To Mary *[handwritten]*,
thank you for the support

Elseerian

[signature]

By Ben Hale

Copyright 2012 Ben Hale

To my family and friends,

who believed

And to my wife,

who is perfect

Table of Contents

Map of Lumineia

Prologue: The Woodsman

"He was still alive when they found him," the woodsman said, his voice raspy, like bark being scraped off a tree. "Alive—but he should have been dead with so much blood seeping from his wounds."

The three soldiers leaned into the firelight, their eyes widening at his words. Cast into shifting patterns of shadow, the woodsman's expression intensified as a gust of chill wind whistled through the clearing, blowing aside his long black hair to reveal an ugly scar stretching from left shoulder to ear.

"Guided by moonlight, the villagers found him in a clearing. Some of them rushed to his side and struggled to staunch the bleeding. The others huddled into groups and watched the dark forest, terrified that the attacker was still nearby. Everyone knew his skill with a blade, but the hero's body lay twisted and crumpled, like an empty sack of flour tossed into a corner. Glittering around him the broken shards of steel were all that remained of his powerful weapon."

"As they pressed against the flowing blood, the dying hero managed to speak four words, 'Death came for me.' They paid no attention to his warning—until a tall form in a black cloak separated itself from the shadows nearby. In his hands a wicked scythe hung—still stained with the hero's life. One by one the villagers froze as they saw the killer approaching, and as the specter of death neared, the cowl lifted to reveal eyes like burning coals."

"Most of them bolted then. The few that remained claimed they saw Death raise a hand of stark white bone to point at them. Their hearts failing, they scattered. As their screams died in the night, Death stood over Valir, watching him take his last breath."

The woodsman paused when one of the soldiers, the new recruit, shuddered and pulled his cloak closer. Another drained his ale and glanced at the dark forest with suspicious eyes, his bald head reflecting the firelight as he turned.

"What happened next?" the large one said, louder than necessary, eliciting glares from his companions and more looks into the trees.

The woodsman flashed a grim smile. "Morning light brought a group of heavily armed men to look for the body and search for the mysterious assassin. They found the body, but there was no sign of his killer. No tracks. No scent for the dogs . . . nothing. Not even a single bent blade of grass."

The young soldier hesitated and then asked, "Is that the same thing that happened to the others?"

The woodsman leaned back into the shadows and considered the question before answering in a low rumble, "Valir is the most recent that I know of, although he is by no means the first. Most of the killings seem to be fighters or leaders."

At this the soldiers started to relax, but the woodsman cut through their calm in an instant, leaning forward with a growl. "No one is safe. There have been other deaths that appear to be random slayings, villagers, merchants"—he paused and the intensity of his voice chilled the air—". . . or a simple group of travelers."

After a moment of stunned silence the large one cut in, glancing uncertainly at his companions. "When did it start?"

"About six months ago," the woodsman replied, his dark eyes glittering in the firelight. "But no one knows who the killer is, even though the king has sent his best troops to hunt him."

He shook his head, stabbing a finger at the three men across from him. "If you ask me, someone is *sending* him out. The deaths are just too convenient, too coordinated. You only take out fighters and leaders if you are planning something . . . something big." His raspy voice darkened at the grim thought, causing them to shudder and pull their weapons closer.

"What about the villagers and travelers though?" the bald man asked in a harsh whisper. "The other murders."

The woodsman gestured wide, his expression fierce in the firelight. "I'd wager a sack of gold that this Death figure is just a killer. The villagers and soldiers must have been on his way—or in his way—to his real targets," his voice shifted as he considered his own words.

After a moment of silence the fire snapped and all three of the soldiers started. "Relax," said their guide, his rough voice turning mild. "We'll be fine, but we should turn in. If we push it, we should reach the king tomorrow before nightfall."

With that said, he drained the mug of ale he'd been nursing before grabbing his bedroll and moving away from the fire. Striding into the cold wind he tossed his blankets next to a large oak tree at the edge of the clearing. Long experience had taught him to sleep with his back to something. It might be a colder spot to sleep, but it had proven to be safer.

The three soldiers remained at the fire for several moments until the youngest rose to his feet and strolled to his own blanket. Attempting nonchalance, the others stretched before sauntering towards their bedrolls. Despite their forced calm, each man subtly moved their blankets a little closer to the fire. They probably would have been more apprehensive if they knew the thoughts of their companion.

The attacks had steadily become more frequent.

The Woodsman

In the beginning they had occurred only once every few weeks, and were scattered in the far eastern villages. Now a corpse was found almost every day, with some only a day's ride from the king's own castle. Messages from towns and homesteads had been flooding to the king, begging for troops to protect them.

The woodsman was one such messenger, and had travelled from the far eastern villages to inform the king of an unknown disease that was spreading throughout that region. Reluctantly leaving his wife and two children, he had already been on the road for over two weeks, pushing his steed as hard as he dared.

Shedding weight to gain speed, he had also elected to get supplies on the way, but food had been unusually scarce. Even hunters or traveling tradesmen had little to offer. In the last town he had passed, the woodsman had met the soldiers at the tavern. Traveling in the same direction, it didn't take long for them to depart together.

Hungry for answers, the men had pried him for new tales, and he did his best to deliver. Having lived through other times of rumor and strife, the woodsman knew well the signs of fear and the whispers of war, but this was different. Something . . . intangible permeated everyone—and everything. You could see it in the abrupt, suspicious looks that had replaced warm, open smiles. Hurried footsteps and jerky movements gave subtle evidence that everyone they met felt it too. Even the woods felt dampened. Birds sang less, the breeze carried a hostile edge, and the shade from trees loomed like the shadows of angry giants.

It was the first time in his life he did not feel at home in the woods.

Rationally, he knew there was nothing to fear. They were not at war with anyone, as far as he knew, and even the northern tribes had been quiet. But he still couldn't shake the sinking foreboding that hung like a shroud. Sighing in a vain effort to shake the unease, he glanced into the shadows—

—a pair of red lights flickered through the trees to the east. His blood froze as he felt his heart begin to pound. Normally he would have passed it off as too much ale, but not with the tales of late. Unable to stop himself, he eased his sword free from its scabbard. Fighting to keep his breath slow, he focused all his senses on the surrounding area, straining for any sign . . .

At first there was nothing . . . then he began to feel the hair on the back of his neck stand up. Like a winter's wind, fear pierced his cloak and clawed at his heart. One of the men straightened—his eyes wide and his hand already reaching for the weapon at his side. The other two finally felt it and were quick to palm their blades as well, twisting when a snort from the horses betrayed their own terror. Smoothly rising and moving towards the fire, the big woodsman readied his sword.

"If we stand together we may have a chance," he growled, and the soldiers stumbled to join him.

Whistling wind and the crackling flames were the only sounds until a sinister shadow drifted out of the darkness. The soldier directly in front of him shouted in alarm and leapt back to the others, who whirled in its direction. Despite the tale they had just heard, the description in the story could not have portrayed what stood before them.

As it moved closer, firelight revealed a menacing figure in a tall black cloak and cowl. Dark red ovals simmered and burned where eyes should have been. Hands of bone protruded from the sleeves, holding the shaft of a long black scythe pulsing with red veins on both handle and blade. A loud snap of leather caused all four of them to jump and look at the horses, only to watch as the three soldiers' mounts disappeared into the trees.

Unsure of what to do, the soldiers moved closer together while the woodsman took a step away. Then the young one leapt in with a yell. "Stop, you fool!" the woodsman shouted—but it was too late. The killer turned aside the thrust and dispatched the man in a single blow. The silent thud of his body hitting the ground caused the group to gasp. Collectively they took a few steps back, placing the fire between them and the assassin before them.

"We might survive if we fight together!" the woodsman said, his voice savage. "Move apart and flank him." Responding better to orders, the men separated. A moment later they attacked as one. A coordinated attack from three sides would have dispatched almost anyone, but the

11

assassin didn't even give ground. Scythe hit steel in a dizzying display of skill, blocking every attack that came near until their initial charge slowed, allowing an opening.

Blocking one slash, Death glided in to cut another one of the soldiers down, slicing him nearly in two. As the bald man screamed his final breath, the survivors fought with the fury of desperation, but to no avail. Finding another opportunity against only two didn't take long. Crying out in agony, the last soldier fell to leave the woodsman alone.

Realizing he didn't have a chance, he spun and leapt towards his own horse, still tethered to a tree. Just as he mounted, a final swing from the scythe gouged deep into his right thigh. Gritting his teeth against the pain, he kicked the horse and yelled for all he was worth. The already frightened animal snapped the lead and bolted out of the clearing to carry his rider to safety.

As the woodsman galloped into the night, Death surveyed the carnage for only a moment before melting back into the shadows from which he'd come. A dying fire and three cooling corpses remained when the only survivor dared to look back.

Chapter 1: Elseerian

Taryn Elseerian's eyes snapped open and he scanned his surroundings for what had woken him. Focusing his attention on his senses, the half elf's slightly pointed ears caught every sound. At first glance, the young man might have passed for an elf except for his eyes and hair. Eyes of dark blue, very unlike the sky blue of the elven race, pierced the shadowed room from under his hair, which hung thick, wavy, and dark red around his face. He had been told too many times to count that his hair looked like a dwarf's.

With his heritage a mystery, he'd always pretended to laugh off the comment—but each time he heard it, he felt something stir and tighten within him. To anyone but his close friends he could pass it off as nothing, but the few who knew him best understood, even if they never voiced it.

Another whisper caressed his ears, and he strained to find the source. The little cabin in which he lived was sparsely furnished. A desk sat in one corner with a few pieces of parchment scattered across the surface. Windows above the desk and bed, typically open to allow an afternoon breeze to cool the room, were now covered to ward off the nightly chill. Moonlight filtered into the room through an opening in the drapes above the desk.

A slight movement in the curtain above his bed caught his keen eyes. Unbidden, an easy smile broke across Taryn's features. *Murai is at it again*, he thought. From an early age, Taryn had been trained by his uncle to wake up instantly if there were any unnatural noise. It had been over fifteen years since someone had surprised him, even when sleeping. That didn't stop his uncle from testing him, though.

In truth, Murai wasn't really his uncle at all, but he had been the one to take him in when his shipwrecked mother had been found twenty-one years ago. Raised by him, it had been natural for Taryn to call him Uncle. Well into his fifth century, the seasoned elf had taught him with kindness and a deep-rooted love. "Always be quick with a smile and a sword," Murai liked to say.

The young man slipped from his bed and onto the floor, keeping his knees under him in a crouch. At the same time he drew the dagger he kept under his pillow, careful to not make any sound. A hand holding an object emerged through the window, followed by an arm. Soon the grinning face of his uncle came into view. Taryn had to hand it to him— for an old elf he was still pretty stealthy. No sound betrayed his presence except the soft rub of cloth on skin as he leaned through the window. His uncle paused before pouncing on the dark bed. At the same time Taryn leapt as well, landing on top of him with the dagger carefully placed with the flat side at his throat.

"I was just coming to get you for breakfast," a muffled voice came out from under Taryn.

"I might believe that, but you brought a knife," he replied mockingly. "You also came through the window. I am sure you know how to use a door."

An arm moved out from under the blanket to reveal the object in his hand to be a spoon. "Breakfast is ready!" the muffled voice said. Taryn burst into laughter as he got off his uncle and moved to open the drapes. Moonlight flooded the room, allowing the young man to get a look at the intruder. Dressed in worn pants and just a shirt, it was clear that he hadn't gotten ready for the day yet. He must have come straight after waking. Elven features were prominent, with eyes of light sky blue, blond hair, and pointed ears. The wiry old elf was short for his race, barely as tall as Taryn's shoulder. You would never suspect that he was one of the best fighters in the history of the island.

Proficient with almost any weapon, he was deadly with a katsana, a long, curving blade about an inch wide. Because of its length and weight, it required both hands—so few elves chose to wield one. He was the only master of that particular weapon on the island and had been Taryn's first teacher. Thinking of that made Taryn look up at the only items hanging on the wall. Sheathed in beautiful black scabbards rested two uniquely crafted katsanas, the only link he had to his parents.

Following Taryn's gaze, Murai looked at the swords as well. "Your parents would be proud of you, Taryn, especially today."

He nodded in response without looking at his uncle, and tried to not show how much he missed not knowing them. Finally of age, today he would be tested and take his rites of passage. He just wished the idea didn't make him feel so alone, and he found himself wondering if others felt the same way.

For as long as the histories had been written, the island of Sri Rosen had been the training ground for elves, who were sent to practice and master weapons from the age of twenty to fifty, when they reached adulthood.

Although most of the fighters had traditionally been elves, there were often a handful of humans and dwarves that were allowed to study with the masters of Sri Rosen. Dwarves, whose life spans matched those of the elves, also trained until the age of fifty, but humans completed at twenty-one.

Without realizing it, Taryn had drawn closer to the swords that were his parents' legacy and he reached up to caress the hilts in the darkness. Drawing both blades in one smooth motion, he left the sheaths on the wall and returned to the beam of moonlight to study the weapons.

The swords were almost identical in every way. Perfectly weighted, they could be balanced on the edge of a chair and remain that way for days. Taryn knew—he'd tried it. Not a single chip marred the razor sharp edges. Shimmering in the moonlight were twin dragons of blue and green, etched down the length of both blades in perfect detail, twined together in an embrace. The only real difference between the two swords was a bright blue sapphire above the hilt in one, and a perfect emerald in the same location on the other. Below the gemstones, black leather had been braided and fastened tightly down the double long hilt, allowing the wielder to fight without losing his grip.

Catching his uncle looking at him, Taryn said, "I wish they could be here for this, Murai."

Without responding, his uncle placed a hand on his shoulder in a token of comfort. They remained there in silence until Murai gently pushed the swords aside while moving to stand in front of him. "You would make *any* parent proud today," he said as a spontaneous grin creased his features, "except me. I can only be proud of you if you eat breakfast with me." At the same time he scrunched his face up in mock haughtiness and looked away.

Taryn grinned. "Just let me get dressed and I will meet you at the dining hall. By the looks of things, you need to as well, so I may even beat you there."

Murai's mock angry face shifted to one that welcomed a challenge. "We will see about that!" Leaping for the bed, he exited in a diving roll through the same window he had entered.

Taryn chuckled to himself and returned the katsanas to their sheaths before preparing for the day. Not ten minutes later the young man stepped out the door and took a deep breath of the cool morning air. Tightening the straps of the two swords on his back, he took a moment to enjoy the view. A light fog hung in the air, although the first rays of dawn could be seen on the horizon and it would burn away soon after sunrise. His little cottage faced south but sat west of the village, nestled into the trees close to the cliffs. To his right the terrain rose sharply to the only mountain on the island, while on his left the ground sloped gently to the sea several miles away.

At just over 50 miles in length, the island was dotted with small villages, most of them hidden in the forest near the mountain. Smoke from other dining halls could be seen drifting lazily out of chimneys and darkening the fog before breaking free into the sky. On the other side of the mountain, to his right, a sheer cliff dropped hundreds of feet to the breaking surf.

Taryn turned and walked briskly through the village, listening to the soft sounds of people waking and preparing for the day. By the time he reached the main street, the early risers were already going about their business. Today would be busier than normal because of the Acabi, an elven word meaning "finish with honor."

Turning towards the center of the village, he nodded at the people he passed as he followed the savory smells coming from the dining hall, grateful that his day to cook was still several days off. Not that he minded helping, but the food never tasted good on his day. Last week it had been particularly dreadful, eliciting more than a few complaints. At least Murai had never seemed concerned. He'd always told him not to worry about his lack of culinary skills because he was 'born to wield a blade'. The phrase had lost its significance though when his uncle had begun to apply it to other things. Frowning at his thoughts, he opened the door and stepped in.

He paused at the threshold until he spotted his uncle in the crowd, with a plate of steaming food in front of him. Knowing he wouldn't be able to escape a ribbing, he moved to sit across from him.

"Took you long enough," Murai said. "I'm on my second helping." Despite his tone, the corners of his mouth were struggling to stop a grin. He was also fully dressed with his own katsana on his back.

"I already finished, but I figured you would like some company," Taryn replied with a smile.

Responding with a loud snort, Murai pointed at the food line. "Get some food; you need to be at the arena in two hours."

"Do you want me to get you thirds?" Taryn asked as he stood. "I don't want you to faint from hunger when you fight me."

Looking up, Murai said brightly, "Of course—although not too much bacon." He leaned in and lowered his voice. "I'm trying to watch my weight, you know."

Taryn smiled and strode to the back of the line to grab his own breakfast. Sly grins and stifled laughter were directed towards him, and he did his best to ignore it. Overhearing someone whisper to another of his latest attempt in the gardens made him cringe. Even though it was expected, the muffled giggle at the end made him tighten his lips.

Avoiding eye contact, he felt heat rise to his neck as he reached for bread, eggs, and extra bacon. It didn't help that he could best any of them with a blade. In every other area, he carried the unfortunate renown as the worst on the island. At one time, Murai had encouraged him to stand up for himself. His attempt could only be described as disastrous, and that had been the end of it. He could count on one hand the few he claimed as friends, and that included his uncle.

Withdrawing into his training had only made it more difficult. Every bit that he excelled only seemed to widen the chasm between himself and the other students, and for some reason he did not understand, many disliked losing to him. The pirate attack four years ago had been a breaking point, and many had yet to forgive him.

Catching someone shaking their head as they turned away, Taryn realized that today might be a chance to redeem himself—if he did well. Everyone knew what he had to face today, and he doubted anyone would be willing to trade places. By longstanding tradition, students completed their training by facing the very people that had taught them, and Taryn had been instructed by four masters—something that was unheard of in written history. Most fighters studied one, or occasionally two, weapons or skills throughout their time on Sri Rosen. A student with three masters had occurred only twice in the last five hundred years.

He just wished it had helped him make friends. Not for the first time, he considered the idea that his mixed heritage had something to do with it. Although not entirely elf, or human, he didn't fit in with either crowd, and apparently, skill in a single area was not sufficient to gain entry to their circles.

Sighing, he returned to his seat and ate quickly to finish at the same time as his uncle. They dropped their dishes off for the daily dish cleaners and stepped outside to allow others to eat.

"Do you want to walk or ride?" Murai asked.

"I think I'll walk," replied Taryn. "It's going to be a beautiful morning."

Murai's gaze lingered on him for several moments before he stretched and smiled. "That's fine, but these old bones aren't up for it. I'll ride and meet you there." With that he turned and walked towards the stables where his horse was kept.

Grateful for the time to be alone, Taryn headed out of the village on the meandering trail to Seascape, the largest of all the villages and the only port. Each year several ships came to trade and drop off or pick up passengers. At least twice a year the new students that had been selected to go to Sri Rosen arrived. Most were very young, between three and five years old for humans. Dwarves and elves arrived at the age of twenty and stayed until they reached the age of accountability for their respective races.

Once on the island, everyone began with the basics of unarmed combat. After that they could select a single master to teach them in a specific style of fighting or continue in unarmed combat. Most elves chose to study the short sword or longbow, the most common elven weapons. The few humans and dwarves usually chose a master of the broadsword, longsword, or battle axe. They would then study with that master until their Acabi ceremony.

Those who passed the Acabi could choose to return to their homeland or stay and advance their studies. Since elves and dwarves could live for several hundred years, many elected to remain. Humans usually returned home as soon as their ceremony was completed. During their training, if any student mastered a specific weapon, they were allowed to select another teacher and learn an additional skill.

While his thoughts continued to wander Taryn strolled down the trail, enjoying the early morning. Frequent breaks in the trees allowed a view of the brilliant sunrise. The sun was already halfway up, with the water reflecting the colors perfectly, making the horizon disappear. Red, orange and yellow shimmered in the water and sky, setting the sea on fire.

By this time of day, students could normally be found running on the trails for their morning exercise. Today being an Acabi ceremony, however, all normal lessons would be cancelled. The trail continued to dip through the light forest at a steady decline, gently turning back on itself when it became too steep. Relishing the solitude, Taryn broke into a run.

Swift and careful, he placed each foot on stone or hard dirt, leaving no sign of his passage. His elven heritage granted him speed and silence—but he also had stamina, which was *not* a normal elf trait. Unending endurance was only common among the dwarves, who were known for fighting for days without rest. Coming to a small stream, he leapt up to grab a thick branch twelve feet above the gurgling water, and swung himself across without slowing.

He smiled to himself. Every day since he was five he'd run a few miles before dawn. It was the only time of day that he could think without being disturbed. At first it was just the isolation that had appealed to him. Later it had become a game to avoid all contact with anyone. Hearing footsteps, he would slip into the woods and ghost past someone without them ever knowing he was there.

Taryn continued to run for ten minutes until he came to one of the villages. Without breaking stride, he used a tree to swing himself onto the roof of a cabin and lightly crossed to grab another branch. Like just another shadow in the morning, he passed through the village without touching the ground. On the other side he dropped softly from a tree and sprinted down the trail. Getting closer to his destination forced him to be more careful as the appearance of one, and then another person, spurred detours. Coming within view of Seascape he slowed to a walk. He had covered almost seven miles in a little over thirty minutes, but suddenly he didn't want to arrive so early.

The city lay sprawled out below him. Cottages and cabins were placed around the outside while the dining hall, arena, and other communal structures were situated in the middle of town. A small strip of forest separated the settlement from the beach. Beyond that, a large dock stretched out into the ocean with the *Sea Dancer,* one of the few ships to come every year, bobbing at the end.

Since he still had an hour before he had to be at the arena, he decided to go down to the dock. Wanting to avoid anyone talking to him, he set a quick pace through town and stepped onto the long pier. Continuing to the very end where the great ship lay berthed, he turned onto a smaller dock for fishing boats. No one was on the jetty itself, but there were several sailors doing various chores on the large ship. Nodding at them, he sat with his legs hanging off the dock's edge, and turned his gaze towards the water.

This close to the sea, the rising sun loomed painfully bright, so he closed his eyes and relaxed. Leaning against a post he enjoyed the soft breeze tugging at his tunic and pants. Any sounds from the city were muted by the crashing surf, and the peace that surrounded him made it hard to imagine the night he was born.

Twenty-one years ago, a storm had whipped the ocean into an angry white froth. For several days a merchant ship had struggled to stay afloat, knowing they were close to the island but unable to find it in the gale. Just as they spotted land a giant wave reached out and smashed their vessel against the reef. An entire side of the boat shattered under the force, and water gushed in.

As the boat sank, many tried to jump to safety inside the reef—but no one made it. At the last instant, two figures appeared on the prow. One placed a foot in the joined hands of the other and using the extra push, was thrown to safety. With the tremendous strength of the thrower, the person in the air cleared the reef and dived smoothly into the lagoon. Surfacing, they began pushing towards shore.

Fate seemed to have other plans. Before they could reach the sandy beach, another large wave hit the boat. The thick mast snapped and hurtled over the reef to crash into the desperate swimmer, who would have drowned then without help. The harbormaster at the time had been the only witness to the carnage and without hesitation sprang into the water. A few minutes later he dragged a pregnant elf maid onto the beach. Fierce wind and rain battered him as he fought to carry her into his home. Laying her on his bed, he relit the candle extinguished by the gust that had ushered them in. The mast had struck her hard, breaking an arm and leaving an ugly wound bleeding through golden hair. She

21

regained consciousness just long enough to give birth and say a name . . . then she was gone.

A long katsana had been strapped on her back with a green gem above the handle. Among the wreckage the following morning, the villagers found the body of a human with dark red hair. Because the newborn's hair matched his in color, everyone assumed this man must have been the father. On his back had been another katsana, this one with a blue gem above the grip.

No one had recognized either one of them, and it had caused quite a dilemma over what to do with the baby. In the end, several people had stepped forward and volunteered to raise him. Murai had been one of them, and oddly the most insistent. In the end his persistence won out and he'd been allowed to become his guardian. To this day Taryn did not know why he had been so adamant.

Taryn had heard the story from the harbormaster many times and never tired of it, but it didn't manage to satisfy the ache he felt to know more.

A sudden weight pressed down onto the board on which he was sitting, causing him to open his eyes and look up to see a beautiful, slender elf sit down next to him.

"I thought I would find you here." Liriana's voice carried a hint of music, betraying her skill with song. Clear blue eyes were framed with thin eyebrows and fair skin. Straight blonde hair fell uninhibited down her back—the gentle wind flicking and pulling at it. She was dressed in riding pants and light chain mail that couldn't quite hide the curves in her figure.

An impish smile played across her face as she focused on Taryn. "You don't have much time before you fight. Are you ready?"

"I don't know. I guess so. What about you?"

"I am more ready to use my bow than my sword." She emphasized her statement by reaching back and pulling her longbow into view. She had made it herself from a supple yew branch and had carved intricate designs into it over the years. Learning how to use a bow had been the

22

most natural thing in the world to her—and the first thing she had chosen to study. Mastering it quickly, she had moved on to learn the elven short sword, but had had a little more trouble with a blade. She had actually helped teach him the longbow and they had stayed close ever since. He had once seen her split a leaf at a hundred paces—a story still told on the island.

On impulse, he decided to voice his thoughts. "Can I ask you something?" He glanced at her, trying to read her expression.

Her eyes pierced his as she shrugged. "Sure."

Looking away, he asked, "Do you remember a few years ago, when I asked Suoh and the others to leave me alone?"

Her brow crinkled as she looked at him. "Yeah . . ."

"Why did they want to fight me?"

She laughed lightly and said, "They don't like that you're better than them. Maybe they saw it as an opportunity to gang up on you, or maybe they were just mad that you stood up for yourself. Either way, you handled it well, even with so many of them."

He sighed and looked away. "I don't think it went well at all. I tried not to hurt them."

She laughed again and nudged his side. "What's this about—" Her eyes then widened as she grinned. "They're still talking about the garden incident, aren't they."

"I only pulled up a few plants," he protested. "I didn't know they weren't weeds."

She shook her head and grinned. "I know you didn't. How could you have known they were the gardeners' prized flowers?"

He frowned at the sarcasm in her voice but she just laughed again.

"It really isn't a cause for concern, Taryn. They can't beat you with a weapon, so they try to tear you down with something else."

"There are certainly plenty of things they can use." He chuckled in chagrin.

"Maybe," she said without taking her eyes off him. "But none of those things matter. Everyone is good at something. If you could, would you trade your skill with weapons for a talent in the kitchen?"

An image of others praising him for his well baked bread came to mind, causing him to snort at the idea. "Of course not, I—" Then it clicked. She was right, as usual, and he had to admit he'd never looked at it that way.

"Even if it meant you didn't burn the bread every time?"

Amused at the similar train of their thought, he replied, "Even then."

She chuckled for a moment. "At least you have grown out of *some* of your awkwardness."

He laughed, taking her bait, "Only some?"

"Only some." She smiled coyly. "You now have a *few* friends."

"A few, but I know I can count on them," he admitted, and then inclined his head towards her. "It must be nice to have so many."

She tossed her hair and looked away, her humor evaporating. "Having friends doesn't mean they are good friends."

He didn't know what to say. Liri, as her close friends called her, was pretty, elegant, poised, and strong willed, and she drew others to her with ease, but he'd never considered the idea that having a host of friends could be bad.

She started to laugh then, a bitter and sad sound. "At least when we leave the island, it won't matter."

"What do you mean?" he asked, leaning back against a post. Although he sometimes didn't know what to say around others, Liri had a way of easing his discomfort.

She glanced at him before responding, and her gaze carried a disturbing depth he had never seen before. "When we get back to the mainland, things will be . . . different. We will be away from all the petty differences here, but there are other things that might not be any better. I . . . will be different."

He blinked and leaned forward. She had never explained her reluctance to return home, and until now, had avoided the conversation of staying or going. "So did you decide if you are staying or going home?" Even though he doubted she would ever favor someone like him, he couldn't suppress a smile at the idea of sailing away with her.

She hesitated. "I decided . . . to go back when you did." As she finished the statement, her crystal blue eyes met his—then flicked back to the sea. They both knew that Taryn was going back on the very ship that nudged the pier they sat on—as long as he passed his test today. He'd had a burning desire to find out more about his parents for as far back as he could remember, and he had only waited to finish training. It had never been a question of *if* he would go back, but *when*.

With his heart soaring at the prospect of her companionship, Taryn rose to his feet and pulled her up to face him. "I would love to—I mean . . . it would be nice . . . to have some company." He knew how he sounded, and felt a wave of relief when she laughed it off.

"Just promise me that you will stay my friend, no matter what you see on the other end." Her wide grin didn't match the serious glint in her eyes, causing him to wonder again what she was afraid of.

"Always," he managed to say.

The impish smile returned in an instant. "You have to finish first— and I don't know if your teachers will pass you. You *were* always the lazy sort . . ."

"Speak for yourself," he said, unable to stop his smile enough to feign a wounded expression. "As I recall, it was you who didn't like to get out of bed for the morning run."

Her pealing laughter lifted his heart even more, and his grin widened as they began to walk towards shore. They both knew his words to be true, and the memory of her grumbling every morning caused him to join in her mirth.

By the time they reached the end of the dock and stepped onto the beach, Liri's laugh had reduced to a chuckle.

"Let's go warm up together," she suggested.

He nodded, feeling a rush of gratitude for her friendship. Falling into step with her shorter gait, he paused only to glance back at the great ship in the harbor.

A surge of confidence washed over him as he realized that as long as he performed well, his journey would begin the following day. He had only to demonstrate the skills he'd honed for his entire life.

It was time to be tested.

Chapter 2: The Acabi

Taryn and Liri arrived at the amphitheatre together and worked their way past several students and masters on their way to the bottom. Shaped like a crescent-moon, the natural depression sloped downward and faced a sheer stone wall. Over the next hour, spectators would continue to trickle in and find seats on stone benches. With each row constructed in descending half circles, there were few locations that did not afford an excellent view.

Between the first row and the rock face, the ground had been cleared, leaving a wide half circle of flat ground. Centuries of battles and ceremonies had pounded the dirt to a rock hard surface. At the moment, four other students were in the bottom of the bowl sparring. Joining them, Taryn and Liri found a section of open ground and unsheathed their weapons. Taryn drew only one sword before facing her.

"Don't worry, I will go easy on you," Liri said with a smirk, the last word barely reaching his ears before she moved in with a quick right slash.

They hadn't really practiced together in a few years—not since he'd stopped learning the bow and moved on to the katsana, but he had to admit she had gotten a LOT better. He parried—but instantly had to twist to avoid her reverse. Taking a quick step backward he swept his sword across to block her next strike—and shifted his feet to attack. She smoothly sidestepped his upward thrust—and then leapt in with a flurry of lightning fast moves.

In moments, their simple warm-up accelerated into a fierce competition. It was clear to Taryn that his counterpart wanted to prove herself, so he resisted the impulse to reveal his own skill. Wanting to really see how much she had learned, he took her through several complicated routines—which she followed surprisingly fast and without any hesitation. Every sweep of her blade was as quick as thought as she danced back and forth through everything Taryn threw at her. This continued for several minutes until Taryn saw out of the corner of his eye that the benches were almost full.

Suddenly very aware of the eyes on him, Taryn nearly missed a block, so he took the next opportunity available. Seeing her shift of feet for another attack, he waited until the last second and darted towards her while her sword extended past him . . . inches from his right side. Without stopping he rolled down her blade and behind her.

Before she could turn to face him, he sheathed his sword and wrapped his left arm around her waist—trapping her body against his. At the same moment, his right hand reached down her sword arm and found her wrist. Before she could react, he pressed on the nerves, forcing her to drop her weapon.

"Sorry, I guess I got lucky," he whispered into her ear.

"No," she exclaimed breathlessly, turning her head to look at him, "you were always amazing with a sword—and a bow."

In that moment Taryn became conscious of her tight form pressed against his and the smell of her soft hair in front of his face. He heard her breath catch as she too recognized the intimacy of their position and abruptly they stepped apart. Taryn swallowed hard against the surge of emotions while Liri stooped to pick up her sword and slid it into its scabbard. By the time she had turned to face him, her easy smile had returned.

"You'll do great today, Taryn, but don't forget I went easy on you," she said.

"I know, I appreciate that," he laughed lightly, still conscious of the many eyes on them. "Thanks for building up my confidence."

Before their conversation could continue, a wizened elf named Daiki, dressed in a ceremonial robe, stepped out from the audience and walked up steps carved into the stone face. Standing on top of the rock, he called for attention. Taryn and Liri joined the other students of the Acabi on the far left bench reserved for them.

The speaker waited a few minutes until everyone had a chance to sit down and the buzz from the audience had diminished. Several hundred had arrived for the event, with groups of people still drifting in. Acabi ceremonies were almost always filled to capacity with late arrivals standing at the back. Today would be no exception.

Once everyone was quiet, Daiki began, "Welcome masters and students to another Acabi. For centuries we have had students demonstrate what they have learned by engaging in combat with the very people that trained them. As you know, victory will prove your mastery of skills and your training is considered complete." He smiled as scattered chuckles came from the audience. It had been over ten years since a student had defeated a master. "If you are defeated, your teacher or teachers will decide together if you have shown proficiency. If you have, then your training is finished. If you have not, then you will continue for another year, at which time you will be eligible for another Acabi."

"Today we have five students that are at the age of testing. Each one is unique in their sphere of study, and it will be an honor to observe their skill and training put into practice. First, we will have the privilege of seeing Maemi. She is from Azertorn, the capital of the elves, and has been studying the elven short sword. By special consideration she is being allowed to test five years early due to her level of mastery." He had to pause as a murmur swept the crowd.

Testing early was very rare and a great honor. Taryn caught her eye and smiled in encouragement. Mae, as her friends called her, had trained in the same village as he had—and had been like a sister to him for as far back as he could remember. Taciturn and serious, she had few friends, so he counted himself lucky to be one of them. She nodded back at him before standing in acknowledgement of the introduction. After she had resumed her seat, Daiki continued, "Following her will be Trin, who comes from the eastern kingdom of humans and has learned the longsword. After that we will see—,"

Murai suddenly caught Taryn's attention from across the arena. Following tradition, he was seated in the front row on the opposite side with the other teachers that would be testing their students. At the moment he was making a face that had the master next to him struggling to stifle a laugh. Taryn smiled to himself. Of all the people he had come to know on the island, he would miss his uncle the most. Hearing his own name, he turned back to listen.

"—and last of all we will see Taryn," Daiki was saying. "As some of you know, he has trained with four different masters." He had to raise his hand to forestall the upswing in noise. "I know it is uncommon for a student to learn four disciplines—but notwithstanding, he has reached a level of mastery in the longbow, the katsana, dual-weapon fighting, and hand-to-hand combat. Today he will be fighting with two katsanas—"

Loud talk engulfed the audience, making it impossible to hear. Despite that, Taryn still heard Suoh and his friends yelling down to him and laughing. Heat blossomed to his face and neck, and he clenched his jaw against his rising frustration. Since the confrontation with them, he'd done everything he could to not tell others about his unique training. Now he would have to endure their mocking even more . . . unless he passed.

Lifting both hands to quiet the crowd, Daiki raised his voice to regain their attention. "It is true that there is no master that teaches a style of fighting with two katsanas—and for good reason. As you know, the katsana is heavy, and normally a two-handed sword. It's also long, which makes fighting with two all but impossible. I have been told that Irela, who has trained him in fighting with two weapons, has helped Taryn create his own style with the two swords—a great accomplishment which we will have the privilege of seeing first hand." Overriding another swell of noise, he called, "So let us begin. Maemi, if you please." He gestured for her to come to the center of the arena and descended the stairs to meet her.

Mae stood up slowly and walked to meet her master. Barely topping five feet, she was the shortest elf Taryn had ever met. In spite of

30

her stature, she was as fast as a snake strike—and just as deadly. Her slender figure moved gracefully, more like a dancer than a fighter. Whenever he'd seen her fight, her body appeared built for unequaled speed. Her soft, delicate features were most often cast in a somber expression, lighting with amusement only on rare occasions. Preferring to train hard, she had few close friends, and even with them she didn't say much. When she did choose to speak it tended to be insightful—and one benefited by listening.

The noise in the crowd dropped as Mae and her master Sani drew their swords and bowed to each other. Daiki, one of the few resident magi, drew some white powder from a pouch and dusted their swords while he muttered some incoherent words. As the powder touched the blades, the dust melted and, of its own accord, coated the sharp edges. When Daiki was finished, he slid his hand down the now dull side to make sure there were no sharp spots. The charm helped, but it didn't completely prevent injuries. Bruises were common and the occasional broken bone was not unheard of—especially if the fight lasted for a while. The spell didn't last forever and would dissipate soon after the match.

Daiki bowed to both of them and returned to his seat. Sani paused for a moment before leaping in, her thin short sword flashing in the sunlight. Mae was just as fast, parrying easily and circling for an opening. Taryn saw the subtle shift of weight in her feet and knew what was coming. Faster than he could blink Mae stepped in with a combination that was so quick her weapon became a blur. Sani struggled to block as each successive thrust or slash came at her in a cascade of feints and strikes.

Sani was excellent, but it was evident that Maemi was faster than her teacher. Each movement of her sword demonstrated precision and speed, like an extension of her own body. Despite Sani being outmatched by her student, she had a smile on her face as she retreated and dodged the attacks. Mae moved in like lightning, subtly beginning to attack from the right with each consecutive technique. Driving her teacher to the left, she kept it up relentlessly until, with a sweeping strike, she twisted around with her sword coming at Sani from the left—

all while Sani's sword was still moving to block the expected attack from the right.

Taryn knew the move was virtually impossible to defeat. To her credit, Sani fared well. She saw it coming and had time to reverse her sword in a vain attempt to block when Maemi's sword stopped . . . on her masters' neck.

The onlookers erupted in sound. Mae's skill and technique were very good, but her sheer speed was stunning. It took several minutes to get the crowd under control after the display. It wasn't often they saw a *student* that had attained such a level of mastery, and the applause and shouts were deafening as the two combatants separated and bowed to each other.

Daiki stood and stepped out to congratulate them. The mage said a few words to each of them, and they returned to their seats as he beckoned for Trin to come forward. Trin's master, Rangel, also stood up and joined them in the center of the fighting area. Both tall and broad shouldered, they couldn't have been a more different pair. Trin had long, dark brown hair, brown eyes and a ready smile that always seemed to be tugging at the corners of his mouth.

He found something amusing in almost every situation, and if he couldn't, he was prone to . . . make it amusing. Rangel wasn't quite as tall as him, but a little stockier, with black hair streaked with silver. They both drew their longswords and bowed before Daiki performed the protection spell on their weapons. Once he was finished, he said a few words of encouragement and returned to his seat.

In a flurry of long sweeps and chops, the battle came together. Trin was excellent with his sword, maintaining a firm grip with both hands while moving forward and back according to the movements of his teacher. A broad smile leapt to his features as he spun to avoid a particularly quick attack. It was apparent he was enjoying the challenge, and a challenge it was. The battle moved all over the arena and lasted for almost fifteen minutes before Rangel feinted high from the right, then swept his sword low to catch Trin on the leg, striking hard enough to knock him on his back. Trin hit the ground in a roll that returned him to his feet. Shaking his head, he spread his hands out wide in a gesture that plainly said, "What did you do that for?"

Rangel let out a guffaw and said, "You shouldn't have been standing there."

Wiping sweat from his brow and feigning out of breath, Trin said, "I got tired and was about to sit down for a break. I knew you needed one, too." They both laughed and clasped hands in congratulations.

Taryn noticed that Rangel was breathing considerably harder than Trin as the two fighters waited for Daiki to calm the audience and couldn't help but wonder how much longer he would have lasted before tiring. It had been a tough fight, and Taryn was impressed with Trin's endurance and Rangel's skill. After a quick exchange between Daiki and Rangel, they announced that Trin had passed his test.

The next student didn't do as well as either Trin or Mae. A tall elf Taryn did not know went next and fought with the short sword, although his lack of skill was obvious in every move. In fact, he looked like he had been training for only a few years. He lost quickly, and Daiki announced they had to consult before they could come to a decision on him. Taryn sighed to himself. If they said they had to deliberate, it almost always meant the student had not passed. Behind him he caught someone talking about how lazy the fighter was. He shook his head. Lazy students on the island did not fare well.

Liri went next. While she and her two masters walked out and waited for Daiki to dull their weapons, a group of other teachers began placing fifteen targets at various distances in the field to the right of the arena. Because she had studied the longbow, she would fight her two masters with the sword first, and then test with her bow after all the swordfights were finished. Taryn would do the same. After Daiki sat down again, Liri and her two teachers squared off. The first time Taryn had seen someone fight two teachers at once he'd thought it wasn't fair on the student, but he had come to realize after several Acabi ceremonies that it was quite practical. After all, how many times were there only two people in a fight?

After their warm-up, Taryn had thought Liri had improved a lot, but it quickly became apparent that she had not been *entirely* forthcoming about her ability during their warm-up either. She was good, her stance was perfect, and her form with each move of the sword was fluid and strong. Sunlight flashed off her sword as she danced left and right to parry her two opponents. Taryn couldn't believe how fast she was, and he found himself admiring and studying her form. She may not have been as lightning quick as Mae had been, but her speed and technique were still impressive.

Darting back from a double strike she continued with a defensive posture. Despite her approach, she still managed to find an opening to slip her sword in and catch one of her teachers in the stomach. Applause broke out as the teacher withdrew from the battle. Liri had been smart, he realized—the teacher she had defeated had been her master of the longbow and probably was not as good with a blade.

Taryn grinned and shook his head. Murai had always taught him to know his opponents—and if he didn't know them, learn fast. His favorite lessons where those in which his uncle would switch techniques mid-match and force him to adapt to a completely different style.

A sudden clash of blades brought him back to the battle before him. Liri fought fiercely, trying with all her might to catch her teacher off guard—but her master was relentless. She backed her student against the rock face, and with nowhere to turn, Liri missed a reverse that came too fast. An instant later it was over. He realized he had been holding his breath and blew out the air as he stood to join applause so thunderous he could barely hear Daiki announce that she had passed. Liri's fight had been one of the best Taryn had seen, and, catching her eye, he grinned and nodded an acknowledgement of her effort.

As the noise began to diminish around him, Taryn remained standing. A chill went down his spine with the knowledge that he was next. At that moment he would have given anything in the world for his parents to be there. Squaring his shoulders and taking a deep breath, he forced himself to focus and walked out to the center of the arena.

Three elves and one human stood up from the master's bench: Murai, his master of the katsana; Elsu, his master of the longbow; Edric,

34

his master of hand-to-hand fighting; and last of all Irela, his master of two-weapon fighting. They all waited patiently as Daiki performed the spell on their weapons. Before his teachers could take up positions on all sides of him, Taryn unobtrusively moved so the rock wall was at his back. He caught his uncle's approving glance at his choice of position as he waited for the four masters to take up positions in front of him.

Taryn closed his eyes and breathed in slowly, gathering his focus, allowing his senses to stretch out to every corner of the arena. Time seemed to slow as he took in everything around him, acutely aware of every sound. A soft breeze played across his face. Muffled footsteps came from his masters' feet spreading out to flank him . . .

—An unusual warmth began emanating from the handles of his swords—

Whispers of conversation could be heard from the crowd. Taryn couldn't help but think about his parents . . .

—The sensation of heat was climbing up his arms—

Someone called out encouragement from the students' bench . . .

—His whole body felt like it was on fire—

Daiki was saying something about the match about to begin, but every sound seemed muted . . .

Taryn struggled to open his eyes and focus on the match, but the world had been erased from his awareness. With all his might, he forced his eyelids open . . .

Intense blue flame engulfed his father's sword in his right hand, making it look twice as large as normal. Green flame streaked up his mother's sword, thinner than the blue flames, but even brighter. The magical fires that wrapped around his hands did not burn, but seemed to caress with surprising gentleness. Taryn looked from one sword to the other in amazement, unable to comprehend what was happening

Without warning white light streaked up his father's sword, leaving behind something written in shining white letters on the blade. A split

35

second later his mother's sword did the same. Unable to move, he watched transfixed as the blue fire on his father's sword intensified and seemed to gather on its cutting edge until the entire length of the sharp side looked like it was melting. He didn't know how he knew it, but he knew the blade was becoming sharper than any weapon could possibly be sharpened with tools alone. Sparing a glance at the green sword just made him stare at it in surprise. Under his left hand the sword was shifting from the beautiful sword he knew, to a magnificent elven longbow with a green arrow already notched, and then morphing back to the sword again.

A sudden cry from the crowd brought his attention back to reality. Instinctively he leapt backwards just as a sword flashed across where he had been standing. Seeing a second thrust out of the corner of his eye, he immediately dodged again. For a few furious moments Taryn dodged and weaved, blocking a strike whenever he could. *They must not have seen what had happened,* he realized. He spared a quick glance at the crowd. No one had a peculiar expression at all; they were just watching the match. No one had seen it—except him—or had he seen anything? Had it been his imagination?

As he brought up the blue sword to block a sweeping attack from Murai, the flame was gone but faint script on the blade caught his eye. Ducking under a thrust and jumping over another low sweep he landed on his back and rolled to his feet. *It had been real*! He thought. Elation filled his heart as he realized that for whatever reason, his parents had left him *magical* weapons. A sudden determination to win the match came unbidden to his mind. For the first time in the fight he truly looked at his four masters.

Murai was the furthest from him after his duck, jump, and roll—but coming in fast. Irela stood only a few feet from him on the left, already starting a combination with her twin short swords. Elsu remained close on his right but was still turning towards him, with Edric sliding behind to try and flank him. The only weapons Edric wielded were the heavy arm guards he used to block weapons, and his fists and feet to attack with—which were just as formidable as any sword. Taryn couldn't allow them to surround him or he would be finished.

36

In one swift move, he turned around to face the rock wall and ran diagonally towards it. Reaching it in three steps, he jumped up, put his right foot against the wall, and pushed off with all his strength. Using the momentum from the run and the push, he twisted his body in mid-air to land a fast kick on the side of Edric's head, sending him tumbling away. Landing in a crouch to avoid the swinging sword of Elsu, Taryn spun his body in a full turn and extended his right leg to catch Elsu at his ankles—sweeping his legs out from under him. With a quick overhand chop to the stomach, Elsu was out of the fight. Not knowing if the magic had removed the protection Daiki had placed on it, Taryn hit him with the flat of the blade just to be safe.

Rising from the crouch, Taryn brought his green sword in an upward slash to keep Irela from getting in range. Extending his other sword towards Murai, he backed away to re-evaluate the situation. Elsu had stood up and sheathed his weapon, a look of chagrin on his face as if to say, "I should have seen that coming." Edric was on his hands and knees, shaking his head, and Taryn felt a twinge of guilt. He hadn't meant to strike him that hard. Murai and Irela were on his right and left, but moving in cautiously.

Deciding that Irela was the more dangerous opponent, he took a step closer to Murai and engaged him with his right sword while at the same time rotating the blade of the left sword to rest along his forearm, reversing his grip. He could now block almost anything with the sword laying flat along his left forearm—without getting in the way of his other weapon. Glancing back and forth between Irela and Murai, he blocked the double overhead smash from Irela with his raised left arm while at the same time attacking aggressively with his right. Unnoticed by the fighters, the crowd was on their feet screaming and yelling—they had never seen anyone fight with two katsanas, let alone in such a manner.

Having fought with Irela many times, Taryn knew what she would do next. Sparing a quick glance at Murai to make sure he wasn't in range, he turned both his swords at Irela, reversing his grip on the left sword back to the original position. Just as he put both weapons vertically on both sides of him, he felt the jarring from Irela's swords coming from the left *and* right. Without hesitation he lifted his foot and leaned in to kick her full on in the chest—hard enough to knock her on her back but not hard enough to hurt her. Before she'd even hit the ground he turned around—but dove to the side to avoid Murai's flashing sword.

Landing again on his back and rolling to his feet, Taryn turned to see Murai already close to him—too close to block his next attack. Keeping most of his momentum, Taryn ducked low and felt the sword pass over his back within an inch of contact. Flipping his right sword to rest on his forearm, he raised his right hand so the sword was vertical as he straightened up—catching the reverse he sensed would be coming. With a simple pull of his fist inward, he sent the blade of his right sword swinging upward to knock Murai's katsana up and away.

Twisting forward and under the raised weapons brought him in close to Murai's body and inside his guard, while at the same time he reversed his left sword so it rested on his forearm as well. Despite his uncle's attempt to throw himself backward and bring his weapon back into play, Taryn continued spinning and tilted his left fist in again, flicking the tip of his left sword out so fast it connected with the retreating chest of his uncle. Again, he turned his hand at the last instant so the flat of the blade hit his uncle's chest and not the point.

Realizing that Edric would probably be back in the battle by now, Taryn finished the rotation and backed away from Irela and where Edric had been—switching both blades back to their original positions. Keeping them horizontally out in front of him, one high, one low, he spun to face the two remaining teachers. It was a good thing he'd turned with his swords out because Edric was sprinting towards him, but Taryn's swords left no room to approach so the unarmed master was forced to leap away.

Ten feet behind Edric, Irela had gotten back on her feet and was on her way to rejoin the fight, a look of determination on her face that he knew well. Wanting to take care of Edric before he had to fight two people at once, Taryn tried to move forward with a quick combination, but Edric blocked every strike with the bracers on his forearms. All too quickly he faced two masters—expertly moving to either side.

38

Still swinging his right sword to keep Edric at bay, he flipped his left weapon back along his forearm to better block Irela. This time they attacked as one. Irela also attacked from two angles with her two weapons, making it impossible to block both strikes with a single sword. Dodging forward to avoid one strike and ducking under the high kick from Edric, Taryn brought up his left arm to block Irela's second attack. Abruptly he crouched and spun towards his unarmed master. As he spun, he sheathed his father's sword, leaving his right hand free to grab Edric's extended leg at the ankle.

Instead of doing the normal block, Taryn kept some of the momentum of his spin and pulled. It was clear that Edric had expected his kick to land because most of his weight was behind it, making it impossible for him to stop his forward motion. Without being able to move, his knee buckled and he awkwardly hit the ground with his right leg still extended. Knowing that Edric would only be on the ground for an instant, Taryn let go almost the moment he'd grabbed the ankle, only hanging on long enough to pull him off balance. Slipping to the left he allowed his left sword to follow Edric down and hit him on the head with the flat of his blade before he even touched the ground.

One more out of the fight.

A quick glance showed that Irela was already darting in. With his back to the rock face he had nowhere to go, so he jumped backwards— and upwards. Using his momentum, he walked two steps backwards up the wall. Just as his body slowed, he threw himself forward and over the top of Irela's head. Knocking her weapons aside as he flipped and twisted over her, he landed and spun in an instant, with both katsanas out and ready.

For several moments they eyed each other, master and student. For the first time, Taryn became aware of the thunderous noise from the crowd. Students were standing on the benches and cheering. Teachers were on their feet and yelling uninhibited. Irela seemed to notice it, too, because she grinned at him. "People are so easily entertained."

Taryn, uncomfortable at the attention yet feeling a rush of excitement, didn't know how to respond, so he shrugged and readied himself. Irela snorted and stepped in to attack again. The sounds of the crowd faded as he focused on the fight at hand. Back and forth they sought for any advantage, but neither of them came close to landing a hit.

Seeing a vague opening he shifted his left sword to be on his forearm to block, and a split second later swung it back, reversing his right sword to parry—then flicked its tip out with a twist of his hand.

Somehow Irela managed to block the strike with her own weapon and tried to slice up and split Taryn's defenses with her second blade. Darting to the right to avoid it, he spun to get behind her—but she whirled to face him. Abruptly he tried to flick his right sword out like he had done with Murai, but Irela was prepared for that and dodged to the side. In a rush they came together with each of them refusing to back down. The intense fighting lasted for several minutes as both combatants displayed dizzying skill, with neither willing to give an inch. The ring of sword striking sword blended together, echoing through the amphitheater until it became difficult to discern individual blows.

Taryn wasn't really surprised that Irela had been the last one standing. He knew how good she was. In the entire time that he had trained with her, he had never beaten her in a fair fight; most battles simply . . . ended. Her technique was flawless and her speed rivaled Maemi's. She'd *also* helped him develop his technique of fighting with the two katsanas, making her practically unbeatable. Realizing that if he wanted to win he would have to pull off something she hadn't seen before, he cast around for something he could use. His glance fell on Mae and an idea began to form.

With a quick step forward and an aggressive combination he was able to drive Irela back and to the right. Using first his right sword and then his left he batted Irela's short swords out wide, taking special care to hit her left sword much harder than her right. After a couple of seconds trading blows, another opportunity came and he did the same thing, hitting both her swords wide but again hitting her left sword a lot harder than her right. The third time he did it, he could see that Irela had a puzzled expression on her face. Seeing another opening, he again swept both his swords out to bat hers to both sides. This time her eyes lingered on her *right* sword.

Good, Taryn thought, she's expecting a feint. It didn't take long before another chance came, but this time instead of hitting her left sword hard, he hit her right sword hard—just as she expected. His unusual swordplay masked his footwork and in an instant he snapped his body around to his left. Before she could react, he'd turned all the way around and smacked the flat side of both his swords on her unguarded torso.

As the final ringing clash from the swords died away, the audience broke into deafening applause and flooded the arena. The tumult was so loud that no one could hear Daiki as he tried to announce his victory and call Taryn and Liri to perform their test with the bow. Taryn barely managed to sheath his weapons before a wave of masters and students slammed into him.

For one long moment, joy engulfed him, and he felt the rush of intense satisfaction at what he had just done. Everyone around him yelled for him, and for the first time in his life, he felt accepted.

Then he caught Suoh's sullen look as he turned away, and just like that his elation evaporated.

Tiral, the name echoed through his mind, cooling his happiness like he'd fallen into a snowdrift, and suddenly the loud praise being shouted at him meant nothing. Unable to stop it, the world seemed to pale at the memory of the pirate attack.

He barely heard those around him.

"That was great, Taryn," Edric had to shout to make himself heard. "My head is going to hurt for a week! I knew you would do something I had never seen before."

Taryn managed a grimace. "Sorry about your head; I didn't mean to kick you so hard."

Before Edric could reply, Murai engulfed Taryn in a huge hug. "You were GREAT! I have never seen anything like it. I would hate to be up against you if you *didn't* like me."

Irela managed to grab his arm. "That was a nice finishing move; I didn't even see it coming."

Elsu clapped him on the back. "I knew I wouldn't last long with my sword, but I hoped to last longer than *that*." He said it in a tone of frustration, but with a huge smile.

A screaming person—who turned out to be Liri—smashed into him from the other side, almost knocking him over. "I can't believe how good you were . . ." The rest of her words were cut off as the crowd pressed in on him.

Despite all the commotion and congratulations directed at him, all Taryn wanted to do was to get away. The emptiness he felt was so intense it ached, and only the thought of his parents enchanted blades gave him a glimpse of hope.

Wanting to make things go as fast as possible, he shrugged his way through the crowd and over to the students' bench to get his bow for the longbow test. When he had finally made it through the throng to the deserted bench he hesitated. Did he want to use his old bow or his mother's sword that could turn into a bow? After a moment's thought he unstrapped his swords and reluctantly placed them behind the bench. He wanted to find out what his weapons could do by himself first, without anyone watching.

Bow and quiver in hand, he pressed through the celebrating group until he found Daiki. "Can we take care of the longbow test?"

Daiki nodded, smiling. "Sure, help me get some of the other teachers to settle the crowd." Then he paused long enough to clap him on the back. "And by the way, that was most amazing Acabi I have ever seen."

Taryn forced a smile and nodded before turning to quiet the mob of shouting people. It took several minutes to calm the jubilant crowd enough to go back to the benches, but everyone gradually started to clear out of the fighting area. Taryn and Liri stayed where they were and waited for Daiki to explain the procedure for the longbow tests. Taryn knew what to do, so he didn't pay attention to the announcement.

The test involved firing fifteen arrows: five at the foot of the benches, about fifty paces away from the targets; five from behind the benches, about one hundred paces away; and the last five shots from on top of the rock face, hitting targets at over two hundred and fifty paces. Targets were generally shaped like animals, with some large ones like deer, and some small ones like squirrels or birds.

Both Liri's test and his own passed quickly. He wasn't surprised to see Liri hit all fifteen targets perfectly. When it came to Taryn's turn, he performed well, even though he didn't take his time. A few of the targets weren't hit in the correct spot, but his mind wasn't on the test. When they were finished Daiki announced they had both passed, but Taryn didn't notice. Already gathering his gear and dodging well-wishers as politely as he could, he slipped out of the arena. The moment he was out of sight, he took off towards the tree line.

Chapter 3: Discoveries

Taryn raced through the woods towards his cottage. Trees and houses blurred passed him, and before he knew it, he'd passed it and stood at the base of the mountain. Without hesitation, he reached for the sheer rock and began to climb. A hundred feet straight up he flew, following the long familiar route. Every handhold was ingrained in his memory; every toehold could be reached without looking.

In a matter of moments he arrived at the top and pulled himself over onto a large ledge. Perfectly flat, the ledge ran back over a hundred paces before hitting another wall of stone. His climb had taken him to the center of a broad, stone shelf. To his left and right the ground tapered back until it disappeared into the mountain. Hardy trees, some as thick as a large man, were scattered along the ledge, somehow finding purchase in cracks or shallow soil.

He had discovered this place when he was eight, and it had become his refuge ever since. Countless hours of practicing had been spent at this spot, and the evidence of mock battles could be seen in every direction. Cuts and holes from his swords, arrows, and other types of weapons marked almost every tree. Older cuts had begun to knit while several new ones still had sap running from them. Scrapes and scratches marred smooth stone where he'd struck it. This had also been the spot where he'd first tried fighting with two katsanas—and perfected it.

Stepping to a tree about five feet from the edge, he turned and sank to the ground, leaning his back against the knotted wood. Before him the entire island stretched away, disappearing into a glittering ocean in the distance. Dense foliage dominated the vista, only broken by the occasional chimney or large structure.

Taryn's eyes gazed without seeing the view, his mind too deep in thought to notice. Tiral, the only student to die during the pirate attack, pulled quickly into the forefront of his thoughts, but as always, he shied away from the lancing memory. Latching instead onto his enchanted weapons, he drew his fathers' sword.

Who were his parents to have weapons like these? And why had they not revealed their true nature before? Magical weapons throughout Lumineia were not uncommon, but Taryn sensed that these weapons were far more powerful than normal. For one thing, he'd never heard of a transforming weapon.

Remembering the flash of white light and the writing that had appeared, he turned his father's sword over in his hands and peered at the writing. Faint silver writing stood out from the shining metal. In flowing script he could make out the word "Mazer."

What could that mean . . .? The thought trailed off as the idea came to mind that Mazer could be his father's name. In that moment the sword glimmered blue as if in answer to his thought and magic tingled up his arm. The more he thought about it, the more confident he became. There was no way he could explain *how* he knew it. He could just . . . *feel* it—so strongly it brought tears to his eyes.

He finally knew his father's name! Grasping his mother's sword, he eagerly drew it and laid it across his knees as well. "Ianna" was inscribed in the same faint silver script. Closing his eyes, he leaned back and reveled in this tiny bit of information he had yearned for his entire life.

Relief and joy spread through him, warming him more than the afternoon sun. For several minutes the strong emotions overcame him, burning into his heart and searing into his mind—and then almost imperceptibly began to fade. Second by second the elation dissipated, left to be replaced with the haggard sadness of one who has caught a glimpse of what they desire most, only to watch it slip away.

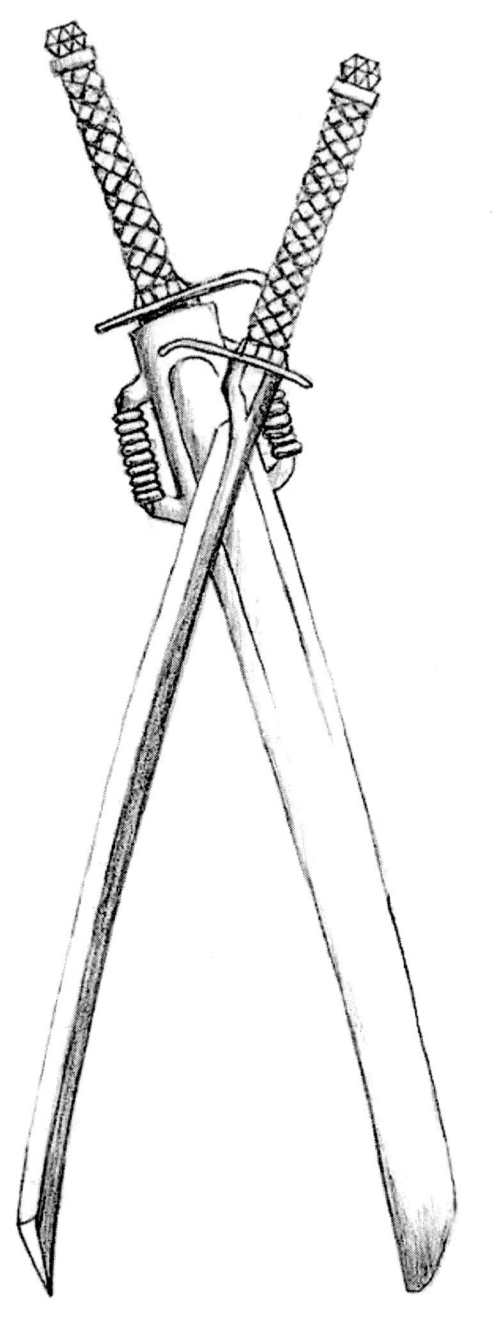

What now? The sobering thought whispered, sending a chill through his heart and chasing the last vestiges of relief away. His entire life he had wanted to return to the mainland of Lumineia to search out his heritage, learn where his family had come from, and why they had brought him to the island. The questions had burned within him from the moment he had understood that Murai was not really his uncle, and now that he knew his parents' names, the prospect of returning felt all too real. For the first time he realized that knowing his parents names didn't quench his desire to know more.

It fueled it.

Sighing at the elusive questions, he looked down at his parents' swords, but the shimmering metal yielded no more answers. Deciding to momentarily set aside his concerns and see what the weapons were capable of, he rose to his feet and returned his father's sword to its scabbard, focusing on his mothers' weapon. Although his training had included little on magic, he knew enough to know that imbued weapons required something to activate. Perhaps he had to say words or incantations?

No, that wouldn't be it. His parents had been warriors; of that he was certain. Warriors would want their weapons accessible, and the same should go for the magic contained within them.

Lifting his mother's sword to eye level, he concentrated on the bow he had glimpsed before the battle in the arena. Before his eyes, the blade began to bend back on itself, while the hilt stretched downward and curved backward. At the same time, the metal faded and began to shape into burnished wood, its dark grain polished and smooth. As the arcing wood neared the end, a string of green light reached out from both ends and joined in the middle. A little taken aback at how easy it had been, Taryn hesitated and then examined it more closely.

The wood of the bow looked to be oak, which was odd, because most bows were made of yew or another kind of supple wood, oak being far too stiff. Intricate designs and runes were carved expertly along the entire length of the curved weapon. Upon closer inspection, he noticed what looked like faint veins of green light twined into the wood. At the end of the bow, the green light extended straight out of the wood to become the string. Reaching for the string, he half expected his hand to pass through it, but instead he found it to be as solid as steel.

Excitement rippled through him as he viewed the amazing weapon, and, seeing that a dark green arrow was already notched, he impulsively turned towards the mountain and drew the arrow to his ear. Smooth to draw, it wasn't nearly as hard a pull as he'd imagined it would be, and he felt a tingle spread up his neck at the sensation. Taking aim at a tree that sat right against the rock, he loosened his fingers . . .

—With a snap the bow released its tension, and in an instant the arrow struck the tree, embedding itself so deep that only the feathers remained in sight—and another arrow appeared to replace it.

Astonished at how fast the arrow had flown, Taryn leapt towards the impaled tree. When he got there, he was even more surprised to see that the arrow had gone all the way through the tree and penetrated the rock of the mountain itself. No bow he had ever seen could make an arrow sink into solid stone. His heart hammering, he returned to where he had shot the first arrow, took aim a few feet from the tree he had hit, and shot another arrow into the smooth cliff. While it quivered from the impact, Taryn raced across the ledge to find it similarly embedded halfway into the hard rock.

For twenty minutes Taryn shot arrows at various targets. Each arrow went exactly where he wanted it to go, and when he pulled the bow back as far as he could, the shafts embedded all the way to the feathers into stone or dense wood. After a few minutes he noticed the arrows he'd shot first had begun to fade away. Transforming the bow with a thought, he sheathed the blade and drew his father's sword. Besides the writing, the weapon hadn't changed, so what could it do? Recalling the glow along its edge, he remembered thinking it was becoming sharper.

Stepping close to a tree with a branch about as thick as his arm, he swept the sword to cut the branch. Yesterday he might have been able to cut the branch with the same sword, but today definitely felt different. The enchanted blade sliced right through the branch like it was a crisp stalk of celery. Turning to a branch as thick as his head, he cut through it just as easily. The sword glimmered dully blue as it cut the thicker

48

wood. The same thing happened when he cut the wide trunk of a tree, except the sword flashed even brighter blue.

He smiled as the whole tree slid off the now angled stump and crashed to the ground. Glancing at a boulder nearby, he hesitated for a second before swinging the sword at the rock—and watching it cut right through.

As it sliced into the stone, the sword flared brilliant blue. So, Taryn mused, the harder the substance, the more magic necessary to cut it. The question was . . . how much magic did the blade contain and would it run out? He smiled as Murai's words came to mind: "Always know the strengths *and* weaknesses of your weapons—and yourself." Deciding it was better to know the limits of his weapons before a battle, and not during, he methodically began to make cuts in the mountain with his father's sword. Each time, it would flash bright blue, but after the twelfth time the weapon only went partway through the cut before stopping as the blue fire extinguished.

The magic had lasted a lot longer than he had expected, and he nodded to himself as he made a mental note of its magical limits. Setting aside his father's sword, he drew his mother's weapon and changed it to the bow. As fast as he could, he drew back the arrows and fired them at the mountain. One after the other they sunk into solid rock. After the fiftieth streaked into place, no arrow appeared, so he began to count. It took thirty seconds for the first arrow he'd shot to disappear from the rock and reappear on the bow. Every five to ten seconds, the other arrows also vanished.

He forced himself to wait until all the arrows had disappeared and then began to shoot again, but this time shot only forty-nine arrows. He carefully counted fifteen seconds before the first one he'd shot faded away. *OK,* he thought, *if I exhaust the magic, it takes longer to replenish.* Turning the bow back into a sword, he sheathed the weapon.

Taryn picked up his father's sword and repeated the earlier exercise of cutting into the mountain. The sword cut only eight times before giving out. It had only been two or three minutes since he had made the first cuts in the rock, so it was reassuring to know the magic of his fathers' sword came back quickly even when it was exhausted. He breathed a sigh of relief; he'd half expected the magic to be gone forever.

With some practice and a little more experimentation it became apparent that he could make Mazer (in that moment he decided he would call his swords by the names on them) cut through almost anything, or *not* cut through objects if he didn't want to. *Good,* he thought, *I won't accidentally cut one of my friends' swords in half while we're sparring.*

His examinations complete, Taryn began to go through routines with his new swords. Linked more than ever, they responded to the slightest movements as if they were just another muscle in his body. Increasing the tempo and difficulty only made the weapons feel more and more connected to his thoughts and will. After thirty minutes he was using the hardest and most complicated techniques he knew without the slightest hesitation. Slipping in between the trees like a gust of wind, he bent and coiled, swinging both swords out to nick trees and rocks alike. In the middle of a combination he shifted his mother's sword, sheathed his father's sword, fired an arrow at the rock wall, and without missing a step changed Ianna back for the next block.

While he stepped through intricate sword routines, his mind wandered miles away from the island he'd grown up on. Out of nowhere, the resolution to find out more about his parents struck him, hitting him so hard he stopped mid swing. He *had* to find out who they had been, why they had been coming to Sri Rosen, and if he had any other family.

He furrowed his brow and shook his head, *Where to begin though?* The only thing he had from his parents was his newfound weapons and the knowledge that his mother was an elf. *Maybe Azertorn, the city of the elves . . . ?* His thoughts trailed off into nothing.

It was time to leave Sri Rosen.

The thought felt like a blast of icy wind, causing him to take a deep breath and look over his favorite spot for what he knew would be the last time. Trees and solid rock were littered with cuts and slices. Arrows had driven holes through trunks and stone alike. The evidence of his fierce battle had extended all across the ledge, and would linger for decades. The sight filled him with sadness, but a thread of excitement raced through him as he turned to get one last look at the view.

More time had passed than he'd realized. It was already early evening, the sun shifting from yellow to red as it sank towards the horizon. Every shade of yellow and orange spilled across the sky and ran together into vibrant streaks of color. Brilliant purple and pink soon appeared, shimmering in the few low-hanging clouds that dotted the view.

Taryn didn't move until every shred of light was gone, and then stayed until stars began to wink and glitter. Only after the moon started to rise did he finally turn and climb slowly down. By the time he got home it was past midnight, but the soft glow of candlelight flickering in one of the windows revealed someone was inside. Without hesitation he opened the door and strode in.

To his surprise, there were several people in his room. He'd expected his uncle, but Liri and Mae were also present. The girls were seated on the bed while Murai sat in the only chair. Empty bottles of ale and crusts of bread sat on the desk and beside the bed.

Nobody spoke for several moments until Taryn broke the silence. He almost didn't say anything, but he knew he had to share what had happened with someone and the people in the room were the only individuals he could imagine sharing something so personal. In halting phrases he began, "I know the names of my parents . . ."

For the next several minutes he explained what had occurred with his swords before the arena fight and a little bit about their magic— enough to satisfy curiosity, but not to reveal everything about their power. He wasn't quite ready to share that, and throughout his tale no one spoke.

"I have to go back," he finished, "now . . . on the next boat."

Almost immediately Liri stood up. "I'm with you, whatever it takes."

Mae wasn't far behind her. "The ship in the harbor is leaving at first light," she said quietly as she rose to her feet.

Taryn hesitated, a little taken aback by the directness of his friends. "Er . . .," he began but Liri cut him off.

"You don't have a choice, Taryn." she said, her jaw set in a firm line that he knew from experience didn't allow for disagreement.

Taryn smiled in surrender. "All right, get your things. We'll meet at the dock an hour before dawn. Liri, would you mind letting the harbormaster know?"

"No problem," she replied as she slipped out the door, a smile of triumph on her lips. Mae simply nodded and followed her out, leaving him alone with his uncle.

It took a minute before Taryn could look his uncle in the eye, so he took the time to place his weapons on the wall. When he finally did manage to face Murai, the sadness he had expected was there, but there was also something else. Was his uncle happy about his leaving?

"I am so proud of you, Taryn. I know . . . I know . . ." But the rest of his words were lost as Murai bounded across the room and embraced his adopted nephew. "I know you will find what you need." He let go and pushed him back. "You will always be my family."

Taryn smiled, swallowing against the surge of emotion. "And you will be mine."

Then Murai inclined his head. "If I may, I have a few final lessons for you."

After Taryn nodded, Murai began, his gaze piercing, "You have not been given an easy life, nor an . . . abundance of talents." He paused and gave an apologetic shrug for his honesty. "But it isn't what you have been given that has made you who you are. It is the choices you have made. There are many that have been gifted with much more but have achieved far less. It is your choices—not your ability, that will define your destiny.

"By now you should know, you have been much more than a student for a long time. I have had the privilege of watching you become far more skilled than any other master on the island. For this reason, you must remember to always trust your own abilities—yet do not allow that confidence to become arrogance."

He paused until Taryn nodded again.

Murai's smile turned sad. "Now for the hardest lesson, the one I cannot teach you." Shaking his head, he took a deep breath. "As such a gifted warrior, you will face many opportunities to take a life, just as you already have."

He sighed, his tone changing to one of regret. "Death by the hand of another destroys many things, but nothing is more damaged than the family. It steals the innocence of children, and shatters the hope of sons. It forever scars mothers, and fathers, and rips apart the very fabric of parenthood. The person's very posterity is erased." He paused and gave a tiny shake of his head before glancing back at Taryn, his eyes bleak. "Taking a life leaves a hole that cannot be measured."

Taryn didn't know what to say. Something in Murai's eyes made him think that he knew firsthand the meaning of his words, but the thought only had time to flicker before his mind was drawn to the pirate attack where Tiral had been slain.

Unknowingly echoing his thoughts, Murai continued, "I know the death of Tiral still haunts you, but you need to know that it is not your fault. He was too young to fight, and disobeyed his master in doing so."

"It doesn't matter," Taryn whispered, barely able to get the thought out. "If I hadn't hesitated maybe he wouldn't have died. We both know the ones I spared were the ones that killed him."

The silence in the cabin stretched for several moments, until Murai said, "I believe there is something in you that rebels against the killing of another, but you should not consider this a curse. Rather it is a gift, and a rare one for a warrior. Unfortunately, many of our trade will kill without a second thought, and their hearts become hardened as a result.

"However, the lesson you will be forced to learn is when a life *must* be taken. Sparing the life of someone can mean others will perish— especially if it is someone who is more evil than good. As horrible as taking a life is, allowing that person to slay many more is indescribably more abominable."

"How do you know when to do it?" Taryn burst out, unable to contain the question he'd wanted to ask since Tiral's death. *Or have I already slain those that deserved life?* For some reason the bearded man from his first battle stood out to him.

Murai just shook his head. "You will need to find your own way to balance this in your life because justice and mercy are—and have always been—opposites. Because of your skill it will frequently fall upon *your* shoulders which to give. Just know that I trust you to make the right choice."

It didn't seem like much of an answer, but as Murai held his gaze, he knew it was all he was going to get, so Taryn nodded.

"Lastly," Murai said, "it is important you recognize that every person is unique, with specific qualities and attributes that make them special. Some are special because of physical skills, sometimes it is a magical skill that sets them apart, but more often than not, it is something . . . else that makes them exceptional. This fact is overlooked by many, and as a result only a few are deemed important."

He paused again, searching for the right words, "Every . . . single . . . individual, is necessary in the battle to do what's right. You are truly the best fighter I have ever seen, so you will be called upon to defend the innocent—but don't ever forget that just because a person doesn't fight, doesn't mean they aren't important to the victory."

When he finished, he smiled and turned away, overcome with a fit of coughing. Something about the way he'd said it made it seem as if it were extremely personal, and for the first time, Taryn realized he knew little about Murai's past. A pang of sorrow echoed through him as he realized there would be no more opportunities to find out.

Taryn's throat tightened. "Thank you, for everything. You were a great teacher."

Clapping Taryn roughly on the shoulders, Murai turned around and grabbed something off the table. Turning back he reached out with a small spoon that had been threaded through a hole in the handle.

"Something told me you would be leaving soon, so I wanted to give you a present to remember your training. This is so you don't forget to be prepared for anything," he said, the corners of his mouth struggling to stay in place.

Recalling the morning's intrusion brought a smile to Taryn's face, but his uncle wasn't finished.

"Actually, I have something else for you," Murai said, still grinning as he reached into his pocket and pulled out a package. "This might be a little more useful."

"I don't know; I'm sure the spoon will come in handy," Taryn replied.

Tossing the package to him, his uncle said, "Maybe, but I thought you might like these in a pinch." Taryn looked at the package in his hands. It was about the length of his forearm, wrapped in cloth, and a little heavy. Removing the cloth revealed a finely crafted belt with five throwing knives in separate sheaths. Sliding one of the little knives free, he found it not only in good condition but also of excellent craftsmanship, with an intricate sea dragon engraved on the blade. Placing it back in its sheath, he pulled out another, which proved to be identical. He glanced at his uncle with a raised eyebrow. No master on the island taught knife throwing.

"I got them off a pirate that thought his *one* ship could attack the island," he responded to the unasked question with a smug grin and a twinkle in his eye that suggested it was utter foolishness on the pirate's part—which Taryn had to admit, it probably was.

"This is a great gift, but I've never used throwing knives before," Taryn said.

"I know . . . neither have I," Murai admitted as he spread his arms out wide, "but I thought you might like to practice on the ship. It's a long voyage, after all. I know that if you could, you would learn every style of fighting there is, and I thought you might like to pick up knife throwing along the way."

"Thank you," was all Taryn managed to say. How do you say goodbye to the person who has raised you?

Seeming to sense Taryn's feelings, his uncle chuckled. "You don't have to say goodbye to this old elf yet; I will be there to see you off in the morning." He paused and smiled. "I am happy for you, about your swords I mean."

Taryn smiled with mixed emotions and nodded in reply.

Murai embraced his adoptive nephew one last time and slipped out the door, leaving Taryn alone in the flickering candlelight.

Feeling numb and drained from the day's events, he blew out the light and lay down, still fully clothed. Despite the hour, Taryn didn't feel tired, and sleep took a long time to come. In a single day he'd found out things about his parents he'd never known, discovered his weapons were magical, and made the decision to leave the island—the only home he had ever known. Overwhelmed by the sheer volume of life changes, he spent the next few hours struggling to let peace overtake him so he could rest.

Sometime early the next morning, Taryn sighed and gave up. Slipping from his bed, he began gathering his things. Aside from the mugs and bottles of ale that his friends and uncle had left, the room contained only a few pieces of parchment, some clothes, a hard leather vest, bracers, a pack, and his weapons on the wall. Everything fit easily into the pack. Then he lifted his swords down from the wall and strapped them onto his back.

Hesitating, he pulled his father's sword out and called forth the blue fire—which came before he'd finished his thought. Drawing his other sword he changed it to the magnificent bow and allowed himself a few moments to admire the weapons. Then, shaking his head at the irrational thought that it had never happened, he changed Ianna back to the sword and sheathed both weapons. Last of all, he wrapped the belt of throwing knives his uncle had given him around his waist and rotated his torso to see how they felt. He would practice with them later—when he had time.

Before he knew it, he was standing and looking at the room that had been his home since birth. A light breeze gently brushed the drapes, allowing a scattering of soft moonlight through. Despite everything that had happened, it was still hard to leave. His heart aching, he turned and slipped out the door for the last time.

Chapter 4: Throwing Lessons

Cresting the horizon in a sudden blast of light, the morning dawn found Taryn standing in the crow's nest of the *Sea Dancer*. The lack of mountains had been unsettling at first, so over the last two weeks he'd taken to spending his time in the only elevated place on the ship. It afforded him a peaceful place to think, along with the occasional ride when they hit rougher waters.

Beneath him, the mainsail stretched in a great white arc as it strained to contain the powerful wind that drove the vessel forward. The *Sea Dancer* had one other smaller mast towards the front of the boat, but its canvas was furled at the moment due to the strong wind. Below and behind him the aft cabin sat with the helm situated above it. A door into the aft cabin led down to the hold and crews' quarters. At the front of the ship, the forecastle housed the captain's quarters, with ready access to the deck. In addition, a large ballista stood mounted at the stern, its wood hardened from long exposure to the salty air.

Even with only one sail, the prow of the large ship crashed through the water with tremendous force, tilting the vessel in either direction without warning. Standing on the deck the affect was slight, but the swaying crow's nest could move up to ten feet to either side in an instant. When he'd first begun volunteering for the high watch, the other sailors had told frequent stories of men who had been catapulted out of the nest when an unexpected wave cracked the tip of the mainmast like a whip—sending the unfortunate men far from the boat.

Taryn enjoyed the tales, and laughed just as much as Liri and Trin. It didn't occur to him until later that the stories were meant for him. By then, the sailors had taken his lack of response as self-assurance, and left him in the unnerving position of being welcomed into the sailors' confidence. They had even begun inviting him to join their games below deck and letting him take the high watch whenever he wanted. One of crew, named Hunrin, or Hun, as the other sailors called him, a squat nugget of a man with a bushy beard and a wide smile to match a wide face, had even offered to show Taryn how to throw knives after seeing the set from his uncle the night before.

A shout from the deck pulled him away from the view. Looking down he saw Hunrin standing at the door to the aft cabin.

"Do ya want to learn how to throw a knife or what?" Hunrin called up.

Without answering, Taryn leapt out of the crow's nest and caught a rope on the way down. With thick leather gloves protecting him from the burn, he slid down the rope almost as fast as he would have fallen. Tightening his grip as he neared the deck, he landed lightly in front of Hun.

The sailor grunted. "Not bad. I can see you've picked up a few things since we set sail, but don't expect it to be so easy to fling a blade." Hun walked across the deck and hung a crude target at about head height on the forecastle. "Not many people are very good, you know, mostly because no one has the coordination or the time to practice. It took me months to become skilled enough to actually *use* a knife throw in a fight." He grinned broadly. "It sure comes in handy now and then."

While he was talking, several more sailors appeared and began going about their morning routine, checking ropes or eating breakfast. Erix, the captain, settled onto the stairs next to the newly hung target and began eating a mess of potatoes. Taryn didn't miss his nonchalance with the knife target only a few feet away.

Hunrin walked back to Taryn, who still stood next to the aft cabin. "I'm just about the best knife thrower I've ever met," he proclaimed,

59

with a smug smile and an over exaggerated wink. At the same time he idly flicked a knife towards the board on the other side of the deck. The small blade went several feet to the left and embedded next to the captain.

With a chagrined "Woah, sorry cap'n," Hun bounded forward to get his knife while the captain glared at him even as the corners of his mouth twitched. The other men within view of the scene laughed until the captain glanced at them.

Hun returned and said with a straight face, "It always helps to look at where you're throwing." He nodded expansively to add emphasis.

Another sailor tightening a rope next to Taryn leaned over to him, "Don't let him fool ya, he's the best o' the crew with a knife."

It didn't take long for Taryn to agree. Like an oiled hinge, Hun whipped out a knife and threw it straight into the board, sinking half the blade just to the left of center. Despite the quick movement, Taryn took careful note of how he threw it. The way he twisted it and tossed it underhand seemed simple enough. A few seconds later, two more knives were in the target within an inch of the first—thrown the same way.

Taryn whistled in appreciation. It was good throwing, and all the more impressive on a rocking boat.

"Are you sure you want to teach me? You never know, I may be a terrible," he said as he pulled out one of the knives his uncle had given him. Even though he had only seen a knife thrown three times, he was pretty sure he could duplicate the move, even if he couldn't do it as well. With a quick turn and throw he sent it digging into the target a hand's breadth from Hunrin's knives. It wasn't quite as good a throw as Hunrin's, but it nevertheless seemed to impress the small man.

"By Ero's staff!" Hunrin shouted in astonishment. "I've never seen anyone be able to do that so quickly."

The sailor that had commented on Hunrin's ability stopped and came over to Taryn. "Five copper says you can't do that again."

Ten coppers and two knives later the betting had spread like wildfire. When Liri and several others joined the group of spectators, Taryn began to regret he'd taken the bet. He didn't care for this much attention, and it left him feeling uncomfortable enough to miss the next few throws. Growling under his breath, he focused on Hun instructing him to imagine sticking the knife into the target and showing him how to angle it down to get the best throw.

It only took a few repetitions of pulling out his knives before he was able to get each blade nearly where he wanted it. Although he felt the heavy scrutiny, he still felt confident that with some decent practice he could master the technique.

Hun seemed intent on teaching Taryn to throw from every possible angle, high or low, on the ship. By mid morning he had managed to strike his target from anywhere—even behind the back or with his body turned. Even though few hit near the center, he performed adequately enough during the fast paced lesson, but he wondered how many others the impatient sailor had successfully taught.

Having learned the basics of knife throwing so quickly, Taryn assumed that the lesson would be over, but Hun returned to where he was standing above the aft cabin and handed him his knives back.

"You've done great, kid, but the real challenge comes next. You need to learn how to avoid a knife getting thrown *at* you."

"How are you going to teach me that?" Taryn asked, but Hun was already pulling two wooden knives out of his pocket.

"I'm gunna throw these at you, and you're gunna dodge them." His smile broadened. "If you want to try to catch 'em you can." His face showed how foolhardy he thought that would be. "But I've only ever heard of one person able to do *that*, and he was a blasted thief. Now, go stand next to the target and I will see if I can hit you," he said as he descended the stairs and took up a position in front of the aft cabin.

As Taryn stepped down to follow him, Liri sidled up close to him. "Are you sure you want to do this?"

"Why not? They are just wooden knives. Besides, it might prove useful."

"OK . . ." Liri sounded uncertain. "But be careful, would you?"

Before he could answer, Hun called to him, "You need to be able to see what it looks like to have a knife coming at you, so I am going to throw these wooden knives a little slow, and then throw them faster once you have gotten used to it, OK?"

Taryn nodded, but he was suddenly very aware of how large the crowd had swelled. Nearly all of the crew lined the rails, smiling and talking to each other. *Let's see you try this*, he thought, not particularly pleased at the turn of events. The flash of coins exchanging hands caused him to glance sideways, but then he did a double take. *Liri was betting too!* He was about to ask her what in *Skorn's* name she was doing, but a quick movement brought his attention back to Hun and the wooden knife streaking towards him. Out of instinct he sidestepped and the fake blade clattered off the captains' door and fell to the deck.

Cheers and laughter burst out from the spectators. Another quick glance showed that now nearly every one of the sailors appeared to be participating in the rampant gambling. *I'm glad I can provide some entertainment during your voyage,* he thought, his brow furrowed in annoyance. Right now, he just wanted the lesson to end so he could escape to the crow's nest.

Like a flash of lightning, he realized for the first time that there might be some benefits to the anonymity he'd had his whole life. Recalling his conversation with Liri on the docks, he thought perhaps there was more truth to Liri's words than he'd given credit.

A split second later the other knife came at him. Distracted and unprepared, he still managed to duck and spin back to his original position.

He smiled to himself. *I can do this,* he thought while stooping to pick up the two wooden knives.

After tossing them back to Hun he readied himself again. This round he did better, and focused enough to watch the spinning knife slice through the air towards him. By the next attempt, Taryn wanted to see if he could catch it. He watched very carefully as Hun leaned forward and threw the knife. Poised as he was, it wasn't difficult for him to sidestep again, but this time he reached out and picked it clean out of the air before it hit the door behind him. Even though he'd caught the wood halfway on the knife portion, he was pretty sure he could do better the next time.

Liri wasn't the only one to applaud at that.

"Kid, you are just too good, ain't ya!" Hun yelled, his voice exultant. "This time I am going to throw it as quick as I normally do."

The next throw really came faster, although Taryn was still able to pick it out of the air without too much of a problem. It was also easier to catch it while he spun to one side or the other, because he didn't have to stop the momentum, but could keep it going. He could imagine himself spinning and whipping the knife back at the thrower. The mental image made him smile inwardly, wondering if it would actually work.

By the time the next two throws came, Taryn was able to see the handle of the spinning knife and snatch it out of the air without even grabbing the "blade" portion of the fake knife.

The watching men were pointing and talking excitedly by now. Trin in particular appeared to be thoroughly enjoying the spectacle, while Mae had her usual inscrutable expression painted across her elven features.

Hunrin caught the two wooden knives that Taryn had just tossed to him. Without hesitation or warning he threw them right back at him in quick succession. On reflex, Taryn twisted and caught one, and then the other—and then without warning a *third* wooden knife appeared out of the corner of his eye.

Looking back at Hun showed him to be already releasing another fake knife in Taryn's direction. Not only was Taryn off balance from the first two, but he was unprepared for the third. Despite this, he dropped the wooden knives and exploded into motion. In a single lightning move, he turned back towards Hun, caught the third wooden knife by the handle, twisted the way he'd imagined, and whipped it straight at Hun—off balance and slow, but still accurate. A split second later a wooden knife sunk quivering, embedded in the door behind Hun a hands breadth from his head.

For a moment no one moved. Then uninhibited applause broke out. Sailors shouted and called out. Hun grabbed his knives and came to Taryn, shouting to be heard over the din, "Well kid, I don't think you still need lessons. Just don't forget who taught you."

Taryn forced a thank you, but what he had just done felt surreal, and caused his stomach to tighten. How did he just do that? It should have been impossible, and he knew he should have just dodged. It would have been the smart thing to do. Why did he try for more? Then he realized the more important question was, why did it work? Oddly, he felt more annoyed than anything else. He had no explanation why weapons came so naturally to him, but as he caught sight of Liri, he just wished something else would be as easy.

Without warning, someone began shouting in alarm, louder than the rest of the group. At first Taryn couldn't pick out who it was, and then he saw the captain standing next to the helm. He was leaning on the rail and looking southward, out to sea. Taryn followed his gaze and caught a glimpse of sails in the distance. One by one the other men silenced themselves and found places against the rail to see.

"Can anyone see what color the sails are?" someone called out.

"Frey, get my glass," the captain ordered. The first mate detached himself from the group and went into the captain's cabin. A few seconds later he returned with the captain's spyglass. As the captain put the distance viewer to his eye, Taryn leaned over to Hun.

"Why is everyone so concerned about sails?" he asked.

Liri, who appeared at his side, leaned in to hear the answer as well.

"We're still a week out from the port at Keese. Too far out for a sailboat, only possibility is merchant or pirate." He glanced at them. "There aren't any shipping lanes to the south of us, and only a few inhabited islands, but nothing high traffic."

"What about the color of the sails?" Liri asked.

"Pirates in this region like to use black sails so other pirates won't needlessly follow them and attack them thinkin' they're a merchant vessel."

"Honor among thieves, huh?" Taryn said skeptically.

Hun snorted at Taryn. "Yeah." Then his face grew serious again. "Pirates have been a little active of late—and they can be vicious. The last few ships have been found barely afloat, with either nothing left on board or dead sailors hanging from the mast as a warning to other ships."

Then he caught sight of the grim expression on Liri's face and his features softened. "Don't worry. Pirates are notoriously greedy. You never see more than one or two ships. They just never seem to want to share, and our crew can easily handle one ship, maybe even two with the four of ya."

"Black sails!" the captain called down.

The light humor evaporated in an instant, and most of the sailors left the rail grumbling before returning to their chores or finishing breakfast.

"Frey, I want you in the nest. You've got the best eyes. That ship moves a finger towards us, you let me know," the captain said as he tossed the spyglass to Frey. "Sabriel, you've got the helm. Markham, Finn, grab some others, get the short sail ready to be raised at a moment's notice and get the emergency canvas out of the hold and tied up, not open, just ready, in case we need it."

Men jumped to follow instructions while the captain came down the stairs to Taryn and Liri.

"Would you mind coming into my cabin for a moment?" His eyes flicked to Trin and Mae. "You too, if you don't mind."

They all nodded and followed him into his cabin. Stepping through the door for the first time, Taryn saw that it was nicer than the crews' quarters, but not by much. Knowing the captain, it wasn't a surprise. For the last two weeks he'd been very organized and decisive, yet with a trace of humility, giving Taryn the impression he was more concerned about his men than himself. His men also obeyed his orders without hesitation or complaint, which always spoke highly of a leader.

The room they stood in was small and sparsely furnished. Dominating the center of the space, a wide desk sat surrounded by heavy chairs, maps strewn across its surface. On one side of the room, a bookshelf rested with a half dozen books on it while a cabinet sat against the other. Small windows on either side of the room had storm shutters opened to allow light in. In the back of the room was another door, which Taryn assumed led to the captain's sleeping quarters.

"I know you have been trained to fight," the captain said as he pulled a bottle out of the cabinet, "but I wanted to know if you four have ever been in a real fight." When they all nodded their heads he continued, "Well, I don't doubt that you are excellent, and if the display by Taryn this morning is any indication of your abilities we will be more than prepared in case of attack. I just need to make sure you won't hesitate, because you had better believe that any pirates you encounter will not be merciful."

The captain's words reminded Taryn of what his uncle had said about justice and mercy, and he wondered what he would do if they were attacked. Since the battle where Tiral had been killed he'd thought often about what he would do next time he was in combat. How would he know if a man was a father? Or a soulless killer? Would his hesitation again cost a life?

Then a darker thought wormed its way into his head. *You will never know the cost of your decision—until it is too late, until you have lost someone you could have saved.* Swallowing hard against the chilling thought, he forced it aside and returned his attention to the conversation.

"We will do what is necessary if the time comes. We have had attacks on Sri Rosen in the past and we know what to do," Trin was saying. They all nodded in agreement; then straight-faced he added, "Although we may not be able to throw a knife as well as Taryn."

The captain gave a slight grin but didn't answer for several seconds. He just looked at each one of them, measuring each in turn before nodding and opening the bottle to pour five glasses. As he filled them with amber liquid Taryn took a moment to study the captain. He was of average build and height, with prominent human features— brown hair, brown eyes, and a round, tanned face from his time in the sun. Probably around forty, it was obvious he had been a sailor his entire life. Generally serious and not prone to joke with the crew, he carried himself in a manner that inspired respect.

Taryn smiled to himself as he guessed the real reason he had wanted to talk to the four of them. To the captain, they presented a variable in an upcoming battle and he wanted to be more prepared. Taryn nodded to himself, satisfied with what he'd seen. The captain would do whatever it took to get his crew home safely, and that included them.

The captain put away the bottle and sat down, pointing at the glasses. "Have a drink of ale." After they grabbed the glasses he continued, "Now, I have a serious question for you . . ." He paused to lean back and put his feet up on his desk. "How much was the take off Taryn's display this morning?" His face creased into a broad smile as he finished the question.

Trin and Liri burst into laughter.

"I made twenty-six silver and fourteen copper," Liri said, glancing at Taryn with a twinkle in her eye. "I think I *somehow* knew to bet on Taryn." She caught his expression and shrugged. "The odds were against you, at least in the beginning anyway."

Trin shook his head in real chagrin. "Of all the days to get up late, I just had to sleep in today. I could have made some coin, too."

To Taryn's surprise, even Mae spoke up. "I made twelve silver and twenty-two copper." She cast Taryn an apologetic look.

"A fine bunch of friends you are," he said with more heat than he intended. "I was just trying to learn how to throw a knife, you know. I didn't mean for it to look like I was seeking praise."

Liri's shoulder bumped into his, as if it were an accident. When he caught her eye, she shook her head slightly and flashed him a soft look.

He realized right then that it was too late for him to do anything about it, so he might as well deal with it. At least he'd learned how to throw his knives, and how to catch them, too, which was an added bonus. That had been his goal and he'd accomplished that, no matter how many people had been watching. Besides, it could have been worse. He could have thrown all his knives into the ocean by accident. Smiling at that thought he let his frustration go and added, "I get half of everything you made."

Liri snorted, "You think, huh? That's not likely to happen anytime soon."

Taryn joined in the laughter and allowed it to wash away any lingering bad feelings from the morning's training.

Trin drained his glass and set it down on the desk. "Thanks for the drink, captain, but we had better finish our breakfast." Taryn and the others were quick to add their thanks as well.

"No problem," the captain said as he stood up and raised his glass to Taryn, "Oh, and nice throwing Taryn."

Taryn could see he was being sincere, so he said "Thank you, but I'm sure you've seen people do that before."

"Not even close," he replied readily, but he changed the subject before anyone could say anything else. "Before I forget, switch with Frey in a few hours would you? I know you like the high watch, so you can give him a break around noon."

"Of course," Taryn said as he walked out the door behind the girls. Liri stopped and turned, allowing the others to pass her.

"Seriously, you really are amazing, you know that?"

"Thanks, and thanks for letting me know I was being . . ., well you know."

She raised her eyebrows. "I don't know what you're talking about," she said, "but you now have a greater challenge."

"Yeah, what's that?"

"You have to teach *me,*" she exclaimed with a smile before turning on her heel and walking away before he could respond. Taryn grinned and followed her, shaking his head. Before he stepped through the door leading below, he stopped and took one last look at the sails on the horizon.

He hoped he'd be ready when the time came.

Chapter 5: Pirates

Tensions had steadily grown on board the *Sea Dancer* in the two days since the pirates had been sighted, despite the crew's efforts to outrun them. The pirates had managed to follow behind them and to their right, or starboard as the sailors corrected Taryn. It didn't help matters that sometime during the night the wind had died down. They were drifting at the moment—just bobbing in the ocean waiting for occasional gusts to fill the sails.

Taryn glanced at the dark sails in the distance in the predawn light. They were just visible, but still lurking. Shaking his head, he turned and whipped a knife across the short span to the target—straight into one of the grooves formed from his repeated strikes. He'd begun waking up early and practicing before the rest of the crew was up and about. He didn't want a repeat of the first day.

With a flip of the wrist he tossed the next knife into the air and caught it deftly by the blade, then threw it overhand into the target next to the first, but his mind wandered elsewhere. Since the knife training with Hun, he'd had quite a bit attention from the other crew members. To his own chagrin, he found he shied away from such a social welcome. He still hadn't decided if his unease came from his training, or a lack of social ability.

Frustrated with himself, he whipped another knife into the target. Hun had told him it was harder to throw overhand but might be worth learning, so he'd taken to practicing both ways. For some reason, throwing overhand felt different, and Taryn had been having more difficulty mastering it.

A quick spin and another knife quivered in the target as the door behind Taryn opened. Turning, he saw Liri's trim figure step out and stretch before she caught sight of him and stifled a yawn into a smile.

"Good morning," she said, strolling towards him. "I can see you are doing your morning routine." She glanced around the deck to ensure no one was about except the man at the helm. "Are you ready to keep teaching me or do you want to throw a few more first?"

"No, that's fine, I was done anyway," he sighed, striding to the target and pulling out his knives. "I still can't quite throw it overhand."

"You will get it soon enough," she replied before her smile became rueful. "At least you can get it close to where you want it."

Taryn handed her a few knives. "Don't say that, you've hit it before." He scrunched his face, thinking hard. "Although I can't remember when . . ."

She opened her mouth in mock outrage and hit him in the shoulder, then with a nimble snap of her wrist threw the knife towards the target. It hit about halfway between the center and the side.

He laughed, "All right, you've hit it once, good job."

Her eyes narrowed and she threw another two in quick order. Both of them hit the target, although neither found the center.

Without warning, brilliant light exploded all around them as the sun came up, causing both of them to squint and flinch away. It always surprised Taryn how quickly the sun rose over the water, and they paused while the pre-dawn light changed to bright daylight in a matter of minutes.

"I would love to continue with you down here, but it's my turn in the nest." He handed her the other two knives from his belt. "You can practice while I am gone though."

71

She nodded and took the blades. "Don't fall off. I still need a teacher."

"Thanks for being so concerned about me," he said as he moved towards the rigging. With a quick smile and an encouraging nod he leapt up and grabbed a rope. Scaling the ropes he reached the nest and slid over the rail. Glancing down, he caught a glimpse of Liri's eyes lingering on him as he ascended. Her odd expression occupied his thoughts until he reached the top.

When he slipped into the crow's nest he was greeted sourly by Frey, who had been up all night with his eyes glued to the distance viewer. Yawning and rubbing his face, the sailor handed him the spyglass.

"It hasn't moved closer or further. I just don't know what they're doing, but I have a bad feeling from my boots to my bald head." He rubbed his bare scalp to emphasize his point. "I'll go get some sleep and relieve you after noon."

Before Taryn could speak a word of agreement, Frey had climbed out of the nest and begun working his thin frame back down to the deck—considerably slower than Taryn had come up.

Taryn shrugged and settled into a comfortable sitting position where he could watch the pirates off to the south. After a quick look to assure himself that they hadn't moved, he relaxed and let his mind wander.

What am I going to do when I get to the mainland? The question that had been bothering him since the voyage began forced itself to the forefront of his thoughts. Try as he might he could not devise a more efficient way to find out more about his heritage. It probably wouldn't be a good idea to just go around asking people if they had heard the names Ianna or Mazer.

The only real hope he had was if there were records kept of people . . . perhaps in the elven city? He was part elf and part human, so maybe he should look for records in the human cities as well? Realizing his shoulders had tightened up, he forced himself to relax and tried to think of another solution to the daunting task.

After an hour of trying in vain, he sighed in frustration. How was he really supposed to find information on his parents when he didn't know anything about them except their names? Then the thought came to mind that the names on the swords weren't the names of his parents. A moment of panic engulfed him, but the same assurance that he'd felt when he'd first seen the names slowly washed away his concern and replaced it with confidence. Ianna and Mazer *were* his parents' names, he was sure of it. He had no reason to believe it, but he still knew it.

Taryn sighed again and let the gentle swaying of the boat lull him as he began think about the pirates. Their behavior seemed odd, and he spent the next few minutes mulling it over. Then an idea sprang to mind that sent a shiver down his spine. *But there's no way the pirates would do that . . .*, he thought. He tried to convince himself it wasn't possible for there to be more than one pirate ship, but the thought kept coming to his mind, pushing against his attempts to quash it. Unable to resist, he stood and, with the spyglass, looked out to sea—not to the south, where the pirate ship was, but to the north.

It took him a few minutes, but after some searching of the horizon he spotted more black sails. "It's not possible," he said aloud, *Hun said that pirates don't work together . . .* But in his heart he knew what was happening, and what was about to happen. Hoping not to find what he expected, he scanned the rest of the horizon to the east, where they were headed. Starting from the first pirate ship, to the south, he rotated a full circle, feeling his heart plummet as he counted. Not including the original one or the one he'd just spotted, he counted *five* more ships, almost out of sight and all to their east—directly in their path.

Unable to believe his eyes, he did the sweep again, but there was no question. They would be facing seven full crews. Shaking his head, he tucked the spyglass into his belt and dropped out of the nest. Descending fast, he put it together.

The first pirates had intentionally allowed themselves to be seen and had carefully driven their quarry towards the waiting trap. It was a good ploy, especially because it kept your attention focused on the one ship until it was too late. *It might already be too late*, he thought as he landed heavily on the deck.

Liri's smile evaporated as she caught sight of his expression.

"What's wrong? Is the pirate ship moving towards us?" She asked.

"Worse," he said, "there's more than one ship."

She blanched. "The captain just got up; he's with the helmsman."

"Fine, take my place in the nest, would you? They are all around us but mostly in front of us to the east. I figure the one ship kept us distracted and moving forward . . ."

". . . and drove us into the others," she finished the statement for him, her expression turning gray. "Smart plan on their part—not so good for us." She caught the spyglass he tossed to her and leapt towards the rigging. "I'll let you know the minute they make a move."

Taryn nodded and hurried to the helm where he found the captain and Sabriel, the second mate. Without any preamble he said, "Captain, we have a problem. There are six more pirate ships. Most are to the east, where we are headed, but a couple are to the north. We're sailing into an ambush."

At first the captain didn't respond, but his face turned to ash. Sabriel just kept staring forward, gripping the wheel so tight that his knuckles went white.

The captain's response was sharp, "How much time do we have?"

"Not much, they could turn towards us at any moment."

Taking the helm, the captain spoke to Sabriel, "Get the men up and armed. Load the ballista and get every bolt we have from below—"

Liri cut off the rest of the instructions, her tone rising as she called down, "They're turning towards us!"

Sabriel looked at the captain. "Go. Now!" the captain said, at which the second mate raced to rouse the crew. Within minutes the boat was

74

teeming with activity. Men rushed about with fear in their eyes, but the chaos had an order to it that rang of frequent training. But how could they fight off *seven* ships?

As Liri, Trin, Mae, and Taryn gathered their weapons and readied themselves, Liri leaned close to Taryn. "There's something strange about these pirates."

"What is it?" Taryn asked, glancing at her.

She hesitated, which made Taryn finish ducking into his hard leather vest and look at her. "What?" he asked again.

"They turned towards us at the same time . . . at the *exact* same moment."

"Are you sure?"

She nodded with a frown. "Didn't Daiki say that instant communication across distances was something very rare?"

"I think so." He paused, trying to remember. "I think he told a story of two brothers that could talk mind to mind across any distance, but I thought he said it was just a legend."

"Whatever it is, these pirates are communicating somehow, which means there is one clear leader." Her brow furrowed before she continued, "If we find him, we might be able to stop this fight without getting killed."

"Agreed, go tell the captain so we can be prepared," Taryn said, tightening his belt.

She nodded and left Taryn to finish readying himself. Sinking his knives into their sheaths, he strapped on his twin curving scabbards and slipped his katsanas home. One last check and he hurried back up to the crow's nest, doing his best not to think about the last time he'd fought pirates.

As soon as he was on top of the mast he made a quick count of the ships to make sure no more had shown up. There were still seven, which wasn't good, but at least no more had appeared. Watching them for a minute, he gauged them to be coming faster than he would have expected. Even though they were still a good distance away, Taryn's sharp eyes narrowed as he peered at one of the vessels. Something was moving on the side of the boat and he pulled the spyglass from its leather case mounted to the rail.

As he brought it to his eye, the ship he had been watching leapt into sharp detail. After a moment's inspection he realized there were oars on both sides of the ship—two banks of oars. At two rowers per oar, that would mean at least a hundred pirates to the one ship. Turning to examine all the other ships, he could see that others had two banks of oars as well, and the few that only had one were even larger vessels. At best they were facing approximately *seven hundred pirates*. A shiver ran down his back . . .

There were only forty sailors on their ship.

In the face of such odds, Taryn's mind turned to his uncle's words. *Do I have no choice? How many will I have to kill?* The questions beat against his skull so hard he had to swallow and shake his head to bring himself back to the present. With all his might he tried to convince himself that the pirates they were going to fight were purely evil and forced himself to imagine sinking his blade into one. In the back of his mind a sinister whisper ripped through him. *What if Liri dies because you choose not to kill?*

Abruptly the wood under his feet snapped backward and he snatched the rail to hold on. As if fate wanted to play a hand in the upcoming sea battle, a strong wind began billowing behind them, filling the sails to the point of breaking. Rocking and plowing forward, the prow of the boat began to buck as it crashed through the water.

A creak of wood behind him brought his attention to a person climbing over the rail. The normally grinning Hunrin's face appeared white under his scruff as he worked himself into the small space. "The captain wants you in his quarters. I'll take the watch."

Taryn nodded and climbed over the rail, leaving the cramped space for the small man. When he arrived at the captain's cabin, he found Liri,

Trin, Maemi, and Sabriel already there. The captain indicated for Taryn to close the door.

"We have a problem," the captain said. "We have forty-two sailors and you four fighters from Sri Rosen. We are going against seven ships with an estimated fifty sailors per ship—"

Taryn coughed and cut in, "Actually, four of the ships have two banks of oars. The others appear to be larger as well." He paused, realizing there was no way to soften the blow. "I estimate at least a hundred per vessel."

The captain's face hardened. "Let me get straight to the point then. I know you four are trained to fight, and Sabriel and I have been in our fair share of sea battles. This is not a fight we can win. We need to come up with something in the next twenty minutes or we will be shark bait by nightfall. Any suggestions?"

The silence was deafening until Mae spoke. "I have an idea I think will work."

The captain nodded, so she asked a few pointed questions about their ship. As she detailed her plan, the others' tense expressions phased to incredulous.

When she finished, Trin asked, "Is that even possible?"

Sabriel's brow knit together as he considered her suggestion, "I . . . think so, but I've never seen it done before."

The captain leaned in. "I think it's our best shot, but it's going to be risky. We will be betting our lives on Liri and Taryn."

Uncertain about his role, Taryn's eyes flickered to Liri. Smiling confidently, she said. "We can do it."

The captain stood up. "We're going to use Maemi's plan. I don't see any other option anyway. You all know your positions, so get to it. Sabriel, inform the rest of the crew and finish getting this ship prepared in any way possible."

Mae leaned forward with an intense expression, drawing all eyes towards her. "Taryn and Liri will do their part. You can count on it."

The captain nodded grimly. "Let's hope so. Our lives depend on it."

Resigned determination mingled with a glimmer of hope as the group hurried to prepare for the upcoming battle, but Taryn found that his heart was not in it. He'd trained his whole life for just such a battle, to defend those weaker than himself against individuals seeking to destroy, to fight the strong preying on the weak.

He just wished he wasn't so afraid to end the life of another sentient being—a sentient being that might still have good within its soul.

Chapter 6: Outnumbered

Taryn looked down from the crow's nest at the crew finishing their preparations. The plan that Mae had presented was going to be tricky, and counted on Liri's and Taryn's skills with a bow. After she'd suggested the plan, she'd explained that there were a limited number of options when faced up against a vastly superior opponent. Hit and run tactics was usually the best option—but they couldn't use that in the current situation. When you are forced to face a much larger enemy, you could either take a superior defensive position—which they couldn't do either—or attack at a weak spot that cripples your opponent.

Prior to explaining her idea, Mae had asked the captain what places on a ship could be hit by an arrow or two that might disable the entire vessel. The captain had answered by saying the rudder might be destroyed by a few well placed arrows. He'd also suggested that cutting the ropes holding the sail down might work as well, but that could easily be repaired.

The proposed plan involved an attempt to disable ships before they could surround the *Sea Dancer*. The oars were the complicating factor. They couldn't really take out the oars, which made hitting the rudder the best option since cutting the sails would only slow the ship. Everything would depend on Liri's and Taryn's ability to hit specific locations on the rudder at the correct angle while both ships bobbed up and down— at unknown distances. But a single vessel disabled might balance the scales for their survival.

"Are you ready?" the captain called up to Taryn.

He leaned over the rail and raised his arm to show his readiness. Liri, positioned at the front of the ship, did the same. The pirates were closing in on them, with the first one only a minute or two from getting within range of bow and ballista. At the moment there were three ships right in front of them. Two of them were in the process of turning to block their way forward. Other vessels were gliding in on the right and left of them, cutting off any escape. *This is going to be close*, Taryn thought.

"Fire as soon as you think you can hit them," the captain called to Taryn and Liri.

Taryn waved in acknowledgement and drew Ianna. In a flash of light it changed to the bow. "I'll take the big one on the left," he yelled to Liri as he raised the bow. Sighting on the ship he'd designated as his target, he waited for the right moment to shoot. He'd picked this particular ship because it was one of the ships that was in the process of turning broadside towards them, which would present the rudder in a couple of seconds.

There! The vessel had finished its turn, bringing the rudder into view. With his elven vision enhanced by the far viewer, he focused on the tail end of the ship. Locating the spot he wanted to hit, he carefully put the far-viewer back into its case without taking his eyes from his target. Taking a deep breath, he brought the bow up and drew back an arrow of solid green light. *This is just target practice*, he told himself—then he released.

It took a few seconds for the arrow to strike, even though it flew so fast it was a blur of green. Hitting hard, it sunk into the wood at the highest spot visible—right next to where the cord that turned the rudder was connected. With a snap that could be heard from their own ship, the arrow went clean through the rudder . . . breaking it completely off. Not only did the rope tear, but also the top wooden pin that hinged it. Now the pirates' rudder hung to the side, barely connected by the second wooden pin at the bottom.

Not a moment later, a second arrow flew from the front of their ship. It didn't travel as fast as Taryn's had, but Liri's arrow still hit its target, and even more accurately, Taryn noted as he looked through the distance viewer. Liri's arrow hit the rope square on, snapping it and embedding into the wood behind it.

A cheer went up from their ship and sailors began calling to Liri and Taryn, but the captain's deep voice cut through their exuberance: "Save the celebration for later mates, we're not out of hot water yet. Taryn, Liri, nice shooting; now do it again if you can."

Taryn waved his arm and prepared to target another ship, but as he began looking for a rudder to target he noticed something strange—and not good for their plan. Even though several other ships had been in the process of turning broadside before, now they were straightening out and coming directly at them—keeping their rudders out of view.

Liri must have noticed it too. "I don't have anything, do you see an opening?" she yelled up to him.

"No, they've all turned towards us," he said, then hesitated, choosing his words carefully. "They responded pretty quickly to our shots; maybe they are watching their own ships."

Her sharp look was still visible to him despite the distance separating them, and he nodded to her. She tilted her head in acknowledgement and left her post, heading for the captain at the helm. He hadn't wanted to alert the crew, but the pirates almost certainly had some form of communication, and whatever it was, it was fast. There was no way all the ships could have seen them hit the rudders, so he'd hoped Liri would catch on and go tell the captain. He was glad to see her hurrying because they didn't have much time. A couple of pirates were already trying to shoot some arrows—which splashed down a hundred feet short of the *Sea Dancer*.

The captain suddenly shouted, "It looks like they're on to us. Taryn get down here. The rest of you lot, prepare to repel boarders." Seeing the fear returning to their faces, he added, "And take courage, they will learn to fear us before this day is out!"

Taryn dropped to the deck and raced to the captain. As he skidded to a stop, the captain said, "Liri explained your theory and it sounds right, so what's our new plan?"

Liri looked at Taryn and he nodded to her. She said, "Normally the only option left would be to try to take the leader…"

"—And that won't work because even if we caught the leader, someone might just kill him to 'advance' themselves in rank," the captain interjected, finishing her statement. "So what are we going to do?"

Liri spoke up again. "I know that *normally* finding the leader of a group of pirates wouldn't work—but, we aren't dealing with a normal set of pirates, are we? If a group has united like this, maybe there is a leader they *will* obey."

"I don't like it, but I don't think we have any other hope," the captain replied with a frown.

An arrow thudded into the railing nearby, drawing all their eyes to the quivering shaft.

"Well, we're out of time, so that's our new plan, but if you see an opportunity to stop a ship, do it." Then the captain raised his voice and yelled to the crew, "Defend the ship, Taryn and Liri have a plan. Don't wait for a command from me to shoot; if you see a target you can hit, hit it!"

The members of the crew that had bows or crossbows immediately turned and aimed over the rail. Pirate ships were all around them now. The two they had disabled were slowly turning with the rowers rowing in reverse on one side. Two ships were on their left, sailing parallel to their own vessel—but getting closer. Three ships were on the right with one of them sailing on an intercept course and the other two mirroring the others on the left. Pretty soon they were going to be surrounded.

A sudden volley of arrows came from the ship on an intercept course. Most embedded in wood, but one sailor cried out when an arrow sunk into his arm.

"Frey, take the injured that are unable to fight below, the injured that can still fight, do the best you can for them. We need every available figh—*everybody get down!*" the captain shouted as another volley flew through the air towards them from the left.

Everyone ducked as pirate ships all around them launched arrows and crossbow bolts in their direction. A hailstorm of deadly missiles rained down on their ship. Sails were ripped and torn, rails and barricades were pummeled relentlessly. Several of the men were hit because it was impossible to find cover from both sides.

Taryn leaned up and glanced over the rail at the ship that was still coming at them. If it didn't turn, it was going to hit them in thirty seconds. Then the ship started to swing sharply to come in line with them. Now coming in at an angle, the rails could be seen lined with villainous looking pirates armed to the teeth with all manner of swords, axes, and daggers. Taryn estimated there to be about seventy in the boarding party, and it was clear they were going to be the first to intercept them. Their oars had been stowed and beams were ready to be put in place between their two ships.

As the ship drew closer the arrows slowed and stopped, allowing him to stand cautiously and look around for something to do. Seeing a stray rope that had been cut by the volley of arrows, an idea flashed into his mind. Brash and dangerous, it just might be brazen enough to take the pirates by surprise. It also might get him killed. With that comforting thought, he sheathed his weapons and sprinted to the rope that was hanging on the side where they were about to be boarded.

Without stopping he snatched the end of the rope and, still on the run, raced towards the back of the boat, wrapping the end of the cord securely around his left wrist as he ran. He streaked past the captain and a few sailors, reached the back rail and leapt off the boat at an angle. The rope instantly went taut and swung Taryn out to the right side of the ship in a wide arc—two feet above the choppy water.

In seconds he was angling out and away from the *Sea Dancer* an arm's length from the pirate ship. Still gliding through the air with astonished pirates looking down at him from above, he drew Mazer and sliced right into the boat. The blade lit up with its magic as it cut through the side of the ship like it was a slice of hot bread. Gouging deep, the curved wood split open, leaving a ragged gap dipping below the water line.

Cries of astonishment turned to anger as they saw Taryn coast by several feet below them, gutting their ship like a fish. Before anyone could do anything, he finished his swing, sheathed his sword, and lifted his legs to fly over the rail of his own vessel. Releasing the rope, he landed lightly next to Trin.

"Show-off," Trin said, his voice laced with sarcasm.

Taryn shrugged and ducked as a retaliating stream of arrows shot towards them again. Through a crack in the barricade he could see the ship that he had sliced begin to settle and fall behind as water poured into the cut he'd made.

A sudden crash from the opposite side punched the *Sea Dancer*, throwing men stumbling to the deck as another ship collided with theirs. Pirates roared and dropped planks of wood between them as sailors and the four fighters from the island rose to defend themselves. Shouts and screams echoed everywhere as the small group struggled to stave off the wave of corsairs. The Sea Dancer's ballistae sent a thrum through the deck, firing as fast as the men could load it. Before long, another ship hooked onto their boat from the right and pulled themselves close—forcing them to defend against both flanks.

Taryn and Liri fought on the left while Trin and Mae helped to defend the right. At first, Liri stood back and used her bow, repeatedly dispatching pirate after pirate until she ran out of arrows, then she drew her sword and moved to stand next to Taryn. For his part, Taryn was using both swords, blocking with first one, and then the other. When he had an opening, one of his swords would dart in, cutting men down the moment they stepped in front of him. His heart clenched as he watched his victims cry out in pain, but he couldn't afford to consider sparing them. Despite his efforts there were times that his sword somehow turned before cutting into flesh, knocking men out rather than killing them.

Perhaps it was the eyes of the dying that gave him pause. Clutching their wounds the pirates he'd struck gasped for life, their bodies shaking in agony as the light in their eyes dimmed. Fury, hate, and finally fear passed through them before they went dark.

84

But Taryn had no choice. For each one that died two took his place, and if he spared them this time their entire ship would be overrun. But the sight of life departing the bodies of those he'd slain seared into his mind. Amidst the desperation and chaos of the battle it seemed like each one bore the same expression.

Disbelief—and blame.

Unable to dwell on it he poured his emotions into his blades, taking three down in whirl of steel. Then he charged forward, roaring as he rammed his shoulder into two men about to jump onto their boat. Smashed into each other, they flew backward and dragged another man into the water between the boats, where all three were quickly left behind by the racing hulls. Turning, he hilt smashed a man that was about to kill Hunrin and sheathed Mazer.

With his right hand free, he changed his mother's sword to a bow and unleashed a barrage of arrows into pirates trying to jump between the ships. Each arrow went precisely where he wanted, embedding deep into shoulders or legs—or hearts when he saw them about to fire back at those beside him. Each man cried out before falling backward onto their own ship. Darting forward, he drew his father's sword again and rejoined the fray.

On the opposite side, Mae twirled and danced, her short sword cutting through any that stood in her path. No one could even get close as she glided in and out of the group of pirates like an avenging wraith of destruction, and before they knew what hit them, they'd been cut down.

Near Mae, Trin stood his ground just as well, although in a far different style. His longsword had a greater reach than nearly all the weapons around him and he took full advantage of its length. Pirates fell left and right as he chopped and swung with incredible strength. Each swing and furious shout plunged fear into any pirate within view, causing more than one to shy away from the tall swordsman.

For a few minutes the four fighters and the sailors of the *Sea Dancer* managed to hold their own—until the other pirate ships drew close and tied on to those already connected to theirs. Now there were four vessels tied together side by side on their left, and two on their right. A moment later, the one he'd gutted managed to catch up and tie on as well. Bloodthirsty pirates howled and flowed across vessels like an unending wave towards the besieged ship in the middle.

Liri ducked an ax swing and cut the wielder down. Continuing her turn, she ended up next to Taryn. "Do you see the little girl by the helm of that ship?" she asked, breathless as she blocked another attack and then whipped around like lightning to slice him across the midsection. The pirate grabbed his stomach and dropped with a groan.

Taryn thought it was an odd question, but he spared a look where she'd indicated, and sure enough there was a young girl next to the pirate at the helm. Between parrying two swords and an axe at the same time, he noticed her hands were tied to the rail.

"Mae says there are other children on the other boats too," Liri said beside him, ducking under his extended sword to fight an incoming charge by several more pirates from Taryn's left.

Taryn reversed Ianna to rest on his forearm and spun to look at the ship on the other side, in the process blocking an overhead chop. Averting his eyes from what he knew was coming, he flicked the tip of sword out and caught the man in the throat.

It took a second, but he caught sight of another child, this one a young man that looked to be about twelve. Taryn ducked underneath a swing from an off-balance pirate and before the man could regain his balance, brought his knee up into the man's stomach. He dropped like a stone, gasping. A hard tap from Mazer's hilt on the man's temple and he went down for good.

Taryn suddenly caught on to what Liri was suggesting. The kids had to have something to do with the way the pirates had communicated—and if they were kids, the leader had to be next to one of them, probably an older child, or perhaps an adult.

"Can you handle this side for a second?" Taryn asked Liri, but before she could answer he sheathed Mazer and morphing Ianna, sent four arrows into the men directly in front of them. Each of them was hit so hard they flew backward, blasting others to the deck.

"Sure," she said ruefully, "but only for a moment," she added as another wave started climbing over the bobbing rail, daggers clenched in their teeth.

Taryn nodded and raced for what was left of the rigging. On the way he punched a man that was about to gut the captain but didn't wait to see the man drop. Sheathing his mother's sword, he leapt up the rigging as fast as he could. In a heartbeat he reached the nest, and in another instant he was running on the crossbeam towards the pirate ship. When he reached the end, he leapt up and out. Sailing through the air above the brutal fight below, he landed hard in a crouch—on the crossbeam of the neighboring ship.

Without hesitation, he stood and sprinted across the spar until he reached the end and leapt again to the next ship in line. In quick order he crossed all three ships until he came to the fourth and last pirate vessel. As he ran across each boat he searched for and spotted a child next to each helmsman, but when he got the last one, he looked down and saw a haggard looking man chained to the rail. Beside him a large pirate stood, shouting orders laced with profanity.

Taryn paused for a moment and studied the pirate leader. Dressed in dark leather, he had long black hair tied back and wore several knives as well as a rapier at his belt. From the deference the other pirates showed him, he appeared to be an epicenter of activity as other pirates jumped to do as he commanded. Seeing a route to the captain, Taryn looked for the fastest way down.

Still in his crouch from jumping onto the spar, Taryn slipped off the beam and dropped towards the deck thirty feet below him. There was no rope to grab to slow his descent, so he landed hard and rolled forward to take most of the force. Finishing his roll he spun in a full circle with his leg extended and dropped two astonished pirates before they could draw their weapons. Giving the others no time to take action, he jumped up the steps to the pirate at the helm.

One man leapt towards him as he came up the stairs, but Taryn angled his body to the left and let the man's sword glide harmlessly past him, an inch from his face. The pirate had evidently expected resistance, because he stumbled as he tried not to fall down the steps. Taryn easily slid past him and tapped the back of his head with his elbow to send him sprawling down the stairs. Racing forward towards the man at the helm, he drew Mazer and smacked the flat of the blade against the pirate's sword hand, forcing him to drop his half-raised weapon. In an instant the long katsana was at the leader's throat.

"Call off the attack," Taryn said in a voice as hard as steel, and hoped the man didn't call his bluff. Killing men in combat was one thing. Slaying a defenseless man was another.

The pirate captain hesitated, at which Taryn dug the tip of his sword into his neck enough to draw blood and make him wince.

After a moment more, the man glared at Taryn and said, "You have no hope. I will have you killed before you can take two steps."

The pirate captain's eyes flicked to the left, and Taryn instinctively snapped his body around. Before his mind had time to register the danger, he had hooked a throwing knife from his belt and snapped it through the air to sink into the attacker's arm with such force that it slammed him into the post behind him, sticking him fast while his loaded crossbow crashed to the deck.

Rotating back before anyone could even blink, Taryn removed his weapon from the man's throat only long enough to smack the flat of his blade into the pirate's face. The sheer speed and strength behind the thrown knife had left the men in view visibly shaken. The pirate captain shook his head and swallowed at the unwavering blade at his neck, eyes wide as he looked at the fire in Taryn's.

"Tell everyone to retreat to their ships," the pirate spoke—not to his shipmates, but to the shabbily dressed man chained to the rail behind him. The prisoner closed his eyes and after a few moments Taryn could hear the sounds of battle slowly diminish, and then stop altogether.

In a flash of steel, Taryn drew Ianna and placed it at the pirate's neck while at the same time he used his father's sword to slice through the chains that bound the man. Mazer glowed dimly blue as it cut the metal chains.

"Your prisoners are no longer yours," Taryn said evenly. Without taking his eyes off the pirate in front of him he addressed the now released man: "Get the children onto our boat."

The man nodded gratefully and left to gather the children. Out of the corner of his eye, Taryn wasn't surprised to see the boys and girls be freed by their captors before the man reached them and work their way slowly over rails until they achieved the relative safety of the *Sea Dancer.*

"What are you going to do, hero?" the pirate said in front of him. "You can't kill us all, can you? Come on . . . my name is Raize, I can make it worth your while if you—."

"No!" Taryn cut him off. "Come with me, and tell your men to jump overboard as we go."

Raize looked like he was about to argue, but a flick of Ianna at his throat and he ordered his men to jump overboard. For several long seconds, no one moved. Truthfully, Taryn didn't expect the pirates to listen. They were pirates, after all, but the way they had coordinated the attack indicated to Taryn that there was something unified about this group, and after what seemed like an eternity of glancing back and forth, one of them dropped his weapon and jumped over the rail— encouraged by the tip of Mazer.

One by one, the others followed the first man into the sea. Several men looked like they were going to resist, but their hesitation cost them.

One moment was all Taryn needed to disarm them and kick them into the ocean. When they were done with the first ship, he retrieved his throwing knife and moved the captain from ship to ship, forcing the pirates of each vessel into the water. As he went, Taryn took the time to disable the helm and sails. Some hadn't seen him before and tried to resist, but Taryn blocked every attack with his father's sword and simply knocked them overboard—all while maintaining Ianna at Raize's throat.

Once he'd cleared all four ships on this side, he returned to his own. As he crossed with his prisoner, he told the captain to get ready to sail as quickly as possible. Every time Raize tried to speak, Ianna cut into his neck a little, making it clear that Taryn wasn't there for conversation. It only took another couple of minutes to empty the last three ships of their crews. For good measure, he cut the sinking one loose from its neighbors. Without oarsmen or anyone to bail water out, it settled deep and began to tip, falling quickly behind.

As soon as he got back on the *Sea Dancer* with his pirate prisoner, Erix called out to cut them free from the pirate's boats. As they began to pull ahead, their surviving crew rushed to repair the sail and rigging damaged in the battle. The experienced sailors worked fast to raise the ragged mainsail into the strong wind and they picked up speed. Before the *Sea Dancer* had even moved off, pirates began climbing back onto their ships, but there was no way they could fix the damage that Taryn had left in his wake—not in time to give chase.

Erix let out an explosive sigh as the pirate ships got smaller in the distance behind them. "Well done, mates. Hun, bind Taryn's friend and take him below. Make sure he can't get loose. I don't want someone getting killed because he frees himself. Frey, lay the dead out on the deck and get the injured below as well. Tend to them as best you can."

"I can help with the injured," Mae said.

"I can too," Trin offered.

"You *are* injured," Liri said with a small smile as she noted a bleeding cut on his arm.

He smirked and shook his head, but followed Mae down to help with the wounded.

"Liri, would you take care of the prisoners that were freed?" the captain asked. She nodded and moved towards the man and the children who were huddled in one corner of the deck.

"Taryn, would you mind helping with the dead?" the captain asked soberly.

Taryn nodded and left the captain giving orders to other members of the crew. He helped Frey gather the sailors that had been killed in the attack, as well as any dead pirates, and lay them out on one side of the boat. Of the forty-two sailors, nine had been killed, twelve were severely injured, and almost everyone else had minor injuries. Few had survived unscathed.

As he sifted through some wreckage, Taryn heard a groan and moved a board to reveal the pirate he'd kneed in the stomach. He was a short man, and young, barely out of his teens, with light hair and stubble on his chin. Taryn cleared some more debris until he could get to the man.

"I found a pirate, and he's alive," he called out.

"Cut his throat and toss him overboard," a sailor said under his breath behind him, but the captain frowned.

"Tie him up as well, but keep him separate from the other one," he ordered. "I don't want them talking."

After Taryn took care of the other pirate he returned to the deck to find the captain had asked the entire crew to meet together.

Once everyone was gathered, he began, "You all fought well. I was proud to fight alongside you." He glanced around and gave a small smile. "We have survived for now, but we are in a tough situation. Our ship is damaged and almost half of our crew is either dead or too injured to help us sail home. From this moment on, every crew member is on double shifts." A hard look at Taryn and his friends showed that they were included in that statement.

"No one is going to get much sleep over the next week, so prepare yourselves." He broke off and looked at the nine bodies that were lined up on the port side of the ship. Shaking his head he said, "We have lost some good men, who paid the price of blood to protect us. Let us have a moment of silence for their sacrifice."

Taryn joined in with the crew in remembering the dead and watched mutely as one by one their bodies were committed to the deep. The captain said a few things about each man before they were reverently slid into the ocean. As Taryn listened to his words, a numbness set into his mind at what had happened, and he found himself regretting something but not knowing what.

Just then, Liri leaned against him and he caught her soft look. Knowing she understood did make him feel better, but the faces of the men that had been killed would stick with him, and he found himself wishing there had been a way to win without bloodshed. Deep down he recognized that hadn't been possible—but he still wondered if any one of the men lying in front of him would have survived if he'd slain more of the pirates.

Out of the corner of his eye he caught sight of one of the children they'd rescued, and he looked at the young men and women crowding around the man. In that brief moment he understood a little of what his uncle had said about protecting the weak, and like a ray of light his profound sadness was softened by a warm feeling of having done something right. It didn't completely dispel the emptiness, but at least it gave a reason for the price paid.

The captain finished his memorials, and the last of the dead sailors disappeared into the dark waters. Each man and woman contemplated the loss of the brave men whose blood stained the deck under their feet. These men had lost their lives so that others could live, and the living recognized the profound sacrifice.

By the end of the day six more would join them.

Chapter 7: Thacker's Tale

By the time they got the deck cleaned up the sun was setting, and some of the crew were off to some much needed sleep. Taryn and his friends stood on the rail looking out at the fading light. No one had said much after the battle with each person focused on the individual tasks to be accomplished, but with the breeze filling the sail and a beautiful sunset in view it was difficult for the seasoned sailors and young fighters to dwell on the dead. In the end, it only took one remark to change the mood.

"I don't think the pirates like Taryn very much," Trin said.

Liri tried not to laugh. She even covered her mouth with her hand in an attempt to stifle it.

Trin saw her and continued with a straight face, "Seriously. . ." He looked at Taryn with a sober expression, "What if they couldn't swim?"

She couldn't help it, and the sound of her lighthearted laughter floated across the ship like the cool breeze that pushed the vessel forward. The soft tinkling sound lifted the hearts of the surviving sailors and washed away the evil morning more effectively than anything else could have. Within a few moments sailors began talking again—subdued conversation, but at least it replaced the silence.

When she had gotten control of the giggles, Liri turned a serious expression on Taryn. "Why did that even work anyway?"

"I was wondering the same thing," the captain spoke up behind them. They turned to see him striding towards them. "Pirates aren't known for their loyalty. At the sight of their captain in trouble, someone *should* have tried to kill you both."

Taryn returned the gaze of the captain and scratched the back of his neck. "I don't know why they didn't just go after me—but it wasn't the only odd thing about the pirates. All of them grouped together like that is one of the strangest things I've ever seen. What would cause pirates to unite like that?"

That statement left all of them scratching their heads. Trin gave up first and blew out his breath in exasperation. "I don't know either, but I'm happy for whatever it is. It certainly saved our skins today."

Erix smiled and nodded in agreement.

"Perhaps we should get some answers," Mae mused.

Liri looked at her and nodded, pursing her lips. "Hmm. Perhaps it is time to get some answers from the family, if they are ready to talk."

The captain was quick to agree. "Let's go see if they're awake. You aren't the only ones with questions for them, but I do believe that the room they're in is too small for all of us to have a quiet conversation. Why don't I invite one of them to join us in my cabin? You can all meet me there."

Several minutes later the man Taryn had rescued walked tiredly through the captain's door and crumpled into the offered chair. As the four fighters and the captain found places to sit around the small office, Taryn took a moment to study him. He hadn't gotten much of a chance before, and the only thing he knew about him was that his name was Thacker. As he looked closer, he began to notice much more than he'd seen at first glance.

Thacker's clothes were light and made of homespun material, and although they were quite dirty, looked to be stitched well, as if they had been tailored specifically for him. Probably made by someone close to him, a wife perhaps? Beyond his stained tunic, his hands and face were darkened by the sun in a way that could not have been recent. This was

95

a man who worked outside frequently. Taryn wondered briefly if he was a farmer, or maybe a fisherman.

As he looked at the man's face, Taryn felt his heart go out to him. He appeared to be exhausted, worn beyond compare. When he sat down he gave the impression of settling into the seat like he would never get up, like he lacked even the energy to stand. Bags under his eyes showed white through his tan and his hunched shoulders carried unseen weight.

The captain cleared his throat. "Thank you for being willing to talk to us and answer some questions. We will try to be brief so you can get some rest."

Thacker nodded and blinked, trying to focus. "What would you like to know?"

"Why were you being held prisoner?" the captain asked.

Thacker hesitated, looking around the room. His eyes were abruptly clear and focused—evaluating. The silence continued as he looked at each individual, taking their measure.

"You can trust us," Mae said in her usual quiet voice. Taryn glanced at her at the same time everyone else did. Something in her eyes or words seemed to settle his concern, because he only hesitated a moment more after locking eyes with the short elf.

"I believe you, but it is still hard to tell a secret that can be used against you." He looked away from Mae's sincere face as if he was in pain. "A year ago my family and I lived in a fishing village a day's journey south of Keese. My wife and I have seven children, and each one is . . . special." He hesitated again, but when the captain nodded at him he continued, "They can talk to each other, mind to mind." He said the last phrase like he was anxious to get it out and at the same time struggling to keep it in. If he'd looked up he would have seen five astonished people in the room.

"They get it from me," he continued. "I could do it with my sister, and somehow it got passed on to my family. My youngest son is very . . . boisterous, and likes to show off. He told one of his friends while they were playing on the docks. I think someone overheard him because a

96

few days later a couple of pirate ships raided our village. My wife . . . was killed." He choked and had to swallow to regain his composure.

"They took my family and forced us to work for them under that villain you have in the hold, Raize. In a different life he probably would have been a great general. He draws people to him, and it didn't take long for more pirates to join him. As he added more ships and men, he began using us to communicate between ships so his attacks would be more successful. I tried to hold out against him. I tried to tell him it wasn't always clear what we tried to say to each other, but he didn't believe me. We have been enslaved by the pirates for several months now, watching his fleet grow, and helping him do unspeakable things…"

He went quiet and slumped into the chair. The silence lasted for several moments while everyone looked at each other, wondering what to say.

"You have your children, and you kept them alive," Liri said, touching his shoulder.

His head snapped up. "Almost all of them. My oldest son is being held by a crew at Keese."

"You have another child?" the captain asked, rising to his feet.

A sad nod confirmed the answer.

"We will help you find your son." The quiet voice of Mae cut through the babble of speculation that had sprung up in the room. Taryn's eyes snapped to Mae's. Her tone had made it evident she was volunteering the four of them, not just herself or the crew on the ship. He felt like he should be annoyed at her, but if she hadn't said something he probably would have. A glance at Trin's and Liri's faces revealed they had arrived at the same conclusion. Smiling to himself, he turned to look at Thacker, who was sitting up with the first glimmerings of hope radiating from his tired eyes.

"Thank you so much. You have done so much for me already. I couldn't begin to pay you back."

Erix leaned away from the wall. "It's settled then. When we get to Keese, we find Thacker's son." Seeing the questioning look in Taryn's face he smiled. "I can't let you four have all the fun. Besides, you seem to be good luck."

A gruff laugh from Trin startled Thacker. "Excellent," he boomed, "I always look forward to a good fight." He looked at Taryn with a pleading look. "Can it *please* be on land, and not on some tiny ship? My sword is a bit long for enclosed spaces."

Smiles and chuckles answered his statement as everyone stood to leave. Liri followed Taryn out, and when he headed for the ladder to the crow's nest she caught his arm. "Do you mind if I join you up there?" she asked.

"Of course, as long as you aren't afraid of heights," he replied with a smile. She flashed him a disparaging look and slipped past him to the rigging. Her graceful movements as she climbed answered his teasing comment better than any words could have.

Then he frowned as a thought crossed his mind. This was the first time she had *asked* to join him in the nest. She had sat up there before, so it meant she wanted to talk to him about something. Shrugging, he followed her up in time to see the other sailor nod at whatever Liri had said and climb out the opposite side. The sight of the human sailor laboring to descend contrasted so sharply with the graceful form of Liri that it brought a wide smile to his lips.

Once they were comfortably leaning against the rail, Taryn spoke. "What's up?"

"So," she began, "when we get to Keese, what's the plan—after we free Thacker's son, of course."

"Hmmm, I'm not really sure," He mused, aware that he was being evasive but he didn't have a ready answer to her question.

After a moment of expectant silence she frowned. "You know what I am talking about. How are we going to find out about your parents?"

He sighed and looked out over the water. "I don't know Liri," he said. That simple confession brought an ache to his heart, and he wished he knew what he was supposed to do. Growing up, he could always focus on his training to avoid thinking about his mysterious heritage. Learn the next move, master another technique. The constant practice had made it too easy to avert his attention. Only in the last couple of weeks had he really looked at the problem of finding more about his lineage, and the challenge had formed an impenetrable wall. The barricade created by his lack of knowledge felt so tangible that his head hurt, as if he'd hit his mind against it.

"I know I have elven blood, so I guess I should start there?" Taryn finally said, but his voice carried no hope.

"That's a good idea for a first step, but if you don't find anything there...?" She looked at him with one raised eyebrow and left the question hanging. When he didn't respond she looked away and whispered, "What if you can't find them?" He heard worry in her tone, and for some odd reason a measure of fear as well.

The silence stretched between them for several minutes while he struggled with that idea. It was a possibility, but not one he'd ever allowed himself to consider. He was too afraid of how easy it would be to yield to the hopelessness of the situation.

"I don't know what to do after that." He paused to watch some light clouds drift past the stars. "Wander around asking questions I suppose," he said with a resigned shrug.

"I think you should go see the Oracle," she said after catching his eye.

That caught him off guard. Taryn didn't know much about the Oracle. What he did know he'd learned from the required lessons on magic given by Daiki. The mage had taught about magic, and magic goes hand in hand with the Oracle. Every generation someone was born with the ability to see energy and magic in *every* form. She (it was always a woman) could then perform magic of every type: wind, water, fire, air, light, earth, animal, and everything else. Because she could see

99

energy in everything, she supposedly could see trends in magic and then predict the outcome of those trends in prophecies.

The Oracle was an incredibly powerful person—magically anyway, and although some elf or dwarf might be more skilled in a specific type of magic, no one could compare to her all-encompassing power and ability.

"How do you think it would help me to see her?" he asked.

Liri shrugged and looked at the half moon that was beginning to rise. "I don't know. My father once said he went to her for help many years ago and she just seemed to know so much." Her gaze focused on him and he suddenly came to the realization that she'd been thinking about his problem a lot more than he would have expected. Then he recalled how she'd phrased the search for his heritage. She'd said *we*, not *you*, and her easy inclusion of herself in his quest brought a flood of gratitude through his heart.

He stared hard at her, lost in thought. When he refocused, he became aware of the incredible depth of her blue eyes. Her soft lips were pursed together and her eyes had a faraway expression in them. Apparently lost in thought, she didn't seem to be aware of him. He resisted the impulse to call her name and took the rare moment to just look at her. A night breeze pulled at her long hair and the moonlight cast soft light on her perfect face. . .

—Her eyes snapped to his and with a start he realized that his mouth was half open. Embarrassed, he turned away to look out into the darkness, taking a slow breath to calm his oddly accelerated heartbeat. If she had noticed his expression, she chose to ignore it.

"I just want to help you figure out what you need to do," she said from beside him.

After a minute of silence he replied, "Thank you Liri. You really have no idea how much that means to me."

"We will find out who your parents were, Taryn, I promise."

100

He turned back to her and nodded but didn't respond. It made him feel better just to hear her say that out loud.

The silence stretched between them for a while and at some point they ended up sitting back to back with their legs dangling through the railing. Warmth radiated from her back into his and he could feel himself somehow entwined with her. He could even feel a slight tension in her muscles as the boat rocked harder than normal, but most of all he could feel her breath going in and out, even and slow.

Creaks of wood and the wind rustling the sails were the only sounds that broke the stillness of the cool night. Twinkling stars stretched across the sky as far as the eye could see in the almost cloudless night— so close it felt like you could reach out and touch them. Taryn couldn't imagine anything evil in the world as he looked at the bright moon. Peace softened his heart and gave him hope that he would find his family . . . someday.

Liri stirred behind him. "What a great view," she murmured.

He agreed in a subdued tone, not wanting to disturb the stillness. As he sat there looking at the peaceful view he found his mind drawn to the contrast between the current peace and the violent battle that morning. Thinking about the fighting reminded him of a question that had been bothering him.

"Did you see me fight this morning?" he asked.

"Of course." Her tone became one of amusement. "Are you looking for me to tell you how good you were?"

He was glad she couldn't see him flush before he answered, "No— that's not what I mean." He stopped, searching for the right words. "Did you notice that I avoided killing?"

For several moments she didn't answer until she said softly, "I did."

"I hate to kill," he said in a rush. "I see them, and I see good in them, and I see their wives, and their children. I see who they could be—who they were meant to be."

By the time she answered, it sounded like she was picking her words carefully.

"I have seen you fight for a long time Taryn, and I don't think you . . . fight . . . the same way the rest of us do."

He turned to look at her again, confused by her answer. "What do you mean?"

She hesitated and cocked her head to one side, her brow furrowing as she said, "When you draw your weapons, you don't battle . . . *against* your opponent, you fight . . . *with* your opponent. The rest of us observe our adversaries movements to find a way to defeat them, but we don't really see the person attacking us. We see move and countermove, while watching their body and weapons to figure out how to get past them."

She smiled affectionately. "You see everything we see—but you also, *somehow*, see the person, who they are and what they are. In that moment, I think you measure the person—and I guess you are able to find some portion of good in them."

When she stopped speaking Taryn felt stunned. Not only was her description accurate of how he fought, it revealed how much she had observed him. It was also something he'd never managed to explain out loud.

"You don't see them like that?" he asked, still surprised by her description.

She shook her head even as she answered, "No Taryn, I don't think anyone has the ability to separate their mind like that. They can't focus on fighting if they are paying too much attention to the person, or at least I can't." Her voice turned sad, "I don't think I could kill if I saw them as a person."

Impulsively he reached out and clasped her hand. "At least you saved lives today. I don't know if my inability cost the crew, or who will die because I failed to dispatch a pirate."

She chuckled, surprising him once again. "No Taryn, if it weren't for you we would have *all* died today. You might not have slaughtered every pirate you faced, but you were the one that saved us. Everyone on board this ship owes you their life." She squeezed his hand to emphasize her point.

Torn between her perspective and his own, he blurted, "But that just means I don't fit anywhere. I am the same as a farmer that can't use a shovel, or a fisherman that is scared to touch fish. It's the only thing I can do, but I can't do it right. It just means . . . I just . . ." He growled at his own inability to voice how he felt. "Where do I fit?"

She gave a deep sigh, her voice turning soft. "Everyone feels that way, Taryn. Those that don't are either lying, or it's only temporarily true. A precious few recognize the value of what they have around them."

Her voice carried such an odd timber to it that Taryn was drawn to ask, "Have you found a place you fit?" For some reason he felt anxious for her answer.

Her answer took longer than he expected to come, and when it did, it was not what he expected.

"No Taryn. Not yet."

The sadness was so out of character for his longtime friend that he didn't know what to say. Unable to figure out an appropriate response, he settled on humor.

Bumping her shoulder, he said, "At least you fit very well in the nest. Have you heard the sailors grumble about how small it is up here?"

He turned away, grimacing at his attempt at humor, and was surprised to hear her chuckle.

"You would think they designed it for smaller people."

He laughed, and tried to allow his tension to melt away, finding it was easy to do so with the peaceful night and the rocking boat. Later, he would think more about her words, but tonight, he didn't want to dwell on such a topic. He sighed in content and leaned back against Liri, happy—at least for the moment, that they were there together. He also found himself glad that Liri had not let go of his hand, and their clasped hands felt especially warm against the cool breeze.

"Hey, can you promise me something?" she asked, turning her head to the side to see him.

"Of course," he replied as he turned to look at her as well, almost bringing their cheeks close enough to touch.

"Actually I have two requests . . ." She trailed off with a questioning look.

"Okay . . .?" he answered with a raised eyebrow.

"I want you to promise me that no matter what happens—good or bad—we'll always remember this view, and how peaceful it feels here." She held his gaze until he nodded.

"—and the second promise?"

She looked at him a little longer before answering, "Someday we will come back and have another night like this." She looked away as soon as she said it, but he could sense that his answer was important.

"No matter what," he said with a smile, and hoped she didn't see his face flush.

She flashed him a grin so wide he could feel the warmth on his face before she nodded curtly and twisted her body to lean against him again.

"Good," she said. Then her tone turned sharp. "You had better not let me down Taryn Elseerian, or I *will* have to kill you."

They both laughed, but Taryn heard the trace of sincerity in her voice. She would hold him to his oath—and he found that he was glad that she would. Leaning back against her, he wondered if he would ever be as happy as he was in that moment.

Chapter 8: Keese

Sunlight blossomed across the sky in a dazzling array of dawn as their ship crashed through the waves at a steady clip. Lights from Keese had been sighted a few minutes ago, and the *Sea Dancer* had gracefully turned towards the port city with a strong wind filling its sails. Sailors and fighters alike were more than ready to get off the boat and stretch their legs. Perhaps the only exception was the captured pirates, Raize and Braglair, the pirate Taryn had knocked out. They were going to be handed over to the guards as soon as they landed, and neither of them were very pleased.

Taryn stood in his favorite spot at the top of the mast—with Liri by his side. With the ship rising and falling several feet in an instant and lurching sideways at any moment, the crow's nest became highly unstable, but Liri just laughed at every sudden dip. Taryn grinned wide as they rode the ship, and found his gaze kept returning to Liri, whose wide eyes and matching smile rivaled the brightness of the rising sun.

Hunrin had said they would be in port in less than thirty minutes, and Taryn wanted to spend every last second he could in his perch. It certainly helped that Liriana had asked to join him—as she had been prone to do more and more in the week since the battle. It would be good to get off the *Sea Dancer* and feel solid ground under his feet again, but leaving the seagoing vessel would be bittersweet.

As cramped as the boat had been, in some ways it had more freedom than Sri Rosen had ever had—where every day had been filled to overflowing with a strict regimen of training and practicing. On the boat they had been free to socialize and relax in a manner that Taryn felt unfamiliar with. It had given him the opportunity to become close friends with Trin, in particular, as well as with Hunrin, Frey, and Erix, the captain.

A sudden call from below pulled him from his reverie.

"All hands on deck," the captain shouted. "Prepare the ship for docking, mates, and make sure that everything is clean and tied down. It's been more than two months, boys, let's look good coming home!"

Cheers and elated laughter burst out from several men as they jumped to ready the ship. Liri started laughing again and her almost musical giggling had a way of lifting Taryn's spirits even more than before.

"Look at the city!" Liri said excitedly by his side.

Taryn abruptly realized that Keese was probably the city she had departed from on her voyage to Sri Rosen, and that she would be just as anxious to arrive as he was. A twinge of sadness streaked through him as he wondered what it would feel like coming home. If he ever found his parents' home, would it feel the same? Frowning, he shook his head to clear the gloomy thought. He wasn't about to let anything mar such a day.

Looking at the approaching waterfront revealed that in just those few moments the city had come into view enough for them to see structures and buildings. Long docks stretched out over the water for several miles to the north and south of where they were approaching. Almost out of sight to the north, the outlet of the Blue River emptied into the ocean, only visible from their high viewpoint. Even though Taryn had never set foot on this land, he still knew about the Blue Lake and Blue River.

Blue Lake was a massive, sprawling lake hundreds of miles across that some said was big enough for all the dragons in the world to take a swim and never see each other. On the southeastern tip of the lake a large river was the only major outlet. The Blue River was so wide that Hunrin had said seagoing vessels traveled up and down from the lake and that fishing was just as large a trade in the lake as on the ocean. To the east and south of the lake were the two human kingdoms, while west of the lake the elves lived in their forests. Dwarves, in their mountain sanctuaries, lived to the northwest. Directly north of the giant lake a barren land devoid of trees and other vegetation stretched. Only trolls or gnomes made the bleak wasteland their homes.

Taryn laughed to himself that he was able to remember so much about the geography of a land he had never seen, but then again it was an area he was sure to traverse in his effort to find his heritage. Daiki had taught quite a bit about the different kingdoms in the few lessons when Taryn was young, and he had tried to absorb as much as possible.

The glorious half hour flew by faster than he thought possible, and before Taryn knew it, they were slipping into a dock. Ropes were tossed back and forth by experienced sailors and dockhands and the ship was quickly tied down. Just as Taryn dropped to the deck to help Hunrin lower the gangplank, the sound of several booted feet striking the wooden pier in unison caught his attention.

Leaning over the rail he spotted a handful of burly uniformed men marching in their direction. The guard in the lead, a large beefy man who looked like he knew how to use a sword, strode towards them, his eyes fixed on the *Sea Dancer* like it was an enemy.

"This isn't a social call," Trin murmured beside him.

Taryn agreed, puzzled at what might be going on, and studied the lead guard, trying to get an idea of what was happening. The guard had dark hair cut short to frame a square face and dark eyes bearing a grim expression. If Taryn didn't know any better, he would have thought they were there for Raize and Braglair, but even as he thought it he knew that couldn't be it. They would have had no way of knowing about the sea battle—but something about their approach made him think otherwise.

The guards walked brusquely up to their ship and arrived just as the plank clattered onto the docks. Before anyone could say a word, the guard in the lead spoke in a firm voice. "I am Dumont, captain of the guard for the City of Keese. We have had reports that there are three pirates on this ship. We are here to take them into custody immediately."

"*Three?*" several people said at the same time, including Erix.

"We do have two pirates in the hold, but not three," the captain responded to the guard's remark.

"We have been informed that their names are Raize, Braglair, and Thacker. If they are on your vessel, please bring them to us for prosecution," the guard replied with an edge to his tone. "If necessary your ship will be seized and searched."

Erix walked down the gangplank and pulled the guard captain to the side. Although their conversation was quiet enough that Taryn couldn't hear it, he could tell that Erix was explaining the nature of the pirate attack. By the unyielding look on Dumont's face and the several times he shook his head, it didn't bode well. After several minutes of conversation, Erix returned to the ship with a frustrated expression on his weathered face.

"They won't take no for an answer; they want all three of them," he said in exasperation. Raising his hand to cut off several objections he added, "I don't think we have a choice, but I have a friend at the council's office. I'm sure he will help us get to the bottom of this."

In another testament to the crew's faith in their captain, not a single crewman argued with him, although it looked like Trin and Mae weren't too happy. The more Taryn thought about it, the more he had to admit he wasn't too pleased either. Now they had to figure out how to keep Thacker out of jail *and* free his son.

Erix cut into his swirling thoughts with some quick instructions. "Frey, you have the ship, assign a few men to stay here while I go sort this out. Hun, go get the scum and explain things to Thacker. Make sure he understands we won't rest until he's out. Then take the rest of the men to the Salty Dog for a few drinks. Keep them ready though; I don't know if we will need to leave quickly or not, but be prepared. Taryn and Liri, if you wouldn't mind, I would like it if you joined me. Trin and Mae, please stay with Thacker's family for the moment. If their father

108

can't be with them, someone reliable should be." He looked at each of them until they all nodded before he continued. "Good. Something tells me this isn't going to be a relaxing stay in port, so take what rest you can get. We may see fighting before the day is out." From the steel in his eyes, it was clear he was determined to do whatever it took to get Thacker and his son freed, and it wouldn't go well for anyone in his way.

Mae snagged Taryn's arm as he was turning to go below.

"Hang on," she said in a hushed voice, and he stopped to listen. Trin and Liri were quick to join them.

"Why is everyone so nervous?" She nodded her head in the direction of the guards, and then pointedly looked at several other groups of men on the docks.

Long experience had taught him to listen when Mae spoke—and she didn't disappoint him this time. Scanning the behavior of the dockhands and guards, he did notice something odd. Nearly every person in view appeared to be extremely wary. Dumont's eyes in particular were constantly roving, as if he were expecting danger at any moment.

Under normal circumstances that could have been passed it off as good soldiers being prepared, but the other dockhands had the same nervous expression. But it wasn't just wariness . . . it was something more. Dockhands moved too stiffly and without banter or conversation. The guards stood ramrod straight with hands twitching towards their swords. It was so subtle he almost didn't believe it for a second, but without exception every individual seemed . . . terrified.

"Bad seafood?" Trin asked with a dry smile.

"No," Liri mused, "that's not it. Something has them spooked, but I can't imagine what it is."

Noticing that Dumont was beginning to shift, Taryn agreed. "Something isn't right here, but we don't have time to do anything without risking a fight with Dumont's men. Let's go with the captain's plan for now—but keep your eyes peeled. Let's not be caught off guard if something does happen. This could get out of hand far too easily for my liking."

Like a spark to oil, he couldn't help thinking.

"That's easy for you to say," Trin grumbled. "At least you get to go ashore."

Mae just stared at him until he put on a false expression of happiness. "Great!" he said. "I get to babysit."

Taryn just shook his head and followed Liri as she turned to go below, and they all ended up helping explain to Thacker—who wasn't happy—why he was about to be arrested. After some tight-lipped conversation, it was Mae who finally calmed him down with only a few words.

"We will get you out by tomorrow—legally or not." Her soft voice carried an unusually intense tone that silenced Thacker's objections. Nodding, he began comforting his family while gathering his things.

Taryn's eyes snapped to her in mild surprise. It was unlike her to suggest breaking someone out of jail. When she caught his questioning look she said in an undertone, "Good families should be together."

Her words carried a bite to them that surprised him, and not for the first time he wished he knew what her life had been like before Sri Rosen. As far as he knew, she had never shared that time of her life with anyone, yet it seemed obvious that shadows darkened her youth. She was the only one he had ever heard of to arrive early at the island.

But her past still didn't explain her willingness to go against guards. As long as he had known her, she'd demonstrated a rigid adherence to rules and laws. Noticing Trin's amused expression, he realized that Mae probably didn't see it as doing something *against* the law, but as correcting something that was morally wrong.

Five minutes later everyone had completed their assigned tasks and Taryn stood watching the two pirates and Thacker being led away by the guards. Every few steps the fisherman kept looking back, worry tightening his features.

"We will figure this out, Taryn," Liri whispered to him. Taryn nodded in return, realizing his stomach was clenched. Forcing himself to relax, he followed Liri as they set out after Erix.

The captain strolled down the long dock with the two of them close behind. Once they stepped onto the wide street that ran along the waterfront, Erix broke the silence. Probably in an effort to lighten the mood as well as show the city, he began a running commentary to the two newcomers at his side.

"That's the Crusty Keel. It's a good place to get some grub but don't go drinking the beer, it's as rancid as week-dead rat in a barrel of water. Over there is the best docking spot on the pier." He pointed towards a wooden pier that looked new—at least compared to some of the others. A lean ship that looked fast berthed there with a few sailors lounging on its deck.

"Aye, and over there is a good shipping company that my brother used to work for. He's not a very good sailor you know." He leaned in and added, "He gets seasick."

Liri started to laugh but several dockhands threw her suspicious looks so she changed it to a cough. Frowning at the men's behavior, Erix continued without waiting for any further response. Taryn only paid enough attention to catch the important parts while he spent the bulk of the time looking over his surroundings. This was the first place he had been to, outside of Sri Rosen, and he gazed at the sights of the unfamiliar town in wonder.

Warehouses interspersed with taverns and pubs lined the street on their right as they strolled along the waterfront to the north. Sailors and dock workers shouted to each other while moving crates of fish or other goods to and from ships. Noise flowed through the air like water over his ears, rising and falling in pitch as someone yelled at a sailor for dropping something, or two individuals in front of an office argued about price. Boats of all shapes and sizes bobbed on the water to their left, with some just arriving or leaving. Due to its proximity to the Blue River's outlet, Keese's location made it valuable for commerce.

Despite the noise, Mae's words still echoed in Taryn's thoughts, and he began noticing other things that made him consider again what might be affecting so many people. Each boat had several guards, all armed and eyeing anyone that came close, and the workers, although shouting to each other, seemed to be communicating as little as possible, only enough to get the message across. The entire atmosphere felt subdued, with a strong undercurrent of tension flowing around them.

Just then Erix turned off the waterfront and led them east through the city. Warehouses and businesses gave way to residences and homes. The area they were passing looked to be well off with some of the homes nice enough to boast small gardens or a porch. Even the clothes of the people in the streets told of prosperity and wealth. The further they got away from the sea the quieter the streets became, and Taryn found that he was glad for the lack of sound. Solitude and peace had dominated his life for so long that the cacophony of noise within the city beat on his ears—even though they had only been on the waterfront for a short time.

Liri suddenly stopped in front of him, forcing him to jump to the side to avoid a collision. In chagrin, he realized that he'd completely stopped paying attention to Erix and it looked like they had already arrived at their destination. Erix was in the process of explaining something about his friend as he leaned forward to ring the small bell that hung by the front door.

". . . is a city council member of Keese and has been for a while. He's well respected and has an excellent reputation. He also used to sail with me before he got into politics . . ." He trailed off as footsteps sounded behind the door. An instant later a short round woman with long brown hair pulled back into a modest ponytail opened the door. At the sight of Erix, a smile blossomed across her features, revealing clean teeth and dimples.

"Erix!" she exclaimed, ushering everyone inside. "It's good to have you back. Will you be staying for dinner?" She whirled and eyed him shrewdly. "Don't expect to stay for drinks though, last time you went through two bottles of our best brandy. By Skorn, the songs you sang would have woken the dead they were so dreadful."

112

Erix grinned broadly and leaned in to give her a hug and a kiss on the forehead. "I missed you too, Molly, but this isn't a social call. We need Rez's help. Is he in?"

At the mention of "we," the woman glanced at Liri and Taryn. Her eyes appraised the two of them for a moment and Taryn caught the trace of fear spark in her eyes. "Yes, of course. Just got home a few minutes ago in fact. You can find him in his study." She kept staring at the two of them until Liri leaned in and smiled prettily. "It's nice to meet you, Ma'am. My name is Liriana, but my friends call me Liri."

A sharp nudge from Liri's elbow and Taryn spoke up as well. "— Er, yeah, my name is Taryn. Nice to meet you too."

She nodded without responding, still frowning at them in a wary manner that was becoming uncomfortably familiar, but then she shook herself and smiled. "Any friends of Erix are friends of ours. Go ahead on up, I have some cleaning to finish." She indicated the wet rag in her hand and brusquely turned away down the hall, calling to someone in the back of the house as she went, "You'd better clean under the rugs or I'll scorch your hide!"

She quickly disappeared and Taryn got his first moment to look at the house. To his left a door led to what looked to be a sitting room and in front of him a hallway trailed straight back towards the door through which Molly had just exited. On the side of the hall a straight staircase led up to the second floor, and he turned to follow the weathered sea captain upward.

When they got to the top, Erix paused and leaned close to them. "Molly is an interesting sort. She doesn't believe in having servants do everything, so she personally helps them cook and clean—and they love her for it. All the other high society types look down on her, though. She's also handy with a dagger if you ever cross her, so watch yourselves."

He chuckled to himself at some memory before turning down the hallway to the last door on the left. Without knocking he opened it and stepped right in. Following him, Liri and Taryn entered a very tidy office inhabited by a short round man who looked remarkably like his

113

wife except for the facial features. Dark blue eyes that were common among humans looked out from under bushy eyebrows and a balding head. What he lacked in physical charm he certainly made up for in personality. Within half a second the chubby man bounded from behind his desk and embraced the thinner Erix.

"Oh, you old sea dog! I haven't seen you in ages." Releasing him just as quickly, he stepped back and waved them in. "Come, come, have a seat, your friends too." He indicated a few chairs, but instead of returning to his own he sat on the front of his desk. "How was your trip? You will stay for dinner won't you?" His tone dropped and his gaze flickered to towards the door. "I have a couple more bottles of our favorite brandy stored away. . ." He indicated the liquor case on the far wall.

Erix cut in with a shake of his head, "Unfortunately not this time Rez. We need your help in a matter of urgency."

Rezko laughed a deep belly laugh that shook his whole frame. "Straight to business as always, my friend. What's the problem?"

As the sea captain introduced Liri and Taryn and then told him their tale, Rezko's eyes darkened and the grin faded. When Erix finished, Rezko sat there for a second with a furrowed brow before returning slowly to his seat. "We have a right difficult problem then. Dumont is a tough man, strict, straight as a rod and just as unbending when it comes to the laws set by the council. If Dumont thinks Thacker's a pirate, he won't let him out of custody until he has done a full investigation—which could take weeks or even months."

Taryn cut through that train of thought. "That's not an option. We have to get him out of there tonight."

Something in his tone brought Rezko up short, and he looked at Taryn with a raised eyebrow. "What if it means you have to break into prison to get him?" he asked, his expression calculating.

Realizing that Rezko was taking a measure of him, Taryn replied, in a tone that left no doubt, "Without hesitation."

114

After a moment, Rezko nodded and the smile returned. "Good, it's been too long since I broke someone out . . . wouldn't you say, my friend?" He looked at Erix with a knowing grin plastered on his face.

The sea captain grinned right back. "This time it won't be so easy. I doubt the guards will be so drunk."

"Please don't mind me asking, but isn't breaking someone out of jail going to be bad for your, er, position?" Liri spoke for the first time.

He chuckled in response. "I wasn't always a politician you know. Besides, it would be nice to get my saber out for a good fight."

Erix nodded slowly, biting his lip. "She does have a point, though. The city won't take lightly to one of their elected officials traipsing all over their laws without regard. I hate to say this Rez, but I think you should sit this one out."

Rez frowned and made one last desperate effort. "Ah, but I know how the new holding cells are constructed. I can get you in easier than you could on your own."

Erix sidestepped his suggestion easily. "You can help us plan it right here without endangering your reputation."

For a brief second a nervous look flashed across Rezko's face and Taryn thought he would protest again, but then he seemed to wilt and conceded. "All right. Let me get some parchment so I can draw you a map." Reaching for a drawer in his desk, he stopped and seemed to consider something, then looked at his three guests. "Let me get some food first, this might take a while."

At a grateful nod from Erix, Rezko stood and left the room. Although the retired sailor tried valiantly to hide it, it was obvious that he was disappointed.

As soon as he left, the sea captain turned with a puzzled look. "That was odd. Rez is usually very optimistically stubborn. I can't believe he gave up so easily on a chance for a scrap."

"He seemed scared too," Liri said to herself.

115

"What? What do you mean? Rezko isn't scared of anything," Erix said, an edge creeping into his voice.

"That's not what she meant," Taryn said quickly. "Go ahead and tell him, Liri."

Liri briefly explained what Mae had said about everyone's behavior on the docks.

When she was done, Erix leaned back in his chair and scratched his chin. "Hmm, I think you might be right. There was definitely something strange today. I have berthed here for almost forty years and I have never felt like so many people were watching me tie up. I thought it was just me, so I didn't say anything—and the way the guards knew we were coming? Something is going on I tell you."

After a moment where they all considered the oddity, Taryn broke the silence. "Have you ever seen Rezko scared?"

"No, never," he replied, his tone emphatic.

"Something has everyone here spooked," Taryn stated matter-of-factly, pointedly drawing attention to the city as a whole rather than Erix's friend. "And it definitely isn't normal."

"What could scare a whole city?" Liri asked in confusion.

"I don't know," Erix said, shaking his head.

A creak in the wood behind them made them all jump and turn to see Rezko in the doorway holding a platter of food. His far-away expression showed he'd heard at least part of their conversation.

"There have been strange tales being told of late." The large man's voice came out in a whisper, barely audible but carrying enough intensity to make Taryn feel the urge to touch his weapons.

"What sort of tales?" Liri asked, matching his tone.

"The sort that scares hardened soldiers and sailors." He paused to wipe the sudden sweat from his brow. "Death is said to stalk this land . . . *personally.*"

"How long has this been going on?" Erix asked, frowning.

"It started a couple of months ago. Travelers and traders from the eastern kingdom have been telling stories of a mysterious assassin—stalking and slaughtering without mercy. No one has been able to stop him. No one knows who it is or why he's doing it—and the assassin's guild isn't behind it. Early on they lost several of their best, including the guildmaster. In the last couple of weeks more and more people have been moving west, and everyone is scared. Some are so scared they come running—but no one is chasing them." He was still standing in the door, staring into space, so Erix stood and led him to his seat. Rezko seemed unaware of his friend's help, and continued with the story as soon as he was seated.

"Soldiers from both human kingdoms have been sent to find him, but to no avail. Some soldiers haven't even reported back. I'm not sure if it's because they deserted or if they were killed, although enough bodies have been found to support the latter possibility." He stopped and took a deep breath. "To make matters worse, a strange disease and lack of food is spreading in the east as well—and now it's reached the southern kingdom." He shivered and swallowed. "Two days ago a messenger was supposed to arrive directly from the eastern king. He never made it."

For the first time Rez looked small. "It's a bad time, I say. Tales of fights and mysterious deaths, of a thief that is so good you can't kill him even if you could catch him. They call him the cheater of death, you know. It's inspired more stealing and robbing than ever. No one can hold onto anything anymore, or trust anyone either. This cursed fear is causing everyone to act as if death is lurking around every corner."

A muffled shout from the first floor snapped them all back to reality.

"She never used to yell," Rezko said, his voice morose. Then he visibly shook himself and smiled half-heartedly. "Let's get to work; we have an innocent man to break out of jail and not much time to prepare."

Taryn and Liri were about to ask for more information, but Erix forestalled them with a look. "OK, Rez, why don't you start with the defenses?" He leaned in to focus on the paper on which the politician had begun to sketch.

Liri caught Taryn's eye with a loaded look that he took to mean they would talk about this later. The odd conversation had sparked far more questions than answers, but there was one question that was on his mind more than all the others. How would this affect his quest to find his heritage? Then guilt washed over him as he realized that a part of him was glad for the distraction.

It was the same part that doubted he would ever find answers.

Chapter 9: Escape

Taryn sat hunched in a darkening alley a couple of blocks from the prison with Liri, Trin, and Mae behind him. While he waited, he reviewed the drawings that Rezko had sketched for them, more than a little apprehensive about the level of security. The councilman had told them that this new complex had been built after the old jail had failed to hold almost anyone. After the description, he wasn't the only one wishing for the old one.

The first thing they had to get past was a high, square shaped wall, built with a single gate facing the sea. Constantly manned by roving and stationary guards, it looked more like a castle than a prison, and surrounded a large courtyard. Barracks had been built inside the outer fortifications on every side and housed more than two hundred men. To make matters worse, outside the wall had been cleared of all trees or buildings within fifty feet, leaving open ground on any approach.

At the center of the courtyard, a small square building contained the only entrance to the underground prison. At the front of the building, an entrance room served to admit prisoners and sat adjacent to Dumont's personal office. Rezko had said that the most difficult door to get through would be the one at the back of the entrance hall. Fashioned of solid iron, the strongdoor could be secured from *inside*, and nothing short of an army would be able to break it down.

At the first sign of an intruder, the two men inside the strongdoor would simply close and lock it before signaling the guards in the barracks to come and deal with the situation. The would-be rescuer would then have no choice but to fight a hopeless battle defending the small entrance room. Behind this last threshold, stairs led down into the holding cells. At the rear of the building, a second strongdoor served as an emergency exit, and was similarly bolted from the inside.

Taryn looked again at the diagram and then glanced at the setting sun. Recognizing it was time to go, he took a deep breath to calm his nerves and stepped out of the shadows. Before he stepped into the torchlight, he began staggering his way towards the outer gate. Appearing to be drunk was difficult for Taryn, who didn't like strong drink and had never really had enough to know firsthand how to act. And with his swords back with his friends, he felt extremely self-conscious. His clothing didn't help either. Trin had 'prepared' them personally, and they smelled like manure and sour ale. Taryn didn't even want to know what he'd done to them. Even Mae had voiced an objection, but Trin had been adamant that the stronger the stench, the more it repulsed.

"Smelling horrible is sort of like . . . armor, and no one will want to come near you," he'd said resolutely.

As Taryn indirectly approached the gate, he focused on the first step of the plan they had come up with—getting arrested. He did his best to calm his pounding heart. It wouldn't go well if he let his nerves get the better of him. Drawing close, he swallowed hard and began the act they had practiced, cursing Trin for coming up with such a line.

"Wur is the stupid gurd that hit me brudder?" he slurred and lurched right into one of the guards at the gate, who promptly shoved him away.

"Get out of here before I arrest you, you filthy dog," another guard yelled while the first one cursed and tried to wipe his hands off from where he'd touched Taryn's cloak.

Taryn's response was to draw a large ladle from within his robe and start hitting the guard, lightly enough to avoid damage but heavily enough to anger the man. He didn't have all day to get arrested; they had a schedule to keep.

On cue the guard raised one hand to block the off-balance blows as he tried to grab Taryn's shoulder with his other and hollered for the other guards, "Oi, get this nutter off me!"

Within moments Taryn allowed himself to be disarmed and was led through the gate and into the field. *Right on time*, Taryn thought, forcing his heart to beat slower.

He staggered and muttered enough to maintain the act but he kept his eyes roving around to look for any snags in their plan. By the time they had crossed the field and gotten to the prison entrance, Taryn had managed to get a good look at the patrols and structures inside the walls. The guard he'd hit with the ladle opened a heavy ironbound oak door and led him into the expected entryway. Five men stood in neat rows against the wall on his left, mirrored by five more on the right. All of them stared at him with hard eyes and hands resting easily on sword hilts. Dumont himself sat behind a desk flanked by five more soldiers on either side of him, also against the walls. Nothing else adorned the bare room except the large strongdoor directly behind the desk and another, smaller, door on the right of the room that presumably went to Dumont's office.

When Taryn and his companion walked through the door Dumont looked up and waved them forward. Taryn was careful to keep up the façade by staggering and lurching. Despite his disguise, he felt a flash of concern as one of the guards from the docks looked like he might recognize him, but just then the smell from his clothing hit the room. Some of the guards blanched as the enclosed space enhanced the odor tenfold. Dumont wrinkled his nose when they stopped in front of his desk.

"What is that horrendous stench?" he demanded, leaning back and gagging.

The guard nodded at Taryn while discreetly keeping his distance. "Got a nutter here, he's stone drunk and I think he fell into a wagon of manure."

121

"Lock him up until he sobers, then bring him to me again—and by Skorn, clean him up before I see him again." He signaled another guard to bring some irons forward.

Taryn took a quiet breath and prepared himself for the hardest part. Because they put shackles on prisoners before they took them through the prison entrance, he had to disable the guards and get through the door before someone locked it from the inside. Finishing his mental preparation, he took a deep breath and promptly slumped onto the desk and started to snore. The guard next to him cursed and tried to pull him off Dumont's desk while Dumont yelled at a few other guards to get him into the shackles.

At the exact moment that the man yanked on his shoulder, Taryn leaned back and smashed his head into the guard's face. Maintaining the act, he flailed around in a seeming half-conscious stupor. As more guards jumped forward in an attempt to restrain him, he spun around and smashed his fists into faces. Guard after guard slumped to the ground, knocked out by subtly precise hits. It didn't take long for Dumont to realize that this was no ordinary prisoner. Seeing the recognition light the guard captain's eyes, Taryn threw off the smelly cloak and kicked the oak desk as hard as he could at the same moment that Dumont began shouting.

Whatever he was about to say never got out, because the heavy desk clipped him, knocking him down as it flew across the room and shattered against the open strongdoor. The force of it blasting apart was so great that most of the guards along the back wall went down with it. Pieces of wood and kindling exploded around the room as everyone, including Taryn, ducked to avoid the wooden shards that ended up sticking into walls or knocking over men that didn't dive for cover.

While everyone froze in shock, Taryn was a blur of motion the instant wood stopped flying. Darting around the room he delivered quick, well-placed blows to the guards' temples, kidneys, necks, or anything else available, knocking them out before they could recover from the shattered desk. As he swept through the room in a controlled whirlwind, he was careful to keep an eye on the strongdoor. As long as it remained open, he could continue knocking out the entrance guards.

In a matter of seconds, most of the men were incapacitated by the desk or Taryn's fists. Only four guards were able to recover enough to present a united defense before he could get to them. Three of them drew their swords and advanced towards him while the fourth dashed behind them towards the jail door. To complicate the situation, Taryn could hear footsteps pounding up the stairs from the inside of the jail. He only had a matter of moments to deal with the crisis before either the guards from inside or the one running towards the door could lock him out.

Taking the initiative, he leapt to the right of the three guards and sidestepped a fumbled thrust from the nearest man. Spinning up the sword to gain momentum, he grabbed the guard's extended sword wrist and a fistful of his tunic. Still spinning, he planted his feet and leaned back. Now continuing to rotate with the guard in his grasp, he stopped hard and heaved the man in the direction of the iron door, leaving his sword in Taryn's grasp.

The guard that had been running towards the prison door glanced back at the same moment the flying man's body collided with him. Yelping in surprise, they both tumbled through the door and slammed into the guard on the stairs. Crashing downward, they ended up in a heap of tangled limbs.

One of the two remaining guards had looked away to watch the body flying past him, and Taryn didn't hesitate . Seeing the distracted guard, he flicked his sword tip into the man's weapon just above the hilt, knocking it flying from his loose grip.

Then Taryn was forced to leap back to avoid a desperate slash from the last guard, giving the now weaponless man time to recover from his surprise and reach for a stray weapon at his feet. Not wanting to lose his advantage, Taryn waited just long enough for the slash to pass his body and then darted in behind the swing. The guard tried to reverse the direction of his sword to stop him, but Taryn reversed his own sword to rest along his forearm and deflected the strike.

Still moving forward, he took his sword hilt and smashed it into the guard's face while the man was still struggling to bring his weapon back into play. As the man collapsed, Taryn turned towards the one picking up a sword and kneed him in the face before he could fully stand up.

By the time their unconscious forms had hit the ground, Taryn was through the strongdoor, landing lightly on the stairs. He needn't have worried. By the bumps, it looked like two of the guards had hit their heads and the only conscious one had been pinned underneath the others. Struggling with all his might to free himself, the trapped guard didn't see Taryn until he felt the sword tip at his throat. The man wilted instantly.

"Please don't kill me," he pleaded.

Looking stern, Taryn spoke quickly, knowing he didn't have much time. "I won't harm you if you do exactly what I say." When the man nodded he said, "For the moment stay still and quiet. I'll be right back."

He turned and ran back up the stairs to the entrance room. Dashing to the front door he locked it, and while he listened for any commotion outside he began checking the still forms. Rezko had made it clear that they shouldn't kill any guards unless in the most dire of circumstances. Worried by how hard he'd kicked the desk, he checked Dumont first. Although he boasted a large lump growing on his head and what was sure to be a wicked bruise on his chest from where the desk had hit him, he was alive. Taryn breathed a sigh of relief and turned to check the others.

As he hurried through the room, he felt a twinge of guilt for the destruction he'd caused. He'd never had a need to use his full strength on anything, so seeing the desk burst apart had been a complete surprise. Then a thought struck him, causing him to pause. Where did his strength come from? It didn't come from training, so it naturally came from his heritage, but who in his lineage had such strength? Elves and humans did not possess such strength . . .?

Without time to consider it, he pushed the thought aside and finished checking the room before entering the jail, locking the iron door behind him and jamming a couple pieces of wood underneath it for good measure. Less than ten minutes had elapsed since he'd first entered the room until he locked the prison door behind him.

A rush of elation burst over him as he realized he'd managed to get past the first part. Until now, he wouldn't have admitted to anyone that he had doubted their plan's chances of success. Struggling to control his sense of triumph, he reminded himself that he wasn't out of danger yet.

Estimating that he was slightly ahead of schedule, he returned to the pinned guard. Taking a moment to check the two men on top of him, Taryn removed all three weapons while the man was still trapped. Sliding the two unconscious guards off of him, he warily helped him to his feet.

Without preamble, he demanded, "How many guards are down here? And don't lie to me."

The man hesitated, swallowing hard, "I . . . I can't help you. I can't afford the punishment."

Taryn suppressed a grin, admiring the man's honest courage. "I'm just here to find an innocent man, and I'm not going to kill you. I don't kill innocent people."

Something in his tone must have convinced the man because he bobbed his head, seeming to believe him. "Lately I have seen a lot of innocent men get taken below."

Taryn gave a tight smile and shook his head. "Please, I just want to get him and leave." Seeing the man still hesitate he added, "And I will knock you out when we're done so no one thinks you were involved."

The man snorted but finally relented. "OK. My name is Danian."

Taryn placed his hand on Danian's shoulder. "Thank you, Danian, for myself and for his family."

The man sighed and asked, "Who are you looking for?"

"His name is Thacker, probably came in earlier today with a couple of pirates."

Danian's face broke into a smile. "I know exactly who you are talking about. They said he was a pirate, too, but he certainly didn't look like one."

"Good. Now how many guards do we have to get past?"

Danian started hurrying down the stairs. "Normally there are twelve, five on each floor with two on the stairs."

Seeing Taryn glance down the stairs, he answered the next question before Taryn could ask it. "The other guard with me stepped out a few minutes ago to relieve himself. He should be back any second." As he admitted this, Danian shrugged apologetically, but Taryn smiled to reassure him, mentally speeding up his timetable. "We'd better hurry then."

The guard obediently turned and continued down the stairs, but pulled up short and looked back. "It would be best if you were dressed as a guard. It's not well lit down here at this time of night and we might be able to walk past the others without raising suspicion."

Taryn considered the idea, realizing that the extra time to put on some guard clothes might stave off a fight. "OK, stay right here and don't move."

Without turning, he backed up the stairs to the downed guards and, picking the one that looked to be the same size, stripped him of his tunic and trousers. Deciding he didn't have time to check if the boots fit, he put on the guard's clothes. They were a little baggy, but would have to do. As he dumped the last of the smelly clothes he'd been wearing he breathed deeply of the clean air. Trin's armor had worked, but he wouldn't care to don it a second time.

Once he had changed, he rejoined his guide and motioned for him to go downward. Keeping his eyes on Danian, he strained his ears for any sound as they descended into the shadows. The guard led him down the steps and turned right when they reached the first basement. Noting that another set of stairs led up in front of him, he turned to follow. Rows of cells disappeared into darkness on the left and right with only a few smoky torches casting flickering shadows around him. Then Danian led him down dim hallways, threading his way past countless barred doors.

By the rustling and clinking in the cells, it seemed that quite a few of them were full, and Taryn wondered how many other innocent men were down here. Suddenly a guard came into view, making Taryn tense, but Danian greeted him without stopping and the bored man passed them with only a nod.

They passed two more roving guards without incident and reached another set of stairs that turned right and went deeper. His guide turned down them without hesitation, although when they reached the bottom he paused to whisper to Taryn.

"Only one guard holds the keys down here." He raised one eyebrow. "You might have to . . . incapacitate him."

Taryn hid a smile and nodded, at which the guard continued, "He is usually in his small office at the center of the cells, but sometimes he roams around checking if the others are awake."

"Take me there and then get out of sight, I don't want him thinking you have helped me." Taryn said.

The man nodded gratefully and turned into the sub-basement, which looked to have the exact layout as the one above him. Only one sentry crossed their path before they reached a small office that Taryn guessed sat underneath Dumont's office.

In contrast to the gloomy jail, the office was well illuminated with several bright torches. A thin man sat hunched over a small desk, writing on a piece of parchment. Muttering to himself, he finished and stretched, finally catching sight of Taryn in the door.

"Is there a problem?" He blinked and focused on Taryn's face. "What are you doing away from your post?" he asked, his voice suspicious—then he stood and reached for his sword, "wait—who are you? You shouldn't be here!"

Taryn launched himself over the desk in a one-handed lift and kicked the man in the chest before his weapon had cleared its scabbard.

127

Papers scattered everywhere and were still floating downward as the captain smashed into the back wall and crumpled to the floor. Landing next to him, Taryn jabbed him on the side of his head as he groggily tried to get to his feet, sending him to the floor.

"Where are the keys?" Taryn demanded of his guide hiding outside.

Danian poked his head into view, shaken at how Taryn had knocked his captain out. "Uh, I think he keeps them in the desk."

Less than a minute later he found what he needed and with the keys in hand Taryn ordered, "Take me to Thacker."

Before they could move, a muffled sound echoed through the jail. They froze and looked upward, waiting. A moment later it repeated itself. It sounded like metal striking metal, and it came from the surface. It appeared the guard who'd relieved himself was back, and probably had more men.

Taryn took his eyes from the ceiling and looked at Danian. "We don't have much time, take me to him."

*****

At the same moment that the guard who'd relieved himself unlocked the outer door and stepped into the room littered with unconscious bodies, Liri was drawing an arrow back and carefully sighting on a guard at the front gate. Panicking at the sight of so many downed men, the guard in the entrance structure ran to the iron door and tried to open it. When he couldn't, he slammed his sword hilt against the door twice to signal any guards below that there was trouble and then ran for help. Exiting the structure, he called for help but was drowned out by several shouts from the entrance gate.

"We're under attack!"

"Get more men over here!"

"Go tell the captain what's going on!"

"What *is* going on?"

128

"Close the gate!"

Commotion burst out as scores of guards rushed towards the front gate, leaving the only guard that knew someone was inside the prison bewildered and struggling to get someone to help him.

Her thoughts on Taryn, Liri performed her diversion to the fullest, launching arrow after arrow towards the guards along the wall and through the now-closed gate. Men ducked and scampered to try to identify the source of the arrows that seemed to be coming from everywhere.

Although Trin and Mae kept their shots high or low, Liri placed her shots so close that they drew blood along cheeks or ripped holes in sleeves. Men all along the battlements dived for cover, thinking they'd almost been killed.

Their combined attack lasted for only a few intense minutes before all three of them melted into the shadows of the streets and strolled towards preselected taverns away from the prison—where they would stay for a short time before reuniting at the *Sea Dancer*.

Liri shot her last arrow and said a silent prayer for Taryn before disappearing into the night, leaving chaos in her wake.

*****

Behind the walls of the jail, three more figures represented the third part of their plan. Erix, Hunrin, and Frey slipped out of their hiding places the moment sounds of alarm issued from the front gate. With practiced hands, the sea captain strung a large bow and quickly shot an arrow over a buttress extending out from the wall fifty feet above them. Fishing twine trailed out from behind the arrow as it reached its zenith and dropped back to earth, leaving the twine over the buttress. Hun grabbed the arrow almost as soon as it hit the ground and, with Frey's help, tied a thicker rope onto the twine. As soon as it was ready the three of them grabbed the twine and pulled the rope up and over the buttress to replace the twine. The whole operation had taken less than a minute, and the three darted into the shadows along the wall to repeat the process further down, effectively giving Taryn two avenues of escape.

Normally the rope would have been discovered almost as soon as it was put in place, but with the distraction up front and Taryn already exiting, they only needed it to be unseen for a minute or two. Just in case the first one was found by some guard, the second would be Taryn's last hope.

*****

While Taryn's friends were buying him a few precious minutes with their distraction, he was hurrying up the sub-basement stairs with Thacker behind him. He'd left his guide locked up in the fisherman's old cell, mercifully unconscious and presumed innocent. Reaching the top, he dashed through the rows of cells with the older man trying to keep up.

With every sense and instinct prepared for a fight, he was surprised that not a single guard showed themselves, until he reached the stairs and heard arguing at the top. *It must have taken them time to get the door open*, Taryn thought.

A split second later he heard booted feet pounding down the steps. Taryn reached back, grabbed Thacker, and yanked him up the darkened back exit stairs to the rear door. Despite the small amount of noise Thacker made as he stumbled behind Taryn, the cloak of darkness enshrouded them not a moment before a score of guards rushed past the foot of the stairs.

Both of them breathed a silent sigh of relief and turned towards the emergency back exit. After some fiddling, Taryn managed to unlatch the door with only a small squeak of protest and opened it a crack. Seeing no one, the two of them slipped out and closed the door behind them. Taryn felt his fear spike as he stepped out into the open, but he did his best to hide it from Thacker. If their plan was to succeed, he couldn't afford for the fisherman to lose his nerve. If he did, they wouldn't get a second chance.

Glancing around, he checked for any sign that they had been detected, but it seemed the diversion still garnered most of the guards' attention. Less importance was also paid to the torches in the back field, because the half dozen or so pinpoints of light were not enough to reveal the whole courtyard.

Taryn leaned in close to Thacker to avoid being heard. "Walk like we are guards, casual but hurried, like we are performing some assignment."

Thacker nodded in response, and they hurried across the field, trying to look like prison guards with business to perform. As soon as they were in the shadow of the back barracks, mercifully empty due to the fake frontal assault, Taryn cupped his hands and boosted the older man onto the wood roof. Once Thacker was up, Taryn jumped the five feet and grabbed the edge. Without hesitation he pulled himself up before Thacker had scrambled to his feet.

Taking a quick look both ways to get his bearings, Taryn guessed that he was about twenty feet to the right of one of the escape ropes that Erix had left for him, so he pulled the other man along looking for a way to climb up the wall.

Seeing a rough patch in the stone wall, he whispered over his shoulder, "Stay here." He reached for a small finger hold and scaled the thirty feet to the battlements. Reaching the top, he peeked left and right for sentries. Seeing none, he pulled himself up and began searching for the rope. He found it not five feet to his left. With nimble fingers he grabbed it and pulled up one side. As quietly as he could he lowered it to Thacker.

"Grab the end and hold on," he hissed as loudly as he dared.

"Why . . .?" Thacker began to ask, but as soon as Taryn felt weight on the end of the rope he pulled the other man straight up the wall. Not waiting for anything, he flipped the rope back over the battlements and whispered, "Climb down, as quick as you can."

Thacker closed his mouth on something he was about to say and climbed over the battlements while Taryn began patrolling to imitate a guard, chafing at the delay. The sounds at the front wall were beginning to diminish as order began to be restored.

Above the shouts and sounds coming from the gate, he suddenly heard Dumont's heavy voice carry across the field. "Check the outside wall, inside and out! Someone escaped and I want them found!"

Wincing at the anger in the guard captain's voice, Taryn glanced down the rope to check on Thacker. Seeing he was almost to the bottom he leapt over the battlements like he was jumping off the crow's nest on the *Sea Dancer*. On the way down he grabbed the rope with his gloved hands and slowed himself enough to land heavily a split second after Thacker let go and stepped back.

Grabbing Thacker's arm, he pulled him into an alley, stripping the guard clothes as he went. Even though he didn't know the city, he kept his eyes high and on the moon to guide him in the right direction. Reaching the waterfront, he slowed to a walk and turned north towards the ship, breathing a sigh of relief.

"That was . . . incredible," Thacker said, winded from the run.

"I'm glad it worked." Taryn replied.

"Hey," Thacker said, grabbing Taryn's arm and stopping him short. "How did you pull me up like that?"

Taryn just shrugged and kept walking, not knowing how to explain. The freed man jumped to catch up and fell into step beside him.

"I know where my son is," he said matter-of-factly.

"How?" Taryn stopped again.

"And why they took me with Raize and Braglair."

"What?" Taryn asked in astonishment. "How do you know that?"

Thacker smiled. "Dumont mentioned to us that a sailor told them there had been a fight at sea, and gave the guards our names. My son also told me while I was in jail that they forced him to tell them what had happened, and then knocked him out before he could tell me they knew. Our communication requires a clear mind and they didn't give him the chance."

Taryn shook his head in chagrin. "We should have known."

"Just before I was arrested I caught part of a phrase from him, but it wasn't enough to tell me anything substantial." His expression became worried. "I think they hurt him."

"We need to get him out fast then, before they hear about tonight," Taryn said. "Where is your son?"

"Seath is being held on a boat up ahead."

At a questioning look from Taryn, he shrugged and continued, "They moved him to a different room on the ship, and he says he can see through a crack. There is a tavern he recognized, so he knows where he is."

"Which one?"

"The Crusty Keel. He says he remembers there being bad ale there."

Taryn smiled to himself, recalling someone else describing the pub the same way earlier that day. "Does he know how many men are on the ship with him?" he asked.

Thacker paused for a moment to communicate with his son. "He says not many. Most went off drinking earlier this afternoon."

Taryn thought for a moment to consider their options. They had already performed one rescue that evening and attempting another might be pressing their luck. On the other hand, they knew where Seath was and that he was in a relatively unguarded position. An idea began to form in his mind as he mulled over the alternatives.

Making up his mind, he changed direction towards the Salty Dog to grab Liri. "OK, we have one stop to make, and then we'll get him."

He was going to need his swords . . .

Chapter 10: Watchers in the Wood

Within an hour of the prison break, Taryn, Liri, and Thacker sat in a small rowboat with Hunrin and Erix rowing quietly behind them. Slipping through the darkness from the seaward side, the small boat eased close to the back of the pirate ship that held Thacker's son Seath. Barely a whisper of sound marked their passage as the small craft drifted near enough for Thacker to reach out and grab the anchor chain. Before the boat had even stopped moving, Taryn crouched and leapt straight up the chain. Grabbing it, he scaled it cautiously while scanning the dark wood in front of him for the marker. Light suddenly reflected dully off a splash of color on the shadowed hull. Upon closer inspection it proved to be a piece of cloth that had been jammed through a crack in the wood.

Taryn gave two sharp tugs on the piece of cloth to signal he was ready, and after a moment three pulls from the other side gave the all clear. Wrapping his legs around the chain to brace himself, he drew Mazer with one hand. He smiled, remembering the dubious expressions when he said there was no need to get *on* the ship. They could enter from the outside. His sword glimmered blue as the enchanted weapon began slicing through the wood, cleanly with little sound. Below him he heard a gasp from someone at the sight of the magic.

After a few moments Taryn sheathed his sword and grabbed the top of the piece of wood as it began to fall outward. It was a good thing he'd cut a handhold, because the wood was too thick for him to grab without both hands and he didn't want it to fall and make a splash. With his legs wrapped tightly around the chain, he had to use quite a bit of strength to tip the bottom of the piece of hull inward and slide it through the new hole.

A young sandy haired youth appeared in the opening the instant it was clear, grinning at the sight of Taryn on the anchor chain.

"Thanks for stopping by," the young man whispered.

Taryn grinned back and reached out as far as he could. Clasping his hand, he helped him climb out and swung him to the chain. A sudden creak from above caused them all to freeze and look up towards the deck to see an unsteady pirate catch himself against the rail. Taryn held his breath until the man laughed at something and stumbled out of view. Waiting for a full minute to ensure he didn't come back, the two hurried down the chain and into the boat. Hun and Erix began rowing with the cloth covered oars as soon as Taryn pushed them free of the chain.

No one spoke until the pirate ship faded into the darkness behind them, but Seath and Thacker sat huddled in the back of the boat, silently communicating their joy at being freed. Taryn watched the father and son, feeling a tightening of his heart at the sight. Looking back at his life he wondered how things would have been different if he could have known his father. Would his father have trained him? What else could he have learned from him?

Swallowing hard at the intensity of the ache, he looked away and found Liri's eyes on him. Her expression pierced right through him as their gaze locked and after a moment a simple understanding passed between them, easing the heaviness in his chest. He forced a sad smile and looked out over the water, still wondering.

By dawn everyone was back on board the *Sea Dancer*, and sailing north. Although some of the sailors were a little irritated at the short stay in port, their disappointment couldn't hold against the sheer joy being displayed by the reunited members of Thacker's family. The few grumbling men were soon smiling with everyone else as they sailed north to the Blue River.

Erix had decided that with the previous night's activities it would be better to leave as soon as possible to avoid any retaliation. Since his next voyage meant crossing the Blue Lake to the eastern capital city of Terros, Trin's home, it would be faster for him to hitch a ride than take the overland route across the southern kingdom. Taryn and Liri would go with them until Tallendale, and then disembark to head for Azertorn. For some inexplicable reason, Maemi had said she wanted to travel a little before returning to Azertorn and had elected to stay on the ship until Terros.

Taryn, confused by her statement, was surprised at the dark tinge to her expression. Although he'd always seen the short elf as reserved, he couldn't recall ever seeing her angry, but the brief darkening of her eyes had been unmistakable for bitterness. Liri then caught his eye and raised a quizzical eyebrow. He just shrugged, unsure of the reason why. Reminded again of his previous thoughts of her past, he considered the possibility that whatever had caused her such pain might still be in Azertorn. Why else would Mae not want to return home?

It didn't take them long to reach the outlet of the Blue River and turn inland. The flow of the current slowed them considerably, although the steady sea breeze kept them moving upstream.

"How is it possible that we are sailing upriver?" Taryn asked in astonishment.

"Ah, now that is an interesting feat of engineering," the captain replied, leaning against the rail. "Many centuries ago, the southern kingdom decided that if they could establish a trade route from the Blue Lake to the sea it would increase profits for their merchants—" He grinned wide. "—and the taxes on the merchants as well." He turned and pointed south. "The merchants of the age had to travel an overland route from eastern Talinor to Keese that took well over two weeks, so the king asked the southern guild of earth magic to figure out how to slow the current of the Blue River enough so a ship could sail up to the lake."

"I doubt that could have been an easy task," Taryn said.

"Exactly," Erix replied, "but the head of the guild was a smart one, and devised a plan to use some kind of hardening mixture to fortify raised barricades on the bottom of the river. He figured that if he could force the water to turn back on itself every few feet it would move more slowly. The enchanted mixture also draws energy from moving water to strengthen itself, causing the river to slow even more."

"Wait, every few feet?" Taryn asked, his eyes widening. "How long is the river?"

Erix smirked and spread his arms wide. "Over thirty miles, and it took the guild more than ten years to complete it. The bottom of the river is like a snake, turning back on itself so many times it almost stops its flow. They called their work the *Danre*, from the elvish phrase meaning 'To pass in safety.' It has been said that before the *Danre* was built, the river was fast and treacherous, taking the lives of many who tried to cross its deadly current."

"Incredible," Taryn said.

The captain nodded with a wry smile then turned away when someone called for him. "Aye, I'm on my way." He shrugged at Taryn and left him to gaze at the view around him.

From where Taryn was standing he had a good look at the immensity of the river. At the outlet it was more than six or seven times the length of the *Sea Dancer*. Thick forests of tall trees stretched away endlessly to the north of the river while to the south the trees only grew along the bank. The water was so blue and clear he could almost see the bottom. Fish swam upstream alongside them, and deer could be seen furtively drinking in the shallows. Birds of different sizes and shapes flew overhead in lazy circles. The lush green world alive with animals presented a stark contrast against the few trees on the south side, which quickly gave way to plains.

It was no wonder that the river was the dividing line between the elven kingdom and the southern human kingdom of Talinor. It seemed so wide that it would be easily defendable from attack from either side, and the forests would be a perfect home for the elves. He smiled at the turn of his own thoughts. Battle readiness had been so deeply instilled in his thinking that even with such a view before him, he still found himself considering defensive strategies.

Liri walked up the stairs to join him. "It's amazing, isn't it?"

"I can't believe how green the forest is," he exclaimed.

"The plant magic of the elves only has effect as far as the river," Liri replied. "Some elves are so dedicated to the trees that they wander the forest, growing and nourishing them like beloved children."

"Do you think we could stop to take a deeper look?" he asked.

"No humans are allowed to enter the forest at this point. There is a bridge and a road up ahead that allow the other races to enter the forest. It's one of the few overland routes to Azertorn from the southern kingdom." She pointed off to the south where a caravan could be seen in the distance on a winding road leading away from Keese. "That road will split a couple of miles ahead. Heading north will take you to the elves, heading east will take you to Tallendale, and heading south will take you to some villages and eventually the southern capital."

"We are getting off at Tallendale, right?"

"Yes, it's the closest spot to Azertorn. Tallendale sits on the southern side adjacent to the river and the lake. In many ways it is similar to Keese. Goods usually travel through Tallendale to the sea. Erix will make a stop there to give his men a longer shore leave before continuing to Terros. We will cross the river there and travel north to the Giant's Shelf and Azertorn."

"How long 'til we get to Tallendale?" Taryn asked.

This time the captain responded, striding back into view, "Two days at the most. It depends on the wind. This time of year it's usually fairly steady."

A little girl's giggle carried to them, and they turned to look at the source. One of Thacker's daughters, who looked to be about ten, had "pinned" a struggling Trin to the deck.

"I win again!" she squealed.

"That's not fair!" he protested. "You are stronger than me."

She laughed again and pretended to let him stand up, but pounced on him the instant he had his feet under him. Taryn wasn't the only one to smile at their antics.

"It's good to hear a little one laugh," Erix said to himself.

His tone was so serious that Taryn caught his eye and raised an eyebrow.

Seeing his expression, Erix said, "There were no children playing or laughing at Keese."

"Hey, I noticed that too," Liri said. "I remember a lot of wide-eyed young ones last time I was there."

He shook his head with a sad expression spread across his leathered face. "Every time we stop there, they are playing on the docks, getting into mischief and the like." He nodded towards Liri. "They love to catch sight of the other races, which normally are not a rarity at Keese. This time though . . ." He shrugged and looked away.

Everyone remained silent for several minutes. Taryn assumed they were all thinking about what Rezko had talked about. He'd almost forgotten about the strange tale of fear being so prevalent in the city. As he looked at the view and pondered the possible causes, each more improbable than the last, he noticed Mae looking towards the forest to the north. Something about her stance told him she wasn't just enjoying the sight, so he excused himself and moved to join her.

When he reached her side he purposefully leaned with his back towards the forest, watching Trin and Thacker's daughter playing.

"Aren't you happy to see your homeland after so long?" he asked in an undertone.

Her eyes flashed at the same time her lips tightened. "A home isn't always happy Taryn."

Her words stung more than he would care to admit, but he didn't want her to see it. The glimpse into her past was a rarity, but revealed little more than he'd already guessed. Then an idea crossed his mind that caused him to cringe. Mae wasn't the only one he knew little about. Liri? Murai? He'd been too preoccupied with his own issues to want to know more. Was he a bad friend? Too self-centered to notice the lives of others?

He winced, sensing there was more truth to the thought than he would care to admit.

"We're being watched," Mae said, pulling him from his brooding.

Resisting the urge to turn around and see for himself he asked, "By whom?"

"Elves. At least a score. They are following us through the trees."

Taryn started to relax, but Mae saw his reaction and her voice gained an edge. "It's a war party."

"What?"

"They are heavily armed, and there are several with bows trained on us at all times. Every few minutes a few of them will run east and take up position ahead of us."

Mae just looked at him and shrugged before walking away, leaving Taryn to ponder alone. After waiting an appropriate amount of time, he turned around and pretended to enjoy the vista. With his elven vision, it didn't take long to spot what Mae had seen. Dark shadows of thin figures darting through the woods as silent as thought— each one with a purpose. Their behavior made it look like they were *defending* their territory, but there was no attacker on the south bank . . .

—The elves were preparing to defend against *them*, he realized.

They expected to be attacked by their ship at any moment. He turned away before he gave away his knowledge of their watchers and strolled back to the helm. Liri must have seen something in his eyes because her expression turned questioning as he approached..

141

Taryn subtly pulled her aside and explained the situation. She nodded at him and asked him loudly, "Care to take a look up top?"

He smiled and followed her up the ropes to the nest. When they were both settled in, she leaned out over the rail and began pointing in different directions, describing different things about the area they were passing. Catching on to her act, he joined in and responded to everything she was saying. Despite her light conversation, he could see her eyes scanning the trees for movement.

After a few minutes of mild conversation she said in a hushed voice, "I see them, and I agree. They aren't just curious about us. They are soldiers prepared for battle. The question is, why are they scared of us?"

Something in the way she phrased the question sparked his memory to Rezko. "They are scared the same way the people in Keese were frightened."

She cocked her head to one side, her brow knitting together in thought. "So someone—or some*thing*, is causing nearly everyone from at least two different races to be afraid?"

Taryn shook his head. "I don't know, but whatever the source, we definitely need to keep an eye on our watchers."

"I'll go inform Erix of our friends. You can stay here and let me know if they do anything."

He nodded soberly and watched her descend. Settling into a comfortable position, he looked to the north and tried to imagine what could cause the elves *and* the humans to be so on edge. More than once, uncomfortable thoughts about what type of friend he had become drifted into his awareness. Each time, he tried to convince himself that there were more pressing issues to address, but the disturbing idea kept creeping back.

For the next few hours, Taryn watched the passing landscape while casting unobtrusive glances at the elves shadowing them. Although they continued to follow, they stayed out of sight in the darkness of the tall trees—until they came to the bridge.

The bridge could only be described as enormous, spanning the wide river in a long arc and high enough to allow ship masts to pass by underneath. Massive stones anchored the foundation on both sides with smaller ones shaping the arch. Worn carvings of dwarves, elves, and humans in furious battles with strange beings could be seen in the few sections of stone not covered by moss or creepers. Many sections looked to be well worn with age, with other pieces crumbling or missing. Despite its ancient appearance, no defining cracks marred its surface. On the north side of the overpass a stone wall had been built, shiny compared to the old bridge, complete with a gate and battlements—and it was occupied by a full contingent of battle-ready elves.

"Taryn!" the captain called in a rising tone when he spotted the warriors. "Get down here! Frey, take his place." Without hesitation Taryn jumped over the rail and caught a rope. Landing heavily, he joined to the captain and his other friends at the helm.

When he arrived, Erix was speaking. "Liri, what in the name of Skorn is going on? That wall wasn't there a few months ago, and there weren't elves armed to the teeth either."

Liri answered with heat in her tone, "I don't know what is going on; the elves have always been peaceful!"

"Relax, it's not the elves we have to worry about," Mae spoke firmly. "It's whatever is frightening them that we need to fear."

"We've already talked about that," Erix spoke in frustration. "We know something is scaring everyone."

"No!" Mae spoke again, uncharacteristically forceful. "You don't understand. There is something deeper going on here. Whatever is causing this is *using* fear to divide people—and at the same time to join people."

"Wait, you lost me," Trin said, shaking his head. "How can fear divide *and* unite?"

Mae responded patiently, as if she were teaching a child, "Fear makes people divide into groups they trust. In this case, the elves are gathering themselves in, just like the humans in Keese—"

"—and the pirates!" Taryn cut in when he finally understood. "They had joined together as well, which is something they never do."

"That's why when you captured the captain, no one killed him," Trin added.

"—and why the elves are ready for a fight," Liri said.

"—and why the people in Keese were acting so strange," Erix exclaimed.

Mae smiled in acknowledgement, but didn't say anything.

Erix nodded confidently. "So the elves probably don't want a fight." He turned to some of the crew that had begun gathering swords and bows. "Put your weapons down, and go about your business as normal mates."

Trin burst out laughing, drawing shocked looks from the crew. "Don't mind the elves that could kill you without a second thought."

No one laughed at his comment, but at least most of them relaxed a little.

Taryn stepped to the rail to get a better look at the approaching bridge. During their conversation they had moved to within a quarter mile of the crossing and the elves that had been following them had all joined the ones at the wall. It looked like two score on the battlements, and at least that many would be behind the wall. Looking towards the opposite side he saw there was a short dock that extended into the river on the southeastern side of the bridge. Besides the elves on the north side, no one else was in sight.

"Liri, do you think it would be a good idea to talk to them?" Erix asked the elf maid at his side.

She considered it for a moment, then said, "Maybe, but it would have to be just elves." She glanced at Taryn with an apologetic look.

He gave a tiny nod and smile to let her know he understood why she didn't include him with her race, hoping the twinge he felt didn't show on his face.

"Whatever you do, you had better do it soon," Erix said as he pointed towards the elves.

They all looked up to see even more elves on the battlements, and a contingent of the lithe fighters armed with longbows streaming out of the gates to line up along the bridge ahead of them. Taryn quickly guessed that there were now over a hundred ready to fight—many of them with arrows already notched.

Liri's expression became determined as she bounded to the front of the ship—with Mae right behind her. Calling out, she addressed her people, "I am Liriana Allasse Tel'Runya of the House of Runya. We have completed our training on the island of Sri Rosen and are returning to our homeland. May we pass in peace?" She finished her formal request and bowed to indicate her respect.

No one spoke on the bridge or boat until the *Sea Dancer* closed the gap to a mere twenty feet. Then one of the elves on the bridge stepped out of the throng of archers and responded in a voice of steel, "You may pass, Lady Liriana of the House of Runya and your sister companion, but know this . . . any non-elf will be destroyed for setting foot in the Forest of Numenessee."

Despite his assurance that they could pass, not a single elf lowered their bow even a fraction. The normally happy elves watched stone-faced as the ship and its occupants passed underneath them into the shadow of the bridge. For a few minutes the creaks of the ship and dripping water echoed in the tunnel until they emerged on the other side to find the elves already watching them—with bows still drawn.

A turn in the river finally put the disturbing sight behind them, and several people breathed easier without it in view. But Taryn noticed that, just as before, they were still being watched from within the forest.

145

His brow furrowed at the continued vigil as he considered the ramifications of the odd exchange. Mulling over the event he felt like there was something he was missing, something in what the elf had said. Despite his efforts, it refused to come to the surface.

For the most part, the next few hours passed in relative peace. Sailors went about their business while the fighters and Thacker's family rested or talked in muted tones. At first Taryn assumed their subdued behavior was due to the encounter with the elves, but as the afternoon passed no one began playing or laughing. No banter or teasing from sailors, fighters, or the family lightened the mood. As time passed it became clear to Taryn that the elves had been a catalyst. *It*, whatever *it* was, was beginning to affect them too. Even as Taryn leaned against the rail to watch the sluggish river, he found that his own heart beat faster for no apparent reason. Try as he might, he couldn't shake the feeling of icy fear that sank deep into his belly.

Liriana's shoulder bumped his as she joined him—causing him to flinch.

"You feel it too, don't you," she whispered.

He nodded and responded without turning, "I don't think we are as bad as the elves, or even the people in the city—but it is definitely beginning to affect us."

She was silent for a long time, long enough for the sun to begin to set. "We do have a problem though," she finally said.

Now he did turn to her, with one eyebrow raised.

"How are we going to get *you* to Azertorn?"

He blinked and furrowed his brow as he realized that *she* could enter the forest but the elves wouldn't allow him. A flood of questions instantly bombarded his mind. Where was he going to start now? How was everything that was happening going to affect him?

Liri must have been able to read on his face what was going through his mind, because she placed her hand lightly on his forearm. "We will figure it out, I promise." She looked at him until his expression lightened and he focused on her. "Together . . . we will go to Azertorn and find your family."

At her statement he sighed deeply, and then smiled and nudged her. "I know Liri, I just don't know how."

They stayed there on the rail until the sun had set and darkness began to encircle them. No one disturbed them, possibly because it seemed they didn't want to be interrupted, but more likely because everyone was too preoccupied with their own fear to notice anybody else.

Taryn spent the time considering options on how to bypass the elves watching their ship . . . in a forest they knew by heart and that he was unfamiliar with. They both knew without saying that their original route to the city wouldn't work. If they guarded *one* ship this well, the elves were sure to be watching roads and cities far more carefully. Their only chance lay in slipping past the elves and heading towards the city *before* they arrived at Tallendale. Tonight, he came to realize, would be their only chance. Smiling sadly, he told Liri what he thought and they began devising a plan to slip past scores of the most alert race in Lumineia.

Chapter 11: The Giant's Shelf

Taryn eased himself down the rope and into the silent water with Liri right behind him. Darkness enshrouded everything around them in the cloudy night—but the two weren't taking any chances at being seen, so they slipped into the river on the south side of the boat. With the *Sea Dancer* obscuring the view from the north, it was a simple matter to let go and sink underwater.

Taryn entered the murky river still holding Liri's hand and took a deep lungful of air before silently disappearing from view. Inky stillness engulfed him like a cold blanket. His pack drifted downward, tugging him with it until he drifted ten feet underwater, suspended in the cool current. Every few moments the clouds would part, casting an otherworldly glow of soft moonlight that penetrated the water and illuminated Liri's form beside him. Counting the seconds as he forced himself to stay under, he tried to allow his body to drift naturally in the slow river and give their ship time to move far enough away that the watchers wouldn't see him surface.

With his whole body screaming for air, he forced himself to gradually empty his lungs and then waited until the last possible second before bringing his face to the surface. Like just another ripple in the water the two of them surfaced for air every few minutes until he felt it was safe to move. Squeezing Liri's hand to let her know he was going to swim towards shore, he took one last breath but this time lifted his eyes out of the water as well. Only rising enough for a quick glance, he chose a dark alcove and ducked underwater one last time. Then he began pulling himself slowly through the water. Thirty seconds later his hands came in contact with the muddy bank and he slowed his movements.

Easing himself above the water, he scanned the darkness for several seconds before lifting himself clear from the river. Once he was out of the water, he darted to the trunk of a large tree to dry himself off. Grabbing the sealskin bag that had been tied to his leg he pulled dry clothes out of the waterproof material and quickly changed—with his eyes searching the darkened forest around him. He had to admit that he couldn't tell if his anxiousness was due to what he was doing or whatever *IT* was . . .

Within a minute Taryn was strapping on his weapons and working his way east to find Liri. They had decided to come ashore in different locations just in case one got caught. Slipping through the forest with the sound of a shadow, he had to go only fifty paces. Hearing an owl hoot, he turned in the direction of the sound to find Liri stepping out of the river with water glistening all over her body. Both of them smiled at the sight of the other. He had always been able to distinguish her owl hoot when they played games together during early training—and the memory of a happier time stood out in stark contrast to their present circumstances.

The memory faded all too quickly, and Taryn turned away to allow her to change clothes. Two minutes later they set out towards Azertorn with Liri in the lead. Uncomfortable silence enclosed them in the dark forest with nothing to mark the passage of time. It only took Taryn a moment to identify that something felt out of place.

There were no normal forest sounds—no animals, no wind, nothing. He resisted the urge to grab Liri's arm to ask her about it, recalling her words before they'd disembarked. She'd shared an elven secret with him, that the trees spoke to the elves and might hear them if they spoke aloud. For some reason he couldn't put his finger on, it seemed like she'd been reluctant to tell him—and not solely because it was an elven secret.

Resigning himself to waiting, he followed her through the maze of trunks. Pushing on until past dawn, they holed up in a shaded gully for the day, electing to set up camp in a secluded cave. Taryn, still wide awake and with senses heightened, volunteered to keep watch while an exhausted Liri slept through the morning. They switched after a quick meal in the early afternoon and he caught a few hours of sleep while they waited for the relative cover of darkness to return. Sometime after dusk he felt a light touch on his shoulder and snapped awake, ready for danger. She shook her head with a yawn so he buckled his weapons on and rose to his feet, stretching.

Stifling another yawn, Liri stood up beside him and handed him some bread, meat, and cheese. For some reason she seemed annoyed so he caught her eye and raised an eyebrow.

She shook her head and leaned over, whispering into his ear so quietly he barely heard her, "You could go forever I swear."

Her pursed lips and furrowed brow made him want to laugh so he bit his lip to avoid making any sound, but he couldn't help his shoulders shaking in suppressed humor. Liri flashed him a frown that didn't reach her eyes and smacked him on the shoulder before gathering her things. With a last soundless chuckle he helped her with her pack and fell into step behind her, trying to finish his dinner in silence.

All night they traveled through the forest, avoiding trails or roads. Taryn also noticed that Liri seemed to be following a very indirect route, moving north, northeast, and then due west before turning north again. Leaning forward and tapping her shoulder he wiggled a hand in a curving route and gave her a questioning look. She nodded and formed her hands into the shape of a house, then slid one hand around it. Taryn nodded, satisfied that she knew the forest well enough to avoid any of the numerous villages that dotted the vast expanse of elven woodland.

Despite their efforts, they still had to detour twice around elven patrols that they barely heard in time. After the second patrol, they decided to try crossing the large road that lead to the great bridge on the Blue River. Avoiding detection in the crossing would be difficult, but once across, their passage should be easier. With wide, empty ocean to the west, there should be fewer patrols, Liri had reasoned. There was less to protect from that direction anyway.

Traveling west, they found the road just before the first rays of dawn streaked the sky. Seeing no one, they dashed across before the light could reveal their presence and continued north towards Azertorn.

Discovering another good hiding spot, they rested during the day once more before continuing on. Taryn found himself enjoying the walk with Liri, but began to understand why she hadn't wanted to tell him about the trees. He felt discouraged by the lack of conversation and guessed that Liri felt the same. She had always been easy to talk to, but he hadn't realized until now how much he liked the conversation. Every time he saw some plant or a track from an animal he had to resist asking a question.

Sighing in frustration, he forced his attention from the elf walking in front of him and looked at the trees instead. Even at night he could tell how beautiful the forest of *Numenessee* was—despite the unnatural silence. Giant trees, some hundreds of feet tall, left little light to penetrate to the undergrowth. Their enormous limbs seemed to extend out protecting arms over the smaller plants and brush, leaving him with the impression that the entire forest lived and breathed as one.

Taryn and Liri continued throughout the night and stopped when dawn began to lighten the forest. Finding a huge tree that had fallen across another, they decided to camp in the cave-like space underneath the massive trunk. Just before Liri fell asleep she murmured, "We only have another hour or so before we hit the Giant's Shelf and the city."

He nodded and whispered, "Good," and then only loud enough for his own ears he added, "But then how am I going to get in?"

The daytime passed quickly with the two of them getting some rest and keeping watch. Before Taryn knew it, Liri was shaking him awake an hour before dusk. When he saw the early hour he looked at her questioningly, but she nodded reassuringly and leaned in close to speak to him.

"I want to show you the city with some light," she whispered, keeping her voice low, her eyes sparkling.

"What about guards?" Taryn asked just as quiet.

She chuckled softly, "They will be protecting the forest. The city has its own defenses and I doubt they will put any scouts this close."

His puzzled expression only made her more amused.

"You will understand when you see the city. *No one* gets into the city without permission."

He opened his mouth to protest that was exactly what he needed to do but her grin widened and she put a finger on his lips. "Except you Taryn."

Her confident demeanor spread to him and he reluctantly set his worry aside, his thoughts lingering instead on the place where her finger had brushed his lips. Still distracted, he gathered the rest of his gear and hurried to follow his guide as the sun began to sink into the horizon. Fading daylight filtered through layers of branches to cast beams of orange and red as the two glided through the deepening shadows.

True to Liri's word, only an hour passed before they pushed through some brush to find themselves on the bank of a large lake. As he looked across the expanse of water in front of him, Taryn gaped openly in wonder as he took in the view of the Giant's Shelf and the city of Azertorn.

A sheer cliff stretched at least a thousand feet straight up in front of him and extended as far as he could see in either direction. The massive plateau blotted out the view of the sky and dominated the vista so completely he couldn't even capture the entire expanse of rock without turning his head back and forth—and yet the city of Azertorn drew the eye far more than the cliff ever could.

Twin waterfalls roughly seven miles apart fell uninhibited the full height of the Giant's Shelf. Slamming into the pool of water with tremendous force and sound, they created huge quantities of mist and fed the large body of water that Taryn and Liri faced. From their position at the southwest corner of the lake, one of the waterfalls fell almost directly in front of them and the other almost out of sight to the east. The elven city of Azertorn had been carved from solid rock *in between* the waterfalls.

152

A bowl of stone had been completely removed to create expanding tiers of rock the higher you looked. Each tier of a hundred feet contained buildings that hadn't been built but rather sculpted straight from the stone. The lowest and smallest portion of the city began a quarter of the way up the cliff face. Starting there, and in the exact center of the bowl, an absolutely massive tree grew at least five hundred feet high with branches so large they were used as pathways to interconnect the separate levels.

With the last vestiges of sunlight and the countless lights glowing on the huge tree and each of the eight tiers, he was able to see that detailed carvings covered the visible stone sections of the citadel—but most of the rock was blanketed with greenery. Trees, flowers, and other vegetation blossomed over the entire city, creating hanging gardens on and between each level.

Below the first tier, only one opening existed. A single large stone door inset at the base of the cliff led to a flat bridge stretching out over the water to the forest. Above the entrance door two hundred and fifty feet of bare stone separated the lake from the city.

Taryn gazed in open admiration at the sheer beauty of the elven city, but he found himself far more impressed at how defensible it was. Protected on both sides by the waterfalls as well as the cliff, with the lake and the very height of the city to the front, the only real place to attack would be from above the plateau—but even there it would be impossible. Liri had told him that the river that fed the two waterfalls split north of the city, forming a fast moving, ever flowing moat around the walls of the city. In every feature, Azertorn had been built and carved to be the strongest fortress ever created, and he found himself wondering how any army could ever breach its defenses.

Liri cut into his thoughts abruptly when she whispered, "The tree is called Le Runtáriel. The elves brought the seed with them when they migrated from the east and it was planted when the city was carved."

Taryn nodded but couldn't respond. He just stared at the magnificent city and tried to comprehend how such an amazing structure had been created.

Without warning the door at the base of the cliff burst open and armed soldiers rushed onto the bridge.

Liri cursed under her breath, "The trees must have heard me. We have to leave—now!"

She grabbed her gear and started to run west, but Taryn caught her arm, spinning her to face him.

"No . . . if you are caught with me then you will be killed for sure," he said, his voice intense.

She started to object but he cut her off. "If they come here and find you, they will be suspicious but may not even look for me. I will find another way into the city, and I will meet you at the base of the tree tomorrow night."

Liri hesitated for one precious second before she agreed, "OK, but don't meet me at the tree. The entire bottom tier is the barracks for the army." She smiled a tight-lipped smile which he returned. "So meet me at my family's house. The House of Runya is on the seventh tier, second from the top in the northeastern corner. Look for a crest with an eagle—but how will you get into the city?"

Taryn glanced at the elves which were already almost across the bridge. "I will figure it out," he said as he grabbed his pack. "If I have to, I will climb the cliff and come from the north."

Her eyes widened. "But I don't think that's ever been done before . . ."

She trailed off as Taryn bolted west without another word. As he ghosted his way through the trees, he guessed he only had twenty or thirty seconds before they found Liri, and maybe another minute or two before they would come looking for him. He darted west first and then threaded his way through the trees and around the lake to the north. When he reached the cliff, he turned west again and sprinted as fast as he could with the Giant's Shelf only a few feet to his right. Wind whistled around him as he raced along the flat rock—but he wasn't running blindly.

155

His eyes scanned the rock above him, searching the face for a path to climb. He saw plenty of handholds and footholds, but not a route he could scale fast enough. Hiding in the forest was out of the question. The elves would find an intruder in their home quickly and efficiently— and he had no doubt that the consequences would be severe.

A shadow in the stone above him caused him to slow down. Peering up he skidded to a stop when he saw that it was a small crack about a hundred feet off the ground. It looked to be less than a foot wide and only a few feet tall, but it would have to do. He studied the rock below it until he'd planned his route and then continued along the cliff for a hundred yards before turning into the forest, glancing backwards as he disappeared into the gloom.

He didn't have much time to leave a false trail and get back to his hiding spot before the elves found him—but the pounding in his ears made it difficult for him to remember what to do. *Would he get caught? What would he do if he did?* The questions swirled through his mind, distracting him even as heat scorched his neck. Woodlore had not been one of his strengths in training, but he did his best to recall what he could, praying it would be enough.

Taking a deep breath, he forced himself to focus and run faster. Rushing through the trees he began touching trees and leaving footprints. Spotting a large tree with strong limbs, he leapt onto the first branch and scaled the trunk as quietly as he could.

Reaching the top, he stopped and removed anything of value from his pack before stashing it into a crook of the tree. Ensuring that everything was strapped on securely, he dropped to a lower branch. The only thing he had kept from his pack besides his weapons was a rope. Once he was done, he stood and ran along a springy branch before leaping to another. Traveling through the trees, he went only thirty feet before dropping lightly to the ground.

With every sense tuned to the slightest indication of his hunters' locations, Taryn returned to the cliff below the crack he'd chosen to hide in. Every few seconds he would stop, listen, and check his trail to make sure there were no signs of his passage. Arriving at the wall, he raced forty feet up a tree that grew close to his destination.

A sudden sound forced him to freeze. Seconds later he heard it again—an elven voice calling out to others. They were on his trail. He glanced at the wall and gauged his time frame. He doubted there was enough time to jump to the wall and climb to his hiding spot before they crossed underneath. He could either wait and hope to make it after they passed . . . or go now and risk being seen on the wall. Resolving to wait, he made sure he was well hidden. Not five seconds later a full company of armed elves came into sight to the east. They raced west and followed his trail to where he'd stopped to look at the cliff.

Taryn breathed a sigh of relief when he saw them stop to look upward. He'd made the right choice to wait; they would have seen him for sure. After a moment, most of the group flew west along his trail, each movement smooth and fluid, silent hunters in the night. One elf spoke to those remaining, and three elves separated themselves before sprinting east towards the city. The rest of them continued to follow his tracks along the cliff.

Their efficiency gave Taryn plenty of cause to admire. This was their homeland and they were stalking an intruder. But it was hard to appreciate with him being the hunted. Waiting until they turned into the forest, he looked at the wall and chose two strong handholds and two footholds to jump for. Mentally he rehearsed how he would land against the cliff several times to make sure he could do it. He had to jump almost twenty feet and catch himself nearly sixty feet off the ground— without making a sound.

Taking a deep breath he pushed off the trunk, ran along a thick branch, and then leapt through the air. Air whistled in his ears as he flew through space straight at the rock face. The instant his hands grabbed stone he clenched his fingers with all his might and brought his feet in to hook the footholds he'd chosen. Using his arms and knees, he cushioned his forward momentum so he wouldn't bounce off the cliff face.

Despite his efforts, his right foot slid free—but he somehow managed to catch himself just before the rest of him followed. After he'd regained his balance, he began climbing the wall with a speed that would have astonished any viewer. Hands and feet reached for the knobs and holes he'd chosen from below, so he didn't have to stop to look where he was going.

Within ten seconds he'd climbed the forty feet to the crevasse and without hesitation squeezed himself into the protective darkness. Cramming himself into the small space, he froze when he heard light footfalls from the east. Peering out of the darkness he watched another score of elven hunters follow his trail underneath him. Realizing he had been holding his breath, he slowly exhaled in a long sigh of relief—but he still didn't move a muscle until the elven hunters disappeared into the forest. Once he felt it was safe to move, he began to maneuver his body into a more comfortable position to watch and wait.

Throughout the night his hiding place turned out to be an excellent vantage point, albeit uncomfortably close to the action. Taryn began to wonder if he would have to stay in his hiding spot all day, but a couple of hours before dawn none other than Liri came into view. Accompanied by a small group of elves, she was led along the cliff face to stop five paces east of his hiding place. Suddenly an elf bounded into view with Taryn's discarded pack in hand. By their behavior, Taryn couldn't tell if Liri was a prisoner or not, but at least she wasn't bound . . . or dead.

One of the elves grabbed the pack from the newcomer and spoke sharply to Liri. As the elf leaned in to ask his question, the moonlight glinted off his light blue armor. Although Taryn couldn't hear the question, it was evident that he wanted Liri to explain the source of the pack. Liri shook her head with a fairly convincing bewildered look. At first Taryn thought the captain would explode in anger, but for some inexplicable reason he visibly cooled his feelings before responding. For several minutes the two of them argued back and forth until another elf cut in timidly with some comment.

The leader seemed angry with the younger soldier, but Liri responded to whatever the young elf had said with another shake of her head. Her response must have calmed the captain somewhat, because he paused for a moment and then gave out some quick orders to several of the elves. As they jumped to obey, Taryn noticed that they appeared to avoid Liri—and not in a bad way. Almost like water slipping around a rock, they flowed past her, giving her a wide berth. The odd behavior spoke of deference, rather than suspicion or fear. It reminded him of the recent conversations they had shared, causing him to consider for the first time that Liri had kept far more from him than he'd originally thought.

Who was Liri?

The next sixty seconds were a blur of activity as most of the patrol returned east towards the city with Liri in their midst. Several of them remained and took up positions along the base of the cliff and, Taryn assumed, in the forest as well. Unfortunately for Taryn, one of the elves decided to stand almost directly below where he was concealed.

Unnatural silence returned to the forest below within seconds of the elves departure, leaving Taryn alone in his fissure with several alert elves spread out below him. Relief flooded through him as he realized that his ruse had been successful. On Sri Rosen, the lessons on tracking had been . . . difficult for him, and despite his best efforts to practice, he'd never once been able to track someone down. But he *had* managed a passable effort at evading capture. He still considered his efforts to elude the elves more luck than skill though, and hoped his luck would hold.

But as more time passed, he began to think he'd made a mistake. The elves below him gave no sign of leaving, placing him in a difficult situation. Considering what to do, he took a few minutes to weigh his options and wonder at the elven leader's actions. The blue-armored elf had done almost exactly as he'd expected right down to bringing Liri to the trail. What surprised him was the fact that he'd left guards. There was no way an intruder would return on the same route by which he had escaped, so why post the sentries?

After a few minutes of considering it, Taryn realized that the elf had left guards because he didn't know what to do—and the strange fear affecting everyone had pushed him to do *something*, even if the action didn't make sense.

Whatever the reason for the sentries, it sharply limited Taryn's options. With the coming of dawn his hiding spot would be revealed for any wandering eyes. He could either risk staying through the day, or start his climb right now and try to make it most of the way before the sun came up. Glancing down at the elves, he made his decision. He would have to make his attempt immediately. At least the sentries were facing into the forest and weren't likely to turn around unless he broke the silence.

Extricating himself from the small crevice proved to take more time than he'd expected, but he forced himself to move slowly to keep his weapons from scraping the rock. Once clear, he took a good grip on the wall as soon as he had the chance and began to climb.

Unfortunately he was unable to use the rope he'd kept. He found no place to tie it, and even if he could it would do him no good, but there was no other option. Dropping it or leaving it in his hold would have revealed his presence, and his route. He couldn't risk it.

Knowing he didn't have much time before he got tired or the sun came up, he scaled the massive cliff as rapidly as he could. Despite his speed he was careful to plan a route, climb, stop, and then plan another route. He didn't end up climbing straight, but his crooked path kept him from hitting the frequent smooth patches that would have taken precious time to backtrack and circumnavigate.

Thirty minutes before the first rays of light graced the horizon, Taryn had scaled nearly half of the Giant's Shelf. By the time the sun had come up enough for anyone to spot him easily, he'd climbed another two hundred feet. He was beginning to think it wouldn't be too difficult—until the cliff abruptly turned sheer.

Eight hundred feet off the ground the stone had been smoothed by the elements, leaving precious few handholds. Pausing for a moment, Taryn wiped the sweat that had begun to sting his eyes and flexed his forearms, trying to restore their weakening grip. It was taking longer and longer to find a route with fewer and fewer places to grasp. His tired hands and sore feet slowed him even further, forcing him to find paths with easier grips. To make matters worse, the wind had picked up, grabbing and tugging at him as it blew past his struggling form.

160

The next hundred feet took nearly two hours of painstaking and exhausting effort. Time and time again Taryn was forced to backtrack, lowering himself to a previous position before taking a second look. Carefully he would climb sideways in search of some tiny ledge or nook that would support his weight.

At nine hundred feet he got lucky and found a ledge nearly four inches wide that curved gently up and to the side. Grasping it gratefully, he looked for something to pull himself up so he could stand—but didn't see anything. No holes or bumps were big enough to grip, no sections of rock offered enough surface for even the tips of his fingers . . . nothing. Looking west he saw that the ledge ran for at least a hundred feet and with its rise in elevation, would take him to within fifty feet of the top. Glancing down he checked to see if there were any toeholds but didn't see anything below the ledge either.

For a second he considered using his father's sword to cut into the rock and pull himself up, but immediately dismissed the idea. He was quite high, but not invisible, and the flash of magic would almost certainly draw unwanted attention. Using his sword would have to be a last resort.

Taking a deep breath in an attempt to steady his tired muscles, he took all the weight off one hand at a time. Clenching and unclenching his hands, he tried to prepare for the only option he had left—let himself hang from the ledge with nothing to support his feet while he inched his way along it.

Tired and sore, Taryn allowed his body to dangle nine hundred feet off the ground . . . and began to work his way along the ledge. Sliding one hand, and then the other, he pushed himself sideways and tried to ignore the angry wind whipping at his clothes. With sweat dripping from his nose, he reached the halfway point. Hoping to find somewhere to place a toe and provide momentary relief he paused to check the wall above and below, but he found nothing and had no choice but to keep going.

As he approached the end of the ledge, it began to taper off, thinning to two inches . . . and then to barely enough for a fingertip. Now little more than a hairsbreadth of stone kept him from plummeting to his death. With shaking arms he reached the end and looked around for something to grip. The only thing within reach was a crack in the wall that started a foot above the ledge. Slightly smaller than his hand, it ran up and curved a little before ending five feet from the top.

Seeing that the crack was completely smooth on the sides, Taryn braced his fingers and lifted himself up. Face smashed into the cliff and clinging to the rock with trembling fingers—he let go with his right hand. Quickly reaching up, he forced his hand into the crack and formed a fist, pressing his flesh against the sides of the crack. Clenching the fist with all his might, he let go with his left hand . . . and began to slide down.

Gritting his teeth, he forced his hand into a tighter ball that stopped him from falling by crushing his flesh against the sides of the split stone. His skin began to tear, eliciting a growl, but he had no other options. Pulling himself up with all his weight resting on his fist, he placed his left hand into the crack in the same manner and was finally able to lift himself up enough to rest his feet on the tiny ledge.

Taryn took the moment to rest and take stock of his situation. The crack would take him close to the top, but it would require his last shred of strength to do so. Glancing at the location of the sun, he was surprised to see that it had already passed its apex. He'd been climbing for almost ten hours.

Knowing his life depended on it, he tried to steady his breath before placing both fists into the crack. By putting his foot sideways into the crack and then twisting his leg until it was upright, he was able to place enough leverage on the rock that it could support his weight. Wincing against the pain in his hands and feet, he drove himself to continue. Fist after painstaking fist, he scaled the tiny crack, and forty feet later he found himself a mere five feet from the top.

With every ounce of strength he had left, he braced his left fist into the very top of the crack and reached as high as he could with right hand. One thousand feet off the ground, Taryn found an extremely good grip that would take him to safety—six inches out of reach. He cursed under his breath and with his face pressed against the cliff, looked around for something else.

All around him the rock had been worn smooth, leaving nothing with enough purchase for him to use. Clenching his eyes shut, he listened to the ragged sound of his breathing, wishing there was another way, but in his heart he knew there wasn't.

Exhausted, he wiped the sweat off his right hand, rubbed it against the wall to get some sense of grip back, crouched on cramped feet . . . and jumped.

Chapter 12: Azertorn

Taryn propelled himself upward only a few inches, but it felt like much further. With muscles shaking in protest, he forced his hand to grab the jutting piece of rock . . . and hold on tight. Knowing he didn't have much time, he reached up with his left hand and grabbed a tiny crack. From there it took two tries before he was able to get high enough to place his left hand on the very top of the Giant's Shelf. Lifting himself up, he inched his way forward until more of his weight leaned horizontal than vertical. Then he rolled himself onto the plateau with a grunt of effort.

Chest heaving from the exertion of climbing for so long, he felt a rush of relief and pride wash over him. Grinning wide he almost laughed, but for some reason his mind turned to Murai. What would he have thought of what he'd just done? The image of his uncle's proud smile caused a pang of sorrow to lance through him, replacing his relief with a bitter taste.

He missed him more than he realized.

Distracted and weary, it took him half an hour before he felt able to continue. Lying flat, he scanned his surroundings, checking to make sure he hadn't been seen. With the exception of a few lonely pine trees, the Giant's Shelf was remarkably barren. Rarely a scrub oak or other plant reached higher than a man's chest. A couple of miles back a forest grew thick and strong, but the space between the edge and the tree line remained dominated by small brush struggling to find purchase in the flat stone. East of his position he could see the trees growing thick next to the river that fed the western falls of Azertorn.

After resting, Taryn took some time to flex his muscles to assess his condition. His arms and legs were sore and at least still functional, but his forearms and hands were another story. In the short time that he'd lain there, they had cramped to the point where he could barely grip with his hands. He could deal with the pain, but his grip had lost most of its strength. He doubted he would be able to hold his swords well enough to fight for a few hours.

Deciding there wasn't much he could do about the situation, he rolled his body over and rose into a crouch to look around. As he forced his legs to respond, he was unable to stop a groan of protest at the effort. Checking one more time for any sign of movement, he attempted to stretch the sore muscles all over his body. It didn't help much, but at least he was able to move in silence.

His immediate position offered some concealment, but not enough to allow him to stay for long. If anyone came within a hundred yards he was sure to be spotted. Preferring to move towards the city, he began to work his way in that direction. As silently as he could, he moved from one barely adequate cover to another, feeling grateful as the movement began to ease his sore body.

Before the sun had begun to set, Taryn slipped into the trees that grew beside the river. He was a little surprised at the lack of elven presence. There should have been guards along the cliff top, but not a single soul could be seen.

Entering the forest, he took even greater care than he had on the plateau—and it was a good thing he did. Within ten steps he encountered a sentry hidden behind the trunk of a tree. Inching past him, he bypassed the soldier without event, but before long found another elf, and then another. Every twenty feet another sentinel would force him to slow down and sneak past. It took nearly an hour to pass the five sentries and reach the river.

The sun was just beginning to sink into the horizon when he came to the flowing water, and he slid into a shadowy vantage point. Fifty feet of white water separated him from the wall of stone that rose up on the opposite bank. The wall rose out of the water for nearly a hundred feet with the first half made of solid rock, while the second half appeared to be built of layered stones to create a strong defense against intruders. Battlements crowned the top, and from Taryn's position he could see numerous guards manning them. No section of ground separated the city wall from the water, which created the illusion that the city grew straight out of the river. Swimming would be out of the question. Not only would the current carry him over the cliff in an instant, there would be no way for him to climb the wall before someone sunk an arrow into him.

Seeing no opening, he began to follow the bank of the river to the north in the hope that another opportunity might present itself. In his heart he doubted the river would really be an option. He'd been hoping the elves would not have been so vigilant above the shelf, but the unnatural fear must have caused them to place more security than normal. As he worked his way through the trees along the bank, he considered his various ideas on how to get into the city—until he walked into a sentry . . .

The elf had hidden himself well, positioning himself in the shadows between two trees adjacent to the river. Taryn bowled right into him as he rounded a trunk. Each bounced off the other as if he'd touched a hot iron, but it was Taryn who responded first. Bolting north, he raced through the trees. The elf he'd surprised raised the alarm in less than a second, and answering calls rang all around him. Turning a corner, he saw a group of elves massing in front of him. Before they could spot him, he reversed direction and darted south towards the cliff.

With trees flashing past him, he tried not to berate himself for being seen and focused on what to do. Knowing he had only seconds, he allowed his mind to broaden and pictured the city with the surrounding area. By using the image in his mind, he looked for a route that would be safe, and preferably take him into the city. Remembering something he'd seen from the foot of the cliff suddenly gave him an idea. It was risky, but he didn't see another option.

Calls and yells snapped his attention backward as he sped up to avoid his pursuers. A sudden shout in front of him made him veer closer to the river. The fading light began to make it increasingly difficult to see, so he raced through the trunks by memory, retracing his route towards the cliff.

—Out of nowhere an elven sentry popped up in front of him with drawn sword. Without missing a step, he twisted and rolled right up the sword thrust, barreling into the elf with his lowered shoulder. Unprepared to withstand the blow, the surprised elf stumbled backward and fell into the river with a grunt. With a glance, Taryn realized that they were only thirty feet from the cliff and the elf wouldn't make it out of the river in time.

Exploding into motion, he drew Ianna, sliced a long, thin branch off a tree, and flicked the end out towards the struggling elf. Just as the elf grasped the end of the branch, Taryn tossed his end towards a trunk hanging out over the water. An instant later his mother's sword became a bow. As the end of the branch touched the trunk of the overhanging tree, a green shafted arrow buried itself into the branch and trunk, securing it and providing the elven soldier a lifeline to the bank.

Without slowing Taryn sped towards the cliff while the branch holding the elf bent and swung him to safety not ten paces from the massive waterfall—but Taryn barely saw it. Still holding his mother's bow, he raced to very edge of the cliff, quickly crouched and leaned out over the thousand foot drop.

Drawing back the bow, he sunk two arrows deep into the rock about a foot down from the plateau. Morphing it back to the sword he sheathed it and grabbed his rope off his back. After tying one end securely onto the arrows, he sprinted away from the falls with only inches between his pounding feet and the long drop. As he ran, he let the rope play out beside him so it stretched between him and the arrows holding the other end.

—Two elves burst into view to his right. Calling for support, they began to pursue him. Within seconds, more elves joined the pursuit so when he broke free of the trees he picked up the pace. Another shout came from behind him, but this time it was a voice of authority.

Looking back, he saw numerous elves lining up with bows drawn. Knowing they would not miss, he gauged what was left of his rope.

Bowstrings twanged behind him and he knew he was out of time. Wrapping what was left of the cord tightly around his left arm and spinning so it looped around his waist, he held on as tight as he could and without hesitation . . . stepped off the cliff. As he dropped from view arrows sliced through the air where he'd been standing—some so close he felt one graze his shoulder as he began to fall, leaving a stinging line in his flesh.

Picking up speed, he plummeted towards the earth until the rope snapped taut and yanked him east—but he wasn't swinging . . . he was running. Sprinting as fast as he could, he raced into the curve and fought to hold on to the rope as the motion put more and more force on his body. His legs blurred almost out of sight as he struggled to keep up with his momentum, speeding faster and faster as the rope swung him like a pendulum at the end of its length. Reaching the waterfall, he leapt for all he was worth . . . and sailed across the crashing water—so close he could feel the spray wetting his feet.

In the blink of an eye he was past the falls and hit the cliff face in a full sprint. Scanning the rock ahead as he began arcing skyward, he desperately looked for what he'd seen from a thousand feet below—a large window.

Suddenly he saw it, and he was going to miss it . . . *if* he didn't adjust his run. By allowing some rope to slide through his fingers, he controlled his angle to point toward the opening as he began to slow. Aligning himself with the window, he drew his father's sword, and just as he reached the top of his arc, jammed it into the cliff—a foot above the window. Letting go of the rope and reaching inside, he found the inside lip with his left hand and pulled himself to safety, drawing Mazer out of the cliff face as he went.

Slipping into a dark room, Taryn allowed himself a brief moment to catch his breath before continuing. His desperate maneuver would probably buy him some time, and he hoped it would be enough. The enchanted arrows supporting the rope would disappear soon enough and hopefully no one would see them. If he got lucky, the elves might not even guess that the intruder had gotten into their city—but even as he thought it he knew that the guards would be searching the city regardless. He had to find Liri's home as quickly as possible.

Once Taryn's heart had slowed and he'd steadied his breathing, he searched the room for a way out. The small chamber turned out to hold barrels containing various foodstuffs. A thin layer of dust had settled over most of the room, so it appeared that no one had been in it for some time. Upon closer inspection he found a rack against the back wall that had pegs. It dawned on him that the room was a lookout post, probably rarely used due to its height. There were sure to be similar rooms lower on the cliff. The rack on the back wall was built to hold bows and arrows in times of attack, but he doubted the room had ever been used for that purpose.

Finding a door behind some barrels, he listened for any sign of movement on the other side. Hearing nothing, he tried the handle— hoping for it to be open—but it proved to be locked. Taryn was sure he could cut through it with his father's sword, but was reluctant to leave such an obvious mark of passage. Seeing that the door swung inward, he used one of his throwing knives to jimmy each of the pegs that held the hinges. When he was done, he inched open the door only tenuously held by the lock, pausing each time the old metal creaked. As the gap widened, dim torchlight cast shadows into his chamber, revealing an empty corridor on the other side.

He waited for several seconds to see if anyone appeared, but his caution proved to be unnecessary. Wanting to leave as little sign as possible of his passing, he lifted the entire door into the room and replaced the pegs, using a stray piece of wood as a mallet. Once the door was back on its hinges, he swung it closed behind him, wincing as the rusty iron squeaked in protest. Even though it wouldn't close all the way because of the locking bar, it should still pass a cursory inspection and, if he was lucky, be passed off as nothing.

Less than ten minutes after his entry into the city, Taryn set out down the unfamiliar corridor to begin his search. Coming to what he'd thought to be a torch he found it to be a piece of wood that cast flickering light from the top, but there was no fire. He'd been taught that the elves used light magic, although he'd never had the opportunity to see a fireless torch. It appeared as if the elves had found a way to duplicate the light from a fire without the actual flame.

As fascinating as it was to look at, Taryn continued down the corridor. He'd entered the room at the end of the passageway, so his path led into the plateau but curved in a long, gentle turn to the right. Heavy doors similar to the one he'd opened were inset into the walls on both sides. The walls themselves were fascinating. No seam could be seen to mar the perfectly smooth stone, and he slid his fingers along the walls just to feel the texture.

After Taryn had passed several doors, the corridor formed a T junction. Taking the path to the right, he made his way to a fortified door. Strong light came out from underneath, causing him to pull up short. Crouching, he peered under the door. No boots could be seen, but it looked like the door led to another storage room, this one well used and clean. Waiting for several moments to ensure that no one was there, he opened the unlocked door as slowly as he could manage. A whine of protest escaped the old hinges, but no one approached at the sound, so he slipped through the crack and closed the door behind him. Ducking some crates, he scanned the room. Three doors led out of the large chamber, two to either side with one right in front of him.

Guessing that the side doors led to corridors similar to the previous one, he cautiously crossed the room and tried the door in front. Only opening it a sliver, he was relieved to see a long darkened walkway that led to a ledge of the city. No lights graced the walls on either side, so he darted through the door, hoping the flash of light from the opened door would go unnoticed.

Placing his back to one of the walls he cautiously slid down the corridor. No sound signaled an approach of guards, but he paused every few seconds to listen as he worked his way through the darkness. Fifty feet from the door, the ceiling gave way to open sky and he continued until he reached the very edge of shadow, taking advantage of the opportunity to examine the city a little closer in the rising moonlight.

Taryn stood on the highest Tier of Azertorn. Above him a low barracks ran along the interior of the high wall. Various stairs led up to the barracks from his ledge. On the tier below him he could see the roofs of tall, ornate buildings blanketed in gardens. At the exact center of the tier below, an extra large building had been carved, much larger than anything else in the city. By the detail and size he assumed it was the governing house of the elves.

He couldn't be sure from his location, but it looked like the buildings in the tier below the palace weren't quite as detailed as the highest tier. All of the lower levels were at least partially obscured by Le Runtáriel, the massive and ancient tree that grew in the center of the bottom level of the city—but it wasn't the only tree in sight.

Trees, flowers, and shrubs grew absolutely *everywhere*—clinging to the stone or free standing, on top of buildings or balconies. Barely a patch of stone was left visible in any direction. Small brooks and miniature canals fed the plants like spider webs of trickling water, imparting life to the veritable forest. In between the trees and buildings, numerous stone arches spanned larger streams. Slim cascades of pure water fell from tier to tier, some only a few inches wide while others were several feet in width. Where the water crossed the base of a level, the stone had been shaped into wide beautiful bridges. Not thirty paces from him he could see a fruit tree reaching out over a rocky waterway that bubbled as it jumped from rock to rock. The sheer volume of moving and falling water lent an almost musical cadence to the environment. Peace washed over him, mixing with the cool breeze, causing him to pause long enough to take a deep breath and close his eyes. The feeling did wonders to combat the subtle fear that felt unnatural in such a place.

After a moment, Taryn returned his gaze to the splendor of the elven city, wondering how it had been built. There was no way elves had carved the stone in such a fashion. Water, plants, and light were their skills. Only the dwarves could have envisioned and hewed the magnificent city straight from the living rock. Shaking his head at the numerous questions in his mind, he resolved to ask Liri when he met up with her. For now, he focused on where to go.

Looking across the expanse to the opposite side, he spotted a particularly detailed structure at the northeastern corner. The building, second in size only to the palace, dominated almost a quarter of the entire half ring. Making that his destination, he began planning a route across the open stone.

As he began to examine different ways to approach his goal, he realized that each level of the city had a lot more to it than he'd thought. For the most part, each larger structure looked to be made up of nine smaller floors built vertically, about a hundred feet tall—at least that is what he assumed based on the number of windows. Each building spanned between two and four windows wide. Between the larger structures he could see the space had been carved out to form flights of stairs. By the signs and decor, the two lowest layers of these structures looked to be shops.

There were four exceptions to these communal structures. The palace was the largest, while the second largest sat on the second tier down in the northeast corner. Two other large buildings were not segmented. One was positioned adjacent to him. Smaller than the rest but even more detailed, the fourth building rested on the third tier down and immediately below the palace. All other structures looked to be segmented into smaller buildings, albeit of varying detail and design.

Just as Taryn was finishing his inspection, several guards came into view on his level. Running in his direction they passed him in a hurry before ascending again out of view. Perhaps the elves had figured out what he'd done? Or were they still searching outside the city? Either way he had to move.

Deciding on a route, he checked for anyone around and then walked casually towards a descending staircase. Hoping his light attitude would help to avoid someone raising an alarm, he forced himself to walk normally through the revealing moonlight. Reaching the stairs without incident, he stepped down the stairs and disappeared into darkness. It turned out that the staircase ran fifty feet before turning back on itself again. On both sides, he passed landings that led to doors, inset into the vine covered stone on either side. The only light came from a single flameless torch on the landing where the stairs turned back to descend further.

He'd expected the stairs to be perfectly spaced and was not disappointed. Each step had been expertly cut, and their almost ten-foot width would allow heavy traffic without feeling crowded. Reaching the bottom of the first set, he came to a balcony overlooking the city before turning around and heading down again—this time facing inward. After several more switchbacks, he came to the bottom of the stairs. Although he'd encountered no elves, he approached the second tier cautiously— and it was a good thing he did.

No sooner had he reached the second level when three elves came into view, marching in unison towards him. Taryn slipped from the shadowed stairwell and ducked into the darkened recess of a doorway, allowing them to pass unmolested. Passing his hiding spot, the elves ascended the stairs out of view. He waited a couple of minutes to make sure he was safe, but just as he breathed a sigh and stepped out the three elves came back into view. Dodging back before they could see him, he watched them return and pass him again. Something about the group seemed different, and a second later he realized that one of the elves was shorter than the other two. The first group had all been the same height. These three must have been following him down without him even knowing.

Realizing his luck could not hold for long, he proceeded even more carefully on his way to the second level. Pausing at the corner, he poked his head out enough to look around. This tier contained the palace in the center, and it appeared to have an extra contingent of guards. He spotted at least two score patrolling the wide stone pathway in front of the building, and there were sure to be more out of view. Between the palace and his goal there would be no way for him to pass without arousing suspicion.

Looking for another route he saw none, so he decided to go down another level in the hope of finding it less protected. He suspected the rotation would be similar, so he kept an eye out for another group of three to go down the next flight of stairs—while at the same time watching for someone to come up his own.

He didn't have to wait long. Five minutes passed and three elves came up the stairs. Realizing he missed the ones going down, he stayed

173

put until this group had turned towards the palace. Employing the same method as before, he sauntered towards the stairs. Descending quickly he kept his eyes peeled for guards but encountered no one. Reaching the third tier, he checked it for sentries.

This level was comprised entirely of the segmented structures, and the security proved to be much lighter. Only three or four patrols could be seen from his position. Hugging the shadowed wall, he worked his way around the bowl towards the opposite side of the city, pausing to marvel at a massive branch that reached out from Le'Runtáriel to embrace the wide pathway. More than once he slipped behind a tree or into a doorway to avoid the roving elves. Before long he reached the eastern side of the city and returned to the second level.

Once he'd found another hiding spot on the palace level, he realized that the ruling house wasn't the only one with extra guards. Elves patrolled the two other large buildings as well. Upon closer inspection he realized that the guards were dressed differently. Even from this distance he could tell that the elves at the palace were more stationary, wore brighter armor, and were much more visible, like an honor guard. The elves at the other two houses wore darker shades of green or blue and were far less visible. One other thing stood out about the large house next to him. It had the crest of an eagle carved into the magnificent double doors.

He'd found the House of Runya.

Quite a few lights cast a warm glow on Liriana's home, but it still took Taryn nearly ten minutes to spot all the elves guarding the house. Some were well hidden while others stood as if they were trying to draw attention to themselves. Something about their demeanor told Taryn that they were well trained and would be difficult to get past.

After a few more minutes of watching the patrol patterns around the house, he thought he saw an opening. There were essentially three groups of elven guards. The first set of ten stood in front of the doors in full view of anyone passing by. The second set of fifteen were hidden in alcoves at different heights all the way to the top and were armed with longbows. Lastly, thirty elves in groups of three patrolled in front of the building and used the stairs. Because the same group of three would eventually reappear several minutes later on the opposite side of the structure, he assumed they circled the building by going up and down the stairs on either side of the large house.

Waiting for the right moment, Taryn stuck to the wall until another group of three passed up the flight of stairs on the right of the structure. Mentally counting, he stepped out from the double doorway where he'd been hiding and sprinted silently to the stairs. Making the distance in less than four seconds, he entered the stairs just as another group exited the opposite flight. Taryn had chosen to follow this group because they were a few steps ahead of the trio following behind them. It had only created a five second window, but it was enough.

Twenty paces behind the group, he stayed against the wall and looked for a door, but none appeared on the side towards Liri's home. He hadn't really expected it to be that easy, but it was always worth a shot. Eight flights of stairs he passed without incident . . . until he came to the last flight. When he reached the bottom of the last set of stairs, something he had not anticipated abruptly came into effect . . . the guards reversed direction at the end of the hour.

In unison, they spun around and started *down* the stairs. There was no place to hide and even in the darkness the keen-eyed elves spotted him in a heartbeat. Shouting for help they raced towards him. Hearing an answering call from below he knew there was nowhere for him to go. He could either surrender or try to fight. Before he could decide, two of the elves drew bows and launched arrows at him.

Instinctively Taryn leapt upward to avoid the streaking missiles. As they sailed below him, he twisted his body to face the wall and grabbed some vines ten feet off the ground—but instantly sprang away. Twisting in midair he landed in a crouch against the opposite wall—but he was now fifteen feet off the ground. Pausing only long enough to rebound, he bounced back towards the first wall. Repeating the process, he ricocheted his way up the stairwell.

Crying out in protest, the elves below him loosed more arrows in an attempt to bring him down—but their quarry was just too quick. Each touch on the wall lasted no longer than half a second before he would jump to the opposing wall. Hearing more calls from below he glanced

175

down to see more guards joining the first three. Soon there would be a flurry of arrows coming up towards him and there was no way he could dodge them all. He responded by varying the direction of his leaps. Still moving upward, he began angling his jumps instead of going straight across. More and more arrows flew past him and he began to doubt that he would make it to the top of the house no matter how erratically he moved. He felt his sleeve and tunic tear as sharp-tipped arrows tore right through them. A moment later one scored his hand, drawing blood as it streaked into the night sky.

Suddenly a small window in Liri's home came into view. Ten feet from the top, it was only two feet square, but it was his only chance. Two more jumps brought him opposite the hole and Taryn dived through it without the slightest idea of what would be on the opposite side. He just hoped there was nothing sharp to land on.

Chapter 13: The House of Runya

Taryn sailed through the window and into darkness, prepared to land on just about anything—except a person. Trying to see, he extended his hands to break his fall in a roll where he guessed the ground would be. Unfortunately for him *and* the elf-maid, an occupied bed sat directly underneath the opening. His attempt failed miserably as he landed on the slumbering form and knocked them both to the floor in a hopeless tangle of legs, arms, and sheets. The elf thrashed around in an effort to untangle herself and cried out for help, but Taryn managed to free one hand and covered her mouth.

"I won't hurt you," he said in a rush. "I am a friend of Liriana and I need to find her."

At his words she calmed immediately, so he cautiously let her go. To his surprise she didn't call out, but rather turned to face him with a quizzical expression.

"Taryn?" she asked.

His look must have given him away, because before he could answer she untangled herself and went to the door of her room.

"Wait here," she said, throwing a drape over her nightgown. "I will call off the guards and summon the lady."

Lady? He asked himself as she slipped out the door. Who could she be to be called a lady? He didn't have long to wait for an answer. A minute passed, and the commotion outside ceased. Daring to peak out the window, he saw the roving guards returning to their rotation. *What is going on?*

The room abruptly flooded with light as the door crashed open and he whirled, ready for danger. Instead, a lithe figure dashed across the room and leapt into his arms.

"Taryn!" she cried, "I never thought you would make it!" Then she leaned back to face him and a rush of words tumbled out of her mouth. "When I got into the city I realized guards had been placed everywhere and there was no way you could get in. I mean, there were so many elves on the cliff and below the cliff and in the city . . ." She stopped, her expression turning suspicious. "How *did* you get in?"

Taryn laughed and looked her in the eye. "*Lady?*" he queried with a raised eyebrow.

She flushed a bright crimson and stepped away from him, tightening the cloak that covered her thin night garments.

"Um . . . there are a few things I should probably explain . . ." She trailed off.

A voice interrupted from the doorway. "Do you mind if I go back to sleep?" the elf-maid asked, her voice full of amusement.

As if someone had snapped their fingers, Liri was all business. In a tone he'd never heard from her she answered, "Taryn and I have some business to discuss. Please inform Stel that we need a room prepared for him."

Nodding at them, she started to turn before Taryn called to her.

"Sorry about landing on you; it wasn't something I meant to do."

She smiled coyly and looked him up and down. "Drop in anytime," she exclaimed before turning on her heel and leaving the room. Something in her response made Liri bristle, but when she turned to Taryn she was all smiles.

"Do you want sleep or answers right now?" she asked brusquely. Before he could decide she added, "And I want some answers from you too, you know, so you had better be ready to tell me how in Skorn's name you got into the city."

He smiled and nodded. "How about you just tell me who you really are and then I can catch some sleep." Raising a hand to forestall her objection he continued, "My story is going to take a minute and I'm worn out. I haven't had any rest since sundown the night we got to the city."

She considered his response with pursed lips. Then she came to a decision. "Deal . . . but you get to explain first thing in the morning." She stared him down as if waiting for an argument, but he nodded and smiled. That was good enough for him.

She seemed to steel herself to do something difficult; then she said in chagrin, "I am one of the princesses of the city."

Stunned, Taryn stood there with his mouth open until his brain processed what she had said. "*What*? What do you mean—?" He meant to keep going, but she shook her head and smiled sweetly.

"Nope, time for bed. We will discuss more in the morning." At that she whipped around and strolled out of the room, leaving Taryn sputtering in her wake

He leapt to catch up to her and said, "*Please* explain that a little more, would you? I will never be able to sleep if you leave it like that."

"I will never be able to sleep until I know how you got into the most fortified and guarded city in all of the kingdoms," she replied.

Still walking beside her, he said, "OK, but let's get something to eat while we talk. Is that all right—*your highness*?" He couldn't restrain a grin as he said it.

She jerked to a stop without looking at him and said. "Please don't call me that. I need to explain a little more before you will understand, but don't ever call me that. I am your friend and always have been." She peeked at him from under a furrowed brow and her eyes were a little wet at the edges. "Don't ever say something that implies you are below me."

Surprised at her emotional response, he took her hands in his and looked at her soberly. "Not just friends . . . the best of friends." She brightened a little, but then he continued, "But I have to tease you about it, or else we wouldn't be the best of friends." His grin was so wide it spread to her and a moment later they were both laughing.

"Fine," she said. "Let's go to the kitchens and get something for you. We can talk there."

Taryn followed her down flights of stairs, past numerous doors, and through a maze of corridors. Most of the flameless torches had been covered or dimmed for the night, but even in the gloom the splendor of the elven home left him breathless. He was surprised to see trees growing everywhere, and any stone left had been colored and carved to make it look like a part of the forest. Adding to the effect, the smooth wood floors left him the distinct feeling of walking through a forest cabin.

"Are those real trees?" Taryn asked as they passed a particular pair of trunks that grew up and branched to form a beautiful arched doorway.

"Actually they are, although I don't think *real* would be an accurate word to describe them." She saw his confused look so she went on, "As you know, our race excels in plant, light, and water magic. Using all three types of magics, our magicians have grown full forests right out of the stone of the city. Traditionally, the status of a home is measured by how much stone is covered by greenery. It requires constant attention by skilled mages to keep the trees healthy and green." She stopped to brush through some hanging vines that formed a doorway that, as far as Taryn could tell, led into the bottom floor of the grand house.

"This is the dining hall," she exclaimed with a smile at Taryn's wondering eyes.

Feeling like he had just stepped outside, he turned his head in every direction to get a better look. On all sides, the view stretched for miles. Countless stars pinpricked the sky above, while clouds drifted past the moon. Southward, he looked out over the dark expanse of Numenessee. To the north, east, and west, he saw the highest tiers of Azertorn, as if the room in which he stood floated in the exact center of the magnificent city, yet high enough that he looked at the palace on even ground.

"Where are we?" Taryn asked, taking a few steps into the room and looking behind him at the opening that led back into Liri's home.

She laughed, delighted with his response. "We are still in the bottom of the House of Runya." She gestured upward. "The ceiling and walls are enchanted to be the view from the very top of the great tree." She pointed to the eastern horizon. "At sunrise or sunset the view is stunning, and at midday it's hard to remember that you are indoors." She sighed happily. "It's like a room in the clouds, and one of things I missed the most."

Now that she had pointed it out, he began to see stray branches in the lowest portions of the walls, bending in the wind. For one brief moment he felt like the entire room was swaying, so he looked at the ground to get his bearings, but even the floor was made of crafted darkwood, adding to the feeling of being in a giant, open air tree house at the top of Le Runtáriel.

"How is this possible?" Taryn asked in open awe at the spectacle,

"Each elven house has at least one mage skilled in magic," she explained. "The house of Runya is the second-largest house and boasts no less than thirty-six, some of which are considered among the best in the city. I am not sure the exact details of how the ceiling was created, but I do know that special vines at the top of the great tree capture the light, and transfer it through their roots to this room. The image is then recreated on the leaves of the vines embedded in the walls and ceiling."

Finally understanding, Taryn began to make out the almost imperceptible outlines of broad leaves blanketing the walls and ceiling, but even seeing them didn't take anything from the sheer majesty of such a place. He stood transfixed, unable to find words to express the wonder he felt. Everything from the view, to the emotions created by such a room, were almost overpowering.

Smiling again at his reaction, Liri put her arm through his. "I know how you feel, this room is my favorite in the house—but you should see it when it's raining." Tugging on his arm, she led him into what looked like branches of Le Runtáriel growing through the floor.

Cultivated, curved and flattened, trees had been grown to look like branches, and had been shaped to both furnish the room, as well as make it more beautiful. All around him, trees had been developed into living furniture, providing chairs and tables of various sizes.

Reaching the other side of the dining area, Liri pulled him towards the back of the room to a partially hidden door. Going through it revealed a room that had a starkly different view from the grand dining hall. The main kitchens had been created with an eye to efficiency, with no greenery in sight. Here the stone had been cut to create everything from counters to stoves to shelves or other storage. Once again, Taryn was impressed by the detail with which the rock had been carved. If there were seams at all, they were invisible to his sharp eyes.

As she led him to some wooden chairs next to a small stone table, he finally voiced the question he'd been wondering since the moment he laid eyes on the magnificent city: "Who *built* Azertorn?"

She nodded as if she'd expected the question. Reaching into a carved cupboard fitted with a wooden door, she responded, "Azertorn was built by the dwarves as a gift to the elves in return for some service, although no one is sure what that service was. The entire city took more than a decade to create, so whatever the elves did for them must have been invaluable." She paused to place bread and cheese on the table with some wine. "Eat, and I will give you some background."

Taryn complied with her request with gusto. He hadn't realized how hungry he was.

Leaning back, she settled into a comfortable position and started with some history. "Most believe the city was carved about ten thousand years ago. It was built specifically as a place where the elves could go, because their home had been destroyed by someone—and before you ask who it was, I don't know. I *do* know that whoever it was affected both of the human kingdoms as well. In fact, back then there was only the one kingdom, Talinor."

"Some great calamity drove the elves out of their ancestral homeland and divided the humans. The kingdom of Griffin formed in the east, while Talinor maintained the south. Other factions also broke off at that time, like the barbarians and the amazons of the deep south. The strange thing is that whatever happened, it must have been catastrophic, but there are very few records that recount anything about it."

Taryn cut in with a question. "Wait, some*one* drove them out? The elves used to live in the forest between the two kingdoms, right? Orlkani—no, that wasn't it. Orláknia?"

Liri nodded and indicated for him to go on.

"Then what people would have driven them out? If it were the humans, or any other normal race for that matter, it would have been recorded, wouldn't it?"

Liri interrupted him, "I don't think it was something . . . normal." Her tone implied something dangerous—and whatever it was, it bothered her that no one knew. She continued while he was still mulling over her words. "I really don't know much more about the ancient elves' migration. All I know is that they came here and that the dwarves built this city for them."

"How *many* dwarves?"

"I think . . . all of them," she said. "Most of the buildings and rooms were carved out by magic you know, although some of it was crafted by hand."

"How far into the shelf does it go?" Taryn asked with his mouth full of bread.

She smirked at his muffled question, but answered it without commenting on his manners. "Several miles at some points, but then only a fraction of all the caverns are in use. Most of the deeper chambers just gather dust." She stifled a yawn before continuing, "The queen lives and governs from the palace—"

"—The large building on the top level?" he interrupted with a shrewd guess.

"Umm, sort of," she replied. "In reality the city has ten levels. Seven tiers form the bowl you saw from the bottom of the cliff. Two are below Le Runtáriel and house most of the army. The last level is actually above the cliff and comprises the wall and the top barracks. Ayame Ser'Tármaril, our queen, rules from the palace on Tier Nine. The House of Runya and House of Keserian are the other two ruling houses, and are almost as large as the palace."

"What do you mean 'the other two ruling houses'?"

"Azertorn is governed by a queen and a council comprised of five members: the respective heads of the army, the home guard, the magic guild, and the Houses of Keserian and Runya."

"Now are you going to explain the princess part?" Taryn asked with a smile as he reached for his glass.

Sighing, she answered, "Whenever a queen passes, the new one is chosen from among the daughters of the Houses of Runya and Keserian by a majority vote of the council. I am one of the daughters of Runya and am eligible with four others. I have two sisters, Arianna, the oldest, and Erianna, in the middle. The house of Keserian has two daughters and two sons, but only the daughters can be considered for the crown."

Swallowing, he asked, "So who is the House of Tármaril?"

"When one becomes queen, they take on the name, as does the rest of their immediate family. Grandchildren return to their original name and house."

"So what are your chances of becoming queen?" Taryn asked innocently. He watched her expression darken and her thin lips tighten before he continued, struggling to keep his face serious, "You know I like to have friends in high places."

184

She burst out laughing, a high musical sound that lightened his heart as only Liri's voice could.

"Of course it's *possible*, but not too likely. I am fourth in age, behind my sisters, who are first and second, then one of the daughters of Keserian, and then me."

Letting some mock disappointment show in his face, he grumbled, "Fine, I guess I will have to *settle* for a princess." Then his expression turned serious as a thought occurred to him. "Why couldn't you have vouched for me when we got to the city? Or at the river?"

She leaned back and furrowed her brow. "I wasn't sure they would have known me, or remembered what I looked like. In either case, it's been a long time since I have been home. I also didn't have my emblem to show who I was—and with the way they were acting, I didn't think it would have been enough proof anyway."

He sighed, accepting her explanation and shaking his head at the memory of the hard faced elves.

Suddenly Taryn yawned and Liri smirked. "OK, that's enough history. Now it's your turn. How did you get in?" She leaned towards him, her eyes sparkling with curiosity.

Taryn briefly recounted the tale of how he'd climbed the cliff and escaped the elven sentries. At the point in the story where he knocked the elf into the river she interrupted, "You didn't hurt any elves did you?"

"Of course not," he responded and explained how he'd saved the elf's life. She calmed and relaxed, allowing him to continue, but when he told how he'd run down the cliff and jumped the waterfall she leaned back with an incredulous smile.

"Only *you* could ever think of something like that," she exclaimed.

He shrugged in chagrin. "I almost didn't make it." He lifted up the torn sleeve to show her the bloody line on his shoulder where he'd almost been hit on the cliff top.

Her eyes sharpened and she leaned in. "*Curse this fear*," she muttered, reaching out to touch the red line.

"Ouch," he said, pulling back at the sting.

"Big baby," she said airily. "It's just a scratch."

He grinned and showed her the cut on his hand. "True, but I received this at the hands of your guards outside."

He caught a glimpse of her lip tightening as she stood and moved to the sink. Dabbing a piece of cloth in water, she returned and without meeting his gaze, began to clean the shallow wounds.

Although it stung, the water felt good against his open skin, but when he thanked her, she only murmured an apology.

"What do you have to apologize for?" Taryn asked. "You didn't do it."

She glanced up at him and he saw the guilt reflecting in her eyes. "I am sorry that you are hurt, that's all."

He laughed. "Like you said, it's just a scratch. Not even worth a healer's time."

Her lips pulled into a grudging smile. "You're probably right, *baby*."

They laughed together and the tension eased. A moment later Liri added, "I still can't believe how you got into the city."

"I don't know." He shrugged. "I guess I just saw an opening and took it."

Her expression turned speculative. "You know . . . the reason no elf or human has ever climbed the Giant's Shelf is because no elf or human has the strength or endurance to do something like that . . ."

She trailed off with one eyebrow raised and her head cocked to one side.

186

"Where *did* you get your strength from?" she voiced her question.

The silence in the kitchen stretched into several minutes as the two of them contemplated possibilities. Taryn's chewing sounded loud, so he swallowed and shook his head—both to himself and to answer her question. He had no idea.

"Well, you have the hair and stamina of a dwarf," she broke the silence with a smirk, "but I'm glad you don't look like one."

He laughed and the mood lightened, "Any more questions, or can I get some sleep?"Liri nodded and stood. "No, I think we are done for tonight. We can talk more tomorrow while I show you the city."

Putting the dishes away, he turned around at her suggestion of a tour. "Will the city guard allow me to pass?"

"Sure, I will give you our house crest and you won't be bothered."

"Thanks, I appreciate your house's protection . . . *princess*."

She glared at him but couldn't hold it for long and shook her head in exasperation. "OK, *dwarf-man*, let's go find you a bed."

He grinned broadly at her response, and followed her back into the maze of corridors, grateful for a safe place to sleep.

Chapter 14: Tallendale

Trin leaned on the rail of the *Sea Dancer* and looked at the approaching city of Tallendale. It had been less than a day since he'd watched Taryn and Liri disappear into the dark waters of the Blue River, and it already seemed like a week. Glancing back at the setting sun behind him, he found himself wondering if he would ever see his friends again.

Although he had lived on Sri Rosen for most of his life, he still remembered his older brother and father, his mother having succumbed to a fever when he was just an infant. On the training island, he had lived in one of the southern villages, and had barely known Taryn and Liri. Mae he'd known only slightly better. But somehow, over the last few weeks of travel, the three of them had become like family to him, and he found that he missed them already.

It was a feeling he wouldn't have admitted to anyone.

Below them, the fading daylight cast long shadows on the water as they glided over the mirror surface reflecting the city. To the south, Tallendale sat on a small rise adjacent to the river. Directly beyond the hill, the Blue Lake stretched in a vast expanse to the eastern horizon. With several islands in the distance and the sheer expanse of calm water, it could easily be mistaken for an ocean.

"Worried about Thacker and his family?" Mae asked, appearing at his side.

"Nah, I think they will be all right," he said, sniffing to hide his emotions. "And it's good to be free of the little rascals."

In an effort to avoid further problems, Thacker and the captain had chosen to drop them off a few miles outside of the city, so they had disembarked an hour ago. It had been a sound plan, but one that meant the family would camp outside the walls of the settlement for at least one night. To his credit, the captain had suggested a fishing village a few miles east of Tallendale that might be a suitable place to settle. Trin had also caught him dropping a handful of coins into the fathers pack.

Mae shifted and caught his eye, her expression unreadable. "I didn't know you were so good with young ones."

Trin laughed, unwilling to admit how much he had enjoyed their company. "Maybe it's because I am one."

"That I won't argue," she said, but her expression was still thoughtful. "Did you see the elves to the north?" She asked.

He nodded without turning around, but his perpetual smile didn't have its usual warmth. The enduring fear had taken a toll on him just like everyone else and for the first time in his life, it took effort to be relaxed. His calm attitude was not reflected by most of the sailors on the ship, who cast worried glances to the north side of the river. The small elven settlement set into the woods would have normally been inviting—but not with the veritable army of elves in view.

Although docks extended out over the water from both the elven and human sides, it could clearly be seen that neither one was allowed on the other's side. Elven sentries with naked blades in hand patrolled the few piers that had not been destroyed, ready for battle at a moment's notice.

For their part, the humans of the southern kingdom had their share of soldiers as well—albeit less organized and armed. These ragtag groups patrolled the south bank with suspicious looks at their fair neighbors—glares which were returned frequently.

"'Tis a sad day to see them like this," Sabriel spoke behind them, and they turned. His expression was somber as he considered the two

189

sides of the river. "Goods used to be ferried back and forth without a sword in sight not six months ago." He shook his head and sighed. "Aye, 'tis a sad day indeed."

Then he turned as the captain called out to his crew, "Make ready to dock boys, we should be welcome here, but be prepared just in case."

"Sad indeed," Sabriel whispered, just loud enough for the two of them to hear as he walked away.

The crew's response to their leader's orders was quick, but they set about their duties cautiously. With weapons nearby and ready, they maneuvered the *Sea Dancer* towards the human waterfront. Gliding over the water, they slid into a pier without incident. Just as ropes were being tossed back and forth in the failing light, Mae leaned close to Trin. "I'll be below until we leave," she said, her tone resigned.

Before he could disagree, she disappeared and Trin didn't go after her. She was right, as usual. There would be no way the humans would allow them to enter the city with an elf, and they needed supplies to cross the lake.

"Let's go, Trin; we might need an extra sword the way things are going," Erix said as he clapped him on the back. Reluctantly he followed the captain down onto the dock and tried not to notice the sharp looks in their direction—but was unable to suppress the desire to tread softly, as if every footfall could light the explosive atmosphere. In an effort to avoid scrutiny, the small group that Erix had selected to get supplies hurried up the slope and through the gates into the city.

Slipping through the doors just before the last vestiges of light vanished, they paused and watched as the gates closed. Lock after lock clicked behind them and Trin swallowed as an unnatural desire washed over him to tear the doors off and run into the night. They were in until dawn; hopefully they could finish their business by then.

"Come on," the captain said in an effort to be encouraging, "let's get some ale and a bed to sleep in, my coin."

It was a testament to how nervous the crew was that no one responded when ale and a warm bed where mentioned.

190

"You're on, captain. But don't start thinking any of you seadogs can out-drink me." Trin said. His broad smile and joking words seemed to lighten the dark feelings that continued to envelop them, and they set out behind the captain's retreating form.

As they trudged through the dim streets, Trin did his best to keep his demeanor pleasant. Despite his lighthearted words, it had taken far more effort than he would care to admit to fight the growing sense of dread. Forcefully he brushed it aside with some help from his deeply rooted sense of humor and focused on the city.

Unlike Keese, Tallendale did not extend to the water. Situated on a small hill, a low wall surrounded the entire city. A stone's throw from the bulwarks, the waterfront contained an assortment of warehouses for holding goods. Docks long and short extended out over the waters of the Blue Lake and the Blue River.

A natural shipping point, the settlement seemed to have grown from a small village into a large city, with no regard for order. Expanding too rapidly, it had been added onto so many times it had become a maze of dirt roads and winding cobblestone lanes. Buildings were mostly leaning, two-story structures made of wood and thatch. Whereas Keese had been lit by numerous lamps, Tallendale possessed only a few smoky torches struggling to illuminate intersections. Most of the light that guided them came from dirty, greasy windows. Even the people they passed were drab, and rushed past them as if they carried some disease. Only one made eye contact, and he had his hand on his sword hilt.

Trin sighed, recalling his childhood home of Terros. As the capital of the eastern kingdom of Griffin, its white granite walls and towering buildings had become a beacon of order and strength. At least, that is the way he remembered it. Now he felt a growing dread at what he would find when he returned to his homeland. Deep down, he recognized that the further east they went, the worse it became. So what would he find in Terros?

Distracted by his thoughts, he nearly ran into Hunrin as he stopped at a structure larger than those around it. Erix leaned over and spoke quietly to Trin: "Keep your wits about you, boy, this isn't a good place but it's one of the few places owned by an honest man."

Glancing at the creaking sign above him, Trin responded lightly, "As long as the ale doesn't actually have hair in it, I'll be fine." The sign above the door read "The Bearded Keg."

Steeling himself for anything, he stepped through the door and took a look around. Surprisingly, it wasn't as bad as he'd expected, although it seemed somewhat more subdued than a normal inn. The common room they'd entered contained numerous patrons eating, drinking, and talking in low tones, with many seated at a bar along the back wall. To one side, a group of men clustered around something at the side of the room, each craning to see into the middle.

"What's going on over there?" Trin asked the captain as they sat down at a table near the bar.

Glancing at the group, Erix shook his head and shrugged.

"They're just finishing up a tournament of Stratos," a barmaid answered as she came to their table.

"What's Stratos?" Trin asked, his eyes on the crowd.

She frowned. "It's a game. Started a few years back and it's become pretty popular among kids *and* adults. Where have you been?" She speared him with suspicious eyes.

"Er, away on business," Trin replied with a disarming smile that did little to assuage her concerns; then changed the subject back to the game. "They're having a tournament of a *game*? Isn't that a little . . . childish?"

She smirked without losing her wariness. "You haven't played it. Adults started practicing it when some captain told his soldiers that they would become better officers if they played—and it worked. It wasn't long before cities were having competitions." Her tone went a little quieter and she stared into space. "I'm glad they let them do the tournament; it's made folk almost happy. They nearly canceled it, you know." She shook her head and forced a smile. "Now what can I get for you?"

"Four plates of whatever you are serving and ale as well," Erix answered. "Oh, and can you tell Folson that Erix is here to see him?"

As she bustled away to get them something to eat, Trin stood up. "I'm going to check out this game," he said, jerking his head towards the gathering in the corner.

"Don't be long," Hun grunted, "or you will miss the food."

Trin nodded and carefully threaded his way through the tables and patrons. It turned out that the group was larger than he'd thought. At least thirty men stood or sat around two individuals facing each other at a table. After several attempts of trying to squeeze through earning him glares, he resigned himself to standing on a chair to see.

With his head above the crowd, he finally managed to get a decent look at the game, although he couldn't see the players. It looked like some sort of wooden board with black and white squares, ten to a side. What seemed to be carved wooden soldiers painted black and green stood at various spots on the board. Upon closer inspection, he could see that black was losing—badly. Taking a quick count, he saw that green had nine pieces and black had only four. Two of the black soldiers were in one corner and the other two were spread out alone. Green had surrounded each of them.

Then the green player reached forward and made a move, taking one of the black pieces. Whatever he'd done elicited murmurs from the onlookers. A spectator moved to whisper to someone, and Trin was finally able to see the black player—who turned out to be a soldier. He was an older man, thin and bearded. It seemed strange that a soldier would be in here playing a game, but Trin was even more surprised when he leaned over to get a look at the green player and saw a kid.

The young man playing green had light brown hair and matching eyes. He was a little on the plump side, and something about his posture told Trin that he wasn't a fighter. In contrast, his eyes surveyed the board in the same calculating way that Trin would look at a group of charging swordsmen. Without warning the chair underneath Trin squeaked in protest, eliciting disapproving looks. Cursing under his breath, he righted himself before he could fall.

After craning his neck for several minutes, Trin was able to watch the black player make several moves but he took only one of the green pieces. Green then took two more black pieces, and the soldier sighed before standing up.

"You are just too good, kid, I swear." He toppled over his last piece. "You win." He then handed the young man a small bag that clinked with money.

The crowd began to disperse amidst loud conversation, and Trin tried to listen in on the two men next to him.

"Amazing game. I can't believe the kid won."

"I knew he would—Braon is the best."

"But he's only fifteen, isn't he?"

"Yeah, but I don't think he's ever lost."

"Why is he in the adult tournament anyway?"

The man guffawed. "Because he beat everyone else."

Trin turned away from the two men and pushed his way through the remaining crowd to find the young man cleaning up the game and putting the pieces into a leather bag.

"Hey kid, what are you playing?" Trin asked as he sat down across from him.

The young man looked up and smiled warmly. "Oh, just a game. It's called Stratos. Ever heard of it?"

"Of course," Trin replied; then he leaned in with wide eyes and a faint grin, "about five minutes ago." The young man laughed a boyish laugh in response.

"I would teach you how to play, but I need to get some rest," Braon replied; then his tone turned worried. "I have to find a ship that is going to Terros tomorrow morning."

Trin spread his arms out wide and grinned. "Hey kid, you're in luck. That's where we're going."

"Really?" Braon asked excitedly. "I haven't been able to find many ships going east. Do you think I could get a ride with you?"

Something about his tone made Trin suspect that the young man was more relieved than excited—but also scared. Braon didn't *want* to go east—he had to.

Sidestepping the question for the moment, Trin answered his request with another question: "Do you have another tournament?"

"Nope, I just need to get home. I'm from Terros."

"Hey! That's where I'm from! I haven't been back in a few years though. Anything changed?"

Braon hesitated for a fraction of a second before responding, "Nah, pretty much the same."

Trin didn't miss the pause, but still figured it wouldn't be a problem to take him with them. "I would think you can come with us, but you'd need to ask the captain. Care to join us at our table?"

"Sure," he answered and finished gathering up the game pieces.

As Braon followed Trin through the crowded room, Trin took the opportunity to surreptitiously study the young man behind him. With a few casual backward glances, he noticed two things. Braon was definitely *not* a fighter; his movement was exactly that of a plump young man. The odd thing was that his eyes *were* those of a fighter: cautious and wary, they took everything in. For some reason he couldn't explain, Trin would bet anything that Braon knew everything that was going on in the room—including any threats.

Stopping next to Hunrin, Trin addressed the captain. "This young man would like to sail with us to Terros."

Erix leaned back and pursed his lips, measuring Braon for a moment before giving his answer. "I don't hold with disrespect," he said firmly. "If you don't follow my orders, I will drop you at the first spot of dry land. Is that clear?"

"Perfectly, sir. Thank you for the ride. I was beginning to lose hope for a chance to return home this week." Braon's attitude conveyed the utmost respect; he even bowed a little.

The captain's expression softened. "Any parents with you, or are you by yourself? And are you riding as a deckhand or passenger?"

"By myself, and passenger preferably," he responded easily.

"Six silver, then, and you have yourself a deal," Erix offered.

Braon answered by reaching into a bag at his waist and handing the captain *nine* pieces of silver. "What time do we leave, sir?"

Erix held the money and looked with crinkled brow at the young man. Six silver was the price of a child. Nine silver was for an adult. "At first light we are going to get some supplies and then leave as soon as possible."

"I will be at your ship at first light. Thanks again." And with that he turned and walked away.

"Do you want to know which ship?" Trin called out to him.

He looked back just long enough to say, "The *Sea Dancer*, I already know."

As he walked towards the back of the inn, Hun spoke for the first time. "That is one smart kid, Captain."

"I'd have to agree with that," Erix replied in amusement, "and there's no question he's used to taking care of himself. I wonder how he knew about our ship."

"The kid's good," Trin said, his tone thoughtful as he watched Braon's retreating form work its way towards the back of the room. As he finally sat down he couldn't shake the feeling that the young man had known who he was and what ship he was on before he'd even introduced himself.

He only had a moment to consider the interesting encounter before the barmaid returned with four bowls of steaming stew and mugs of ale.

"Folson said he would talk to you in the back in half an hour," her tone dropped, "*alone*. He said to give you a room as well. Upstairs, third door on the right." Then she disappeared without waiting for a response.

"Do you have a friend in *every* city?" Trin asked as they began to eat.

"At least one," Erix replied with a small smile.

They finished the meal in silence with each of them wrapped up in their thoughts. Finishing first, the captain stood. "I am going to talk to Folson. I'll meet you in the room."

He strode towards the back and disappeared through a door. A few minutes later the three of them climbed the stairs and found their room. Trin wasn't the only one yawning as they climbed into the rickety beds and quickly fell asleep.

It felt like only an hour before Hun shook Trin awake.

"Time to go. The others are already downstairs eating breakfast," he said.

"Why didn't you wake me?" Trin said, irritated, but sat up and pulled his boots on.

"We tried, but you refused to stop snoring," Hun exclaimed with a bark of laughter.

Trin snorted and finished strapping his longsword to his back before following Hunrin down the stairs. Entered the dining hall, he stopped short at the feel in the room. Whatever levity the previous night's games had provided was long gone. Men and women alike cast suspicious glances on each other, and few were speaking. Despite the warmth from the fire, Trin felt a chill go down his spine.

Grabbing a plate from the bar, he joined the others and ate fast enough to finish at the same time. He wasn't surprised that no one else

197

teased him about not waking up. The tension in the room made even him lose his sense of humor.

Erix slapped some coins on the table and stood. "Let's get some supplies and get out of this place," he said in an undertone.

Trin nodded in relief and followed them back into the streets. Streaks of light were barely piercing the darkness and the early morning chill still held frost on windows as they hurried down dim alleys. It was even earlier than he'd thought. Dawn was still at least half an hour away. He smiled to himself, *No wonder it was hard for them to wake me.*

Light continued to chase away the night, but the few people they passed refused to lighten with it. By the time they got to the city wall and the markets, Trin had to suppress the desire to run out of the city. Without a word, the four of them lengthened their strides and arrived at the shops just as they were opening.

Erix spoke to a few merchants and ordered several crates and barrels of supplies. The sun finally broke free of the horizon just as the four of them were walking onto the ship with a few dockhands rolling barrels behind them. The moment his boots touched the deck, Erix barked for his first mate: "Frey! Get this ship under way as soon as possible."

Frey's bald head popped into view from behind the helm, and he began shouting instructions to the crew who jumped to get the ship back on its way to Terros. Within minutes the *Sea Dancer* pulled away from the dock as the crew efficiently finished their assigned tasks. Before long they were sailing into the huge lake.

Trin leaned on the rail and forced himself to relax as Tallendale finally began to sink out of view. The horrible feeling that had dominated the city didn't seem to extend onto the clear waters, and he felt his heart lift as the wind filled the sails. Sunlight danced on the blue water that crashed against the prow as the strong breeze drove the vessel forward.

A light voice spoke beside him. "I love the lake."

Looking at the source, he found Braon next to him. Chuckling in chagrin, he realized that he'd forgotten all about the lad—but wasn't surprised to see that he'd made it on the ship.

"How did you get on board?" Trin asked the young man.

Braon shrugged, "They were suspicious of course, but it's easy for me to not appear as a threat."

Trin laughed and shook his head. He didn't doubt for a second that the chubby youth could play the innocent card well.

On the other side of him a musical voice spoke up. "I thought he was rather resourceful," Mae said with a rare smile.

They enjoyed the view for several minutes until Trin looked at the young man beside him. "So, are you going to teach me your game, or am I going to have to throw you overboard first?"

Braon laughed easily, and Trin got the impression he was just as glad to be out of the city. "Follow me," Braon said.

Trin glanced at Mae with a raised eyebrow, but she refused the unasked invitation. "I will let you boys play," she said with her gaze directed towards the lake and a small smile still on her lips.

Shrugging, Trin followed Braon down to the tiny galley and helped set up a couple of chairs next to a barrel. Braon then pulled out the bag containing his game and laid the flat wooden board onto the barrel. He then placed several pieces onto squares. Some were black or green while others were red.

Looking at Trin, the young man began, "Stratos is a game that simulates a battle between two generals. Each player first chooses a different color." He swept his hand at the pieces, and then pointed at one of the small soldiers. "Then each player selects an army. You can choose to be elves, which are green, humans, which are black, or dwarves which are red. Each one has its advantages and slightly different soldiers." Handing Trin a green piece that looked remarkably like an elf with a longbow, he continued, "This is an elven archer. They are better than the human archers and can attack further pieces."

Pointing to several others in turn, he said, "This is a human swordsman, this is a human knight, this is a dwarf with an axe, this is an elf with a short sword. Any questions so far?"

Trin shook his head, so Braon continued. "The field of battle is made up of squares, with ten to a side. Each player moves a single piece on his turn. To attack another piece, you simply move your piece to the same square. We begin by each choosing a race and ten pieces from that race. You have to show me five of the ones you have picked. The other five you won't show me until we reveal our side of the board. You may place your pieces on the first three rows on your side, but cover what you are doing with this," he indicated a piece of cloth, "so I can't see where you place your army or what other five pieces you have selected. We won't play that rule though until you have a feel for the game."

"Can you explain a little more about the different pieces and races before we start?" Trin asked.

Braon bobbed his head and pointed at the piece in Trin's hand. "Each piece moves in a specific pattern. The elven longbow in your hand can attack four spaces straight, and one to either side." Placing it in the center of the board, he indicated the squares that the elven longbow could move to by sliding his finger straight four, then to the side one. "The elven longbow, just like the dwarf axe throwers and human crossbowmen, can't attack straight in any direction, or any other square in between. The red axe throwers move two straight, and one to the side, and the human crossbowmen move three straight and one to the side. Do you understand how the ranged attackers work?"

Trin nodded slowly, trying to commit the movements to memory. "I think so. What's next?"

Braon had already begun separating the different pieces of the human side, and once he was finished he pointed to the three piles. "Each race has five ranged pieces, such as the elven longbow, the human crossbow, and the dwarven axe throwers. Then each race has five foot soldiers, which can move in any direction but are limited in how far they can go. The human knights move only one space, the elves can move two spaces, and the dwarves move three spaces in any direction."

Trin was smiling. "The dwarves move furthest because of their endurance, the elves move second furthest because of their speed, and the human foot soldiers are slowest so only move one space."

Braon grinned. "Correct. Most soldiers are quick to recognize the reasons behind the different races' strengths and weaknesses."

"So what are the last pieces?" Trin asked, pointing to the last group.

Picking one up, he gave it to Trin. "The third set is the special group, and the one in your hand is the human cavalry. They can move straight in any direction as far as they want, but can't move diagonally."

"Sounds powerful," Trin exclaimed.

"They are, just as the special abilities of both the others are stronger as well." He picked up a red piece. "This is a dwarf guardian. As you can see, they are armored and carry a double edged battle axe. They can move in any diagonal direction as far as they want."

"OK, so what about the elves' special group?"

"Ah, the elven mage," Braon said with a smile, "one of my favorites, even though many players think of the elves as weaker because the mages have a handicap."

"What do you mean?"

Braon placed the elven mage onto the center of the board and laid other pieces on different squares around it. "The elven mage can move diagonally or straight as far as they want, *but* they cannot attack players first. They can only defend other pieces. This means that the only way an elven mage can take another piece is if an opponent killed one they were covering, like this." He moved a red guardian to take an elven longbow, then took the red guardian with the elven mage. "Understood?"

Trin laughed in delight. "It makes perfect sense. The elves' magic is more defensive than attack oriented, so it fits."

Braon grinned. "Exactly. Last of all is the general." He handed him the most ornate piece of a human man on a horse carrying a raised flag. "All three generals can move only one space in any direction and also carry the flag of your troops. If the general is killed, the game is over." When Trin nodded Braon asked, "Any questions or are you ready to play?"

"I think I'm ready," Trin answered, and after a moment's thought, chose the elves. Braon then showed him how to choose ten of the fifteen pieces and explained how it was better to have a well balanced army.

After a minute of examining the pieces, Trin placed his three elven archers on the row closest to him and two elven swordsmen at various points on his side. Lastly he placed the five mages to cover the rest of his army. When Braon was done placing his human army, they started.

Trin had to laugh at himself. It didn't take long before the human cavalry had crossed the board and decimated his elves. His archers were able to shoot four squares, but it wasn't enough to bring down the armored humans. The game ended quickly with Braon the victor. Trin smiled in chagrin, but took notice at how the young man had used the foot soldiers defensively, the crossbowmen as backup, and the cavalry as attackers.

"Want to play again?" Braon asked as he took the last elf.

Trin started laughing. "Of course, but something tells me I'm not going to win, am I?"

Braon smiled, but sidestepped his question. "Which race do you want to be?"

"I'll try humans," Trin exclaimed.

Braon's smile widened and he gave him the human pieces. Trin watched him set up his side with the dwarves. Five minutes later, Trin was watching his general get pinned on the wall and killed.

Laughing again, he tried the dwarves next, but lost to the humans— and then the elves right after. Once he felt he had the hang of the game, Trin asked, "So, why do you have to go back to Terros?"

Braon didn't take his eyes off the board to respond. "My father still lives there, and he doesn't think I am old enough to live on my own."

Trin caught just a trace of bitterness, and wondered what kind of father he had. "What about brothers or sisters?"

He shook his head. "None. You?"

Trin grinned at the memory of Aroet. "One, an older brother. He is probably captain by now. He's several years older than me, and was a sergeant in the guard before I left. Even then, his men called him Captain Arrow. I don't doubt that by now he has achieved that rank."

Braon raised an eyebrow. "I think I have heard of him. I believe he rides with the cavalry, and if my memory is correct, he is quite popular with the ladies."

"That would be him," Trin laughed, "but I doubt he realizes it. We used to say that he got the looks, the skill, and the sense of responsibility, and I got the fun." The nostalgia quickly faded and was replaced by a sadness he did his best to hide. "My father was very proud of him, which was why he helped Arrow get into the army. At the time, the better soldiers were given ranks. Those less . . . skilled, were either sent home, became common soldiers, or if the family could afford it, were sent to train with elves."

Braon's expression revealed that Trin hadn't managed to keep the bitterness from his tone, so Trin grinned wide to soften his words. "I consider myself lucky," he said. "I got to go to an island in the sea with beautiful elves. Aside from daily, brutally exhausting training, it was like a vacation."

"I'm sure," Braon said with a grin that shrank to a tight-lipped smile. "At least you got to go. I came from one of the less fortunate families, so my training did not go as well."

"What happened?" Trin asked, moving a piece forward, only to see it be taken immediately.

"Let's just say that I did not excel in weaponry, and my . . . other skills . . . only cultivated enemies."

"That must have been hard," Trin said, realizing that despite his familial problems, he probably did have a better life than many of the other students at the early training in Terros. "So how long will you stay in Terros?"

Braon laughed. "Until the next tournament."

Looking down, Trin watched him take one of his last pieces. "Well, you are certainly winning this contest. Care to start over?"

The kid nodded and they began to reset the board, but Trin found his mind returning to their conversation. Something about it left him feeling unsettled, until he realized that the young man had learned a great deal about him, while revealing very little about himself. The little he did say had served to reinforce a perception of youth and vulnerability. Yet there was something entirely too concise about the way he'd expressed his words.

Never one for subtlety, Trin asked with a sly smile, "Do you always work conversations to your advantage?"

Braon paused and looked at him, his expression calculating. "Most of the time," he admitted, and then shrugged. "It helps to know those around you."

"—and for them to not see you as a threat."

Braon's eyebrow peaked. "When you are not good with a blade, invisibility is your greatest weapon."

Trin started to laugh, a deep belly sound that shook his entire frame. "Kid, you would make a fine general."

"If they ever let me be in command."

For the first time since he had known the youth, Trin heard a true insight into Braon's personality.

"It'll be their loss if they don't," he said. "Now are you going to move or not?"

Braon's smile returned as he moved his first piece, and as they played the conversation shifted to lighter topics. Trin, however, was left to wonder what kind of life lay in store for such a unique young man. No army would ever rank a person without a shred of combat skill, yet the overweight youth in front of him, even at his current age, would far surpass the strategic ability of anyone alive.

But would anyone ever see it outside of a child's game?

Chapter 15: Impregnable

Taryn awoke groggy and sore. Recalling the previous night's conversation with Liri, he realized he still had a few questions for her. Resolving to ask her when he had the chance, he made to sit up but the soreness in his body caused him to wince. The effects of climbing the cliff would take time to heal, and until then he would just have bear it. Gingerly stretching, he stifled a yawn and checked his weapons before getting dressed. Unbidden, Murai's words came back to him: "Always keep your weapons close at hand. They are your life."

The memory of his uncle elicited a pang of regret. He missed Murai more than he thought he would, and for the first time he considered whether his quest was worth it. He knew in his heart that it was unlikely at best that he would discover anything about his family, and perhaps he'd said goodbye to the only family he would ever have. Despite its shortcomings, Sri Rosen had felt like a type of home, and he wondered if he would ever feel that again.

Sighing, he strapped on his katsanas and went to the door before realizing he had no clue where he was in Liri's home. Hoping for direction, he swung open the door to see an armed elf standing at attention. Eyes narrowing at the sight of him, the lean figure said, "If you are ready, the Lady Liriana requests you join her for breakfast before a tour of the city."

Taryn responded with a warm smile. "Lead on," he said, indicating his readiness with a sweep of his hand.

Instead of heading down the corridor, the elf gave a short bow without taking his eyes off Taryn and replied, "You may go first, guest of Runya, and I will direct your path."

Smiling at the elf's choice of a tactically superior position, Taryn nodded and headed down the corridor. Approaching a turn, his guide would quietly indicate a direction. As Taryn led the way, he pondered the behavior of the elf behind him. His demeanor had been controlled, but there was a layer of extreme caution just beneath the surface, as if he expected to be attacked at any moment. He was left to ponder on the odd behavior for only a few moments. On a particularly long corridor, his guide broke the silence.

"I heard about your effort to scout the walls above the cliff."

Ah, Taryn thought, *that explains everything.* Then he stopped and turned around. The elf dodged a step back and palmed the hilt of his short sword.

"And . . . ?" Taryn asked with raised eyebrows.

The elf's eyes were hard. "So how did you get into the city? Last anyone saw, you dropped off the shelf. When the home guard reached the edge, you had disappeared, and even when they searched with magic, you were nowhere to be found."

Taryn furrowed his brow, considering whether or not to tell the young man. Impulsively he answered, "I used a rope and swung in front of the falls."

The elf snorted in disbelief but his demeanor appeared to lighten. After a moment of silence he said, "I can't believe you made it."

Taryn laughed, uneasy at the exchange. "Me neither, but it was the only way in, so I took it."

His guard slowly removed his hand from the sword, "My name is Rokei. I am one of the personal guards of Lady Liriana."

Taryn smiled as the conversation shifted to a more comfortable topic. Moving to stand beside the guard, he ignored him when he stiffened and grabbed his weapon again. "Then we shall get along fine. There is no one I am more dedicated to protecting than Liri."

Rokei's eyes went wide at the familiar use of his princess's name. In that moment he seemed to decide that Taryn was no enemy, and his posture relaxed. "Let me lead you to breakfast then." With that, he moved in front of Taryn and led the way down the corridor.

When they arrived at the now familiar dining hall, the enchanted ceiling shimmered and glowed as sunlight danced into the vaulted space. Somewhere above, a flock of birds winged its way west, their small shapes reflected deep in the blue sky. To the south, the rolling green of the forest of Numenessee stretched as far as he could see, and when the wind rippled the treetops, Taryn almost felt the breeze on his face. He looked at the clouds and the rising sun on the eastern wall, shaking his head in wonder until a sudden call broke him from his amazement.

"Taryn! It's about time you got up. I can't believe you slept for *ten* hours." Liri stood halfway up the hall with another guard standing behind her. Her tone of astonishment made Taryn grin, and he moved to sit across from her. Rokei discreetly moved to stand behind his ward.

"Grab some breakfast quickly," she said. "I want to show you around." She emphasized her point by retaking her seat and resuming her meal.

He nodded with a grin and wolfed down the bread and fruit placed in front of him. Liri waited for him to finish, but as soon as it looked like he was satisfied she bounded to her feet with an impish grin. "Let's go."

Something in her second guard's eyes quelled a part of his excitement, but it was hard to stay discouraged next to Liri's bubbling joy at showing off her beloved city. She could barely contain herself as she raced to the front gates of her house—towing him by the arm.

They burst into the sunlight, and Taryn laughed out loud. "Is there any way I can see the tree first . . . what did you call it?"

"Le Runtáriel, and no, we can't go see it first. I am going to take you from the bottom to the top and show you each tier. Just hitting the highlights we will need to hurry if we are going to make it before dark." She bit her lip to consider something and then pulled him towards the nearest stairs, fastening an emblem onto his shoulder as she went. "This will keep you safe in the city and identify you as a member of the House of Runya." Something about the way that sounded made her chuckle to herself and blush ever so slightly.

Taryn thought her behavior odd, but didn't have time to dwell on it as she led him down multiple flights of stairs. It seemed like she was leading him away from the bowl so he didn't get many chances to see the great tree. The whole time he was very aware of two pairs of feet treading softly behind them, and he didn't need to turn around to know it was Rokei and the other guard, which reminded him . . .

"Why was Rokei so strange earlier?" Taryn asked.

She slowed down enough to walk beside him. "What do you mean?" she asked as she cast a dark glare behind her, and he heard someone's footfalls falter.

"Nothing big, it just seemed that he was a little bit . . . wary."

"Oh," she chuckled, "the Home Guard is a little bit . . . er, *angry* at you. They don't know what you did to get into the city. They saw you fall off the cliff but had no idea what happened to you. When they found out you got into the city somehow, they were . . . furious, to put it lightly." She glanced at him with a wry grin. "Azertorn is impossible to get into under normal circumstances—and last night was *not* normal. Home Guard and almost the entire army were on alert and prepared. I do believe you are the first person to *ever* sneak into the city, or at least with everyone on high alert."

Taryn coughed and changed the subject from himself. "So remind me why you have two guards today?"

She grimaced. "Two is better than ten." Seeing his confused expression, she explained, "My mother wanted to send *ten* guards, but I talked her down to two. She was less than pleased that the intruder just

209

happened to be *my* friend." She laughed at the memory, her eyes sparkling.

The two of them turned a corner and encountered a large ironbound door flanked by two guards. Liri's expression changed to serious as they approached the armed elves.

"I am Liriana Alasse Tel'Runya of the House of Runya. I have come to inspect the city's defenses. Let us pass."

Her tone allowed no room for dispute, but the elven sentries still hesitated and Taryn didn't miss the loaded glance in his direction. After a moment one of them gave a curt bow and replied, "I will ask the leave of our captain."

Liri's expression darkened but she nodded in response, so the guard knocked on the door and slipped through when it was opened from the other side. A few minutes later another elf, dressed in blue armor, came through the door and addressed Liri. "I beg forgiveness, my lady, but we are not prepared for someone to see the fortifications of this city . . ." He trailed off with his eyes on Taryn.

Liri's expression clouded in fury, and her voice turned to a steel that Taryn had never heard before. "Captain, that was not a request— and please do not disrespect a guest of the House of Runya." He started to protest, but she cut him off before the words left his lips. "An immediate response would be appreciated, *Captain.*"

Furious at the rebuke, the elf nevertheless signaled for the door to be opened and Taryn followed Liri through. With her personal guard behind them, she began leading him through a maze of barracks and armories.

As they walked, Liri began explaining their surroundings in more detail. "This is where the Second Legion is housed, on the second tier of Azertorn. In a minute we will go down to the Hall of the First Legion. Technically there are four arms of the elven military: the First, Second, and Third Legions comprise the army, and the Home Guard protects the interior of the city. Each legion boasts twenty thousand elves and the Guard contains half that number. Most of the time there are only a few thousand of each legion on duty at one time, while the rest live in the forest in any one of the smaller elven settlements."

Her expression shifted to thoughtful. "In times of war or danger though, the entire army is brought in. For some reason that no one can explain, now is such a time. This tier alone contains the entire Second Legion living, training, and readying themselves for battle at a moment's notice. Each tier, if necessary, could house three times that number, although as far as I know those areas have never been used. "

"What do the different colors of armor represent?" Taryn asked as they passed a scowling elf outfitted in blue.

"Green armor indicates a soldier, blue armor represents an officer. The darker the shade of color, the higher up the chain of command."

"So a captain and higher wear blue?"

She nodded and then pointed to a corridor that curved away from them to the north. "These bottom tiers mirror the shape of the city, a series of half circles that wrap around a large, open space. The only difference is that down here the center is a cavern. Each of the rings house the soldiers' quarters and the armories, while the center cavern contains mess halls, training areas, and other structures for the general use of the army. We are passing through the rings now," she said as she indicated the rooms on either side. Each one looked to have two beds and was relatively small.

"These tiers are built so that the elves can retreat backward through the barracks before going up a floor. There are only three entrances to the barracks from above, the eastern, northern, and western gates. We came through the eastern gate."

It took them longer than he would have expected to reach the center of the second tier, but when they did, he realized that the level was *taller* than he'd imagined. The center cavern, or the Second Great Hall, as Liri was in the process of describing, stretched at least fifty feet high, and at least a half a mile across. It was extremely well lit, although he couldn't place the source of the light. At the moment they were facing west, so the cliff must be immediately to his left.

"How thick is the cliff face?" Taryn interrupted her description of the Second Great Hall.

She pursued her lips in disapproval to which he shrugged sheepishly. "I just explained that. The rock behind the face is fifty feet thick at every point below the sixth tier." Then she turned and directed his attention to the rock structures carved out of the walls and the massive pillar in the center. "As I was saying before I was interrupted . . .," she continued, grinning at him, "the center column is the main command of the Second Legion, and it helps support the roof. You'll notice it is located directly below the great tree Le Runtáriel. It is called the Second Pillar because it is carved from a single pillar of stone." She went on to describe the four floors of the Second Pillar and the structures ringing the open space.

Taryn only half listened to her description, his attention drawn to the thousands of elves in the cavernous space. Lean fighters were spread out in various activities, but by far the bulk of the activity could be described in a single word—training. Swords clashed in hundreds of sparring matches while the twang of longbows could be heard as a soft backdrop to the ring of steel. Taryn had trained with weapons his entire life, but he'd never seen so many people training at one time. The sight of so many elite warriors perfecting their craft was impressive—and intimidating.

Liri finished her description of the Second Great Hall and indicated for him to follow her to the First Legion, still describing the defenses. "Right now we are a little over a hundred feet above the forest floor. As we go down to the First Great Hall, you will see even stronger defenses." She smiled at his expression and led them to a descending ramp that led back into the cliff. They had to pass several gates and portcullises before they reached the bottom—again at the rear of the barracks. It then took another few minutes to go through the First Legions' quarters—passing even more gates. It was clear the corridors of both barracks had been designed to bottleneck an invading army and allow the defenders an advantage during every inch of a retreat. Taryn shook his head in amazement. He couldn't imagine any army to *ever* breach the city—let alone take it. The city's fortifications were just . . .

overkill. It would a take an army centuries to defeat even an unprepared people.

They arrived at the First Great Hall and Liri gave an abbreviated description of the few differences between the two halls. "The First Legion unquestionably has the best warriors, and it is a great honor to be a soldier or an officer within its ranks. Other than that, the only real difference is the wall and the main gates of the city." She led the group past several training rings, and as they approached the First Pillar he saw what she meant about the wall.

A wall, shaped like a half moon, curved out of the back of the cliff, merged to the First Pillar, and then continued its curve until it fused into the rear of the cliff. Formed of interlocking stones instead of solid rock, it served as an extra line of defense behind the front gates. Soldiers were prominent at strategic battlements, with longbows in easy reach. Liri led them through the first floor of the First Pillar and under a massive gate to pass through the only opening in the wall. A hundred feet of flat stone separated the wall from the back side of the cliff face—except for the contingent of elves armed to the teeth. With a start Taryn realized the elves in this position would have been the ones that chased him the night before. Their eyes certainly betrayed their suspicion of him, and a few shifted uneasily.

Liri touched his arm. "Don't worry Taryn, they won't attack you."

As she said it, he became aware of his own tense posture and that his hands were moving towards his weapons. Taking a deep breath, he forced himself to relax. After a moment she tugged on his arm and pulled him towards the enormous main gates. At first he was surprised that the gates were open, until he realized that these were only secondary gates, not the large doors he'd seen from the exterior. Through the opening he was amazed to see in place of a corridor, a pillar of solid stone blocking their view. Past this reserve gate, wide corridors to either side curved around the column towards the cliff face. Following Liri they walked down the left path until they promptly came to a dead end.

A little confused, Taryn looked at Liri with a raised eyebrow. She laughed mischievously and pointed towards the blank wall to their right.

Several elves moved forward and opened a hidden stone door. Taryn's eyes widened as he watched the portal open to reveal the side of the road. When they walked through the secret portal, he was astonished to see that the outer doors at the end of the bridge were actually false. Liri saw his expression at the sight and laughed lightly.

"Amazing isn't it?" she asked with a twinkle in her eye.

"Amazing doesn't cover it," he breathed.

From the front, the main gates were set *into* the wall about twenty feet—but the ironbound wooden gates were actually backed by a column of solid rock. On either side of the false main gates were smaller doors that were made of the stone itself and, when they were closed, blended in perfectly with the surrounding rock. To get into the city you had to walk towards the false doors and then turn left or right to go through the hidden real ones. After going through the hidden entrance, you would curve around until you came to the second gates set directly behind the first gates—fifty feet behind the fake ones.

A battering ram would never truly break through because it would be hitting doors backed by *thirty feet of unyielding stone*. Taryn shook his head, stunned at the sheer magnitude of the city's fortifications.

Liri chuckled in satisfaction. "Only the elves are aware of the false doors. That is why no other race is allowed entry through this way."

That reminded Taryn of a question that had been bothering him. "Liri, did you get a chance to find out why everyone is so afraid?"

She turned to face him with a thoughtful expression. "I did ask my mother when I arrived within the city, but she had no answer to give. She said she could 'feel the fear seeping into the city like a thick smoke,' yet no elf knows its source."

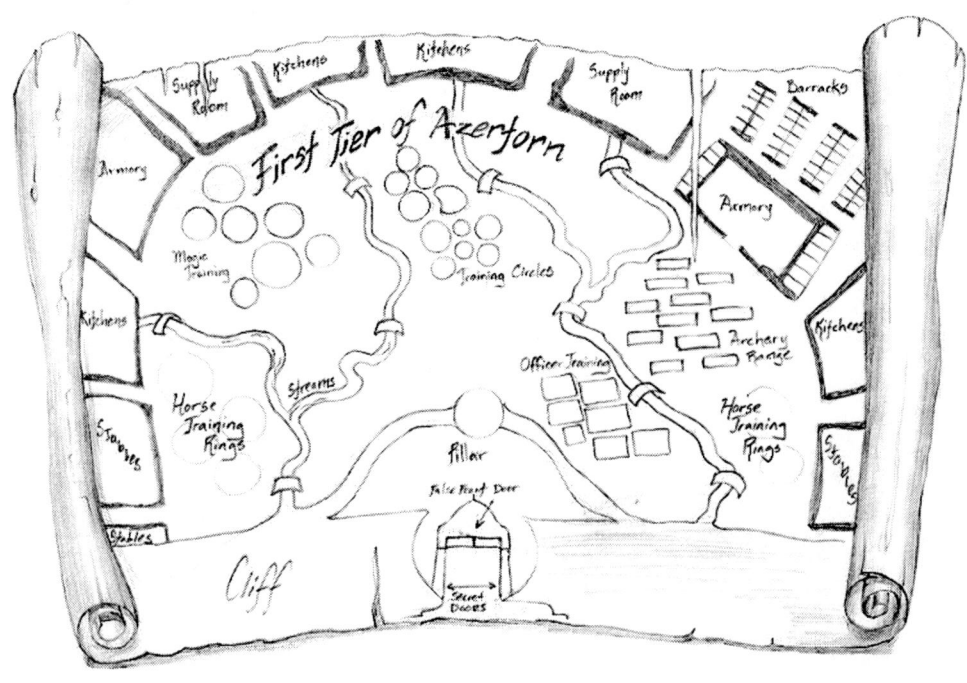

He bit his lip in thought. Not even the elves know what causes this unnatural dread.

Liri shifted next to him. "We had better go back into the city, or we are liable to be shut out."

Startled, he looked at the elves standing outside the gates, waiting for them. Their rigid posture and darkening expressions told him exactly what she meant. In fact, they appeared to be inching towards the hidden doors and there was no doubt in his mind that once they were closed . . . they wouldn't open easily.

They hurried their way through the secret doors and wound their way around the training circles. Without stopping, the trip up to the third tier was considerably shorter than their way down. Liri only paused as they arrived at another strongdoor.

"We are about to enter the bowl of the third level . . . and Le Runtáriel," she told him, her eyes bright. "This tree is sacred to the elves, so watch yourself."

He nodded, trying to contain his excitement, and followed her through the door. As he stepped out of the artificial light of the corridors and into the lower bowl, Taryn's eyes were drawn toward the most *enormous* tree he'd ever seen. From the exact center of the half-circle, the massive tree stretched over five hundred feet skyward. At its base the trunk grew thicker than fifty feet in diameter and its branches had grown so large they spanned the western and eastern sides of the city. These incredible living arches created walkways at every level, with multiple smaller branches shaped like stairs between them. A huge spiral staircase wound its way around the central trunk to further connect the different levels. The breathtaking tree's beauty could only be matched by the wide garden at its base.

Lush gardens, at least a mile across, contained thousands of smaller trees, plants, and flowers of every kind. Water came to the grove by way of several waterfalls that cascaded down from the upper levels. The streams wound its way through the garden via numerous small creeks and ended in a large pond to his left that covered the entire space between the two sides of the cliff. Startled, he realized that the pond didn't have an opposite edge at all, creating an illusion that the pond must form a waterfall on the cliff face—which he knew didn't exist. He would have seen it from the outside. The invisible edge pool of water shimmered and danced with the light of the sun, reflecting the garden and tree to any passerby.

Liri spoke softly beside him, cutting into his reverie. "Le Runtáriel is the pride and joy of the elves. It was brought with two other trees when the ancient ones migrated to the city. This is the one that survived and flourished. Centuries of elves have nurtured it with their magic and have shaped every inch of growth. It is a living legacy of the elves' ancestral homeland."

"It's stunning, Liri." he replied in awe. "I've never seen anything like it. I mean, I saw it from outside the city, and again from above it when I entered the higher level, but I never dreamed that it would be so *stunning.*"

Suddenly he couldn't help himself: "How does the pool not have an edge? Where does the water go? How old is the tree? What are the gardens called? What—"

She flashed a broad grin and interrupted him, "Be patient, let me answer those questions first. The pond is called Mirror's Edge, and it doesn't have an opposite side because the water runs over a small ledge and into a trough. Then it drains into the barracks below. The tree is at least ten thousand years old, probably far older. I don't think anyone knows when it was first planted. I do know it was already a tree when it was transplanted here, and what was your last question?" Before he could answer she continued, "Oh yes, the gardens are called the Céius Gardens." She smiled a soft smile and caught his eye. "It means 'Light and Enlightenment'."

He nodded, satisfied for the moment, and asked, "Mind if we take a look around?"

Liri's smile widened and she nodded. "Let's go; there are a few places I wish to show you." And with that she led him into the wondrous grove.

For twenty minutes, the two of them, followed by their guards, strolled through the labyrinth of hidden walkways. Every few minutes they would cross a small bridge over a gurgling brook, or duck under low hanging fruit trees with their fragrance hanging heavy in the air. Paths branched away from theirs and each walkway hid ensconced benches of both ornate stone and living trees, many of them occupied by elves seeking peace or knowledge in the gardens of Light and Enlightenment.

During their exploration, a peaceful silence stretched between them as both considered the beauty around them. Taryn found himself wishing he could come here every day, and for the first time wondered what he would do after he found his heritage. Would he settle into a home? For some reason that thought caused him to glance at Liri. He'd always harbored strong feelings for her, but had never noticed anything to indicate she favored him . . . had he? That train of thought occupied his mind until Liri reluctantly cleared her throat.

"We should probably get going," she said. "There is quite a bit more I would like to show you today."

He nodded with a sad smile, disappointed at the short visit.

"We will come back, I promise," she said earnestly.

Taryn grinned at her easy reading of his expression and sighed. "What's next?"

She matched his grin. "We go up." Then she turned towards the center staircase several hundred feet away. Arriving at its base, they began to climb. As they ascended, Taryn took the opportunity to view each facet of the wondrous city as they slowly rotated around its midpoint. At each separate tier, multiple paths separated themselves from the trunk and arced over to the city. Railings had been shaped and woven out of smaller branches growing out of the larger ones. Taryn looked from one wonder to the next, stunned by the sheer grace and beauty that Le Runtáriel gave to the city.

"Hang on, we have a stop to make," Liri said, interrupting his fascinated study of the elven city as she turned onto one of the massive branches that spanned several hundred feet. She lead him down the gently sloping wood until they came to the end of the branch and stepped off at the point where it had been grown into the path of tier four, the first level above the gardens.

"Where are we going?" Taryn asked, smiling when he realized that despite the subtle feeling of unease and fear that dominated the city's inhabitants, he felt wonderful seeing the magnificent city with Liri.

"You'll see," she replied, but her expression carried an odd contrast. At the same time she looked amused and . . . disapproving?

Before he could ask her what she meant, she stopped in front of a stone structure that boasted very little greenery. With mostly tan stone walls, it appeared odd and out of place. Glancing up, Taryn saw a battered sign hanging above the door.

"The *Drunken* Elf?" Taryn read aloud, surprised at the name. Now he understood Liri's disapproval. Elves didn't drink much, only light ale or fruit drinks. It was rare and frowned upon for an elf to be inebriated. He glanced at Liri and caught the wry smile.

"It's the one of the few taverns in Azertorn, and the only one that serves hard liquor."

"Why do we need to stop here?" he asked, incredulous.

"We need to speak to Aléthya, and before you ask who she is, I will tell you." She paused for effect and said, "She is the greatest healer the elven race has ever seen."

"And we will find her *here*?" Taryn asked, shocked that a healer would frequent such a locale.

"She owns the place."

And now he understood her amusement.

Chapter 16: The Drunken Elf

Taryn stepped through the door into the well lit tavern. It was still early in the morning, but there were quite a few elves in the room, drinking and talking. It felt odd to be in such an establishment with *elves* all around him. Liri surprised him further.

"I believe this crowd is the group from last night."

He looked at her, shocked that elves would behave in such a way, and by her expression he could tell she was enjoying this far too much.

"They will clear out in an hour or so; then it's pretty quiet until evening when the party begins again."

"This place is that popular?" he asked, lowering his voice in an effort to hide his surprise. He didn't want to get into a fight . . . wait, what was he thinking? A bar fight with elves? That thought was too strange for words.

"It's surprisingly one of the favorite places for the soldiers . . . and *others* . . . within the city." Her tone left it clear she didn't want to talk about the others. Perhaps it was someone in her family?

Taryn snorted and shook his head, trying in vain to understand. "Which one is Aléthya?"

Liri nodded towards the bar. "She's the one with brown hair."

"Brown?" he asked, surprised again.

"Her mother was a human, and she has the brown hair and dark blue eyes from her. Everything else about her is elven." Her lips twitched in a suppressed smile. "She is part of the reason many of the soldiers are in here."

Taryn spotted her right away and immediately understood what Liri was talking about. An impossibly beautiful elf worked behind the bar, bustling back and forth while serving drinks and witty remarks with equal measure. Her brown hair had been pulled back in a human style ponytail. Dark blue eyes set in a pixie face burned with subdued fire that hinted of an unyielding spirit. He found himself staring until a sharp elbow in his side brought him back. Glancing at Liri, he shrugged an apology, a little abashed. "She's pretty," he mumbled.

Liri snorted derisively and looked back at the bar. She seemed like she was about to start forward but stopped. She nodded towards the bar, "You might enjoy this."

He looked back at the bar and noticed an inebriated elf trying to reach across and grab Aléthya's arm. Before Taryn could move to intervene, Aléthya grabbed the elf's hand and wrenched it over in a hold he knew well from his training, slamming his head down into the bar.

Her voice was as sharp as a daggers tip. "I think you should leave." Without waiting for an answer she used her hold to shove him from the stool. He tumbled to the floor, and landed in a heap. Staggering to his feet he was helped towards the door by a couple of friends. One of them called out an apology.

"Sorry Thia, it won't happen again."

"It better not," she stated as she watched them stumble away. Then she caught sight of Liri and her face lit up. "Liri! You're back." She bounded around the bar and rushed towards them, engulfing Liri in a spinning embrace.

"I knew you'd be coming soon, but I must have lost track of time. Has it really been thirty years?"

Liri laughed her high tinkling laugh and allowed herself to be spun around. "It's good to see you too, Thia."

She finally set her down and took a step back to look at her. "You look good, and I'm delighted to see you brought home a *man*." She looked meaningfully at Taryn and smirked in a fashion that made him flush.

Swallowing, he reached a hand forward. "I'm Taryn."

She smiled and offered her hand in response. Her grip was surprisingly firm as she flashed him a dazzling smile, her eyes sparkling. "And a *strong* man, too. Something tells me he knows his way around a fight." She eyed him in a way that made him feel like he was about to be eaten until Liri and he both shifted uneasily.

She laughed out loud and released his hand. "And it's good to know the two of you are together as well."

Taryn's mouth opened but no sound came out while Liri began to sputter a protest, but she cut them both off, "Oh well, if not now then soon enough." Then she changed the subject before they could respond. "Come, let's have a seat and something to eat, shall we?"

Taryn nodded, relieved when she turned around and walked to the bar, calling out for someone to take over. She was too beautiful to look at, and it made him extremely uncomfortable. He was well aware of his difficulty in talking with women, but it had been a while since he had felt so utterly frozen. Not since the first time he'd met Liri in fact. Just then Liri caught his eye in a way that suggested she could guess what he was thinking, causing him flush.

She fought to hide a smile. "She has that effect on most males, so don't feel bad."

He laughed off his tension, relieved that she couldn't read his mind, and followed Aléthya into a back room furnished with a table and a few chairs.

"I'll get some food," she said, and a moment later returned with three bowls of steaming soup and hot bread that smelled delicious.

Sitting down, they began to eat while Aléthya bombarded Liri with questions about Sri Rosen and her life there. Taryn found himself impressed at how skillfully she talked and ate at the same time. Then he realized she must have had training in etiquette and again wondered how a healer had ended up here.

When the conversation shifted to him, her first question was how he'd gotten into the city. Although her eyes were innocent her mouth twitched, so he suspected she already knew. Avoiding eye contact, he explained how he'd managed to cross the waterfall and enter the storeroom, secretly pleased at her expression. He found himself considering how easy it would be to impress her, but one look at Liri's knowing smile and he quelled the urge to embellish the story.

When he finished, she leaned back and blew out her breath. "Unbelievable, Taryn. If I didn't know Liri so well, I would have doubted your tale."

"Er . . . it seemed the only way in—but I am curious about you. How did you end up here? Especially since you're a healer, right?"

She made a face, "*Was* a healer—no more."

His expression begged her to continue, so she settled into her seat with a frown on her lips—which were slightly more full than an elf's— *By Skorn, get a grip, Taryn,* he told himself.

"Do you know anything about healing magic, Taryn?" Aléthya asked.

"Just that it is the only magic that can be found in any race, and that it uses the healing ability of the person's own stored energy, weakening the sick or injured person but healing them earlier than the person would over time," Taryn responded using almost the exact phrase that Daiki had taught on the island.

"Correct," she said with a sigh, and he realized she was reluctant to tell her story.

"It's OK, Thia, you can trust him," Liri said, her expression soft.

Aléthya nodded and her smile returned. "There is a school of healing called the Sheleiam in the southern human kingdom of Talinor that many healers are sent to. I was sent at an early age because I showed an aptitude for the art. Excelling quickly, it wasn't long before I'd mastered all of the healing skills they had to teach. One of the reasons I learned so much was that *I* have a natural healing ability. Disease has no hold on me and wounds would knit and disappear in seconds. The leaders of the Sheleiam tried quite hard to duplicate it, but to no avail.

"When their experiments became more . . . desperate, I escaped and returned to my home in Azertorn, and although my mother was a human I was accepted here. Soon after my arrival the queen got sick, and no one was able to heal her. I was asked to come. I was still young, and I wanted to remove the queen's disease so much that something awakened within me. In that moment I found that I had the ability to transfer the sickness to myself. I chose to do so, hoping that my own ability would destroy the disease. Despite the tremendous pain, my body healed and I survived. Everyone was more than grateful, and many began to come to me . . . but something had changed. I could no longer heal someone else unless I took their ailment upon myself. With all the pain and suffering I had to endure to help others, I . . . I decided to quit—to give up healing."

She paused and Taryn realized he'd become lost in the tale. After a moment she sighed. "I haven't healed anyone in many years, although I do teach and aid other healers when necessary."

Silence returned until he asked, "So how did you end up with an e*lven* bar?"

Chuckling she said, "At one time this was my father's house, and after he died I decided to ask the Oracle what I should do with my life, live in Azertorn as an elf, or live as a human. She was very wise, but must have had a sense of humor. She told me it would be good to bring some human . . . culture . . . to the elves. Eventually I took her advice and turned my father's house into a pub." Then she laughed out loud. "The elven high council didn't approve and tried to stop me, but I had healed the queen, so I had too many supporters." Her eyes lit up when she talked about the disapproval of the governing body.

Liri laughed with her and after a moment Taryn joined in. It was just too much to imagine the high council of the elves trying to stonewall the formation of a drinking establishment within their city.

Liri suddenly stopped. "Oh, before I forget, I was wondering if you'd mind helping my sister. She needs to heal someone who broke their leg, but it seems to be a complicated break. Do you mind assisting her?"

Already nodding, she said, "For your family, anything. I'll stop by this afternoon."

Liri thanked her and stood up. "I'm going to show Taryn the rest of the city. I'm sure we'll see you later."

The beautiful bartender stood up and embraced her warmly. "It was good to see you, and you had better believe I want to see the *two* of you again." Her eyes narrowed at Taryn. "I think you owe me a drinking game."

Liri laughed. "Now that I would like to see, although you might have met your match, Thia."

Taryn smiled and nodded amicably, hoping such a contest would never occur. "Thank you for the meal, Aléthya."

"Call me Thia," she said. "All my friends do."

With that they departed, leaving her to tend to other duties. As they walked through the door, Liri leaned over to him. "Well, what did you think?"

"Of Thia or the bar?" Taryn asked with a grin.

"Of both."

"The bar is nice, and I would love to come back . . ." Taryn trailed off, letting her fill in the blank, but she refused to bite.

"And her?" she asked with a smile, but he could tell there was something else she wanted to know.

"She was great, and *very* pretty." He paused for a second. "I'm sure she'll be like a sister to me." The subtle tension in her body evaporated at his words, but Taryn couldn't figure out why.

"That's what she's like to me," she said, and then began walking briskly back to Le Runtáriel. "Come on, I want you to see the view from the top of the tree."

Her humor was infectious, causing Taryn to grin as he hurried to catch up. Reaching the trunk, they began to climb. For a few moments she pointed out features of the tree or the city that were visible, but after they passed the next tier she fell silent, allowing him to look at the view unhindered as they ascended. For three hundred feet they worked their way up the wide spiral staircase, passing quite a few elves that hurried past. At some point between the third and fourth tiers—fifth and sixth tiers, Taryn corrected himself, he kept forgetting the two sub levels—an elf racing behind them caught up and exclaimed breathlessly, "Lady Liriana, your presence is requested by the queen—immediately."

Liri hid her confusion well, only twitching her eyebrows in a manner he knew well. "Inform her I will be there directly."

The messenger bowed and hurried across a northern branch. Watching her response, Taryn was just beginning to understand certain nuances about her that he'd never really understood before. She'd always been adept at hiding her emotions and it finally made sense why.

Liri sighed deeply. "We are going to have to cut this tour a little short." Then her face brightened. "Do you want to come with me? You could see the palace."

He smiled wide to let her know he wasn't disappointed. "That would be great. I've wanted to see it since last night—but I can't imagine it surpassing the House of Runya."

She grinned. "Perhaps, but I think you will enjoy it, nonetheless." Turning, she led the way down the same giant limb that the messenger had taken.

227

Following in her wake, he fell to pondering her change in behavior. She had been so open and . . . personal with him before they arrived at Azertorn. Since they had arrived, he'd watched her shift from the Liri he knew, to the Lady Liriana. It was odd, seeing the other side of his long-time friend that he'd only caught glimpses of. At the same time it felt revealing . . . and unsettling. Something about the way Liri reacted to her role led him to believe she disliked her position. Glancing back to ensure the two guards following them were out of earshot he decided to voice his thoughts. "Do you not care for your status in the city?"

She glanced at him and sighed. "No," she admitted. "In the twenty years of my youth here, I never felt free. Training on Sri Rosen with you and Trin and Mae was . . . liberating, and it is difficult to try to be myself with you here and also be the person everyone expects me to be."

She leaned closer to him as she walked. "Don't let me forget myself, will you Taryn?" She looked at him with her beautiful blue eyes full of the desperate pleading in her voice.

He felt his heart flutter, but did his best not to let it affect his response. "Of course Liri, what else would I do?"

She flashed him a dazzling smile, and Taryn saw some of the old Liri in her eyes. "Forever, then?"

He responded with a lighthearted laugh. "Deal. Now let's go see what your queen wants of you. Then you can finish showing me your city."

"It shouldn't take long," she said, an oddly triumphant expression on her face as they strolled down the massive branch.

Taryn nodded, but something about the way her lips tightened when she said it gave him a different impression. Whatever the reason the queen had summoned her, it wasn't good . . . and Liri knew it.

Chapter 17: The Queen and the Quest

The two of them soon arrived at the palace on the ninth level of Azertorn, not stopping to view anything else. With Liri preoccupied Taryn said little, unsure of what to say. Instead of leading him to the massive and intricate doors at the front, Liri turned toward a small side door, relatively hidden behind strategically grown trees. Without hesitation, she slipped down the thin path and through the door. If she noticed the several hidden guards in the brush, she gave no sign.

Entering, she led them through various corridors and up several flights of stairs. As in the house of Runya, vines, plants, and trees grew everywhere, but it seemed that there were more flowering plants here.

"Why all the flowers?" Taryn asked.

"The queen likes them, and requested for additional flowers to be grown throughout the palace."

Taryn nodded and allowed her to return to her thoughts. As he followed her soft footsteps, he compared the two homes. The sweet smell of different flowers hung thick in the air in the palace, and although it looked nice, he preferred Liri's ancestral home. The House of Runya looked more natural, and felt more comfortable as a result.

Liri finally stopped at a door guarded by another couple of sentries. Bowing, she exclaimed, "Liriana Alasse Tel'Runya, and guest, to see the queen, as requested."

With an openly hostile expression, one of the guards responded, "You may enter, but your . . . *guest* . . . must wait outside—and surrender his weapons."

"Out of the question," Liri snapped with no trace of softness. "If the queen wishes to see me, then my friend comes as well."

"Liri I—" Taryn started to protest, but she cut him off with a fierce glance. He'd known her a long time, so he understood by her look that she wanted him to be with her when she met with the queen—with his weapons.

The guard shook his head and scowled. "I shall request the leave of the queen." Striding down the hall and through another door, he left the second elf looking disgruntled at the situation. Taryn suppressed a laugh; one elf would be no match for him and Liri if it came to a fight. He caught her expression, and the glint in her eyes revealed she was thinking the same thing.

They waited for several minutes until the guard returned and said stiffly, "I ask your apology, my lady, you may now enter. She has been expecting you." He seemed to hesitate and then added with a pointed look in Taryn's direction, "You will be held personally responsible by the guards for his actions." Liri nodded with a sly smile that only succeeded in infuriating the guard even more, but he opened the door without another word.

Following her into the room, Taryn took in his surroundings. They appeared to be in a sitting room large enough for several people. Just as in the House of Runya, trees had been bent as they'd grown to form living chairs in a circle. Gurgling water flowed in several small channels around the room, and countless flowers grew from the floor, walls, and ceiling.

"This is the personal receiving room for the queen," Liri said. Then her lips twitched into a smile. "Be on your best behavior."

"I will behave as well as I always do," he replied, uneasy at the prospect of meeting the queen of a city he'd just snuck into.

She chuckled quietly in response but fell silent when a secret door on the opposite side of the room opened to allow three elves to enter. Ornate blue armor and two short swords identified the first man as a warrior. Even without the weapons, Taryn would have seen him as a fighter. The elf's eyes were gray rather than blue and set in a lean and pointed face that appeared weathered by time and elements. His gaze never left Taryn as he strode into the room.

The second elf entering the room couldn't have been more different. She wore a layered green and purple gown that appeared at the same time magnificent, yet simple. Eyes of clear light blue gave the impression of ancient knowledge and wisdom. When she met Taryn's gaze, he could see a firm line to her mouth and a beautiful face surrounded by almost white blonde hair. Her very presence breathed authority, grace, and intelligence.

Last, a smaller elf entered the room. At first glance he appeared to be just another guard—until Taryn took a closer look. Despite the elf's diminutive stature, his carriage screamed his skill with a blade. Instead of strolling into the room, he seemed to glide in, almost slipping into a half crouch at the sight of Taryn. No visible weapon appeared on his back or side, but there were conspicuous bulges about the length of daggers or knives along his thighs and forearms—and there were sure to be more weapons even better hidden. After a moment's thought Taryn assumed this was probably the queen's personal bodyguard—certainly here due to Taryn's presence.

The three elves seated themselves in a strategic arrangement, with the queen slightly behind the other two. The first one to enter the room spoke first. "I am Deiran, general of the elven armies. Despite my objections, the queen has requested this meeting." He shifted to look at Taryn, his eyes narrowing. "But before we begin I wish to say something to you. Watch yourself, *half-breed*, in this room, or you will find yourself cut down before you can take half a step in any hostile act!"

The queen shifted, subtly drawing attention to her. When she'd caught Taryn's eye she gave a wry smile. "Forgive my general; he has been very irritable of late and slightly overprotective." Her voice sounded light and smooth, like a summer breeze through the clouds.

"*Overprotective!*" Deiran exploded, but she silenced him with a glance before continuing.

"My name is Ayame Ser'Tármaril, but you may call me Ayame. I am told your name is Taryn Elseerian and you know little of your heritage. I am most curious about where you come from, but unfortunately that conversation will have to wait. We have more pressing matters to discuss."

Her gaze shifted to Liri, and her voice softened. "Liri, my dear, it is good to see you after so long."

Taryn was surprised by her familiar use of Liri's name. During their training only a handful of very close friends had called her Liri.

"You have returned at a strange time in our lands. In place of the light-hearted and cheerful people when you departed, there is now a fierce and battle-ready nation. We do not know what has caused this recent change, but we know it is worsening. I feel the tension increase almost daily now."

She composed herself with a sigh and returned her gaze to Liri. "I fear if this continues we will be at war with the druids, the humans, or the dwarves—or even all three—at any moment. As the saying goes 'The kindling has been laid' . . ."

Taryn finished the statement in his mind, *and only needs a spark.*

Ayame's tone suddenly became urgent. "We must solve this dilemma before it destroys us all."

Deiran interrupted in a pleading tone. "My lady, I am confident we will be victorious in any engagement. Our people have nearly all been gathered in, and the city of Azertorn will never fall to enemy hands."

She patiently allowed him to finish before responding, "I believe you, General, but I do not care for *any* battle to occur, especially when the only driving force is an unnatural fear that possesses us. Every life is precious, and I refuse to allow any to be lost needlessly. Unity is necessary in the face of fear, not battle."

Turning back to Liri, she said, "We are in a troubled time. Fear and terror spread faster than the wind across our land. A thief we cannot catch has somehow managed to steal from us on several occasions. Trusted nations have turned against us. It is even more baffling how suddenly this has come to pass. In a handful of weeks, we have gone from a peaceful race to a hardened angry one."

She sighed and shook her head. "I cannot help but draw our country in to protect it, but I recognize this will not solve our dilemma. That is why I have decided to send an envoy east, to the Oracle. Hopefully she will have some wisdom in this dire time. Unfortunately, few elves have traveled outside the boundaries of our lands in recent months, and even fewer are willing to do so now. The two of you seem to be less affected by this plague of terror, so I wish for you to accompany them."

For the first time, the smaller elf on the right spoke up, his voice as hard as steel. "My lady, I must protest, this man is an outsider and must not be allowed on this journey."

She smiled affectionately at him. "Ren, you have always protected me well, but I must insist. They will be traveling in human lands, and if there are any needs of the party, they will need him to speak to humans. I also want you to go with them, as my personal representative."

Momentarily flustered, he still responded with a nod, "Yes, my lady."

She continued speaking to him. "Take Denithir and his command with you. I have chosen them specifically for this purpose, and he will lead this quest with valor." Her slight emphasis on the word *lead* sent a not-so-subtle message of who would be in charge. She obviously wasn't taking any chances with an authority struggle.

Ren nodded and flashed a triumphant smile in Taryn's direction. "Yes, my lady."

Something about Ren's reaction to the elven captain's name left Taryn feeling unsettled. His instincts told him it had something to do with him, but he saw no apparent reason why it would.

Liri leaned forward and asked, "Ayame, what exactly would you have *me* do?"

She smiled at Liri's question. "Leave at first light and go to the Oracle. Ask her what is happening within our kingdom, and everywhere else—and do so quickly." Her tone dropped, "Or we may be at war when you return."

Despite his previous feelings, the queen had an aura of trust, causing him to ask, "I am . . . grateful for your confidence, but I feel I must ask why you would have me go? It must be more than my human heritage."

The queen smiled. "I sense that you will be needed, perhaps it is because you look human, or perhaps it is something . . . else, but you are as crucial for this mission as anyone. It is evident that Liri trusts you completely, so despite my fear that you will destroy us, I will place my faith in you as well." Both the general and Ren shifted at that statement, and she added in an amused tone, "That may not be enough for others, but Liri's faith in you is sufficient evidence for me to fight my fear."

Taryn found himself nodding in sincere gratitude. "I will do whatever is necessary."

The queen's face warmed and her smile spread. "I do not doubt it." Then she looked at Liri, sadness returning to her gaze. "This quest is vital to our survival. Do not fail us."

The queen gave a brief bow and Taryn recognized it as a dismissal, so he bowed in turn without taking his eyes off Ren—who watched him with unblinking eyes. Taryn's wary look seemed to amuse the small warrior and his lips slid into a smirk. Ren knew, that Taryn knew, that they would have a fight sometime in the future—and that both were certain that they would be the victor.

Liri and Taryn stood together and watched the three elves exit through the same door they'd come in. Ren's eyes remained locked on Taryn's form until the door closed with a soft click.

Liri blew out her breath and exclaimed, "Well, isn't that just *great* for us, huh?"

"What?" he asked quizzically, "I thought it sounded like fun, and at least we'd get to find out what is going on."

"I don't know if I *want* to know what is going on."

Taryn chuckled. "Do we have any choice?"

She sighed. "Not really."

"Then let's go and talk to the Oracle. Besides, maybe she will have some answers about my parents . . ."

"Exactly!" she said. "Then we have preparations to make, don't we?"

"Why is the Oracle in the east anyway? Isn't she an elf?" he asked.

"Well yes, but apparently the Oracle didn't participate in the elves' migration. For some reason she decided to stay." Her expression turned thoughtful and she said, "I would think that her presence in the east has served some good. I know that the humans started seeking her counsel. It's partially due to her that the elves opened their borders and allowed humans and dwarves to pass freely through the Forest of Numenessee and use the Lake Road, which runs along the Giant's shelf as it climbs the plateau. Before all this mess, humans, dwarves, and druids were allowed to travel freely on the Lake Road—but I doubt it is permitted now."

"I would like to see the Blue Lake," Taryn exclaimed with a sigh, "and the road would be impressive for sure. "

"I will show it to you sometime, but we should probably prepare for the journey. With the kingdoms on the brink of war I doubt it will be an easy one," Liri said.

No sooner had the words left her mouth than the door slammed open and the same ornery guard stepped into the room. "Thank you for your visit."

The two of them strolled past the guard and back towards the hidden entrance to the palace. As soon as they were out of earshot, Liri began talking animatedly about what they should ask the Oracle but Taryn only listened with half his mind. Despite his earlier show of nonchalance, he was worried. Something serious was undermining the stability of nations, and whatever it was, it was getting worse—especially further east. One thing was certain, though, when they did reach the Oracle he was going ask about his heritage.

He only hoped she had some answers.

Chapter 18: Test of Loyalty

Sunrise shimmered on the early morning dew in the small meadow that Taryn's group had chosen to camp in—but it felt far from peaceful. Somehow the innate tranquility of such a place had been stolen, replaced with a sinister feeling in the air that had persisted throughout the unnaturally silent night and into the morning. Each member of the party, whether asleep or on watch, had shifted uneasily whenever the fire crackled.

It had only been a day since they'd met with the queen, but it felt like another life. Taryn rolled up his bedroll amidst the score of Denithir's hardened elves around him, feeling more than one set of eyes on him. The personal guard of the queen, Ren, had camped close to Liri and Taryn on their first night away from the elven fortress. But Ren wasn't the only one to be hostile.

Denithir's attitude towards Taryn had been openly antagonistic since the moment he'd laid eyes on him. The elven captain seemed remarkably similar to Ren, and Liri had informed him that they were related somehow. Small of stature but well balanced in his stance, he was certain to be a formidable fighter. Intense blue eyes in the lean elf's face were restless, never stopping as they searched for signs of danger. In fact, there only appeared to be one real difference between the two. Denithir was a fighter *and* an excellent commander. It had been obvious in every move he'd made—especially the position of his soldiers for the night. Not only had there been a defensive layout that left them prepared for an attack from without, he was also prepared for an attack from within.

Four of the company had laid their bedrolls in a strategic four-point pattern around Taryn's. The lack of trust had left Taryn recalling painful memories of Sri Rosen. Unfortunately, he hadn't handled those chances well, giving him little experience on how to cope with the situation. The one thing he knew was that it did not bode well for their chances of success.

"Captain?" Taryn broke the stillness in a respectful tone.

Denithir turned his head to regard Taryn, surprised that he'd spoken so directly. He hadn't said a word to him since they'd left the previous morning. "Is there something you need, *guest* of Runya?"

Liri bristled next to Taryn when Denithir pointedly didn't use his name, but Taryn did his best to ignore it and pressed forward, "I don't think it's a good idea for us to continue this *perilous* journey at the request of the queen unless we can trust each other."

At Taryn's blunt statement, the captain turned completely around to face him and studied him for several moments. Taryn had chosen his words with care, stressing the hazardous nature of their quest hoping it would appeal to the strategic side of a military commander. He'd also called attention to the fact that this mission came from the queen, and that his presence had been personally requested by her.

Denithir chewed on his comment, and then reluctantly said, "I agree that our current predicament could prove . . . difficult, if we are unable to work effectively together. What do you have in mind?"

Taryn fought the wave of relief. Denithir had responded the way he'd hoped. "A truce, for now, but if there is anything I can do to show my loyalty to the House of Runya, and the elves, name it."

Instead of Denithir, it was Ren that answered, pouncing on his words, "A test then, a test of your loyalty."

The sudden eagerness in the dangerous fighter's eyes set Taryn instantly on guard. "If that is your wish," he responded carefully.

238

Denithir chewed his lip, apparently lost in thought, although his expression appeared just as eager as Ren's. A sinking feeling settled into Taryn's abdomen as he realized that this was something they had been waiting for. Liri shifted beside Taryn, and a glance in her direction revealed her expression had shifted to one of concern.

Appearing to come to a decision, Denithir looked hard at Taryn. "Do you know the first law of the elves?"

His heart tightened. "Never spill the blood of another elf."

Denithir's voice rang out, "How many will stand to test his loyalty?" After a moment, every single elf except for Liri stood and took a step forward, including Denithir and Ren.

Taryn swallowed against the knot that had formed in his throat. He was going to have to fight the entire company—and he couldn't actually *hurt* any of them. Glancing around at the hard eyes facing him, he suddenly realized that they did not view him as an elf, and therefore not subject to the first law of the elves.

They were looking to kill him.

How had he gotten himself into such a mess, *again*? Did he lack the basic social ability that so many others possessed? Why couldn't he be more charismatic like Trin or Murai? What would his uncle do in such a position?

The questions bombarded his mind even as he cast about for some way out of the pointless engagement, until his eyes found Liri's. For some inexplicable reason, her expression carried amusement.

Taryn felt the anger rush to his head. How could Liri laugh at him now? Before he could say anything through his churning emotions, Liri spoke up.

"As the law states . . . never *spill the blood* of another elf," she called out, allowing the implication to hang in the air.

In that moment he saw what she meant, and it seemed like a small light had appeared through the clouds. He couldn't cut them, but he could hurt them. "Don't hurt them too bad, Taryn," she added with a mischievous chuckle, "except their pride—you can hurt *that* as much as you want." She began to laugh before sitting against a tree and munching on a piece of fruit, as calm as a summer's breeze.

His anger towards Liri had begun to dissipate, but he still didn't appreciate her cavalier attitude. Frowning, he turned back towards the stone-faced elves. *Fine*, he thought darkly and met the elven captain's gaze. "Let's get this over with then." He sighed in resignation and slowly reached for his weapons—

Exploding into action, Taryn leapt to the left at the nearest elf ten feet away—strategically the opposite side from Denithir and Ren. Before the elf could draw a weapon, Taryn smashed a fist into his temple. Time seemed to slow for Taryn as he turned to a small group of elves reaching for their swords. In the half-second it took for the first elf's unconscious form to hit the ground, he ghosted his way through and around the elven guard while knocking out several more. Edric, his master in unarmed combat, had taught him several ways to incapacitate an opponent. In this current battle he couldn't use lethal or severely damaging points—but that still left several places to target.

Taryn used every one of them.

Slipping between elves like a leaf in the wind, he led with a knife edge of his hand, leaving still forms in his wake. When the last in line managed to turn towards him, Taryn smashed his forehead into the elf's face and he crumpled without a sound.

The first elf's unconscious form hit the ground and time sped up. About a third of the elves were already out of the fight, but that left more than half a score of furious elves with weapons drawn. Unsure if he'd be able to restrain the magic in his father's sword, he drew Ianna and threw the sword out to block strike after strike. Knowing they would move to flank him, he allowed them to move around his sides before abruptly leaping into a high forward flip that carried him over the heads of those still in front of him. Twisting in midair and landing facing the backs of several elves, he heard a low chuckle from the side of the meadow and knew that Liri was enjoying herself.

The unexpected maneuver left quite a few surprised and struggling to turn around, but he didn't give them the chance. The instant his feet touched the ground, he darted to their backs and took out three more with precision blows before anyone could put a blade in his direction— but the elves were quick to adapt. A desperate, off-balance thrust forced him to dodge backward and allowed the others time to attack.

Suddenly a thin sword darted in, seeking his heart, but Taryn swatted it aside with the tip of Ianna, and leapt in with a lightning fast punch that sent the attacker sprawling into the elf next to him. The two went down in a tangle of arms and legs while the rest of the elves rushed to flank him again.

Again he allowed them to surround him while whipping Ianna as fast as he could to block the cascade of blows in his direction. Once they had circled him, he made to jump and watched as they tried to thrust upward where he would have been. The second their eyes lifted skyward, he dropped to the ground. Extending his leg, he spun and dropped several that were too close. Before the others could react, he dove towards two elves that were on the ground next to each other. Snapping his sword out and up, he blocked a weak strike and managed to land on the other side of them in a quick roll. Rising to his feet, he smacked the flat of his blade against one elf's head and he dropped with a groan. One sharp kick knocked out another elf on the ground, but the last one rolled away before he could get him.

Only a handful of elves still remained with their captain and Ren— who he'd purposefully left no opportunity to close with. Hiding a smile, he watched as they tried to surround him again. They had evidently been trained to surround a numerically weaker opponent so he could be decimated—and Taryn didn't hesitate to exploit their tactics. This time the remaining elves approached with more caution, slowly moving in without striking. A quick head count in the lull revealed only seven elves left standing.

Hoping for a quick ending, he asked, "Has this been a sufficient test?"

Without responding they all struck as one. Deadly blades reached out high and low towards his body. If he hadn't been moving he would

241

have been sliced by several weapons . . . but their blades only found his shadow. Ducking under a high blade that had been aimed at his head, he crouched and whirled towards the ring of elves. In one fluid movement he continued the spin between two elves, grabbed an elf's leg as he slipped through the deadly circle, yanked him off balance in the direction of his companions, and, as they fell, stood and smashed his gloved hand into his temple.

Ready for the instant response, he backed away with his sword extended towards the four elves in front of him. The elven captain looked furious, but Ren's expression actually appeared amused as he advanced on Taryn with his daggers up and ready. One of the elves Taryn had tripped stood up groggily and tried to rejoin the fight.

With so few opponents left he could not ignore his greatest adversaries, Ren and Denithir. Locking eyes with Ren he said quietly, "I haven't cut anyone yet, and I am not going—"

In a flash he batted aside an extended short sword and leapt towards its wielder. Elbowing him in the head, he turned back around in time to quickly parry three blades in succession. Another sword reached out to cut him, and he was forced to jump backwards to avoid the flashing blade of the captain.

Instead of continuing to retreat, he barely touched his feet to the ground before knocking a sweeping attack aside and leaping forward. Rolling his sword around the elf's blade in a circular motion, he slipped past his guard and slapped the end of his sword against the elf's hand hard enough to force the blade from his palm. As it spun into the shadows, Taryn blocked the three remaining swords in a ring of steel. The weaponless elf tried to back off and search for another weapon, but Taryn didn't give him the opportunity. Bolting towards him, Taryn blasted past him with his free arm extended, hitting him in the chest hard enough to knock the wind out of him and smashing him brutally to the ground, gasping for air.

Knowing the remaining three elves would be at his back, Taryn did the thing they least expected. Crouching, he jumped high, flipping backwards over the expected charge. Only Ren reacted quickly enough to get a blade up while Taryn flew over their heads. In midair, Taryn twisted and knocked the weapon away before landing in a crouch behind them. Denithir and Ren were already halfway turned around, but the third elf hadn't responded fast enough. Ianna's long steel flashed in the sunlight, reaching out towards the elf and smacking him on the side of the head.

Only two left.

Ren sidestepped to get some room and chuckled. "Not bad Taryn, not bad at all."

Taryn backed away from the two fighters. Allowing a group to get around him was one thing but letting these two at his sides would be deadly—at least with only one sword. Reaching back, he slowly drew his father's sword and extended both weapons towards his two remaining adversaries. At the sight of the second katsana they both hesitated, glancing at each other uncertainly.

"Are we going to finish this so we can continue our quest?" Taryn asked, unable to keep the sadness from his voice.

An instant later three weapons leapt for his death while he spun to defend himself. Reversing his mother's sword he carefully blocked each strike from Denithir on his left while using the bulk of his attention to parry Ren's lightning fast daggers. Mazer whipped back and forth to block the shorter weapons before they could get close enough to strike.

Ringing filled the meadow as steel clashed for several minutes while all three looked for an opening. Ren found one first. Feinting, he knocked the longer weapon aside and leapt in with his other dagger, a cry of victory on his lips—but the opening had been a ruse. Taryn had shifted his feet and sidestepped the deadly thrust for his chest, sheathing his mothers sword at the same time. Ren was so close that Taryn could feel his breath on his face as he rolled around the elf's body, hooking his left arm around Ren's neck as he went. The small form struggled in his grip in an effort to reach back and stab Taryn in the leg, but to no avail. Taryn braced his feet, and stopped hard, transferring his momentum into Ren's body. With a twist of his upper body he tossed him like a sack of flour to land several feet away. Continuing his roll until he faced Denithir, he bought himself time to parry his attack.

Suddenly Taryn was sick of fighting his allies. Drawing his mothers' sword again, he brought both swords to bear, relentlessly attacking the elven captain from all sides. Overwhelming his defenses in moments, he disarmed him and kicked him full in the chest. Tripping over a fallen elf and flying backwards, Denithir landed in a heap almost ten feet away. In a heartbeat Taryn snapped around to face Ren as he slowly stood up, pointing Mazer at his rising form.

Ren stared at him; then snorted and shook his head. "I think it's safe to say that if you were an enemy of the elves you could have killed us all."

Denithir coughed and sat up, fighting to breathe. "You have proven your loyalty . . . Taryn Elseerian."

Bowing slightly in acknowledgement of Denithir's concession, Taryn sheathed his swords and grabbed a water skin. He took a quick drink for himself before tossing it to Denithir, who caught it deftly as he stood, massaging his chest where Taryn had kicked him.

"I am here to serve, my captain." Taryn said, and the sincerity in his tone set the elven captain aback.

In that moment, Denithir seemed to come to a conclusion and his attitude shifted. "I will never question you again, Taryn. Welcome to my command."

For the first time he saw a hint of warmth in the captain's eyes and realized that he may have finally managed to prove himself. Ren welcomed him as well, although in a different way—with a hard punch to the shoulder.

"I had to hit you at least once," the small elf said gruffly without looking at him. Despite the bluster, Taryn saw it for what it was—an honorable warrior conceding defeat.

In response Taryn gave a cautious smile. "You are quick with those daggers, my friend, and I want you to show me some of your techniques."

Grinning for the first time since he'd met Taryn, Ren responded, "Only if you can show me some of yours in return." Something in his tone and eyes made Taryn realize there was a deeper meaning to his comment, but he couldn't put a finger on it. A groan from the ground distracted him and looking down, he saw Liri trying to revive an elf. Guilt washed over him and he stooped to help.

Before he could say anything, Liri murmured, "Ren doesn't know how you did it."

He met her gaze with a raised eyebrow, so she added, "You were far stronger and smarter than he expected"— her brow furrowed—"and faster . . . than even I expected," she said, her brow still creased in confused concentration, trying to puzzle out what she'd seen.

He shrugged and started to drip some water on the half-conscious elf, but Liri grabbed his elbow, forcing him to look at her again.

"You were faster than I have ever seen you, Taryn." Her intense gaze burrowed into him. "You were better today than any time I have seen you fight, even at the Acabi."

"What do you mean?" he asked, surprised by her comments.

She shook her head in confusion. "I'm not sure. You have always been fast and strong and smart, but this was different. You were so fast that I could barely see you, and you just knocked out a score of the best elven warriors in a matter of minutes—like they were children."

Further conversation was cut off as Denithir called to them, "Let's wake them up, we have a quest to complete."

Taryn moved to another elf and began reviving him while he mulled over what Liri had said. Thinking back on the test, he realized he *had* been faster. Then a memory came to mind that pulled him up short. Something Murai had said a few years ago, what was it?

After a particularly tough practice fight, Murai had peered at him and said, "You are getting better Taryn."

"Thank you," he'd responded with a courteous bow, but Murai had cut him off.

"That's not what I mean—although you are getting better with a blade. I mean that your *innate* abilities are getting better, your speed, strength, and cunning. Those are the skills that you can only train to a certain point." His uncle had just stared at him with his eyebrows knitting together. "But you don't seem to have a limitation—or at least we haven't reached it yet." His eyes had then focused on Taryn, seeing his embarrassment for the first time, so he smiled disarmingly. "Let's work on your techniques against an axe shall we?"

Coming back to the present he pondered the fading memory. Had he still not reached his limits? Would he get even faster and stronger? How was that even possible? No person was limitless. He suddenly saw how the fight would have looked through Liri's eyes. Taryn had taken down an elite elven guard without even using all of his skill. It should have been an impossible fight, unwinnable by all accounts.

For the next several hours he pondered the question that had no answer while helping to revive the elves and preparing to continue their journey. The questions kept leading back to the overriding dilemma of his heritage. *Where did he come from and who were his parents?*

He knew in his heart that that question was the source of everything else. The problem was . . . that answer was the most elusive.

Chapter 19: Terros

A week had passed since they'd left Tallendale, and Trin had played Stratos with Braon almost the entire time—especially when he introduced the other races. Braon had four other sets to play with. Druid, gnome, barbarian, and rock troll, each with different pieces and moves. The young man had explained that the other sets weren't allowed in official tournaments, but they were a lot of fun, and helped to practice strategy. Once Trin had memorized how the other races moved, it became something close to an obsession. It didn't matter though, he still lost.

Peering down at the small soldiers, Trin studied the layout again before moving his rock troll to attack the elf on the side of the board. Even though he was able to kill it, another elf destroyed his troll. Try as he might, he couldn't figure out how to defeat Braon, although this game was going to be closer than normal. He thought he had the advantage because he had more pieces.

His contemplations were interrupted when Mae poked her head into the small cabin. "Something's up, Trin, you might want to come take a look."

Torn between finishing the game and following Mae, he hesitated, but Braon solved his dilemma. "Don't worry about it. This is what you would have done, right?" The young man proceeded to play both sides of the board, and within twenty seconds his elves won. Glancing back at Trin, he looked sheepish. "That was the best you could have done anyway."

"Do you know everything your opponent is going to do?" Trin exclaimed in exasperation.

Shrugging without answering, Braon swept the pieces into his bag. "Let's go see what the trouble is."

Trin stepped into the bright sun and blinked to let his brown eyes adjust. Regaining his vision, he saw most of the sailors leaning out over the rail to look east. He slipped through the throng to join Mae at the front of the ship and finally got a look at what was going on.

At first he thought they must be approaching land, but after peering towards the horizon for a few moments he was able to make out that it wasn't the coast, it was ships—thousands of them. By the different sizes of the sails, it looked like everything from small schooners and fishing boats to larger sea-going vessels and cargo ships. There were so many that they blocked out the horizon.

"By Skorn . . .," Trin breathed.

"Something isn't right." Mae spoke quietly beside him.

"You got that right!" Erix exclaimed from the other side of him. "Get back to your posts men, and stay sharp!"

The men went about their business, but an air of tension prevailed all over the *Sea Dancer*. Trin remained rooted in place with Mae at the front of the boat and watched the approaching fleet.

Braon appeared beside him. Seeing the cause of the commotion, his face went ashen. "Something happened to Terros."

"What?" Trin asked sharply. "How could you know what happened in Terros?"

Braon answered without looking at him, "If it was an army, there wouldn't be small ships. If it was something normal, there wouldn't be so many. They are retreating . . . and by how many . . . I would say it's practically everyone in the eastern kingdom." He finally turned to Trin with an expression like death. "They're refugees—and they've been driven out."

248

Trin could only stare at him. To his surprise, he realized he trusted him completely. If there was anything he knew about the young man, it was that he knew strategy. Braon was right.

"Let's go tell Erix." Trin grabbed his shoulder and led him to the helm. "Tell him," he said, giving the young man a slight push.

Braon explained his theory well, but Erix's response was skeptical. "How can you possibly know that?"

The young man opened his mouth to reply, but it was Trin that answered first, "Trust him captain. He knows what he's talking about."

At Trin's firm tone, the captain seemed taken aback. Then he came to a decision and nodded. *"OK . . . that changes things a bit."* He looked ahead and seemed to consider his options before saying, "Tell Mae to go below; I don't want to spook anyone with an elf on board. Trin, go to the front of the ship and try to hail one of the vessels. We need to find out what happened. I know you left Terros when you were a kid, but keep an eye out for anyone you might know. Braon, go with him and let me know immediately if there is anything else you see."

Jumping to the front of the ship, Trin let Mae know her role. She grimaced but didn't complain as she left the two of them watching and waiting. After several minutes of silence, Braon asked, "Do you have family anywhere else in the Griffin Empire, or just in Terros?"

He felt his heart tear as he thought of his father and brother. Would he ever see them again? Were they already dead? A sense of loneliness swept over him, causing him to swallow against the growing knot in his throat. The sliver of fear felt sharp and painful, and it took all his effort to quash it. Doing his best to keep his voice even, he said, "Just in Terros."

A few moments passed until he added, "You?"

"Same," Braon answered in a surprisingly even tone.

Glancing at the young man he realized that he was hiding his emotions well, but the way he rubbed his left thumb into his forefinger betrayed him. Trin placed his hand on his shoulder and squeezed, but if Braon recognized it he gave no sign.

The two of them watched the approaching ships in silence until they got close enough to see faces—but seeing their expressions only made things worse. Haunted eyes looked back at them with no hint of warmth, and when he tried to hail them, there was no response. After a few attempts he fell silent, realizing the effort was futile. Ship after ship passed them on their way west, without a single soul saying a word.

Halfway through the pack they began to see the wounded.

Men, women, and children, wearing makeshift bandages, were crowded onto the heavily laden vessels. Blood soaked rags covered injuries of every size and shape. Each vessel they passed carried more wounded, and by the stillness of some forms, not all had survived. Many mourned over the wounded or dead, their grief too intense to voice.

The sight grated at Trin's heart in a way he'd never imagined possible, clawed at his natural born faith with such power it threatened to engulf him. Somehow his hope fought back, walling itself deep inside where the despair could not touch, where it would have a chance to survive. Numbness then began to replace the anguish, until Trin, and everyone on board the *Sea Dancer*, joined the refugee armada in bleak silence.

Two hours crawled by, and to Trin it felt like an eternity while the dull ache settled deep and refused to budge. Finally the mass of ships began to thin, until only a few stragglers passed them, loaded to the brim with the bloody and the lifeless.

Erix appeared at Trin's side. "We *have* to find out what happened." His voice echoed unnaturally after the lack of sound, and Trin wasn't the only one that winced.

"How long until we get there?" Trin whispered to the captain.

"An hour, no more."

"So whatever happened, happened this morning." Braon said, his face drawn.

250

Erix nodded at him, his expression stony, before turning away and heading towards the helm. *"Ero save us,"* he said under his breath as he turned away.

Still frozen in place, Trin felt Braon switch feet and end up closer to him than before. The two continued to watch the coming horizon without a word, and barely noticed when Mae joined them a few minutes later.

She was the first one to see the smoke.

"Something is burning," she said, leaning forward.

"Are you sure?" Trin asked.

A second later someone called down a warning from the nest, and a few minutes later Trin and Braon could see the smoke as well—but by then it was difficult *not* to see it. No land was in sight, but vast plumes of black smoke lazily drifted skyward from the eastern horizon.

Braon's words mirrored his thoughts: "Terros has been razed." The avowal was offered with no emotion, but a glance at his hand revealed the skin of his thumb was white as it rubbed his fingers. Trin waited for tears from the young man, but none came.

"We should not get too close to land." Mae's tone was uncharacteristically sharp.

Braon instantly agreed with her. "Whatever or whoever did this is probably still nearby. We need to come about."

"No," the captain said, appearing behind them again. "We must see what happened, so we may bear witness." His gaze was so intense that Trin briefly wondered who in Terros the old sea captain had cared about.

"But—" Braon started to protest before the captain stopped him with a glance.

"We will get close enough to see the city—but not too close." He paused, and then added, "Just close enough to see."

251

Three solemn nods answered him, so Erix left to organize his men. Mae caught Trin's eye and hissed, "Every moment we delay, we put ourselves in danger."

"I know, Mae, but we have to trust the captain."

Mae shook her head in disapproval but returned her gaze to the column of smoke without another comment.

As if the Sea Dancer itself could feel the increasing tension, it began to pick up speed. The wind started to gust and howl, and many sailors around them cast fearful looks at the darkening sky. Ash and soot drifted down to them like warm snow, tingeing the air with its acrid scent, and the very air began to pulse with the mounting tension of the crew.

It didn't take long to see the burning structures. As they got closer, they were finally able to see the portions of the capital city of Griffin that were still on fire. Most of the city wasn't actually burning—but very little was left that could. Every stone building that wouldn't burn had been violently torn down. In many places it was impossible to tell what the structure had been. Debris and broken stones were scattered over the remains of the city—and some stones looked to be shattered . . . or even crushed to dust. Taller buildings were no more than piles of blackened wood and rubble. Defensive walls and living quarters alike had been utterly devastated.

Fear crawled in Trin's veins as his heart thudded in his chest. His home had been erased. There was nothing left. He couldn't imagine the destruction being any worse—until the haze cleared and the corpses came into view. Bodies of men and women littered the ground like fallen autumn leaves. Thousands of them lay broken and still bloody, smashed under rocks, buried in rubble, or torn asunder. Behind him someone gasped, but he couldn't tear his eyes from the carnage to find out who.

Braon broke the silence, his words horrified. "The army tried to protect their escape."

At his words, Trin noticed that the majority of the dead wore broken armor and tattered uniforms. Many of them lay on or near the docks. They had bravely given their lives to allow the ships to escape, knowing they would never survive.

Was his father or brother among them?

Mae suddenly asked, "Where are the attackers?"

Someone behind him cursed, and he glanced back to see half the crew peering into the gloom surrounding the city.

But that wasn't what Mae had meant . . .

"Where are the *bodies* of the attackers?" she hissed furiously.

Trin spun back and scanned the dead. Panic bubbled inside him when he realized that there were no bodies of those who had killed them—none at all. All the men looked to be Griffin defenders. There were no bodies of *any other race* lying with the dead.

Who could have done this? Trin thought in horror.

"We must leave this place," Braon yelled, "or we will join them!"

His remark seemed to release everyone from their hold. Panic and utter terror engulfed the men. Scrambling, they leapt to the sails or the helm, their eyes crazed and full of fear. Several men roughly shoved the captain out of the way and struggled to turn the helm. Stumbling, Trin grabbed a railing as the *Sea Dancer* listed sharply to port in response to the sailors' actions. Whipping around, the ship groaned in protest to the sharp turn. Without orders, men raced around the ship in chaos, shouting and yelling, mad with fear. Some leapt to put every scrap of sail onto the mast, while most of the sailors lost control and began exchanging blows. Within moments the ship dissolved into a brawl.

Trin fought to keep his feet under him and saw Braon grasping the rail. "Find a place to hide kid, I don't want you getting hurt," he yelled.

The young man nodded, his self-control obviously shattered by the chaos, and began working his way towards the stairs. Without warning

253

the ship swung in a different direction and they all lurched to the side. Someone at the helm had almost succeeded in turning the ship around before another man tried to knock him out of the way and the two traded blows. With so many hands to guide it, the ship began to careen in either direction at the slightest touch.

"Wait!" Mae shouted beside him as she clung to the rail.

Trin turned to her in astonishment, but instead of responding she pointed out to the water.

Looking where she directed, it took him a moment to spot what she had seen—a rowboat, and it had a single passenger lying in it. It was so close he couldn't imagine how they'd passed it, but then, no one had been looking at the water. Looking around he saw there was no chance to stop the ship, and they only had moments before they would pass him.

"There's a man down there!" he cried desperately, but even if they could have heard him over the screaming wind, no one could have done anything.

"They aren't going to stop!" Mae yelled over the commotion.

Trin staggered away from the rail, trying to keep his balance as the ship careened out of control. Grabbing a rope for support he looked at the helm and saw that four men were fighting to control the wheel. "They've gone mad!" Mae shouted beside him.

Some part of Trin's mind wondered how they had kept their wits while everyone else had lost theirs, but a wild-eyed sailor came out of nowhere and lunged at him. Ducking the blow, he came up behind the man and without a second thought elbowed him in the back of the head. Watching him drop like a sack of potatoes gave him an idea.

"I'll knock out the crew. Mae, hook that rowboat. We can figure out how to get him on board as soon as we have the ship under control."

Without waiting for a response he lurched towards two men trading blows nearby. Drawing his sword, he quickly smashed the hilt against each sailor's head in turn. The men crumpled to the deck and he looked for someone else. Hunrin abruptly appeared at his side and Trin turned to defend himself.

"I'll help," Hunrin growled though clenched teeth, and without waiting for an answer he leapt to a group of crazed men.

At least someone kept it together, Trin thought.

Without warning the deck swung to the side as one man got knocked headlong into the group at the helm, causing them all to go down. Spinning freely, the wheel caused the *Sea Dancer* to bounce wildly north.

A lithe figure caught his eye as he grabbed the mast for support. Mae danced down the tilted deck like it was flat ground, knocking people out with quick, sharp blows as she passed. Stopping at a boat hook strapped to the railing, she yanked it free and deftly tied a rope to the end.

Trin was forced to catch himself when the deck jerked again. Looking toward the bridge he saw Erix, with a bleeding lip and swollen eye, back at the helm—his face white with fear and fury. As the ship straightened and curved back west, Trin regained his footing just in time to ward off a blow from a makeshift club.

Training took over and he dodged behind the mast to avoid another strike. Whipping his longsword out and up, he smacked the flat of the blade against the man's leg so hard it buckled under him and he cried out as his knee hit the deck. Reversing the blade, he rotated around the mast and smashed the pommel into the back of his head.

A half-second later he felt something tug on the ship. Staggering he looked back at the burning city, afraid they had been attacked, but then saw that Mae had thrown the boathook like a spear, hooking the rowboat behind them.

Seeing she had things well in hand, Trin turned to help Hunrin— who had just been tackled to the deck by two men. Leaping to his aid, he tried to kick one man off—but the attacker shrugged it off. The two men continued to pummel Hunrin mercilessly for the precious seconds it took for Trin to incapacitate them. Shoving the unconscious sailors

255

off, he reached down and pulled Hun to his feet. His face was bleeding in several places and bruises were beginning to form, but the knife thrower simply shook his head.

"Is that all of them?" he asked, spitting blood through his teeth.

Looking around, Trin saw that most of the fighting had stopped. The first mate and the few others who hadn't lost their heads were finishing up.

Erix suddenly began issuing crisp orders: "Frey, tie up anyone who caused trouble. I don't want them freed until we know they've come to their senses. Mae, get up here and tell me why you threw a spear overboard. Hun, clean yourself up and help Frey tie 'em up. Anyone else who hasn't gone crazy, get this ship moving!"

Without specific instructions, Trin followed Mae to the rear of the ship and listened to her explain about the boat to the captain. Glancing behind them for the first time, he saw the body in the boat and nodded. "Trin, Mae, grab the rope and pull him in. Find out if he is alive. If he is, take care of him and, by Ero's staff, try to find out what happened to Terros!"

The two fighters sprinted to follow his instructions. Mae reached the rope first but she needed Trin's strength to pull the small craft closer. Huffing, he pulled for all he was worth until the little boat bounced in the wake behind the *Sea Dancer*.

"We won't be able to pull it alongside us with just the two of us," Trin exclaimed. "Let's drop a rope off the back and bring him up."

The elf beside him nodded in agreement and they set about rigging a harness to pull the man up. As soon as they were ready, they hurried to the rear of the ship and lowered it. In moments Mae slid down the rope and lightly dropped into the bucking rowboat. Wrapping the makeshift harness around the man's arms, she quickly climbed back to the ship and helped Trin pull the man up. As soon as he could, Trin reached over the railing and grabbed the man's tunic. With a grunt he managed to roll him over and onto the deck.

256

The captain glanced back. "If we don't need that boat, cut it loose. We need every bit of speed we can get."

Mae stood up. "I got it," she said as she turned towards the rope, drawing her short sword.

Trin rolled the man onto his back and bent to examine him. The man was alive, but barely. Two shallow wounds were visible. His head had been smashed against something and was still bleeding a little. The shoulder wound was a little more severe, but still wasn't bleeding enough to account for the man's condition.

Looking closer at the right thigh, Trin realized there was a thick bandage on the man's leg that was soaked with dark blood—old blood. By the coloring it looked like it was a few days or even weeks old. Peeling back the torn leggings, he saw that whatever had cut him in the leg looked to be poisonous—his leg was streaked with dark grey lines where the veins should be.

As the man's head lolled to the side and his black hair was lifted by the breeze, something caught Trin's eye. A long, ugly scar on the left side of his neck ran from ear to shoulder.

This man was a fighter, Trin thought.

"Is he alive?" Mae asked as she kneeled beside him.

"Yes, but he needs some care." He showed her the leg bandage. "Look at the thigh. Something bad did this for sure."

She shook her head and a worried expression flashed across her elven features. "He looks like death already came for him, but he refused to go."

"He's a fighter, this one," Trin replied, but then he looked at the clothes for the first time. They were worn leather, and the brown and green colors suggested something else . . . "Not a fighter," he mused out loud, "more like . . . a woodsman."

She nodded in agreement. "Let's get him below and see what we can do for him."

Trin lifted the man's shoulders while Mae grabbed his legs. As they carried him below and laid him on a bunk, Trin cast a prayer skyward that the woodsman would survive . . . and hopefully have some answers when he awoke.

Chapter 20: A Thief in the Night

Long shadows cast by the setting sun blanketed the small copse of trees where Denithir had chosen to camp. Each of the elven guard went about their duties while an air of quiet tension seeped through them, causing furtive glances into the darkening trees. Taryn looked around at the elves and wondered how much more they could take before someone snapped.

A week had passed since the test of loyalty, and the only good occurrence since then had been the acceptance of Taryn into the group. Ren, more than any of the others, had talked quite a bit with him, sharing tales of his own life and young family. It helped to ease the overshadowing tension, as well as pass the time. Sometime over the last few hours the talk had shifted to their training on Sri Rosen. Upon hearing that Murai had practically raised him, his eyebrows shot up.

"I remember Murai. Is he still as strict as a steel sword?" he asked. "I'd wager that was a rough upbringing."

Confused, Taryn shook his head. "What do you mean? Murai was like family. I don't think I can even recall him giving any sort of punishment."

"Are you certain? I heard tales of him long before even I went to training. Before he went to Sri Rosen he worked for the Home Guard of Azertorn as a Setarian."

"What's a Setarian?" Taryn asked, annoyed with himself for never trying to know his adoptive uncle.

"A Seeker, and it's a special office in the Home Guard. Only two or three are ever allowed the honor at any one time. From what I heard he was one of the best, and they called him Longblade because of his sword. He was renowned for his sense of unyielding justice."

"What does a Seeker do?"

Liri, who was walking beside him, answered before Ren could, "They work directly with the Queen, and carry a rank only surpassed by the Captain of the Home Guard or the General. When something is stolen from the elves a Seeker is sent to return it—and bring justice to the taker."

"Did you know he was one?" Taryn asked, trying to keep the annoyance from his voice. He couldn't believe she didn't tell him.

She flashed an apologetic look. "I thought you knew. Murai hasn't gone by the name for more than a century, and I'm sure few remember it now."

Taryn felt the frustration mounting, but couldn't explain why. Was he angry at Murai for not revealing more . . . or at himself for not asking? He was beginning to wonder if he knew anything at all about his adoptive uncle. Again, he considered the possibility that he had given up a real home for the fleeting prospect of one. The thought chilled his blood, and left him with a shaken resolve.

Liri nudged him and he looked at her. "Huh?" he asked, attempting to pull himself from his swirling thoughts.

"Ren asked if you would like to see an orb of his daughter?" Liri's lips pursed as she flicked her eyebrows towards Ren on the opposite side.

"Er, yeah," Taryn said, doing his best to recover from his momentary lapse in attention, but it proved to be unnecessary. Ren apparently hadn't noticed, and was digging through his pack as he muttered to himself.

"Where is that blasted . . . ah, here it is."

Withdrawing a small memory orb, he handed it to Taryn. Despite the size of the glass ball, the image of a blond, curly haired elf stood clear inside. Grinning wide, the elf child couldn't have been more than a few years old.

"She's adorable," Taryn exclaimed, and Liri echoed his statement.

"Just turned four a couple of months ago, so my wife had this made for me. I think the mage overcharged her, but I can't dispute the results." He took it back from Taryn and gazed at it with pride before returning it to his pack. "Denithir is about to have his own you know," he said, reseating his pack and turning back to them.

"Really?" Liri asked, "He's in his fourth century isn't he?"

Ren nodded towards the captain's back and lowered his voice. "They had trouble conceiving for quite some time. I don't know how they did it, but he found out just a few days ago that his wife was with child. Before he was summoned on this journey they were discussing names. I've never seen him so proud."

—A hurried call hissed from the lead scout, and in an instant they were all on guard. Diving into the brush on either side, the entire command of elves evaporated in a heartbeat, waiting and barely breathing for fear of discovery. A moment later a whisper came back that it was only a deer, but the false alarm had had just as much effect as a real one.

Returning to the trail, they lapsed into silence, their attention focused outward once more. Still trying to calm his pounding heart, Taryn knew the conversation was over. The oppressive feeling of fear had surged back like a blast of hot air, and it would be some time before it would change—if it changed.

The further east they traveled, the more difficult the journey had become.

Traveling through the southern lands had provided a chance for Taryn to see more of the southern kingdom of Talinor, but had proved

261

hazardous on multiple occasions. Heavily armed patrols of humans roamed the country like they were at war—which he had to admit wasn't far off the elves' attitude. Villages they had managed to pass boasted makeshift palisades and watchful guards. They had been forced to circumnavigate several times to avoid encountering humans. There was no doubt that if they were discovered a fight would be unavoidable—and would result in humans flooding towards them within hours.

Now patrols had increased in size and strength, with many of them mounted on long-legged horses. Avoiding them had become almost impossible, and without Kryll they would have been discovered and killed long ago. Dour and exceptionally strong for an elf, he had lived in the Forest of Numenessee his entire life and felt more at home in the woods than in a city. His uncanny instinct for trouble had more than once saved their skins when they would dive into hiding and watch men gallop by not a moment later.

But the constant vigilance was taking a toll on everyone, including Taryn. With hardly a word spoken for the rest of the day, the tension just seemed to build. By nightfall, nerves had been rubbed raw and tempers were on the verge of explosion as they bunked down a day's journey from the Oracle's temple.

Taryn gnawed on his dinner of cold meat and dried fruit, wishing he could identify the source of his agitation. What he wouldn't give for a hot meal, but they couldn't risk a fire being spotted. Deep down he found he was still grateful for the excuse so he wouldn't have to start one. Early in their journey, he'd been tasked with both the fire and the preparation of the evening meal. On both counts, he wasn't asked again.

Laying down, Taryn sighed and looked up at the few stars just beginning to twinkle in the inky sky. He glanced at Liri to tell her something, but on spotting her tense expression he realized she still wasn't in the mood to talk. With a sigh he forced himself to relax and fall asleep.

It felt like only a minute before he felt a silent footstep beside him. In a fraction of a second he palmed his sword and rolled into a defensive crouch before seeing Kryll's arm extended to touch him. Shock emanated from Kryll's darkened face.

"How did you hear me?" he whispered in confusion, "I made no noise."

Taryn shrugged, not wanting to explain his uncle's teachings. The older elf waited for a second, but seeing Taryn wasn't going to answer he whispered again, "Denithir said you can take the second watch if you'd like."

Hiding his surprise, Taryn nodded and worked his way to the position on the perimeter that the elf had indicated. Settling into place with his back to a large oak, Taryn checked his surroundings before pausing to consider Denithir. After the battle in the woods he'd still been standoffish, but not overly so. Taryn had volunteered to take a watch every night but he had been politely turned down. This night marked the first that Denithir had relented and allowed Taryn to be one of the four sentries that were posted each night. A glimmer of hope blossomed as he realized that perhaps the strict elven captain had begun to trust him as an asset, and not just as a guest.

Glancing at the moon, he guessed it to be about midnight. He had to keep watch for three hours, so he shifted to get more comfortable and checked his body to ensure that he was completely in the shadow of a massive oak. Rather than continue to ponder the host of questions that had been bombarding his mind, he focused on the darkness in front of him. Time crawled by as he checked and rechecked his quadrant for any sign of intruders.

—Without warning something caused the hair on the back of his neck to stand up. Casting about for the source, he neither saw nor heard anything—but the feeling persisted. Something or someone was out there. A trickle crawled up his spine as he felt an alien presence nearby.

There! *Behind him?* He'd heard something so quiet he almost doubted it, but in his gut he knew what it was . . . the whisper of skin on leather. Taryn whipped his head around and looked into the camp, scanning for anything out of place. One of the elves sat up and stretched—perhaps that had been it? But it wasn't.

263

Then he saw it. *His* bedroll was occupied. Maybe another elf had taken his spot . . .? His instincts screamed otherwise, but he had to be sure. He scanned the camp to find what didn't sit right. *What was it?* As the elf laid down again, Taryn realized what it was. There were twenty-one prone forms in the clearing. Denithir commanded a score of elves plus Ren. With Taryn and Liri that came to twenty-four . . . and there were four sentries. *Who was the extra person?*

Taryn's eyes snapped to his own blanket beside Liri and he suddenly saw a slight movement of a hand moving in Liri's direction.

Adrenaline kicked in and Taryn charged into the camp, leaping over still forms and arriving at Liri's sleeping form a split second later. Amazingly the person had already gotten to his feet and leapt away, almost as if he'd sensed the sudden approach. *How would that be possible?*

Taryn wasn't about to let him go. With the speed of thought Taryn raced across the clearing to overtake the intruder at the edge of the woods. Reaching out to him he snatched his hand back as a dagger flashed out and almost sliced into his palm. Without stopping he lunged and wrapped both arms around the figure's chest, pinning his arms. The intruder struggled and tried to bring his dagger up to cut the entrapping arms, but Taryn twisted his body in midair and tried to slam him into the ground.

Somehow the intruder got his feet under him and darted into the shadows with Taryn right behind him. Realizing his opponent had training in combat, Taryn sped after him more cautiously and began to overtake him again.

Whirling, the intruder flung an arm up, sending something spinning towards him. Instinct kicked in and Taryn reached out his hand without slowing down to snatch the throwing knife right out of the air. Flinging it straight back at its thrower, he heard a low chuckle from the fleeing form as he also caught it.

Out of nowhere an arrow zipped past Taryn and caught the thick cloak on the intruder's shoulder, pulling him up short as it pinned him to a tree. Taryn bounded straight forward, knowing what was coming.

Only Liri had the skill to shoot into darkness and hit a speeding target. He wasn't disappointed. Two more arrows sped past Taryn's head to embed themselves, further fastening the intruder to the tree—until he shrugged out of his cloak and bolted.

But Taryn had caught up.

Without preamble he launched his clenched fist into the side of the man's head, expecting it to end there, but he managed to roll with the blow so it didn't knock him out. Dazed, the man struggled to keep moving.

Despite himself, Taryn was impressed by the person's sheer tenacity as he bounded after him. The man had dodged behind trees and begun to run in a zigzag to avoid more arrows. He certainly would have escaped then—except Taryn was faster.

Instead of chasing him directly, Taryn leapt to the side and raced parallel to his path. Seconds later the intruder passed Taryn and dodged in front of him. Coming around a tree, the man ran straight into Taryn's outstretched arm, and the force caused him to do a back flip before landing flat on his stomach with a low "*Ooof.*"

Not wanting to give him another opportunity, Taryn used the knife edge of his hand to knock the man out. Even then he'd already begun to roll over and get to his feet.

Taryn reached down and lifted the unconscious man to his shoulder. Checking to make sure he was truly out, he carried him back to the camp where Liri had roused everyone to full alert. When he entered the clearing he laid the man down and motioned for someone to tie him up before he could come to his senses.

Denithir darted to his side. "*By Skorn,* what was that all about?" he hissed.

Taryn took a moment to catch his breath as he shook his head. "I have no idea. I spotted him in the camp and ran him down." He glanced at the elf tying him. "Watch him, though, he's wily and a good fighter."

A light touch on his elbow drew his attention to the opposite side. Liri looked up at him, her eyes full of gratitude. "Thank you so much, Taryn. He'd taken my mother's pendant!"

She bent and rifled through the man's clothes until she found the thin gold chain and reverently returned it to her neck. "I hope it hurt when he took you down," she said to the still form, her tone uncharacteristically venomous.

Questions bubbled around Taryn as more elves gathered around the thief, preventing Taryn from saying anything to Liri.

"Who is he?"

"What was he doing here?"

"How did he get into camp?"

"He didn't get past me!" Three different elves said in unison.

Denithir cut through the chatter with a growl, "He got past somebody." He glared at his soldiers for a moment. "Get back to your posts or back to sleep, we will figure this out in the morning. Kryll, put two on our guest. I don't want him leaving us before we can have some answers."

Taryn slipped to Liri's side and whispered, "Thanks for the support earlier. It's always nice to know that you're watching my back."

She smiled and stifled a yawn. "You know I'll always be right behind you."

Unable to resist he added, "Thanks for missing me, too. A couple of those arrows came pretty close, you know."

Liri furrowed her brow and pursed her lips, but that only made her look cute. "Not close enough," she said in exasperation. Then she lightly punched him in the shoulder and laid down.

Taryn chuckled and returned to his sentry position. Their playful banter really had been their way of ensuring that each was all right. But their light conversation hadn't been able to dispel the tension that still blanketed the night like a fog. As he settled into his previous position behind the oak tree, he asked himself the same questions the elves had, and added a few of his own. Who would enter a heavily armed group of vigilant elves to steal something? And what was more, who had the *ability*? To Taryn, the latter question would be far more important.

*****

A light touch woke Taryn from a dream-filled sleep. Recognizing the touch made him smile before he opened his eyes. "Do I have to get up, Liri?"

A small fist slugged him in the shoulder; then its owner chuckled. Sighing, Taryn opened his eyes to the dim, early morning light. Stretching and yawning, he sat up and rubbed his eyes. His watch had ended around four in the morning, so he'd only been asleep for a couple of hours.

Automatically his eyes sought out their prisoner and found him at the edge of the camp, bound and gagged.

"Why is he gagged?" he asked Kryll.

The elven soldier shrugged. "They said he wouldn't shut up. I think he got on their nerves."

Taryn smirked at his response and caught Liri's eye, knowing she wanted some answers as well. She caught his raised eyebrow and nodded towards the food that had been laid out. *Food first, then answers*, he understood her unspoken suggestion, so they quickly ate a breakfast of dried fruit and nuts before approaching the prisoner. The two elven guards nodded in his direction, with newfound respect in their eyes.

Crouching in front of the man, he took a moment and looked him over. For a human he'd been incredibly agile the night before, and his instincts and speed had been more like an elf than a human—but his features held no trace of elven blood. A strong, firm jaw, handsome face, and the dark blue eyes of the human race looked back at Taryn without fear. Short black hair, at the same time trimmed and a little wild, hung freely without cap or armored helm.

Taryn unbound the gag, and he immediately spat out the cloth. "What's with all the hostility?" he said and then pretended to glower at Liri. "I thought the elves were supposed to be peaceful?"

Taryn couldn't help but smile at the true statement. "You could say that the times have called for more . . . caution than normal."

Liri leaned towards him, her expression intense. "Why did you steal my necklace?"

He shrugged even though his hands were tied behind his back. "It was pretty; I thought it would fetch a price."

Surprised by his frank honesty, Taryn exclaimed, "You're a thief."

"Guilty as charged," the man said with a wide grin. "The name's Jack Myst, one of the best thieves you'll ever meet." He winked and smiled roguishly at Liri.

Something about the man's demeanor suggested that the ladies usually liked him, and for half a second Taryn thought Liri would fall for him as well. She didn't disappoint him, however.

"Thieving scum," she scowled. "I ought to gut you right here." A blade had appeared out of nowhere in her hand.

"Easy," Taryn said, although he was secretly pleased that she hadn't been attracted to the thief.

"Aren't you a feisty one," Jack said, chuckling without the slightest bit of fear.

She almost lunged at him, but something held her in check, and she managed to compose herself quickly. "You aren't worth it."

With that she stood and strode off, ignoring his parting comment.

"Yes I am." He half sang the words in amusement.

Taryn spoke softly. "How did you get into the camp?"

For the first time Jack became serious, eyeing Taryn shrewdly. "You're the one that caught me, aren't you?" The thief's tone implied he didn't get caught very often.

Taryn nodded in response.

After a moment where the two looked each other over, the man said, "It isn't hard to slip past sentries. Their eyes are always on the ground, and never in the trees."

Taryn grinned. Jack had answered honestly, again to his surprise, so he chose to answer honestly as well.

"Too true; it's probably what I would have done."

The open humor returned to Jack's face as easily as it had gone. "It takes a fox to catch a fox." Then he asked Taryn a question: "How did you know I was here?"

"I heard you and then saw there was an extra body in the camp," Taryn said.

"You *heard* me?" he exclaimed in genuine astonishment. "I'm truly impressed, my friend."

Suddenly the elven captain cut into their conversation, his low growl carrying across the camp to everyone's ears. "We march in five minutes. Ren, bring our guest—and watch him carefully. Kryll, take the lead, let us know if there is any danger. We should reach the Oracle by nightfall, so be on your guard. I don't want this mission to fail on the last day."

"Their respect for their captain is the only thing controlling their fear," Jack said in an undertone that only reached Taryn's ears.

Taryn looked back at him, intrigued by his statement. Meeting his gaze he matched his tone, "I know." He sighed and added, "I wish I knew the source of the fear."

Jack smiled without humor, "So do I, mate, it would make it easier to steal from elves."

The complete seriousness in his tone made Taryn snort loudly. Several of the elves nearby looked at him, but he shook his head.

"I guess you are coming with us friend, so we might be able to find out together."

"You know I could escape at any moment."

"I have no doubt, but I believe you are just as curious about this disease of terror as I am. You won't escape until you get some answers—now that you know who we are and what our quest is."

The thief gave him a knowing smile before Ren appeared at his side.

"On your feet, human, and watch yourself. I will end your life before you make a move to escape."

Jack nodded in mock seriousness. "I will obey," he said, his voice laced with sarcasm.

Taryn nodded at Ren, trying not to grin at Jack's comment, before turning to grab his bedroll and take his place within the elven formation. He found himself pondering the unusual exchange. It was evident that the man had enormous ability and skill, both in fighting and stealth. After their conversation, Taryn oddly felt like he'd just been in a sparring match, with both of them testing their opponent.

However, that wasn't the strangest thing about their conversation. The strangest thing was that in Jack Myst the thief, he'd found a kindred spirit . . . and probably a friend. The thought unsettled him more than a little, but he knew it to be true.

There was also something about the fight the previous night that kept nagging him, refusing to go away. When he finally realized it, he found it didn't surprise him. The thief had thrown a knife at him, but it had been aimed low rather than to kill. The implication was clear, and at the same time in line with the sense he got from Jack.

As he mulled the thought over throughout the day, he finally had to admit to himself that after talking to him, he knew that Jack would protect the innocent—and probably without an invitation. A thief he may be, but he had *some* code of honor that he lived by, and Taryn wondered where it had come from.

And where stealing had become part of it.

Chapter 21: The Oracle

Reaching shadows deepened the gloom as the sun sank below the horizon. Dismal and dank, the forest of Orláknia contrasted sharply with the bright trees of the elven homeland. In place of flowers and vines, moss and decaying wood lent a darkness that could not be attributed solely to the heavy canopy. Instead of shrubs or other green undergrowth, mushrooms or fungus spread across stones and the spotted boles of trees.

"Orláknia began to decay after the elves migrated west," Liri whispered sadly beside Taryn.

Taryn didn't know how to respond. They had entered the forest only an hour ago, but it seemed like much longer. Everything about the dying wilderness gave the impression of a once majestic and enlightened place that had been drained of all life. The very air felt like all light had been taken out of it, like sunlight was no longer permitted to enter.

"Why would the elves' migration affect the woods?" Taryn asked Liri softly, somehow feeling like speaking normally would be unfitting in this forsaken place.

"My mother believes that the forest lived too long with elven magic to sustain it, and without it . . ." She swept her hand at the surrounding shadows.

Silence echoed around them until the sun finally slipped out of sight, but there was little discernible change in their environment except for a slight deepening of the shadows. However slight the change in light level, each elf felt the sun's absence.

Unseen tension blanketed the elven patrol as they drifted through the trees. Every noise, no matter how small, caused them to jump and reach for their weapons. Taryn unconsciously moved in front of Liri in a protective pose, and for once she didn't protest.

After an hour of traveling with the utmost caution, Denithir held up a hand in a fist and everyone stopped.

"We're here," he growled. "Stay sharp."

Working his way forward, the group passed an imperceptible line marked by a visible lightening in the trees around them. Most of the elven soldiers visibly relaxed as the decay gave way to life. Blooming flowers and other manicured vegetation stretched away from them, illuminated by soft moonlight filtering through pruned trees. Paths of crushed stone wound their way through the garden and off into the darkness.

Surprised by the visibility, Taryn looked skyward. The sliver of a moon appeared much brighter than it should have, almost as bright as a full moon. Did the elves have the power to brighten the moon?

Kryll caught his puzzled glance skyward and said, "It's an illusion. The light is only magnified, the moon isn't actually enchanted."

"It's still stunning."

Kryll grinned with unmistakable pride in his race, and then turned and followed the rest of the patrol through the paths.

Liri brushed Taryn's arm and murmured, "Can you feel it? The fear is less here. Perhaps the Oracle can affect it somehow?" She seemed to be musing more to herself, so he simply nodded and stepped into the beautiful garden.

Rose-colored gravel crunched underfoot and he breathed deeply of the clean night air, enjoying the feeling of temporary relief from the rest of Orláknia. It left him feeling odd. At the same moment, he could sense both peace and fear fighting for dominance within him.

An instant later the fear returned in full.

A shout rang out in front of him—a shout of fear and warning that dispelled any semblance of tranquility. The whole group bounded forward, rushing through the gardens in the direction of the call. Within seconds a giant structure of living trees woven together came into view.

The few that had arrived ahead of Taryn stood at a pair of open doors with weapons drawn, whirling towards him as he exploded into view. Recognizing him, one elf simply turned and pointed downward. Then Taryn saw it and the fear tightened in his chest. Several bloodied bodies lay strewn about in the open doorway. All were armored elves—guards of the Oracle with fresh wounds clearly visible, only minutes old.

One by one the rest of the elves materialized into view, halting sharply when they saw the dead sentries. Not a second later Denithir arrived and took command.

"Ren, advance with your five and search the first floor. Kryll, take your five and check the cellars. Don't be stupid. You find resistance, you call for help. The rest of you are with me, we need to check the upper levels."

Thin forms sprang to obey orders as Taryn leapt to follow Denithir into the structure. Smokeless lanterns revealed a long hallway stretching away from them. Several more dead elves could be seen in various poses, bearing witness to their last moments of valor. Like ghosts in the night Ren and his command peeled away to search around them. Moments later Kryll and his group disappeared down the stairs to the right.

Denithir led the remainder of their group up the woven branches that formed the staircase to their left. Forced to leap over even more dead, they raced forward, listening for any sign of trouble. Sadness snapped through Taryn as he passed the still forms of several women and children among the dead soldiers, whose postures showed their last, fruitless efforts had been to protect those weaker then themselves.

There! A sudden ring echoed from above. A split second later it repeated, and this time Taryn and his companions heard the unmistakable sound of clashing blades. Without a sound, the entire group sprinted upward, bounding over the wreckage and dead forms that had borne the brunt of the merciless attack.

One part of Taryn's mind wondered why he didn't see any dead intruders. Surely they had defeated some of them? He couldn't imagine any race killing so many well-trained elven sentries without suffering severe casualties. But he didn't have time to stop and ponder the mystery. Turning up the last flight of woven stairs, he took them in a single leap and exploded through the opening at the top. Before his mind fully registered what was in front of him he landed in a crouch with both weapons drawn.

A moment later Denithir skidded to a stop next to him, as did the rest of the elite elven patrol. Thirteen fighters armed to the teeth took in the bloody carnage before them and finally got a look at the single intruder . . . who could only be described as the living specter of Death.

The dark-cloaked figure spun to face them the moment Taryn had burst into the room. Eyes like burning red coals looked out of a black hooded cloak. Hands of pure white bone reached out of dark sleeves and held a black scythe that pulsed with red veins of light—its blade still dripping from its latest victim. It was a testament to the supreme courage of every elf around him that not a single one ran at the very sight.

Steel suddenly flashed behind Death but he spun the scythe behind his back and blocked the strike in an almost lazy effort. In that moment Taryn's mind went into battle mode and registered several things at once while the world slowed to a crawl: slain warriors around him would cause the footing to be unsure, he would have to be careful not to trip;

behind Death a single defender remained standing and had been the one to try to attack Death when his back was turned; behind that soldier a raised dais contained a single occupant, a very, very old blind elf with white hair—the Oracle.

The half second ended and time sped up as Taryn leapt forward, a single thought in mind. Nothing was going to stop him from discovering who he was.

Denithir shouted in vain behind him, "Stop fool, we fight together!"

Death glided towards Taryn, whirling the Scythe so fast it became a blur of red, black and deadly steel—but Taryn was just as fast. Mazer and Ianna struck and blocked, parried and cut—as quick as Death's weapon and just as deadly. Taryn's gaze locked on the evil figure before him as he leapt over a low sweep and whipped his own weapon out like a snake strike, which was blocked by the equally fast scythe. The two danced and spun in a ring of blades and dark cloaks. Razor sharp edges came inches from contact on both sides with the two straining for an advantage where none was given.

The sheer speed of the battle prevented any other elf from joining. Each skilled elven warrior instinctively understood that they were overmatched, and would not survive on their own. Only Taryn had the ability to endure even a few seconds. Denithir, Liri, and the rest stood rooted in place, unable to assist and awed by the supreme battle before them.

Light footfalls suddenly announced the arrival of the rest of the elves and the increased number finally loosened them from their hold.

"Back him against a wall Taryn, I have an idea!" Denithir shouted and then turned to the score of elves around him. "Elves of Azertorn, draw your bows!"

Longbows and arrows appeared—but Death was quicker. Seeming to understand the tactic, he leapt away from Taryn, and before Taryn could charge him down he did the unthinkable. Spinning like lighting he brushed past the last elven warrior, knocking aside his swinging katsana as he went, and struck the Oracle. In one clean sweep the scythe blade cut through both the wooden dais and the old elf's body.

Both crumbled to the floor . . . lifeless.

Before the stunned elves could respond, Death whirled to face Taryn once more, and then drifted backwards until he faded into the shadows. Taryn charged after him and furiously swept the darkness with his swords, but to no avail. Somehow, he was gone. They had failed, and there would be no answers. Everyone in the room watched his desperate efforts to find Death, shocked into immobility. Some of them had bows half drawn or arrows still in hand, and for one terrible bleak moment, all hope seemed lost.

The fury suddenly drained out of Taryn and he sank to the floor, overcome with his emotions. Liri took a step towards him but surprisingly the last remaining oracle guard got to him first. He leaned over and whispered something into Taryn's ear.

In the blink of an eye Taryn was on his feet, completely serious. "We must leave. Now."

The guard nodded in affirmation. "There is a secret way we can go; follow me." Without waiting for an answer, he brushed through the shocked elves and descended the stairs. Taryn and Liri followed but everyone else hesitated, glancing towards Denithir. After a moment's consideration, he gave a sharp nod before turning to follow them, and the rest of his command quickly fell into line behind him.

The guard hurried down the flights of stairs and when they arrived at the ground floor he continued straight to the cellars. Bypassing multiple rooms of foodstuffs and barrels, he stopped at a bank of crates set into the wall. Reaching behind one of them the Oracle guard fumbled for something until there was a soft click and several crates swung out from the wall. The false wall led to a tunnel that stretched away into darkness, but the guard made a movement with his hand and light blossomed in several wall brackets. He slipped into the tunnel and the rest of the group were quick to follow. Soft footfalls and the creak of weapons enveloped them in near silence as they hurried down the long corridor.

After several minutes the group came to a set of stairs which ascended steeply to a hidden exit in a dead tree. Swinging it open, the guard and Taryn burst into the oppressive darkness of Orláknia and turned, heading due north.

Within seconds they came to the edge of a swamp, but the guard stepped into the murky water without stopping. Looking back he whispered, "Follow my steps *exactly*. If you step to either side your life is the price."

Taryn fell into step behind him and found there to be a firm invisible path a few inches below the water line. He heard several muttered curses behind him followed by a quiet bark from Denithir to keep silent. No elf would ever be happy in a swamp, that was certain, but Taryn knew there was no other way. What the guard had whispered had changed everything, but there was no time to explain, and despite the burning eyes on his back he kept walking.

The hidden path wound through the bog, repeatedly making switchbacks before continuing north, towards the Blue Lake. Each treacherous step told Taryn that this was not a good place to be. Every few minutes he could hear movement in the thick waters, and he could tell by the sound it was something big—or *several* things.

After an hour of travel they came to a small island in the swamp and the guard finally stopped. Striding forward, he slipped through twisted trees until he came to the center of the island. In place of the scrub trees and hanging moss, there were four great oak trees reaching towards the sky, creating a protective canopy overhead. The trees were so out of place in the foggy marsh that it was obvious they had been grown for a purpose . . . a refuge.

Stepping under the trees, the guard turned and waited until everyone had arrived. Facing the group he reached up and stripped the helm from his head.

Long golden hair fell around the young *female* elf's angular face. Amid the gasps and shocked expressions, she proclaimed fiercely, "I am the Oracle."

Taryn was just as stunned as everyone else; the only thing the guard had whispered was, "That was not the Oracle. I will take you to her."

Before anyone could say a word, she whirled towards Taryn and frowned in disapproval. "It's about time you got here, brother."

Chapter 22: Heritage

The Oracle smirked at Taryn's expression of shock. "Well . . . half brother would be more accurate."

His mind whirled to process the new information while a host of questions tried to find a route to his lips. *Who are . . .? Where did . . .? What do you . . .?* Unfortunately the only word that came out was, "How?!"

She laughed and said, "We have the same mother, of course."

"Who were they? And what is your name? What were their names? How do you know this? Why did they take me to Sri Rosen?" Taryn blurted out most of his big questions before he could stop himself. Then he caught a look at Denithir's expression and flushed at his behavior.

"Hold on," she said, putting her hand up to forestall his questions. "My name is Siarra, but the rest of your questions will be a bit harder to answer, so give me a moment." She turned towards the group of elven warriors and asked, "May I ask your captain's name?"

Denithir stepped forward. "Denithir Lorosian, Arch Captain of the First Legion," he responded with a short, formal bow.

Her tone turned firm and authoritative. "We must leave immediately. He won't take long to realize that the old elf he killed was just an illusion. I'm afraid we are still in danger—even here."

"He could find us in the swamp?" Denithir asked, surprised.

"I believe he could find someone anywhere—and he will never give up," she responded in the same matter-of-fact tone, as if a proficient killer hunting her didn't bother her at all. "If we stay here, he will find us in a few hours and then strike from the shadows. His skill—" She nodded towards Taryn. "—is the only reason he left before. This time he will pick us off more carefully—if he can find us. We must flee."

"Where can we go, then?" Denithir asked.

"We can take a trail west from here until we leave the swamp. It's not far. Then we must hasten to Azertorn. Perhaps we may find refuge that far west."

Denithir nodded and began issuing crisp orders, but abruptly stopped and looked around. "Where's the thief?" he demanded.

Taryn had forgotten all about Jack Myst when they'd rushed into the Oracle's home. Casting his eyes about, he searched for him in vain. One of the elves stepped forward, his eyes on the ground. "He disappeared somewhere in the Oracle's gardens. When the warning was given, I took my eyes off him for a moment, and when I looked back he was gone."

"Was he *securely* bound?" Denithir demanded.

The elf nodded in response and answered in a small voice, "I don't know how he did it, Captain. I tied the knots myself, and I have never seen them bested."

Taryn chuckled, drawing everyone's eyes to him. "Don't worry about Jack. I believe he could have escaped at any time. He only stuck around because he was curious about us." Taryn watched as Denithir scowled, and then nodded and continued with his instructions. Taryn sighed in relief. He desperately wanted to talk to Siarra and knew it wouldn't happen until they were on the move.

Within moments the group organized itself under their captain's firm leadership and headed back across the swamp with Siarra as their guide. Taryn and Liri stayed close behind her as they all attempted to follow in her footsteps. Every so often someone would slip off the hidden path, but there was always one quick to grab them before they could sink into the muck.

Taryn couldn't settle his mind, and he kept twitching in an effort to keep his pace even. It felt like a fever had taken hold of his head as his mind buzzed with the enlightening information that Siarra, his . . . sister—he struggled to wrap his mind around the new concept—had given him. Unfortunately, the tantalizing bits of information presented far more questions than answers. For one thing, who was his father and why did they have different fathers? The brief moments when he'd gotten a chance to look at her had not been enough to determine much about her, especially in the darkness. How much older was she? How did she know about him?

Liri brushed against him in a not so subtle manner, and her soft touch went a long way towards helping him be patient, but it was maddening to have the truth literally in front of him, and still have to wait.

Luckily, it only took thirty minutes to reach the swamp's edge. The moment they were on dry ground among the trees of Orláknia, Taryn moved to walk beside Siarra—who also fell back beside him.

Siarra spoke first. "Do you mind if I start at the beginning? I promise when I am done you can ask any questions I have not answered." She glanced sideways at him to watch his response.

Taryn nodded readily, eager to hear anything she had to share.

"Our mother's name was Ianna"—Taryn sighed in relief when she said her name—"and she was the previous Oracle. I guess the story begins about fifty years ago, before I was born. I am not sure if you are aware, but the Oracle's husband is chosen by the elven guild of magic. It is always an elf with tremendous magical power that is chosen and it is a great honor. My father was chosen from among the guild and sent to Orláknia to be joined to our mother. She soon conceived and, as is customary, had a girl. Of course, I was to be the next Oracle."

For some reason Taryn could sense irritation as she proclaimed her birthright. Was it something she did not want?

284

She sighed. "Unfortunately, my father was not a very good elf, despite his magical ability. He frequently . . . visited . . . with other elf maids and traveled whenever he had an excuse. He was careful to keep his exploits secret, but our mother knew. If nothing had changed, I believe our mother would still be alive today, but without hope of life, or love, to brighten her existence.

"Around this time a certain man came to see her. He was a troubled individual and came seeking guidance, as men are prone to do with their brief lives. Despite his problems, strength and virtue were two of his greatest qualities. His name was Mazer."

Taryn let out the breath he realized he'd been holding but made no sound, not wanting her to stop.

"Our mother took a liking to this man and the man felt something in turn, but it is expressly forbidden for an Oracle to deviate from her given path. Despite this, Mazer visited often, always with questions and issues for her to help him solve. I was still young at this time, barely twenty, but I could see she was falling in love with him. I encouraged her to see him more." Her voice softened. "I wanted her to be happy."

"Who was my father and why was he troubled?" Taryn interrupted.

She frowned at his interruption. "I was getting to that. Have some patience, little brother." Shaking her head, she smiled to take the sting from her words. "First I have to describe what your father looked like. He was enormously strong but short for a human, and he had red hair." She looked at him with an amused expression. "Much like yours, anyway. The truth is he was half dwarf and half human."

Taryn heard a gasp and then a low tinkling laugh from behind him as Liri overheard his ancestry. She smothered it quickly and went quiet, but he knew she would have things to say about it later.

Siarra looked at him again with a soft expression. "I believe you have a great deal of him in you, at least in looks, but I am curious if you have his dwarven attributes of endurance and strength."

Before Taryn could respond, Liri caught up to them and proclaimed in a serious tone, "He is unmatched in either category, against human, elf, or dwarf."

"Really?" Siarra's eyes sparkled with interest. "Interesting . . . very interesting . . ." She trailed off with a faraway look.

Jumping to avoid the conversation shifting to another topic, he asked, "So how exactly did my father and our mother end up together? I mean, I thought you said it was forbidden, and why isn't it allowed?"

She shook her head to clear her thoughts and returned to her story. "It is not allowed because if an Oracle becomes pregnant a second time, she loses the ability to see energy—and therefore cannot use magic anymore. She stops being the Oracle."

"Did she know this before she got pregnant with me?" Taryn asked, shocked that his mother would give up her abilities to have another child.

"Yes, but let me back up." She pursued her lips and continued where she'd left off. "It didn't take long before our mother tired of my father's behavior and decided to leave with Mazer. One night she was there, and the next . . . she was gone. You cannot imagine the uproar her disappearance caused amongst the elves. Never before has an Oracle run away. Search parties were sent out, and not just from the elves. Many people wanted to have her back. Once every month or so someone caught up to them, but it didn't matter. She was too powerful and he was too strong a fighter. No one could force them to return." A ghost of a smile spread across her features as she recalled the story. Then her face grew somber again.

"One night she secretly returned to visit me. She told me they had decided to have a baby and that she wanted me to know that it didn't diminish how much she loved me. I was furious with her but at the same time glad she was doing something that would finally bring her joy. That was the last time I saw her."

No one spoke for several minutes as they walked through the dark forest, both thinking about long past events.

Taryn broke the silence. "So how did you know it was me?"

"The ability to *see* and feel energy is enhanced with individuals that I know well, or that I am related to. I have felt your presence for a few weeks now." She glanced at him with a raised eyebrow. "Have you been taught about magic and the Oracle?"

"Briefly," he admitted, "I know that magic comes from existing energy within a substance, and that the user has the ability to *see* that energy and manipulate it. I also know that each race has different kinds of magic that they predominantly use. Light, plant, and water for elves, fire and stone for dwarves, animal and earth for humans, and so forth. The Oracle"— he nodded towards her—"can see all types of energy and can use all types of magic."

She smiled in approval. "Very good, but allow me to fill in some holes in your education." She furrowed her brow and her tone took on a lecturing ring. "Many individuals can see energy but cannot manipulate it. Fire is a perfect example. Humans can see the flame but cannot manipulate it. A dwarven cleric will see the flame and can cause it to do his bidding, such as stoke it or weaken it, without adding or removing fuel. The better the magician and the more training they've had, the more they can do. Essentially, they draw upon heat in the surrounding environment to increase the flame."

She lifted an arm and wrapped her fingers into a fist, then opened her fingers like a flower and a small flame burst into life within her cupped hand. "More advanced users can *create* fire from heat, adding only a spark of energy. This particular flame comes from the heat within the surrounding air and my own body."

She let him watch the speck of light for a moment before extinguishing it. "Some types of magic are easier than others. Anything fluid, such as light, fire, water, or air, is easier to manipulate. Stone or earth, on the other hand, take a great deal more training because the energy within them is contained in their form and structure. If a dwarf can move even a small amount of stone, he is a great mage."

She reached out with her hand facing palm down. In a sweeping gesture she flipped her palm upward, bringing a piece of earth out of the ground in front of her. It lifted in a column about the thickness of his arm but continued to move in front of her, sliding along the ground.

"Notice that this pillar of earth still touches the ground. If I try to take it off the ground," she lifted her hand higher and the column lifted off the ground, disintegrating into dust in an instant, "it can't hold its form."

Two questions occurred to him. "Why didn't you fight Death with magic? And when did you train with a sword?"

She was already nodding as he asked the questions but paused to step over a large root in the trail before answering, "A young oracle has power and ability, but does not reach her full potential until she comes of age, turning fifty years old. At that time, on her birthday, she is unbound and the full extent of her abilities return." She blinked and shook her head, understanding flashing across her features. "That is why he attacked today."

"What?" Taryn asked, not following her meaning.

"My birthday is in two days. Whoever sent the assassin sent him now before I came of age because I wouldn't be powerful enough to defeat him with magic. He will do everything he can to destroy me before that moment."

Confused, Taryn asked, "But doesn't he think the Oracle was your illusion of the older woman on the throne?"

"Then, yes. Now . . . I'm not sure. As soon as Death entered our chamber he went after the false oracle rather than me. I doubt he was instructed any further than to *kill the Oracle,* and an old blind elf is what most people think of as an oracle. He will certainly return to confirm a kill of this importance and when he does . . ."

She shook her head at the impending result and added. "He would have eventually found me and destroyed me if you hadn't arrived and fought so well." She inclined her head towards him, "Thank you for that by the way."

Taryn nodded, "Anytime." Then his expression turned serious. "But something tells me you will return the favor before this is done."

She chuckled without humor. "Unfortunately that is probably true—unless he catches us before I come of age. That is why we are running. I will not be strong enough to defeat him until after my unbinding."

"There might be another way . . .," Taryn mused aloud. He glanced back at Liri and she stepped forward to join them. As soon as she was close enough to hear, he said, "When I fought him, I learned a few things."

Siarra looked intensely curious, and Liri's expression matched hers.

"He has just about my skill on speed, strength, or technique with a weapon, and if those were the only factors I honestly don't know who would emerge victorious . . . but I believe my father's katsana is more powerful than his weapon . . ."

"Why?" Liri asked beside him.

He shrugged, "Early on I tried to smash my blade through the shaft of his scythe, but he managed to deflect it off at an angle. It still took a chunk with it though. I also think Death knew he couldn't take a straight blow because he didn't give me another opportunity to strike his weapon straight on."

Liri nodded, confident in Taryn's skill, but Siarra looked doubtful.

"If he knows he has a weakness, he won't be likely to expose it for any reason, unless you think you could force him to open himself up . . .?" she said, then seeing his unsure expression she shook her head. "No, I think we must keep that as a last resort."

A sudden shout came from behind them and all three of them turned to see that Denithir had stopped everyone. They were quick to join him and caught the end of his quietly furious question.

"—want to know who saw Kryll last? And who else is missing?"

289

No one responded, but quite a few cast furtive looks into the dank forest.

Taryn did a quick head count and was surprised to see only sixteen people huddled together. He counted again to be sure, but got the same result. Where were the other eight?

Ren spoke up, "Kiest is also missing."

Another elf added, "Glyn and Tari are gone, too."

"By Skorn, what happened to them?" Denithir hissed.

Siarra answered his question in a grim tone, "Death has found us . . . and he's been picking us off one by one."

Fear gripped each member of the group as realization finally dawned. The assassin had hunted them, a highly alert and battle-ready elven patrol, and still managed to kill *nine* of their group without a single person noticing. When had they been taken? Somewhere in the forest? The swamp?

Taryn's spine tingled as he covertly checked the darkness around them, knowing the killer was nearby and probably watching them for another opportunity to strike. He knew exactly what Death would be doing—stalking them and silently taking out anybody that wasn't being watched, whittling them down to nothing.

Denithir swore under his breath and barked, "Partner up, and don't leave your partner for anything. Taryn and Liri, protect the Oracle. We *cannot* afford to lose her."

The surviving elves began marching again, but their confidence was shaken. A ruthless and deadly killer followed them, and they knew they were no match for him. Each elf huddled next to his partner as if proximity to another person would ward off Death's strike, but their efforts proved to be in vain.

Six more elves disappeared before dawn.

Chapter 23: The Ravine

Beleaguered and exhausted, the ten survivors finally stopped at the edge of a deep ravine a mile outside of Orláknia. Each member of the group had been awake for over eighteen hours, and the constant strain and lack of rest was beginning to take a toll on everyone except Taryn.

"Lucky dwarven dog," Liri grumbled, sitting down in a huff and leaning against a tree in the small stand where they had taken shelter around noon.

He shrugged at her. "It's not my fault I can go longer than you." He'd said it with an attempt at humor despite their grim situation, and Liri smiled weakly in acknowledgement.

Denithir appeared beside him and asked, "Taryn, can you take watch for the afternoon while everyone gets some sleep? I don't think our assassin will attack during daylight, and not here where we could see him coming, but still . . ."

Taryn looked at the elven captain. Denithir's face was drawn and bathed in a sheen of sweat, but his mouth was set in a firm line to hold his emotions in check. It was a good thing he was managing to hide his despair, or his soldiers would have lost all semblance of courage. It was evident, however, that he keenly felt the death of each member of his command.

He wasn't the only one.

Over the last week Taryn had gotten to know quite of few of them, Kryll in particular. Now most of them were gone, and their bodies lay somewhere behind them. It made him angry to think of leaving them like that, but Denithir had made the tough decision to keep moving. Now as he looked at the elven captain and Ren behind him, he realized they could both be dead by nightfall, leaving their children fatherless.

It was a life he knew far too well.

Suddenly Taryn realized he hadn't answered Denithir's request. "No problem captain," he said with a solemn nod, knowing that he'd been asked because he was the only one capable of remaining alert. Elves were not known for their endurance.

Denithir nodded tiredly and turned away. Watching him go, Taryn again felt the grizzled warrior's pain. Three quarters of his hand-picked and elite fighters had been killed in a single night by an invisible and far superior hunter, one by one disappearing without a trace. A capable and determined warrior such as Denithir had faced countless desperate fights and still emerged victorious, but this was different. His soldiers were being slaughtered like cattle . . . and he was helpless to save them.

Taryn swallowed the knot in his throat and turned to Liri to ask her a question, but she was already asleep. Her blonde hair hung lightly around her pixie face, which appeared troubled even now. Bending down and gently grasping her shoulders, he moved her off the tree and onto the blanket she'd laid out. Except for a slight twitch she stayed asleep when he gingerly slid his own bedroll under her head for a pillow, brushing her neck in the process. For the first time, she smiled and seemed to be at peace.

Self-conscious at the intimate posture, he rose and scanned the camp. Not a single elf remained awake. Strewn all over the small clearing, their forms appeared as if they had collapsed where they stood, which some of them had.

He sighed and silently circled the perimeter, checking every approach. Their camp sat nestled in a small grouping of oak and fir right next to the Blue Lake with a deep ravine blocking their path west. To the north, the trees grew right to a high cliff that dropped to the lake, sunlight sparkling off its waters as it stretched away into the distance. West of them the ravine had been gouged out by a small but fast-moving river that flowed north. As he passed that side, he glanced down into the deep chasm and could see crashing water racing over large boulders. Looking at the other side, he gauged the distance and wondered if he could make the jump, but it seemed to be outside even his ability. Turning away, he continued his route, not spending much time on the north or west approaches to their hiding place. Both would be difficult to scale and very defensible. South and east were a different story.

The east approach held scattered trees as the ground slowly sloped downward towards the dark forest of Orláknia a few miles away. South, the ground climbed into large hills that he knew contained several human settlements they had passed on their journey to the Oracle's home.

Taryn found a comfortable spot on the southeastern corner of the trees and settled in to wait for dusk, taking the time to plan. Unfortunately the stop could not be avoided, even though he would have preferred to descend the cliff and cross the river during the day. The elves needed to rest, and would not have had the strength to scale a cliff in their current condition. As much as he disliked the proposition, they would have to make the attempt during the early twilight hours and hope to finish before nightfall.

A thought crossed his mind and he circled the camp again. As he came to the western edge, he saw what he'd remembered. Close to the edge of the ravine a huge dead tree about three feet thick reached into the sky. Most of its branches and bark had been broken off, and it had hardened into a pillar of smooth dry wood. Looking back and forth between the tall tree and the expanse to the west, he could tell that it was taller than the ravine was wide. It helped that the base of the tree rested only a few feet from the edge.

Taryn grabbed one of the few remaining branches and tested its strength. Using considerable force, he checked to see if it was rotted and saw that it was not. Satisfied, he held onto the branch and leaned out over the ravine. A few feet down, a small ledge, invisible from above, ran north and south. In both directions it tapered off to a few inches within thirty paces or so.

Leaning back he looked at the tree again and wondered if his plan would work. He would have to cut the tree with his father's sword in such a way that it fell across the ravine and didn't roll into it. Tricky at best, it would still be worth a try when the time came. Returning to his post, he scanned the approaches but saw no one, so he settled in to wait, circling the camp every few minutes.

*****

The sun had already begun to set when Taryn touched Denithir's shoulder. It was a testament to how tired the captain was that it took two shakes to wake him up, but after the second he rose quickly, automatically buckling on his weapons.

"Rouse Ren and he will get the rest up and going," Denithir ordered, his voice hoarse as he rubbed the dark rings around his eyes. "I want to be across before it gets dark."

Taryn spoke up. "I might have a better way across—if it works."

Denithir paused and looked at him speculatively for a moment, and then nodded. "Show me, but wake Ren first and have him place a few soldiers to the south and east. I don't want to be surprised."

Taryn woke the small elf and let him know what to do. Within moments Taryn returned to the elven captain's side. "Follow me."

They came to the dead tree and Taryn explained his plan of forming a bridge, adding, "If it doesn't work, we are no worse off, and if it does, we can cross and cut it into the ravine. Maybe it will slow the assassin."

A shadow of a smile crossed the elven captain's face. "Wait until we are ready to leave," he conceded, "then do it." For the first time the captain seemed to have hope in his eyes as he glanced east. Taryn could almost see him calculating how much time they might gain.

It took only a few minutes to get everyone up and ready. The ten remaining members of the party gathered at the base of the dead tree, still tired, but ready to press forward. Prudently, Denithir still had some of his elves face outwards so as not to be attacked from behind.

Liri brushed Taryn's arm as he passed her, and he caught her eye. She smiled and raised her eyebrows, mouthing, "Good luck."

Taryn understood she was telling him it was OK if his plan didn't work, so he smiled back, but he didn't intend to fail. Standing to the south of the tree, he slowly drew Mazer and raised it high, gauging his strike. Blue flames erupted from the long blade as it swept down and sliced right through the tree from east to west. In a flash he reversed the blade and came again high from the west. Again magic flashed in the twilight sky as the second cut separated a large wedge of wood that slipped out and thudded to the ground, leaving the tree with no support on the ravine side. Wood creaked and groaned in protest as the ancient tree shifted and slid off its base.

The giant wooden pole hung for a long moment until it gained momentum as it fell across the ravine. A loud crack of splitting wood echoed around them as it crashed to the earth with tremendous force, bouncing off the ground before hitting again . . . and slowly starting to roll. In a flash Siarra leapt forward and swept her hand palm up. A column of dirt rose on both sides of the tree, trapping it and holding it fast. She kept her hand palm up for a moment until it stopped quivering.

Suddenly someone let out a breath—then someone else, and then everyone blew out the air they had been holding in.

Denithir shook his head. "Excellent job, Taryn, Siarra. Ren, tie a rope around Liri's waist since she's the lightest. It might have cracked when it landed and I don't want someone to fall."

Taryn's throat tightened as he saw them ready to put her in danger, but the assessment was accurate. If anyone had a chance of making it, Liri, with her light form, did, so he kept his concerns to himself. Once she was ready, two elves anchored the other end of the rope to a tree, and without hesitation she stepped up onto the trunk and began to walk. Inching her way forward, she advanced across the unstable bridge.

She didn't look down, but her shoulders were so tense they almost shook as she worked her way outward. Without warning the tree began to creak in protest and dipped in the middle, causing her to crouch and wait anxiously. When it didn't snap she bravely moved forward, slowing even more to negotiate past a long branch that extended straight up. Once clear, she continued until she reached the other side and hopped down, already untying the rope from her waist. With no trees or rocks near enough to tie it to, she let it fall and the elves pulled it back in.

"Oracle, you next," Denithir said.

She nodded and allowed the elves to tie her the same way. Carefully she stepped up onto the smooth wood and began to advance, her eyes on the hundred foot drop. She reached the straight branch and held onto it for support with her free hand while she leaned out and began to edge her way around it.

A sudden flash of movement caught Taryn's eye and he took his eyes off Siarra in time to see a black figure race along the small ledge under the makeshift bridge. Before Taryn could call out a warning, a scythe snapped out and sliced through the earth column holding the tree in place. It instantly crumbled to the ground and the tree began to roll.

Siarra lost her balance and had to desperately grab the branch for support. Without her magic the tree began to roll faster and she almost rolled right off, but she crouched and clung to the branch with all her might as the tree accelerated towards the edge.

Half a second later she would have been thrown to her death, but as the massive tree rolled towards the brink, Taryn leapt forward and planted himself in front of it. It smashed into him and the sound was like wood crashing into stone, but the stone held. Taryn wrapped his arm under the trunk and braced himself against the tremendous weight. Muscles like knotted cords strained against the massive bulk, and sweat immediately began to bead on his forehead. Indeed, Taryn's raised heels actually extended into space while his toes held the bare edge of the cliff.

Death appeared on the northern edge of their circle and his weapon began its grisly work. Two elves went down before anyone could react, and then Ren leapt towards him, calling for aid. Denithir shouted for his remaining soldiers to help Ren while he reached for the rope holding Siarra, but Death was too quick. Rolling around the elves he sliced through the rope before returning to the battle.

"Oracle! Get across!" The elven captain bellowed, watching helplessly as the lifeline fell away into space.

She scrambled to her feet and across the bridge as fast as she could, but ten feet from the other side the unthinkable happened. Taryn slipped an inch. Roaring in rage, he pushed against the tree with all his might and managed to slide it back, far enough for him to regain his footing—but the damage had already been done.

Siarra had misstepped the moment the tree had shifted, and her foot slid right off the smooth wood, sending her body angling out into thin air. This time there was no branch to grab, and she screamed as she began to slide into the ravine. Liri tried to reach her in time but was too slow. . .

—Another figure in black burst into view on the other side of the ravine. Quick as lightning he leapt fifteen feet out and landed in a crouch on the log. The same moment she began to fall, he reached down and caught the Oracle's arm while stabbing a knife into the tree with his free hand. Holding onto the hilt, he managed to drag her back onto the log. As soon as she was safe the two of them sprinted for safety.

The precious moments to save her had a price, and two more elves paid it, leaving Ren, Denithir, and only one more elven soldier still fighting. For one breathless moment it looked like they might be able to hold their own, until Death smashed the shaft of his weapon into the last soldier's chest so hard you could hear bone snap. A split second later the soldier's lifeless body tumbled into the gorge.

Ren screamed in anger, "Captain, go! I will hold him off." His daggers were a blur of defensive moves as he stepped in front of his captain to forestall any protest. Denithir hesitated, but understood the situation clearly. Roaring in frustration, he turned and sprinted towards the fallen tree. Leaping onto it, he barely slowed as he raced across. Before he reached the middle, Ren finally went down under the spinning scythe, never to rise again.

The thump of his body hitting the ground sent chills of agony down Taryn's spine, but his heart rent in two as he spotted a glittering object rolling under him. Knocked loose by Ren's fall the memory orb bounced by, the image of the now fatherless babe smiling sadly up at him. The open blue eyes burned into his, forging an indelible image in his mind as the orb sailed into the ravine and plunged out of sight.

Never had he felt such anger at another creature, and the desire to plunge his blade deep into the assassin's body coursed through him, lancing across his heart and mind like a delirious fever. As clear as the midday sun, he recognized in that moment what Murai had tried to tell him. Destroying such evil would save countless lives—but in that moment he was powerless to move.

Denithir hadn't crossed yet.

Roaring against his rage and helplessness, Taryn could only stand fast to ensure the elf captains' survival. Rooted in place, he was left to wait for Death to finish him, knowing the seconds it took for the elven captain to reach the other side were more than enough time for the assassin to get to him.

Death sped towards his helpless form, scythe rising for the killing blow—but an arrow streaked across the expanse and he paused to block it. Arrow after arrow flew towards him, so fast it actually forced him to retreat as the scythe whirled defensively. Earth rose up on all sides to smash into him and wind forced him back even further.

Liri and Siarra had joined the fight.

The reinforcements granted him a tiny window of opportunity, and the idea of vengeance flashed red across his vision—but then he saw his friends. He couldn't leave them alone, and if he failed, they would certainly be slain. Liri's fierce expression as she launched missiles calmed his wrath enough for him to make his choice.

298

He had to get across the ravine.

Knowing he had only a few precious moments before Death slipped past the attacks and killed him, Taryn anchored his toes into the rock, gathered every ounce of strength he possessed, and pushed against the tree. Straining and roaring, he poured his fury into his muscles, and rolled the log far enough back to buy himself some time. In an instant, he leapt onto the log and sprinted across the tree at the same time it began to roll underneath him.

Before he'd gone half a step he felt a tug as the evil scythe tore his cloak from his body, but he never stopped to look back. Five feet from the midpoint, the log rolled into space and began to fall, taking him with it.

Gritting his teeth, he leapt forward and grabbed the lateral branch. Using it to gain momentum, he yanked on it and desperately threw himself upward. As the makeshift bridge plummeted into the ravine, he sailed through the air towards his friends and safety—but began falling *just* short of their outstretched hands.

Picking up speed, he did the only thing he could think of. In a flash he drew Mazer and plunged it into the stone in front of him. Blue magic flared as it cut through the vertical rock. For twenty feet Taryn fell before he extinguished the magic and the sword stopped, brutally slamming him into the wall. Wincing, he grimly held on.

Below him a sudden *snap* echoed up the canyon when the long tree bounced off a wall and split in two. Looking down, Taryn watched the massive pieces of deadwood continue to crumble as they plummeted downward. Breaking apart from the force, they smashed into the rocks below with a tremendous crash that reverberated upward, sending a tremor through the stone.

Taryn closed his eyes and sighed in relief that he hadn't been with it. Not ten seconds later a rope unrolled itself beside him. Letting go of the sword with one hand he grabbed the cord and withdrew Mazer from the smoking gouge it had left. Before he could begin to scale the rope, he felt it being pulled up, and in seconds his tired form was brought to safety over the edge.

Liri crushed him in an embrace. "Are you OK?" she whispered into his ear, her throat tight.

He blew out his breath, still feeling the rush of anger and frustration pounding in his ears. "No, but I will be," he said, his eyes drawn to the still forms on the other side of the ravine.

Other worried faces appeared in view: Denithir, Siarra . . . and *Jack Myst*? Taryn thought the lightning movement had been familiar, but he couldn't imagine where Jack had come from or why he would help save them.

The thief interpreted his expression correctly. "Happened to be passing through and couldn't let a beautiful girl fall to her death, now could I?"

Siarra hit the thief on the shoulder, but he ignored her blow and rolled his eyes, "Fine, not passing by; I followed you."

Taryn reluctantly let go of Liri and looked across the gorge in time to see Death melting into the long shadows cast by the setting sun.

Jack sniffed. "I don't think he likes you guys."

"Ya think?" Siarra replied, and then turned to face him with her hands on her hips. "I appreciate your saving me but in the two minutes since I have known you, you have just been annoying."

The thief smirked at her expression and Taryn wondered what he had said to her when he saved her.

"Hey, if he comes again, I'll hold you if you get scared," the thief said with his arms out wide.

Siarra's expression turned murderous, but Denithir put up a hand to forestall her next comment. "Stop," he said, still out of breath. "We must leave."

"He's not going to give up . . . .is he?" Liri said to herself, but everyone heard.

Taryn stood and wished he knew a better way to comfort her. "We'll be fine, Liri. Don't worry." Even to himself his voice sounded doubtful.

Denithir muttered something beside them that sounded like a prayer, and as Taryn looked at those that had paid the price for their survival, he felt the dread in his heart, and wondered if they should all be praying.

Or if that could even help.

Chapter 24: Life and Death

Taryn's eyes snapped open the moment Denithir touched his shoulder. In an instant he was on his feet with his sword half drawn.

"Easy," the elven captain said. "You only slept for an hour and I hope it was enough. It's almost dusk."

Taryn nodded and gathered his things. They had pushed themselves through the night and into the early afternoon before they collapsed from exhaustion. Taryn had kept the first watch, but Denithir had relieved him so he could get at least some rest. Rubbing his head he tried to ignore the growing headache from the lack of sleep. It had been nearly sixty hours of running and fighting and he could feel his body protesting.

Liri strapped on her longbow beside him. "Now what?" she asked seriously. "He is going to come after us tonight, right?"

"Without question," Siarra said with a frown. "I come of age tomorrow, and he has to kill me before then." She hesitated, and then added, "He will find us, and I don't think he will give up until we are all destroyed."

Jack Myst spoke up. "Why don't we just kill the bugger?"

Siarra growled and looked at him. "What are you even doing here? You saved me. I said thank you. Now you are free to go. Why would you choose to die with us?"

"I'm just here for the adventure." He grinned and spread his arms out wide. "And something tells me this group will have plenty."

The Oracle stared him down until his grin started to fade. When she spoke, her voice was dangerously soft. "Do you feel the fear?"

The thief's arms slowly dropped to his sides and the remainder of his smile evaporated. "Of course I feel it. It's everywhere."

She nodded at him. "The *source* of that fear is what is hunting us."

"What?" Taryn blinked, swiveling to stare at her.

She looked at him. "This assassin spawns this unholy fear, and he has been spreading terror for a while. It has taken time, but by now it has seeped into *every* heart of *every* person throughout the five kingdoms, although it is worst in the east, where it began."

"*Why?*" Denithir asked, his voice crackling with desperation. "Who is he and where does he come from?"

"I don't know." Her head dropped slightly as she answered. Taryn could sense her frustration that she didn't know the answer. "I can just feel evil and fear growing in the eastern kingdom. I don't know its nature or source. The only other thing I can tell you is that this is only the beginning. He has been sent to weaken resistance for whoever, or whatever, sent him—"

"Wait." Liri raised a hand. "There is more than just him?"

Siarra nodded. "Something is gathering an incredibly powerful force. Whoever is doing it sent him to kill us, and others, before we could fight back. Not only does he kill strong leaders, he also spreads terror to separate and blind people."

"So even if we beat Death, we still have to contend with whoever sent him—which is probably worse," Denithir stated, struggling to keep the mounting fear out of his voice.

Siarra looked away and her voice became as cold as ice. "I believe far worse than we can imagine."

Deafening silence echoed around them for several moments until Denithir growled and visibly shook himself. "Enough. We are not facing who sent him; we are facing him. Let's focus on that and hopefully we will learn more after Siarra comes of age."

"—And that won't happen until *after* he kills us . . . correct?" Jack said acidly.

Denithir glowered at him. "You may leave at any moment." He made it sound like a command, but the thief ignored him.

"I think I will stick around." He seemed about to say more but his eyes flicked to Siarra and he closed his mouth with a click.

Liri nudged Taryn, and he understood her thoughts with a glance at her expression. She knew there was something else the thief wasn't saying, and that something had pushed him to risk his life. Before he could wonder what it was, the Oracle cut in.

"We don't have time for this," she exclaimed. "We cannot outrun him, so we will have to fight. I suggest we choose our battleground rather than push ourselves throughout the night again and face him weary and unprepared."

Denithir nodded in agreement, glancing at the setting sun. "We have an hour then. Let's find somewhere to make our stand."

Without waiting for a response, he stepped out of their small camp and strode off to the west. Taryn and the others were quick to fall into line behind him. For several minutes no one spoke while they trudged along a game trail in the foothills south of the Blue Lake, each of them searching for a defensible location.

Despite the grim outlook, Taryn felt eager to continue his conversation with Siarra, but the prevailing mood didn't seem like the right time. *Although there might not be a later,* he thought darkly. Forcing the discouraging thought aside, he looked south. The ground rose and fell in gentle hills that provided little cover. Trees grew in scattered groves in many locations, but few seemed a suitable spot to fight. North, the ground sloped down to a beach on the Blue Lake. Trees stood tall and thick close to the lake but he didn't like the idea of having water at his back.

Darkness continued to deepen and the sun turned a brilliant orange as it began to set, casting long shadows around them. Rather than peaceful, the deepening darkness left an increasing feeling of panic growing within him—and left more and more places for a killer to hide.

"Perhaps among the trees?" Denithir said, but his voice held no hope and no one responded.

A few minutes later Taryn began to think the trees along the shore would be their only option as the last streaks of light began to fade, but just as full darkness fell, his keen eyes caught a glimpse of something to the south.

"There," he said, pointing to indicate the direction.

"What did you see?" Denithir asked, tense and ready.

"Just before the light disappeared, I saw a place we might be able to hole up in."

Siarra cut off the elven captain's response. "Lead the way, quickly."

Taryn took the lead and leapt off the trail into the sparse vegetation. Glancing up, he saw clouds moving to cover the moon, blocking out the little light he had to guide him. Slipping through the trees by memory, he hurried to lead them to what he'd seen, hoping it was there. Approaching the steep rise to a small mountain, he rounded some rocks and came to what he'd seen—a small stream. Over centuries it had cut a path through the rock, leaving a thin corridor into a thirty-foot cliff.

Without stopping, he turned upriver and followed the bank as it wound into the stone crevasse. A small amount of light fell from thirty feet above where the gap opened to the sky, and smooth rock rose up on either side of them, so close you could touch both sides at the same time. Taryn plunged his boots into the cool water as the pathway tightened, but he continued to press forward.

Someone started to protest behind him, but he heard an elbow striking a gut and then silence returned. A moment later they came to what he'd heard from outside the cut. The sides opened up to reveal a waterfall as tall as a tree cascading into a shallow pool. On one side of the pool the water had washed out a large portion to leave forty feet of dry ground in the shape of a half circle, surrounded by thirty feet of smooth vertical stone. Taryn nodded, satisfied at what he saw—a grotto hidden away from sight that would be perfect to defend.

As the others came up behind him and stepped out of the water, they each smiled.

"How did you know this was here?" Liri asked.

"I didn't. I saw light flash off the water near the opening and hoped for something, but I didn't know what would be here. I also heard the waterfall but didn't see one, so I thought it was worth a shot."

Denithir looked up. "You think he can get to us from above?"

Surprisingly Jack was the one to answer. "Most definitely."

They all looked at him and he shrugged. "If I could do it, I'm sure he could."

Taryn nodded at him. "If we are sure he will attack then there is no point in trying to hide. We need a fire, fast. He could be here any minute."

"I'll go get some wood," Liri suggested bravely, but Taryn cut her off.

"No, it would take too long and would be too dangerous," he exclaimed.

Siarra gazed at the rim thirty feet up where some trees were in sight. "If one of you can get up there and get some wood, I can get a fire going."

Jack smirked and looked at Taryn. "Need a boost?" he offered, stooping down and cupping his hands together at his knee.

307

Although Taryn knew he could probably make the jump on his own, he accepted Jack's offer and took the two steps to him in a rush. Placing his foot in the cupped hands, he leapt upwards, assisted by Jack's effort to launch him skyward. The two of them proved to be more than enough as he sailed ten feet above the rim and had to windmill his arms to keep his balance. Still unstable he managed to land in a crouch and scanned the darkness for a hint of their killer.

A low chuckle from Jack could be heard from below, but he ignored it and hurried to lop off thick branches with his father's sword. Blue magic glimmered as he sliced through enough wood to make several fires and dropped it to the ground below him. Finishing quickly, he hung from an outstretched branch and dropped, rolling to absorb the impact.

Light flickered around him as Siarra pulled the heat from the surrounding stone and focused it until the wood burst into flame. One by one she lit the piles around her until firelight chased every bit of darkness from their grotto.

She finished her work and turned to the group. "I will do what I can when he attacks, but I only have a fraction of my ability until tomorrow. You will have to depend on yourselves." She blew her breath out and added fervently, "But pray to whatever god you believe in, for we truly have little chance in this fight."

"Is that supposed to be encouraging?" Jack demanded.

"You can still leave whenever you want," the elven captain said fiercely with a hand on his short sword. "With help if necessary!"

Jack started to respond, but Siarra cut him off. "No. We need him in this, at least for his blade."

"Did you hear that?" he asked Denithir innocently. "She wants me to stay, and I bet there is more than one reason . . ."

She glowered at him, muttering something under her breath which only made his grin widen.

Liri looked at the thief and said in a deadly sweet voice that Taryn knew well, "You don't have to hide your fear with humor; we all know you are scared. But don't worry, we will protect you."

Apparently her comment hit home because he took a step towards her, anger darkening his face for the first time, but Taryn stepped between them in an instant.

As he glared at Jack and started to say something, a flicker of movement over the waterfall caught his eye. Turning, he saw the dark figure of Death rising out of the water behind Siarra, droplets cascading off his dark form. Already knowing it was too late, he cried out for her to move, trying to reach her in time. The scythe descended in a blur as she turned around, plunging itself deep—

—into Denithir's shoulder as he slammed into her, throwing her out of the way.

His effort saved her life, but cost him his. The elven captain fell with a bellow of anguish, mortally wounded, but knocking the Oracle into the rock wall. A crack echoed through their grotto when her head crashed into the stone and she slumped to the ground, still.

Taryn leapt towards Death with a cry of rage on his lips, with Jack only a step behind. The assassin met Taryn's rush in kind, spinning his scythe to block his lightning blows. Remarkably, the thief joined the fight almost as fast as Taryn, a thin curving blade from his back in one hand and a dagger in the other. Four blades sought to strike the assassin down, but the red-veined weapon somehow managed to deflect everything that came its way.

Despite the assassin's speed, the sheer force of their charge drove him backward, almost to the water's edge, before he finally stopped their efforts. For several furious moments the three of them battled, the ring of blows echoing in the enclosed grotto and amplifying the sound a hundredfold.

Suddenly Death spun sideways and whipped the shaft of his scythe out, striking Jack so hard he was knocked backward. Scrambling to stay upright, he tripped over Denithir's body. Death blew past Taryn and followed the thief down with the blade of his weapon. Unable to stop himself, the thief hit the ground hard and immediately tried to roll away, but the deadly scythe was too close.

The evil weapon plunged so deep into the man's side that it scraped stone underneath and his tunic burst into bright crimson. Jack cried out in agony and writhed on the ground while Death withdrew his weapon to block Taryn's retaliating strike.

Liri abruptly joined the fight after seeing she was unable to revive Siarra. Her short sword bravely whipped in, but it was far slower than Death's or Taryn's speed.

"No!" Taryn cried as she attacked.

Almost lazily Death reached his scythe out to hit her—and at the same time revealing the length of the shaft to Taryn. In that split second Taryn knew two things: that it was an opening that Death had left on purpose, and that if he didn't take it Liri would be dead.

He didn't hesitate.

With all his strength he brought Mazer down on the shaft, sending a jarring shock through his hands and arms. Blue light flared as it came in contact with the wood, shattering right through the red-veined handle and sending a blast of energy outward. Taryn felt like he'd tried to cut through thick wood with a butter knife, and his arms ached from the blow, but he felt a moment of triumph as he saw the weapon in two pieces in Death's hands.

Triumph faded to despair as Death used the momentum of the blow to spin the remaining wood around and smash it into Taryn's right hand. Mazer flew from his grasp, landing several feet away, out of reach. Taryn immediately backed up and clenched his mother's sword with both hands, but he knew the battle was over. Death had used Liri to force him into a move he couldn't resist. Hope drained from his heart as he slipped the tip of Ianna out to block the incoming strikes.

As quick as thought, he whipped the katsana back and forth to parry blows from the weapon end of the scythe and the piece of the shaft while Liri struggled to slip past Death to reach Taryn's sword, but the assassin stayed firmly between them. When at last Taryn was able to draw him out enough for her to bolt past him, the assassin spun and threw the shaft piece. With a crack it hit her in the head and she dropped, her hand inches from Mazer's hilt.

Taryn roared at Death and struck with all his might, driving him back. Ianna may not have been as strong as his father's sword, but Death only had a fraction of his weapon, and Taryn knew how to use the two-handed katsana.

Death parried Taryn's sweep and swung the scythe in a whirl meant to take his head. Ducking at the last second, Taryn leapt in, attempting to get inside Death's guard—but the evil weapon snapped back and forced him away. Trying to throw Death off, he reversed Ianna along his forearm and flicked the tip out at his side. In an instant, the scythe blade crossed to block the blow. As it lowered, Taryn reached to his belt and threw one of his knives at his head.

Impossibly fast, Death twisted to the side and the knife passed a hairsbreadth from his cowl, clattering off the rock behind him. The burning coals that were his eyes seemed to pulse at the near hit and he charged Taryn. Hard pressed, Taryn didn't even have time to bring Ianna back to its original hold for several seconds, and was left to block as he retreated. At last he had an opportunity when Death swung the scythe blade towards him, attempting to gut him. Jumping backwards he whipped Ianna back to hold it with both hands.

He growled and darted forward once more, trying not to think about the quiet forms that littered the grotto.

Death spun the remaining piece of his weapon with both hands, so fast it blurred in the air, while Taryn struggled to get past his defenses. After a moment the scythe flew out like quicksilver and he was forced to leap away. The instant he moved back, Death glided back as well, and before Taryn could stop him, he picked up the other piece of his weapon. Placing the broken pieces together the red veins pulsed and the wood knit together, whole once more.

Taryn morphed his mother's sword to a bow and sent arrow after arrow towards Death, so fast that two arrows were in the air before the first one reached him. The full whirling scythe deflected the arrows into the rock around him, sending each embedding deep into stone. Arrows reached out towards Death as Taryn struggled to keep him at bay, knowing that once they closed again . . . it would be over.

Pinned, the assassin could only spin his weapon to deflect arrows until Taryn ran out. His red eyes burned, but he seemed patient to wait until Taryn launched his last arrow. Within ten seconds, the last arrow flew from Ianna and sped towards the impenetrable defense—

—Out of nowhere a dagger plunged into the back of Death's hood, the tip actually poking out where his face would have been. The whirling weapon stopped spinning as Death crumpled to his knees and an unholy screech pierced the night, so loud that Taryn had to cover his ears as it echoed and reechoed around the fire-lit grotto.

The scythe's veins pulsed violently red until suddenly the shaft exploded, throwing everyone backward. As Taryn bounced off the rock and landed on his knees, he watched the red coals inside the hood flicker and slowly go dark, watched as the cloak disintegrated into dust and crumpled before him.

Relief flooded him and he looked to see who had killed Death. His eyes widened at the sight of Jack Myst on his feet with the dagger still in his hand, looking at the pile of dust and fragments of dead wood that had been a supreme assassin only moments before.

"I thought you were dead!" Taryn said, shocked that Jack could stand with so much blood wetting his chest.

The thief shrugged like it was nothing and reached down to his side, pulling back the cloth to reveal that the weapon had penetrated the clothing but had barely grazed his skin.

"But the blood!" Taryn exclaimed with his mouth open. "I heard you cry out as you died!"

Jack reached into the hole in his tunic and pulled out a wineskin with a deep gash through it. "My favorite skin," he said sadly. "Pity, I will miss it. I had to put on a show, you know, and wait for the chance to strike."

Taryn shook his head, utterly at a loss for words. Then he remembered Liri. With a bound he crossed the intervening space and knelt at her side. Touching her throat, he sighed in relief to find a pulse, weak, but there. A glance to the side revealed that Siarra too was still breathing. Then he leapt to Denithir.

Crouching next to him, he was surprised to see him still alive. Instantly he tore a strip of cloth and began to put pressure on the gaping wound, but a feeble hand reached up to stop him. "Don't . . . it doesn't matter." He coughed and nearly lost consciousness, but somehow had the strength to pull Taryn closer. "Tell . . . Eressa . . . I love her."

Recognizing there was nothing he could do, Taryn blinked and spoke through the tightness in his throat. "I will."

Denithir relaxed at his words and his eyes began to close. "I am sorry I doubted you Taryn."

He watched as the elven captain took his last breath, and then succumbed to his wounds, leaving Taryn to his grief. Looking down on him, his heart rent in two.

How many will lose a father before the end? How many would grow up like him?

For the first time he saw more to his own life than a desire to find his family. Settling deep into his gut, a steel resolve to defeat this enemy spread through him. No more children would go fatherless because of him.

No more children would be alone because of him.

A stirring nearby yanked him from his thoughts, and he darted to Liri's side. Carefully, he carried her to the water's edge and cupped water in his hands to drip onto her. After several endless minutes she coughed and her eyes fluttered.

"Er . . . wha' happened?" she slurred and tried to sit up, but he forced her to stay down.

313

"You were knocked out. I fought until Jack—who wasn't really dead—managed to surprise and kill him."

"Really?" She was slowly coming to her senses, so he helped her sit up. "You didn't kill him?" She seemed disappointed for some reason, but he smiled at her.

"Nope, all Jack," he said, flashing a weak smile.

Gratitude flooded him as he heard Siarra's voice from close by. "Stupid thief." But her voice was kind, and he could tell she was smiling, too. Looking back, he saw Jack wiping her forehead with a wet cloth he'd torn from his shirt. Inexplicably, they both had goofy grins plastered across their features.

"I don't feel the fear anymore," Liri said next to him, and her flashing smile lightened the grotto more than the fire ever could.

In that moment, a feeling of intense hope surged through his frame, blossoming into a joy that brought tears to his eyes and wrapped his heart in a warm soft blanket. For the first time in weeks he was released from the cold chains of terror that Death had wrapped around him and he had to swallow at the overwhelming happiness.

"Neither do I, Liri. Neither do I," Taryn exclaimed, joy coloring his tone.

Liri suddenly started to laugh as elation flowed through her. Taryn, Siarra, and Jack joined her, all of them laughing. The light sound, restrained for so long, washed over each of them, cleansing the magical oppression that had yoked their emotions.

In the back of Taryn's mind he knew they shouldn't be laughing, that too many had died already. But the very lack of fear after feeling it for so long caused him to swell with joy. They had won, they had defeated the greatest assassin—and Liri and Siarra were still alive.

The feeling of supreme happiness lasted only a few minutes before it began to dissipate, and each one found themselves remembering Siarra's words.

Someone had sent Death—someone far more powerful.

Chapter 25: Answers

Trin leaned back against the bench and sighed. Constant stress and tension had left the crew on the verge of snapping with several sailors starting fights on the slightest pretext. Patrolling the ship with weapons drawn, Trin and Mae had been tasked with keeping the peace, a grueling and thankless effort. Their presence had gone a long way towards preventing bloodshed in the endless week since they'd seen the desolation of Terros.

"Want to play a game?" Braon asked half-heartedly, already knowing the answer.

"Nah, maybe later," Trin replied, too weary to consider concentrating. In just the last hour he'd prevented two stabbings, three beatings—although one sailor had broken his arm—and a man being thrown overboard—but that wasn't the worst part. The worst part came from seeing the utter terror in each man's eyes . . . reflecting his own. Almost every moment he felt the desire to hurt someone else, with the exception of Mae and Braon, and it required all his willpower to stop others doing what he felt the desire to do. He'd given up wondering why he didn't have any animosity towards Braon or Mae. He just didn't have the energy to consider it further.

Braon stooped and peered at the still unconscious form on the bunk beside them, "Any change?"

Trin shook his head. "Maemi said he still didn't wake up today." Looking down at the man, he wondered how much more he could endure before simply wasting away. The gray from his leg had streaked all the way to his chest now, and it looked like it was headed for his heart. "I'll keep an eye on him tonight, you should get some sleep," Trin said to Braon, who had taken to watching over the woodsman.

A rapid shuffle of booted feet above them signaled another conflict brewing and Trin listened for the sign that Mae had stopped it. The muted thud of a flat blade coming in contact with a head was followed by silence.

"How soon until we get to Tallendale?" Braon asked, a tremor running through his voice. On the first day after Terros someone had tried to gut the boy, screaming that he was a spy. Since then he'd stayed below and out of sight.

"One week," Trin said, but he knew Braon had only asked to make conversation. The boy was scared out of his mind, too, and Trin wished he could do something to reassure him.

"Get some rest kid; I'll be back in a minute," Trin said and stood up. Slipping through the door, he returned to the deck and joined Mae against the rail. She gave no sign that she heard him until he stood next to her.

"You should be sleeping. You know I have the night watch," she said in low tone.

"I wanted to get some air."

She didn't reply and they stood facing south in silence, broken only when footsteps passed behind them. Both tensed and reached for their weapons, but the man didn't stop so they relaxed and continued watching the black sky. The clouds deepened the darkness as they slowly covered the moon and all light was extinguished.

Despite his exhaustion, Trin stayed by her side for several minutes, enjoying her company. It felt right when they were together, like the whole crew was against them and they could only count on each other. He knew it didn't make any sense, but that was how he felt.

Suddenly Mae tensed beside him and pointed out over the water. "Did you see that?"

He looked where she pointed. "See what?"

"There was a flash of something . . . like a flash of darkness?" Her tone carried confusion and doubt.

"What do you mean—" He stopped when he saw a dark mist explode towards them. It moved so fast that before he could say anything else it blew right past them. And abruptly every shred of fear that had been suffocating his heart . . . evaporated, disappeared so completely that he gasped at the gaping hole left behind. Without warning the natural hope that resides within all beings returned with a fury, surging through his soul like a warm spring wind, lifting his heels off the deck by its sheer intensity.

Trin reeled as the feeling of hope and faith flooded his frame, and found himself gripping the rail for support—and he was not alone. All over the ship, hearts struggled to handle the tremendous outpouring of happiness as the chains of despair were stripped away. Some sailors started to cry, some collapsed to their knees in grateful prayer, and others simply laughed out loud.

After several moments, Trin finally got his emotions under control and opened his eyes. Mae stood next to him, just grinning and looking at him with a very non-Maemi expression . . . *joy.*

Trin grinned right back, happy for the first time in weeks. A door slammed behind him and he turned to see the captain stride out of his quarters calling for information, but he was smiling as well.

"Frey, what just happened? Trin, Mae, did you see anything? Does *anybody* know what is going on?"

Several people called back that they had no idea what was happening until Mae stepped forward and happily explained what they had witnessed. Her explanation only seemed to cause more questions than answers, and Erix scowled. "So no one knows anything," he stated.

"Pretty much, captain," Trin said with a trace of his normal sarcasm. (It was good to have *that* back.)

The captain abruptly relaxed. "Well, whatever happened, it must have been good." He shrugged and looked at the two of them. "It doesn't mean you are off duty for the night. Stay sharp." With that he shouted for Frey to stay awake in the nest and returned to his quarters.

Mae chuckled. "Wow, I had forgotten what it was like to *believe*."

"What do you mean?" Trin asked, cocking his head in confusion. The feeling of euphoria had already begun to diminish, but the fear hadn't returned.

"That evil feeling, it slowly took away every belief I had that things would work out."

"Aaah, I'd lost all hope as well—*and* my sense of humor." He voice was full of anguish at losing the latter.

She laughed out loud, probably the first time he had ever heard her open up so freely, and he discovered he liked it tremendously. He laughed in response, and they both returned to the rail to look south. The feeling of exhaustion was creeping back, but he fought it. Leaning against Mae, he keenly felt the absence of tension from moments before and the blanket of peace that had replaced it. A board creaked beside him, and Braon appeared next to him.

"It's safe to come up . . . right?" the young man asked tentatively.

Trin smiled and nodded. "I think so."

Braon sighed deeply. "Good. It's nice to have fresh air for once."

The three of them stood together and stared over the dark water for over an hour, each of them reluctant to let the moment end. Braon finally broke the stillness. "Sleep well, Trin, I know I will." With that he left and went below, his steps much lighter than before.

"I should go too," Trin said sadly, knowing he was *very* tired.

Mae nodded and turned away. It seemed her usual reserve had returned, and Trin felt a sharp pang of sorrow to see the moment pass. Descending the stairs he went to his bunk and fell asleep in seconds, slumbering peacefully for the first time in weeks.

A muffled cry came from above and he awoke groggily, taking a few seconds to remember what had happened. Someone yelled again, a cry of warning, and he rolled out of his bunk, cursing as he smashed his knee. Roughly he shoved his boots on and fumbled for his weapons before bolting up onto deck to see what the commotion was about.

Stepping through the door, he was surprised to see it still night, without even a hint of dawn. Silver light from the moon cascaded over everything and Trin wondered when the clouds had cleared. Stifling a yawn, he asked the time from a passing sailor.

"Just after midnight," he replied before hurrying to the port rail.

"Wait—what's going on?" Trin demanded and followed him to the rail to look south. It only took him a minute to see what the fuss was about.

In the distance, a wave of water—impossibly only a few feet wide—streaked towards them at incredible speed.

"By the gods. . ." someone breathed beside him, and then he saw it, too.

There was someone on top of the wave, riding it towards them. It had to be magic, and whoever it was had to be powerful. After several moments, the person came close enough for them to see in the moonlight and it became clear that it wasn't a person . . . it was *persons*—apparently headed in their ship's direction.

"Get ready for a battle mates! We got a mage comin' at us!"

Men jumped to prepare for battle but Trin stayed where he was. There was something familiar about them . . .

Mae suddenly spoke excitedly beside him. "It's Taryn and Liri!"

320

"Are you certain?" Trin asked, and she gave him a disapproving look.

"Never doubt an elf's vision," she said.

He grinned widely. "Captain," he called, "they are friends; don't worry about a battle."

The captain stood up from where he'd been stringing a bow. "What? Who are they?"

Trin grinned wider. "It's Taryn and Liriana."

Erix guffawed and called off his men before eagerly coming to see for himself. Trin looked back at the incoming wave and saw they had gotten much closer. Now he could make out four individuals riding a log at the crest of the wave. A female elf stood sideways on the precarious ride, her long blond hair billowing behind her, while Taryn, Liri, and an unknown man straddled the log behind her.

Within another minute, the magical wave carried the log right onto the ship, causing water to crash over everyone. Taryn was on his feet in an instant and jumping towards Mae, picking her up and embracing her warmly.

"Maemi! It's so good to see you!"

Others stepped forward to greet the old friends but the female elf that had been standing on the log called out, her loud voice carrying over the ship, "Captain of this ship, we have no time to waste, how fast can your vessel go without coming apart?"

Erix responded with pride, "As fast as the wind can push her."

She didn't smile but one eyebrow lifted upward. "We shall see." With that she faced the front of the ship, leaned back, and took a deep breath. Something intangible seemed to gather around her and everyone warily took a step back. Abruptly she took a step forward and slammed her foot down at the same time she swung her arms forward in a ringing clap. Instantly the wind began to pick up, stronger and stronger. Within seconds it howled and screamed to push the sail forward, forcing the

321

thick mast to bend as it strained to transfer the momentum into the large ship. The *Sea Dancer* protested loudly but began to crash up and down as its hull split the water.

"Tie her down mates," the captain called, exultation evident in his voice as he accepted the challenge. "We've got a gale to ride!"

The sailors jumped to their tasks and before Trin could ask what was going on, Taryn turned to the elven maid and exclaimed dryly, "So . . . I see what you meant about having more power." He swept a hand that indicated both their ride and the high wind.

She smiled and relaxed for the first time. "It feels good to be unbound."

Trin stepped forward, speaking loudly over the howl of the wind. "I take it nothing new happened with you guys . . . right?"

Liri laughed. "Not exactly. But let's go below so we can talk."

The reunited friends led the way to the galley, the only place large enough for all of them. As soon as they were as comfortable as possible and introductions had been made (including Braon), Taryn spoke first. He began where he and Liri had left the ship and explained what had happened up through meeting the Oracle.

"You're the Oracle?" Mae interrupted, her tone sharp.

"And Taryn's sister," Liri said with a smile.

Trin's jaw wasn't the only one to fall open, but before he could respond Taryn jumped in, "Half-sister, but let me finish before you ask any more questions."

Without waiting for a response, he continued with their tale, describing each battle with the figure of Death and their eventual triumph in the hidden grotto.

"After we buried Denithir, we thought we'd camp for the night, but sometime after midnight . . ." He glanced at the Oracle and tilted his head, inviting her to finish.

"After midnight, the rest of my magic was freed, and I became whole. It didn't take me long to sense the extent of what is happening in Lumineia and who sent the assassin. Now we must hasten to Azertorn. Every second we delay, lives will be lost."

Trin started to ask the question but Braon beat him to it, "Who *sent* him—you mean it isn't over?"

The Oracle smiled kindly at him. "No, it's not over. Death was just the forerunner of the war."

"Who was this assassin?" Braon asked, his expression calculating.

"I can't explain everything right now, but I will say this. Death was sent to do two things. Kill specific people to ensure victory, and spread fear—"

"—that would divide people so they would be easier to destroy." Braon finished her statement with a nod to himself, and she looked at him with newfound respect.

"Very good." She appraised him for a moment and then cocked her head to one side. "You have a very . . . unique power, young man. I've never seen anything like it." She spoke softly, as if she didn't quite understand what his power was.

Jack spoke for the first time. "Is there anything in here to eat?" he queried, seemingly oblivious to the conversation as he looked at the counters of the galley.

Siarra lips thinned, but Trin pointed to a drawer. "Meat and bread should be in there, if you want it."

Jack nodded and, finding the food, dug in without another word.

"How did you know where we were?" Mae asked.

The Oracle smiled. "We weren't actually looking for you, but we were looking for the others. I could feel a multitude of people heading west, many of them mages, and we wanted to catch up with them. When

323

we got close, Taryn and Liri recognized this ship so we came to you." She leaned in. "Why are there so many people heading west anyway?"

Trin grimaced at the memory of the carnage at Terros. Briefly he described what they had seen. By the time he finished, they'd turned pale.

"Terros is gone? I can't believe it." The Oracle seemed shocked and shook her head in confusion. "Something isn't right. They weren't ready . . . wait, that *might* give us more time." She sighed, and for the first time Trin noticed how worn they all looked.

"Let's get some sleep," he said firmly, ignoring his craving to know more. "I'm sure we can figure it out in the morning."

Siarra yawned. "We should get to the coast of the elven homeland by tomorrow, or is that today?"

"Today of course," Jack exclaimed through a mouthful of food, and she glanced at him in irritation. Trin wondered who he was and where he fit into the picture. They hadn't been very clear about where he'd come from. Reluctantly, Trin ignored the impulse to ask and stood up. "I think it's time for bed, then."

Each of them nodded, so Trin led the new visitors to bunks or hammocks where they could sleep. As they settled into some spare beds, he nudged the Oracle. "Mind if I ride a wave like that sometime?"

She chuckled tiredly. "Sure," she said as she lay down.

Before he even left the room, she was asleep, along with the rest of their party. Trin yawned and returned to his own bunk, expecting to fall asleep right away. But one thought kept repeating itself until he finally fell into a fitful sleep.

The assassin had been killed, but who had destroyed Terros?

Chapter 26: Healing

Taryn kicked his heels into the horse again, urging his mount even faster. Beside and around him Siarra, Liri, Trin, Mae, Jack, and Braon, who was a surprisingly good rider, urged their animals faster as well. The only other person with them was the unconscious man from the ship, whom Siarra had insisted be brought along. He lay strapped to a spare animal behind them. As Taryn rode, he couldn't imagine how they'd gone so far, so fast. Less than twenty-four hours ago they had been over a week's voyage from Tallendale, but the magical wind had pushed the *Sea Dancer* faster than it seemed possible. They'd sailed right past the refugees' ships like they'd been anchored and arrived at an elven port that would give them the fastest route to Azertorn.

No one in their party clearly understood the Oracle's urgency to get to the city, but something in her firm lips and set face had convinced them that they had no time to waste. Upon disembarking, Siarra had literally sprinted to the stables, and grabbing a horse she'd bolted into the forest of Numenessee. The others had been right behind her, and within minutes of landing, the eight riders were pounding through the elven forest in a blur of green and brown, their horses' unnatural gait informing Taryn that Siarra's powers were still at work.

He glanced behind him and saw Braon holding onto his horse, his face tight with concentration as he rode high in the saddle. Siarra had also insisted the young man be brought with them, but hadn't taken the time to explain why—despite chafing at every delay as the pudgy young man tried to keep up with them.

Normally the trip between the elven port and the elven capital would have been at least a full day's ride, but not four hours had passed before they reached the wide bridge between the magnificent waterfalls.

Siarra crossed the bridge at a full gallop with the seven of them right behind her. She reined in her horse at the last minute and dismounted even as it skidded to a stop. The surprised guards had their weapons out, but she spoke in the ringing tone of authority. "I am Siarra Kelrára Elseerian, the Oracle of the Elves. Send word to the queen immediately with your fastest runner to gather the high council."

They gaped at her for a moment until she barked, "Now!" and the elves jumped to do as they'd been told.

Jack dismounted from his steed, which still shook from the run, murmuring just loud enough for Taryn and Siarra to hear him, "Ah, the voice of a powerful woman."

She bristled, and unseen energy seemed to crackle around her. The thief only chuckled and handed the reins of his winded horse to one of the elves coming out to meet them.

"Gather the human and carry him with us," she commanded an elf hurrying towards them. It was obvious she partially meant Jack, but the elf went to the unconscious human and gingerly began to unstrap him.

Taryn dropped to the ground and hurried to gather his things before following them into the city, admitting to himself it felt good to enter the citadel through the front door—and without the fear that had prevailed during the last visit. The presence of compassion and hope in its place felt so strong it brought a smile to his lips.

Behind him, Taryn heard Braon gasp as he came through the secret doors. The boy began bombarding Trin with questions, but Trin shrugged and suggested he ask Taryn. The young man huffed to catch up to Taryn and redirected his flow of queries in his direction. Surprised by Braon's immediate grasp of the impressive strategic layout and defensive capabilities of the lower barracks, Taryn answered him as well as he could. But when Liri joined in the conversation, he let her take over. She certainly knew more about the fortress than he did.

326

As they were led through the lower levels of Azertorn, he could tell Trin in particular wanted to know more about the city, but he didn't get a chance to ask many questions with the group hurrying to follow Siarra. Surprisingly, Jack didn't seem at all curious about Azertorn . . . perhaps he'd already been here? Taryn suppressed a laugh as he realized the better question was, how many *times* had Jack been in Azertorn, and how much had he stolen? For a brief moment Taryn remembered the queen of the elves telling them about a thief they couldn't catch.

The next surprise came when Siarra led them, not straight to the palace, but rather to *The Drunken Elf.* Without hesitation, she walked right through the doors and up to the bar where Aléthya stood lazily wiping a glass. At this time of day there were only a couple of soldiers in the tavern, drinking their day away.

"I need your help," the Oracle exclaimed to Aléthya.

Aléthya eyed her with an amused expression, her brown hair shimmering in the sunlight that streamed through the open windows. "You're the Oracle," she stated, not even bothering to stop cleaning glasses. "I knew your mother, you know."

Taryn was suddenly aware that the Oracle who had helped Aléthya had been *his* mother as well, so he barely heard his sister's response.

"Yes, and I need you to heal someone." Siarra's voice softened. "It is of the utmost importance."

"Couldn't you do it yourself?" Aléthya's question held no rancor.

Siarra grimaced. "Healing magic has always been a weakness of mine. His wounds are beyond my ability."

For some reason Taryn couldn't explain, he felt like the fate of the world rested on Aléthya's response, and he found himself holding his breath for the answer. Knowing how she felt about healing people, he didn't have much hope, but after several agonizing seconds where the two locked eyes, the healer shrugged and put down the glass.

"I am at your service, Oracle." Aléthya inclined her head in a demonstration of the utmost respect and came out from behind the counter. "Who is it?"

Siarra waved for the human to be brought forward and laid on a table. "I don't know who he is. I just know we need answers, and he is the only one that has them."

The man looked wretched, his face gray and drawn, his leg streaked with dark black, and when Taryn helped lay him on the table he could feel the cold, clammy skin. *Death's door is already open for this poor soul*, he thought.

Aléthya drew in a breath and leaned over him, murmuring so quietly to herself that even Taryn's sharp ears had a hard time hearing.

"Poison . . . that's for sure . . . what kind? Something dark . . . a magical poison? . . . it must be. . . wounded in several places, but the leg . . . hmm . . . the source was here . . . something struck him here . . . something deadly . . ." She trailed off and stood straight. Without looking at anyone, she sighed to herself, "This is going to hurt." Then she turned to Taryn and Liri. "Hold me up so I don't fall—and don't let go no matter what happens."

Without waiting for an answer, Aléthya took another deep breath and placed both hands on the leg. White light immediately shimmered through her hands and into the man's leg. Several seconds passed before anything happened, but then the gray lines reluctantly began to recede. At the same moment, the healer cried out in agony and her right leg buckled.

Taryn and Liri caught her in an instant, but it only got worse. The gray lines grew lighter and lighter as they disappeared, only to reappear on Aléthya's body, darker and longer. Blood also began to drip onto the floor as her flesh split. Frozen in place, they could only watch as her body began to tremble and shake under their arms, but the white light continued to transfer the wound from the man's body to hers. She screamed again, a cry of pure anguish, and then slumped into their arms.

Taryn lifted her feather light form and laid her on another table as everyone gathered around.

"Do something!" someone said to Siarra, but she shook her head.

"I cannot. There is nothing I can do."

Taryn swallowed hard and was about to say something, but the gray on the leg slowly, ever so slowly, began to lighten and disappear. It took a full five minutes for the death lines to completely recede and the wound in her thigh to knit. With a gasp she sat up and took a few deep breaths.

"Are you OK?" Liri asked, worry etched in her voice.

"I'm fine; just give me a minute," she said hoarsely as she massaged her leg. Then without a word she jumped down and moved to her bar. Slopping amber liquid into a glass she drained it with a wince. After another moment she gave a small smile. "I'm fine, but I can honestly say it would have been less painful to tear my leg off piece by piece and then grow a new one." She shuddered at some memory and asked, "How did he get hurt anyway?"

A deep voice behind them answered: "The assassin came for me."

They all turned to see the human sitting up on the table. For the first time he looked alive, and he was quick to stand and test his legs.

"Well that chicken soup definitely helped," Trin said with a grin.

The man snorted in agreement. "Who healed me?" His said, his voice dead and raspy.

Aléthya stepped forward and moved to stand in front of him. "I did. You had been poisoned by something dark."

"*How* did you heal me?"

Aléthya smiled wryly. "Technically, I didn't. I transferred your wound to my own body, and then I healed myself."

The man dropped to one knee and kissed her hand, exclaiming in a voice choked with emotion, "I am deeply sorry for the pain you must have had to endure for me . . . thank you, my lady."

For a moment there was silence as everyone in the room began to understand the depth of the man's pain over the past few weeks.

Siarra exchanged a grateful look with Aléthya and then stepped forward. "What is your name, sir?"

The man rose and looked at her, his frame strong and tall once more. "I am Ryben, the woodsman of the East, a tracker and guide for all eastern villages . . ." His face turned grim. ". . . at least until Griffin was invaded and Terros annihilated."

Trin opened his mouth to say something, but Siarra cut him off. "I am Siarra Elseerian, the Oracle of the elves. There is much we must know, and precious little time. It would be best if you only explain this once today, to the high council of the elves."

Ryben nodded and said simply, "Lead the way." He gestured for the Oracle to walk in front of him and fell into step the moment she swept past him. In an instant she returned to her desire to hurry and began to lengthen her stride. The others struggled to keep up with her magically enhanced steps as she headed towards the top of the city.

They hastened to the palace and Liri led them through the main entrance and up a huge stone staircase covered in greenery. Once again Taryn couldn't help but be amazed at the sheer volume of flowers and other vegetation growing out of the very walls and floors.

She led them through corridors and guarded openings deep into the plateau until they finally came to a wide set of ornately carved doors. Two guards nodded at Liri and ushered them through. Entering the room, they saw several older elves already seated on chairs of beautiful curving trees surrounding a massive stone table in the shape of an oval. Each elf, dressed in formal clothes showing their rank, studied them as they came into view, and Taryn immediately felt self-conscious of his torn and dirty travelling clothes.

As the Oracle approached the table, she beckoned to a guard and when he moved close to her, she whispered quietly, "Summon the arch historian from the archives." He bowed and left the room.

Drawing near to the table she stopped and looked directly at the queen seated at the head. The other five members of the high council sat around her, but it seemed Siarra disregarded their presence.

"My queen," she said in a ringing tone, "there is no time for formalities. We have six weeks, three days, and fourteen hours to prevent the inevitable."

"What do we face?" The queen asked solemnly.

Siarra shook her head, and for the first time since Taryn had met her he saw unparalleled terror sweep across her features.

She breathed out slowly and said simply, "*Extinction.*"

Despite her quiet tone, the word echoed through the chamber like a thunderclap, stunning everyone to silence. After several long moments someone managed to gasp, "Of the elves?"

Voices bubbled up but Siarra cut them off with a raised hand.

"No." Her tone carried such intense horror that all eyes locked on her expression until she spoke softly in the stillness: "Of everyone."

Chapter 27: Council of War

Deiran, the heavily built general of the army, swept to his feet. "What do you mean, *everyone*?"

Siarra started to respond but the queen stood up, her very presence silencing the room. "One moment, I ask of you. Please be seated and introduce our visitors so we may start at the beginning."

Her tone held no animosity yet carried the weight of authority, and even Siarra found a seat with the others in their group. After nudging a hesitant Braon, Siarra moved to sit at the foot of the table with Taryn on her right, followed by Liri and then Jack. To the Oracle's left Braon settled uncomfortably into a seat while Trin sat himself next to the young man. Mae slid smoothly to his left and Ryben, the woodsman from the east, sat next to her small form.

Once everyone had found a place to sit, the table felt considerably more crowded, with only a few chairs still empty. The queen remained standing and addressed the group. "I recognize the need for urgency, however this moment should be thought through, so let us begin by introducing ourselves, shall we?"

Without waiting for a response she said in her light voice, "I am Ayame Ser'Tármaril, the Queen of the elves." She smoothly sat and indicated for the elf on her right to stand.

"Deiran Tandril, high general of the elven armies," he said shortly, bowing to the group. The general's eyebrows were gathered in what

Taryn was beginning to think of as a perpetual scowl. Broad shouldered for an elf and tall as well, his form once again reminded Taryn of a human.

Standing next, a soldier dressed in dark green armor announced himself quietly as Keiko Ker'isse, captain of the home guard. Like Deiran he stood slightly wider than the average elf, but his movements were far more fluid, and his clear blue eyes constantly roved the room—and the new individuals seated at the table. He gave Taryn the impression of contained fire that could explode at the first hint of danger.

The next elf to stand bore a striking resemblance to Liri, and when she said her name was Lariel Tel'Runya, he wasn't surprised. Almost identical to his long-time friend in every way, she carried the same beauty and grace, accentuated by her light eyes and even lighter hair. The only perceptible differences were the hair had begun to turn silvery, indicating that she was at least a few centuries old, and her demeanor appeared more somber than Liri's, no less fiery, simply more disciplined. Taryn found himself wondering if he was looking at Liri in five hundred years. With his dwarf and elf blood he was glad he would be around to see it.

From their group, Ryben stood first, his frame large yet somehow gentle as he pronounced in his deep voice his name and his position as the woodsman of the east. Maemi stood and said her name so fast that Taryn barely heard it and he fought to hide his smile. She didn't like formal functions.

Trin stood next and seemed completely at ease, although Taryn could almost feel his suppressed tension. After him the short, overweight Braon appeared awkward and out of place. Siarra then spoke and abruptly it was Taryn's turn. Despite his self-consciousness he straightened and said his name without title or origin. Liri followed him and smiled at her mother when she stated the name of her house.

For a moment Taryn watched the two, mother and daughter, obviously proud of each other and still close, despite the thirty years without contact—and wished he knew what that was like.

Jack fluidly stood and with a smug expression said, "Jack Myst, formerly of the thieves' guild. It's good to be in Azertorn again." He winked slyly at the captain of the home guard but before he could sit down, Keiko was on his feet.

"He is not welcome here," he said firmly. "He should be in chains, or executed."

Before the queen could respond, Siarra mildly stated, "And yet he is, and has been, vital to our cause." Keiko's eyes snapped to the queen, who shook her head slightly, so he reluctantly sat down, his expression fiercely disapproving. Jack ghosted a smile before bowing to Siarra and sitting. Taryn suppressed a grin and leaned forward a bit to see the next elf, who was already saying his name.

Ladarius Re'Keserian proclaimed himself to be the head of the house of Keserian, the second ruling house of Azertorn. Although he said as little as everyone else, his tone and his robes spoke volumes about his character. Speaking with a subtle tinge of aloofness, especially when he announced his title, he wore robes far more ornate and expensive than those of anyone else at the table.

The last one to stand proclaimed himself to be Teleriel Sur'Maegrian, archmage of the guild of magi. His expensive robes rustled slightly as he stood, and it was evident the colors were amplified by magic. A glance towards Siarra when he said his title revealed an air of superiority.

The queen finally stood and thanked the group. "Liriana of the house of Runya, please start at the beginning when you left the city, and then perhaps the Oracle can finish the tale and explain her previous words."

Siarra fidgeted beside Taryn, and he could feel her frustration at having to wait further, but she didn't comment as Liri stood and began to tell of their journey to the Oracle's home. She conspicuously left out both Taryn's test of loyalty and Jack's attempt to steal from them, so it didn't take her long before she nodded graciously to Siarra and allowed her to take over the tale at the point when they had arrived at her home.

Siarra virtually leapt to her feet and explained Death's attack on her home, including the full details of the destruction and slaying of everyone there. When she described the assassin, several people shifted, including Ryben, who subconsciously rubbed his thigh where he'd been injured by the same killer.

Siarra continued by describing their flight from the swamp and the elves that had disappeared during the night when Deiran interrupted.

"That's impossible! No assassin could take so many elves unaware—especially Denithir's command." His face tightened in fury, but diffused slightly when Siarra began nodding at him.

"You are correct general—no assassin could catch so many elves unaware . . ."

"Then how could—" he blustered, but she cut him off in a voice of ice.

"They weren't unaware, general, they were *extremely vigilant*—and he still killed them *like they were children!*" By now she was leaning forward, her voice thick with anger. Silenced, Deiran sat with his mouth agape.

Her voice rang throughout the chamber, and for the first time the true danger of the assassin came into focus. Those that didn't know the end of the tale tensed and looked around as if Death was already lurking around them. Surprisingly, the queen's soft expression didn't change except for a slight tightening of her eyebrows.

"Please proceed with your tale," she requested, serene despite the upswing in tension.

Siarra thanked the queen with a glance and continued with the desperate battle at the ravine and the fall of Ren. Taryn glanced at the queen and saw her face go rigid upon the news of her bodyguard's death. She swallowed hard, but didn't interrupt. Taryn felt a pang of sorrow as well, and the image of the memory orb falling into the ravine flashed across his eyes.

When Siarra came to the battle in the grotto, she stopped and inclined her head towards Taryn, saying, "I was knocked out early in the fight. I believe Taryn can explain the rest of the battle. She sat and looked expectantly at him. Surprised, he stood slowly to organize his thoughts before speaking.

Beginning with Death's attack, he told of Denithir's valiant effort to save the Oracle. Catching the saddening expression on the queen's features almost made him stop, but he forced himself to describe the feigned slaying of Jack Myst and then his own battle with Death, followed by Jack's rising to destroy the assassin.

A palpable sigh went through the room as he sat, and several people tried to speak at the same time. Teleriel, the archmage, spoke the loudest. "Why was *he* able to destroy the creature?" he demanded over the babble of voices.

Everyone quieted again and looked at the Oracle, who shook her head. "I cannot say."

In that instant something clicked in Taryn's mind. "But I do," he said hesitantly.

Every eye turned to him but he just stared off into space, trying to remember a conversation in Keese. What was it that Rezko had said about a thief being . . . *the cheater of death*. That was it!

He snapped back to the present and looked at Jack. "Have you ever been called the cheater of death?"

Jack smirked and nodded.

The captain of the home guard snorted, still angry. "I think we've tried to kill him at least a couple of times."

Jack's smirk widened. "Six actually, in different guises."

Keiko glowered at him, but Taryn spoke loudly, drawing attention back to himself. "Don't you see? He was *supposed* to kill death. Perhaps the only one that could."

"Are you trying to say that this . . . thief . . . is the only one who could have killed the assassin?" Ladarius Keserian challenged, his voice full of scorn.

"My uncle on Sri Rosen said something to me before I left," Taryn said forcefully, knowing his words to be true. "He said *everyone* was important in the battle against evil, that everyone had a specific place and a specific purpose."

"But he *is* the evil," Ladarius scoffed.

"No," Siarra said quietly, drawing attention to herself. "He's not." She looked at Taryn. "Thank you, Taryn, for helping me to understand." Then she looked directly at the queen and stood up once more. "The true evil is the source of power that sent the assassin."

"Who?" several people asked, but instead of answering, Siarra turned around and indicated for a wizened old elf, who had slipped into the room unnoticed, to come forward.

"Father of records, please come and tell us about the one who commanded Death."

The old elf walked forward slowly and stood next to Siarra, gazing at each of the high council in turn.

"His name is Draeken, the demigod of chaos, my queen." His voice was whispery, like two scrolls being rubbed together, and the sound matched his wrinkled face perfectly. He was perhaps the only elf Taryn had ever seen that truly looked ancient.

Teleriel, the archmage, snorted and gave a dismissive wave. "That's impossible, he was destroyed during the holocaust ten thousand years ago."

The elderly elf shook his head. "No; I believe he was not killed. I believe he was only imprisoned." He coughed and Siarra touched him briefly. Energy seemed to flow into him and he stood straighter. Thanking her with a glance, he continued, "For those of you who do not know, Draeken was cast out by the gods for conspiring to destroy them. He was cast down here and bound. As a final mockery, Skorn told him

337

he would be freed 'when chaos reigned upon the earth.' Without being able to implement his own desired result, he could only languish, trapped and helpless, able only to hope for the races to bring about this destruction on their own.

"But the gods did not know how close Draeken was to destroying them. Unbeknownst to them he had created an army, so vast it could destroy everything in the heavens—and he'd gathered the fiends into a place where he could open a portal to bring them in.

"Furious at his banishment, he found a way to open the portal from within his confinement, and the holocaust began. Death was the forerunner, killing leaders and other key warriors. However, his ability to take lives was far surpassed by his power to spread fear and divide the races. This terror was his most effective weapon to keep people separated and easier to conquer. He was the perfect assassin, and until now, I believed nothing could kill him." He inclined his head towards Jack Myst before continuing.

"Famine and Plague came next. Riding separately, they swept through the countryside to weaken the population by destroying food and spreading disease. The closer they came, the weaker armies became. Food became spoiled and rancid; men and women were too sick to fight. There was no defense and no way to stop it.

"Last of all rode War, general of the fiend army. Leading the countless hordes he swept the land, killing everything and everyone that had survived his predecessors' attacks. We do not know much about him because the army disappeared before they had gone very far."

Ryben suddenly interrupted, his deep voice resonating through the room, "I saw him—I saw War." His big frame twitched and he swallowed at the memory. "When they wiped out Terros, he was there."

The historian coughed. "It has begun then, the beginning of the end."

"Can Draeken be killed?" Ladarius asked, his voice full of bluster, but a sliver of fear had seeped in.

338

The wizened elf bobbed his head. "The Oracle of that age prophesied that only if the races combined could Draeken truly be destroyed. Lakonus, said to be descended from the elves, humans, and dwarves, sought the Lord of Chaos, and gave his life to destroy him—at least that is the way the legend goes."

At the mention of the blood of the races in one hero, a shiver of foreboding crawled up Taryn's spine and he almost missed what was said next.

"But you don't believe he was killed." Lariel spoke for the first time.

He nodded again. "I believe that Lakonus didn't kill him, but he somehow managed to close the portal. In that moment, all the fiends were pulled back to their home, disappearing in an instant."

"Why do you believe this, Sirfalas?" the queen asked.

"Because it is the only explanation. All the signs are the same. Draeken has certainly opened the portal again. I understand this only now that I have heard of the destruction at Terros and Death's demise." He wheezed to a stop and fell silent.

After a moment of silence Siarra broke the stillness, "As with all Oracles, most of my power was chained at an early age to prevent misuse, so I did not understand the full extent of the danger until I was unbound two days ago. As soon as I knew, I hastened to this high council so we can prepare with all speed."

"Is there any hope for us?" the queen asked, a desperate glimmer in her expression.

"Some," Siarra answered. "We have more time to prepare than before." She nodded towards Ryben. "The woodsman has given us that."

He started and leaned forward. "Me? How?"

"When Death didn't kill you, you were able to warn Terros. War then moved up his plans and tried to wipe out the eastern kingdom before he was ready, before his full army had come through the portal.

It's because of you that so many refugees from the eastern kingdom made it out alive. *You . . .* "—she leaned in—"are the Watcher."

"Ah, yes!" Sirfalas smiled for the first time. "The ancient prophecy spoke of a Watcher who would warn the kingdoms to prepare. No one seemed to fit the role at the time, so that part was dismissed as an error."

"How much time did we gain?" Keiko asked.

"We would have had a month, but thanks to Ryben we now have a little more than six weeks before he reaches this city. While we gather and fortify here, Taryn must find and destroy Draeken."

Taryn snapped to look at her, shocked. "Me?"

She returned his gaze with kind eyes. "You, brother, are the one in the prophecy. Only you can kill Draeken, just as Jack killed Death."

Taryn started to protest but Ladarius beat him to it. "That boy!" He said with a wave of his hand. "We don't even know who he is. There is certainly an elven warrior that can best him."

The archmage echoed his comments, but trailed off when Liri began to laugh scornfully. The harsh sound caused several in the room to look at her oddly until she stopped and met Telerial's gaze. "You are indeed a fool if you think someone can defeat Taryn."

She rose to her feet when the mage's face clouded with anger, preventing him from speaking. "Think about it magi," she said, her tone shifting to persuasive. "The greatest skills of the dwarves, stamina, endurance and strength, added to the cunning and shrewdness of humans, and joined with the speed and agility of our race . . ."

Many eyes looked at Taryn with newfound intensity, but all he felt was dread. How could he be the one to perform such an act? He couldn't do anything but swing a weapon. A tidal wave of discouragement threatened to engulf him, and he looked away from the searching looks at the head of the table, only to meet the gaze of his friends.

Confidence radiated from each of them, bolstering his courage enough that he managed not to reveal his despair. Then Liri sat down, her expression triumphant as she looked at Taryn, and the worry evaporated as quickly as it had come, replaced by the warmth of confidence—weak, but growing stronger. In that moment he thought of Denithir's dying words, and the promise he'd made to himself.

Now was the time to fulfill that vow.

Returning to the conversation, Taryn heard Deiran interrupt Siarra.

"So we have six weeks to prepare the city?" the general asked.

She nodded and then he looked at the archmage. "How many can you gather?"

"At least ten thousand battle magi," he responded with pride.

"I can summon three legions of twenty thousand each and have the city prepared within the time frame," Deiran said, looking at Teleriel. "We can be ready to defend the city against any force by then. I can lead the defenses indefinitely within the walls of this city."

The archmage nodded, smiling. "Then it's settled. We gather, and hold out until Taryn can kill Draeken."

"Or until we defeat the invasion." The general nodded sharply.

"FOOLS!" Siarra's voice thundered through the chamber at the same time her fists smashed into the table, cracking it all the way to the queen.

Before the sound had died away she lifted a hand and clenched her fist. Energy arced through the general and the archmage and seemed to clamp their mouths shut. Everyone froze at the sight and watched the two elves desperately struggle to part their lips. When she spoke again, her venomously soft tone shook with contained fury. "This army was created to destroy the *gods*! They will number in the *billions* and you will be nothing more than flies to be swatted. If Deiran leads the defenses,"—she jerked a finger at him and he flinched—"you will fall in a single *HOUR*!" She finished in a low hiss that shook everyone at the table.

Blue energy abruptly crackled all around the Oracle, and Taryn wasn't the only one to lean away from the awesome display of power. Before anyone could move her hand shot out, making them all jump, but it stopped and pointed at Braon. With her voice still furiously quiet she said, "If *HE* leads the defenses—of *every member*—of *every race,* all gathered upon this cliff . . . then—and only then—you *might* last *seven days*. That is longest you can hope to survive, *seven days!"*

Despite her low tone, her words echoed and re-echoed throughout their minds, and the weight of understanding finally settled on every person in the room like the rock ceiling had suddenly crashed onto them. Every race had to be *convinced* to come, then gathered, then prepared to defend, and they could still only last seven days?

Responsibility suddenly crushed Taryn as he realized that thousands of lives would be lost every minute until he defeated Draeken—who hadn't been killed the last time. He swallowed and bowed his head, humbled once again by his calling in the coming war.

The silence stretched on as Siarra's magic dissipated, and still no one spoke. Finally the queen slowly rose to her feet.

"Every person has a purpose, no matter how small. We must collect every life of every race in the coming weeks. Our lives depend on this as much as theirs. My brothers and sisters . . . we must commence the greatest gathering in the history of our world as we fight for the survival of our race. Let us not fail our descendents.

"General, gather the troops. Archmage, gather your magi. Braon—" When she said his name he blinked hard and swallowed. "—lead us . . . and gather everyone else. I have always trusted the Oracle, and so I shall trust you." Her tone became one of ringing authority and she cast a sharp look at Deiran. "As of this moment, I relinquish all military command to Braon. He is now, and will be, our battle commander until we either survive by some miracle, or perish. Let us pray the Oracle has chosen him wisely, for every life in Lumineia now rests in his hands." Her eyes flicked to Telerial and Ladarius, both of whom looked about to protest. Her gaze was wide and challenging, against which their eyes dropped to the table.

With that said, she nodded sympathetically at Braon and swept from the room. Again silence enveloped them as everyone looked at the individuals around them, wondering who would survive the coming conflict.

Taryn found himself holding Liri's hand and looking at the young man bowing his head in front of him. In his heart he wondered if the two of them would be able to perform their assigned tasks, for quite literally the weight of the world rested on their shoulders.

Taryn had never felt so small.

Chapter 28: The Prophecy

"Do you think we have a chance?" Taryn asked Siarra as they stood at the battlements on the highest level of Azertorn. She didn't respond for several minutes, and they both watched the sun begin to set on the horizon. Bright light gradually faded from yellow to orange and then slowly to red before the sun sank below the horizon and darkness blanketed the countryside.

"I honestly don't know, Taryn." She sighed and looked at him. For the first time he felt like she was his older sister and he realized he had missed her while he was growing up. "I can feel them coming," she said, her voice soft, "and I can feel us fighting, but after that there is . . . nothing. There is simply too much that our survival depends on, too many factors for me to sense past."

"Do you think I can do it?" Taryn asked, unable to meet her penetrating gaze.

"No question," she replied with a compassionate smile on her lips.

He sighed, and neither spoke for several minutes until Taryn asked a question that had been nagging him. "I asked you something before, but I didn't get an answer. I was wondering why you trained with a sword, especially considering your magical abilities."

She glanced at him, her expression tender. "Because our mother's weapon was a blade, a katsana, and I guess I wanted to be close to her." Her eyes seemed to stare right through him for a moment. "I used to train with her, you know. We would as often as we could, both with weapons and with magic."

"Is it common for Oracles to train in combat?" he asked. For some reason it seemed odd for a magi to use a weapon.

She shrugged. "Normally they were taught the basics, although I don't think very many had to *use* their battle training. Despite that, there have been quite a few Oracles in the past that have chosen to train extensively with a weapon and enchant one of their choosing. Any such items are exceptionally rare and incredibly powerful."

Taryn drew Ianna from the sheath on his back and laid it on the stone in front of them. "Was this hers?"

Siarra's eyes lit up at the sight of the glimmering weapon, and she gently took it from him. Reverently, she slid her finger up the flat side.

"I haven't seen this sword in many years—and yes, it was hers." She morphed it to the bow and back again, sighing in deep satisfaction before returning it to him.

"I was there when she enchanted it to become a bow." She smiled at the memory. "This particular spell of transfiguration is no easy feat— even for an Oracle, but I believe she meant for you to have it. She made it a few months before she left with Mazer."

Taryn returned Ianna to its scabbard and drew his father's sword. "What about this?"

Gently she took the long katsana, musing to herself. "Hmm, now this is new." She stroked the sharp edge, eliciting a dull flash of light that cut her finger.

Chuckling she rubbed her finger and it healed quickly. "It's a sharpening augmentation, plus a few other . . . enhancements. The sharpening enchantment alone is one of the trickiest imaginable and requires the utmost skill and focus in metal magic, a highly advanced type of stone energy." She paused and ran her healed finger along the engraved name. "Mazer . . .," she murmured. "She must have added her touch to it before her power was lost." She palmed the hilt and flicked

346

the tip outward. "Perfectly balanced, but I do believe it was like that before she added her touch." She met his gaze. "It's definitely your father's weapon."

Taryn smiled sadly and took the offered hilt. "I wish I could have known them."

Siarra nodded, her expression mirroring his own. "I know how you feel. I wish Ianna were here to help me figure out what I am supposed to do."

"I think you are doing pretty well on your own."

She looked dubious, but that only made him laugh. Struggling to speak he said, "I know you made a permanent impact on the High Council's table."

Her brow furrowed. "I just can't abide stupid people," she said, "especially in our current situation. I guess I just don't have much patience." Then she laughed. "Mother used to tell me that it would take me centuries to learn to hold my tongue."

"Don't worry about them," Taryn laughed. "I think they understand what is coming now."

All their humor evaporated in an instant as the thought of Draeken returned. "Well, we definitely have some work to do," he said.

Behind them a familiar voice spoke up. "Yes, we certainly do." They turned to see Liri approaching. She leaned against the wall beside them with a worn sigh.

"I had to wrap up the council while the rest of you got to scatter."

She sounded jealous at their freedom, but Taryn decided not to tease her. Instead he asked, "Where did Trin and Mae head off to?"

Finally she chuckled, "They went with Jack to Aléthya's bar. I think I heard Trin saying something about needing a stiff drink and Jack agreed with him wholeheartedly."

Siarra smirked. "I don't think they were the only ones. I'm pretty sure some of the high council are drowning themselves in a bottle right now."

He grinned at the image. "How'd you find us, anyway?"

She laughed and nudged him affectionately. "I know about you and high places, especially when you want to think. I knew you would be up here."

Taryn flashed her a wry smile, unsurprised that she'd read him so easily. Liri then added, with an edge of seriousness behind the quip: "You aren't supposed to be predictable you know. It makes you easy to kill."

A gust of chill air blew past them, and she leaned against him for warmth. After a moment she murmured, "But only be unpredictable to your enemies. Your friends should know where you will be and what you will do, so they can be there to help."

He chuckled at her comment, knowing it to be true. For several minutes, silence stretched between them, each of them contemplating their thoughts of the previous few hours.

Without warning, lightning flashed behind them and they all turned to see that a storm was brewing in the east. Knowing that the weather had nothing to do with Draeken did little to ease his mind. The ensuing thunderclap felt like a physical blow, and Taryn couldn't help glancing behind him, wishing the sun hadn't gone down so fast. It felt like the storm in the dark had chased away the light, and he found himself worrying that the light would not return.

The ominous clouds lit up every few minutes as more lightning streaked through the black night. Stars began to disappear, slowly eaten up by the encroaching gale.

—Suddenly Taryn felt a current of magic begin to flow around him and into his sister. Subtle yet powerful, it steadily built into a tidal wave of sheer force. Invisible, the swirling energy pulsed with forbidding strength, until finally Siarra broke the stillness, her tone dark and soft, but ringing in the voice of prophecy.

"For seven days the light will fight the dark, with all races gathered against the endless night. If night should fall on the last day, with darkness still undefeated . . . it will be eternal. The end of days will have come and all light will be extinguished forever, never to return . . ."

He shuddered at the image of evil stronger than good and clenched his teeth against the wave of panic that threatened to engulf him. Liri quivered beside him and sought his hand in desperation. Together they fought to hold onto their hope.

Siarra abruptly growled and smashed a fist into the stone battlement, snapping them out of their despair. "I will NOT let us fail," she said so fiercely that Taryn and Liri jumped. Immediately the swirling magic dispersed back into the night, leaving the three of them alone with their thoughts.

"I hope so," Liri replied in a voice so small that Taryn put his arm around her and squeezed her hand, vainly trying to ward off the premonition with his grip.

The brooding silence stretched between them for over an hour with the three of them staring mutely at the lightning storm in the distance. Finally Siarra pushed herself off the wall with a deep sigh. "I'm going to have dreams tonight, I can feel it. I just hope they're pleasant."

Her voice held no hope, but Taryn wished her well anyway as she bid them goodnight and headed towards the House of Runya, where Liri's mother, Lariel had invited them all to stay for the night. She trudged away and Taryn slid down to sit with his back against the parapet.

Liri sat next to him so he put his arm around her. She snuggled to his chest in response.

Taryn broke the silence first. "Denithir didn't die right away."

Liri leaned back, her expression quizzical as she asked, "What do you mean?"

Taryn winced at the memory. "He said to tell Eressa that he loved her. Now I have to find his wife and tell her I failed him."

Tears sprang to Liri's eyes as she choked out, "Eressa isn't his wife . . . She's his unborn daughter."

Taryn's throat tightened and his eyes lifted to the heavens, his heart unable to bear what he had just heard. How could he tell a daughter why she would never know her father?

"I'm sorry Taryn," Liri murmured. "I will help you tell them if you wish."

Clamping down on his surging emotions, he accepted her offer. "Thank you Liri. I don't think I could do it without you." Reaching out, he pulled her to his chest and hugged her.

She sighed and shifted to get more comfortable. "I wish we didn't have all this going on," she mumbled into his tunic.

"I feel the same way, Liri," he said.

"We have to leave in the morning, don't we?" she asked tonelessly.

"*We*?" he asked in surprise.

She thumped his chest with her hand. "Of course." —Her expression displayed frank annoyance. "—Did you expect me to sit around here?"

"Um, sort of," he said, half-heartedly wishing she would, at least for her own safety.

"Not likely," she scoffed. "Where you go, I go. We're in this together."

He took a moment to respond. "You know . . . what happened to Lakonus . . ." He couldn't bring himself to finish the thought, so he tried

351

to explain a different way. "Something tells me anybody with him died too."

"This time will be different—I am sure of it." Liri's voice sounded almost confident, like she was struggling to convince herself. Then she leaned away from him and her eyes locked with his, her expression so intense he would have backed up if his head wasn't already against the stone.

"One thing I am sure of, Taryn: I know you can kill this evil. If there is one thing I have learned, it's never to doubt your ability."

Her complete and unwavering confidence in him was honest and genuine, so he smiled and pulled her back to him. "Thank you for trusting me, Liri." He hesitated for a moment, and then relented. "And I'm glad you'll be with me for the journey."

Even though he couldn't see her face he could feel her smile. Sighing, he said, "So tomorrow the gathering begins."

She stirred and said softly, "Riders are already being dispatched." She looked at him with eyes full of profound sorrow. "The gathering has already begun."

###

Excerpt from The Gathering

Siarra forced herself to breathe as she advanced between the snarling fiends on either side of her, knowing they were only held in check by their absolute fear of her—and that it wouldn't last long. She just hoped it was long enough. With cautious steps she worked her way past the various evil creatures trembling in their desire to tear her asunder.

Quare dominated the vicious army. The man-size fiends boasted a mane of dark red fur that barely showed on their ink-colored skin. Although they carried no weapons, they had slaughtered thousands with their bare hands. Rippling muscles bunched and clenched throughout their bodies, and their fur stood on end as she passed, their manes flaring in anger. She knew they could tear a man in half, and they would try to do the same to her.

Sipers, dogs the size of lions, growled and snapped at the air swirling in her wake. Lightning fast, they were the first to close off her path behind her, blocking her in. The hard, arrowhead scales that covered their bodies shimmered from pure black to deep crimson as they sensed the kill. Opalescent eyes glittered as she passed through a pack of them, and she willed herself not to shudder.

In between the Sipers and Quare, the Kraka captains towered over the other fiends. Blanketed in white bone armor that grew from their own flesh, they dragged massive obsidian swords as if they were too heavy to carry, until they whipped the sword through an elf like the snap of a whip. Earlier in the battle she'd seen a single Kraka annihilate an entire company of humans before a lucky ballistae bolt finally took it down. A hundred dead in a matter of minutes, and there were hundreds of thousands of Krakas around her.

Lastly came Skorpians, huge beasts as large as a wagon with tails that grew black bone spears in minutes, spears that could be launched with a snap of their tail to embed into solid rock. If that wasn't enough, their dual pincers could cut through armor and bone like it was parchment. Their exoskeleton had prevented all but the most powerful attacks from penetrating . . .

A Siper lunged at her, fury overcoming its fear. As quick as thought she sidestepped the lunge and lifted a spike of earth to impale it mid-flight. She turned from the dying creature and stared at the black horde, until once again their fear overcame their boiling hate. For one brief instant she relished in the feeling of power. She had faced down an army of billions, and they had retreated.

But the thought was fleeting, and her courage waned, so she resumed her steady walk forward. Heat blossomed in her chest as her fear spiked, but she clenched her jaw and focused on each step as she worked her way further from the broken gates of Azertorn. Each precious step moved her farther from the city, but it wasn't distance she needed, it was time.

The cliff and city had been under siege by an almost unlimited host of fiends for less than six days. *How could so many have died in six days*? And they still had to survive for another thirty-six hours before the light fell on the seventh day. Part of her recognized it wasn't her fault, but she couldn't shake the great weight that hunched her shoulders. As the Oracle of Lumineia, she was the most powerful mage throughout the kingdoms, and had guided the races to unite.

Somewhere, somehow, she had failed.

Before her thoughts could continue, a ripple coursed through the army and she came to a halt. Like the wind had shifted, she knew. This was the spot of her last battle. The fiends around her snarled and growled, roared and pawed the ground, each waiting for her to attack. She stood firm, hoping the extra seconds might make a difference. If she moved first it would only be a matter of time before they overwhelmed her. She had to give the allies time to fortify again, to prepare for the next onslaught.

Deep down she knew it wasn't enough, that her desperate bid to give them time would fail. She knew she couldn't hold them off, but it just wasn't in her to give up. She knew she would die, and then everyone in Azertorn would perish. Looking at the curled muzzles and dark, bloodthirsty mass surrounding her, she wondered where they had lost, where she had made a wrong decision.

What in heaven or earth could have turned aside this holocaust?

Siarra took one last look upward at the vast cloud of black that had enveloped the sky, leaving only a column of sunlight from the city to the clouds, piercing the encroaching darkness and causing the heavens to shine on Azertorn. Even as she watched the black roiled and pressed against the waning light and she knew it was time.

Bringing her tired gaze back to the roiling sea of black, she listened to the fiends gathering their courage and readied herself for the fight of her life. The unnatural peace lasted only a few seconds, until a huge Kraka began to charge. From deep within the enraged army he roared, a bellow of rage that echoed off the scorched and broken cliff as he began to pick up speed. The entire host seemed to take a breath in unison, ready to strike when the armored warrior reached her tiny elven form.

Barreling towards her the massive fiend captain roared in defiance and pumped its legs faster. Its obsidian blade bounced through the dirt behind him, kicking up a spray of soil as he thundered across the ground like a galloping steed. Fifty paces away . . . then twenty . . . then ten, and finally the huge beast snapped the giant sword high—but Siarra was quicker.

Lifting her fingers she raised the ground in front of the beast only a few inches, and tripped him before he could get within range. The fiend's roar turned to a cry of pain as it slammed into the unforgiving ground and tumbled towards her. Before the impending wave of creatures could descend she used a gust of air to push the dark blade underneath the rolling body, forcing him to land on his own sword.

355

When he finally came to a stop, he didn't move . . . but Siarra wasn't there to see it.

The catalyst had shattered the calm, and billions of fiends flooded towards her, bent on wiping her from existence. In an instant she became a whirlwind of action. Her hands blurred into motion and air flew into enemies, knocking them flying. With a stomp of her foot the ground exploded outward, thundering into anything nearby and crushing them into each other. Clenching her fist she sent waves of ice missiles lancing through armor and bone alike. The sharp ice dropped them where they stood, but more fiends jumped over their twisted forms before they had even stopped breathing.

Siarra spun and twisted, blasting magical attacks into the bodies of her enemies. Fire exploded and burned when she pulled heat from the air, lightning jumped and arced as she gathered the charge from the surrounding area, stone rose up to obliterate dark forms at her command, and the very light from above scorched them where they stood . . . but it was not enough.

Bit by bit the encroaching wave pressed inward, over the bodies of hundreds of their dead comrades, and slowly grew closer. Each strike now came within feet of hitting home, then inches . . . then it was too late.

A Siper dodged every attack and leapt at Siarra from behind, taking her down. Tasting her fear, she rolled and blasted him away, but other claws were already descending towards her. She called on what was left of the forest of Numenessee and long roots sprang up from the ground to crush the nearest fiends, but they came too late. Something had gouged into her leg, causing her to cry out in pain. Seconds later her arm was almost ripped out by a Quare, and she burned him to ash. The heat from the magical fire shimmered off her skin before another form materialized through the dust and smashed into her, throwing her backwards.

Her frail body tumbled through ranks of fiends, barely protected by a thin film of energy that shocked anything that tried to strike her, but some of the more determined attempts made it through. When she finally came to a stop, her right side had gone numb, two ribs were broken, and she could feel blood seeping from her body in too many places to count.

A giant Kraka stood above her as she coughed and fought to bring her magic to bear. Shrugging aside her effort to throw him back, he took a moment to cut down a Siper that had slunk past him. Fighting for breath she squirmed as he brought his black weapon up. His roar caused her to flinch and lose what semblance of focus she'd regained.

She had probably killed several thousand in the last few minutes, but now she could do nothing but scream and watch the blade descend towards her neck . . .

The Gathering is currently available for purchase on Amazon. Look for the explosive finale, Seven Days, to be released Christmas 2012.

Author Bio

Originally from Utah, Ben has grown up with a passion for learning almost everything. Driven particularly to reading caused him to be caught reading by flashlight under the covers at an early age. While still young, he practiced various sports, became an Eagle Scout, and taught himself to play the piano. This thirst for knowledge gained him excellent grades and helped him graduate college with honors, as well as become fluent in three languages after doing volunteer work in Brazil. After school, he started and ran several successful businesses that gave him time to work on his numerous writing projects. His greatest support and inspiration comes from his wonderful wife and three beautiful children. Currently he resides in Florida while working on his latest writing and business endeavors.

To contact the author, discover more about Lumineia, or find out about the upcoming sequels, check out his website at Lumineia.com. You can also follow the author on twitter @ BenHale8 or Facebook at Facebook.com/Elseerian.

CPSIA information can be obtained at www.ICGtesting.com
Printed in the USA
LVOW08s0305280913

354495LV00001B/7/P